SIX
IMPOSSIBLE
THINGS

By Elizabeth Boyle

Novels

Six Impossible Things
The Knave of Hearts
The Viscount Who Lived Down the Lane
If Wishes Were Earls
And the Miss Ran Away With the Rake
Along Came a Duke
Lord Langley Is Back in Town
Mad About the Duke
How I Met My Countess
Memoirs of a Scandalous Red Dress
Confessions of a Little Black Gown
Tempted By the Night
Love Letters From a Duke
His Mistress By Morning
This Rake of Mine
Something About Emmaline
It Takes a Hero
Stealing the Bride
One Night of Passion
Once Tempted
No Marriage of Convenience

Novellas

Mad About the Major
Have You Any Rogues?

ELIZABETH BOYLE

SIX IMPOSSIBLE THINGS

❧ Rhymes With Love ❧

AVONBOOKS

An Imprint of HarperCollinsPublishers

SIX IMPOSSIBLE THINGS. Copyright © 2017 by Elizabeth Boyle. All rights reserved. Printed in the United States of America. No part of this book may be used or reproduced in any manner whatsoever without written permission except in the case of brief quotations embodied in critical articles and reviews. For information, address HarperCollins Publishers, 195 Broadway, New York, NY 10007.

First Avon Books mass market printing: May 2017
First Avon Books hardcover printing: April 2017

Print Edition ISBN: 978-0-06-267478-4
Digital Edition ISBN: 978-0-06-228399-3

FIRST EDITION

17 18 19 20 21   LSC   10 9 8 7 6 5 4 3 2 1

To my longtime editor, Lyssa Keusch.
Thank you for your steady presence
and gracious help all these years.
You always get it right.
My deepest gratitude and sincere appreciation.

SIX
IMPOSSIBLE
THINGS

Prologue

"*Girls cannot join the Foreign Office.*"

"*No, Roselie, girls are never spies.*"

"*Grow up to be a diplomat? I fear, child, that is impossible.*"

No matter that Miss Roselie Stratton spoke six different languages. Read several others.

That she could decipher the letters her father received from his far-flung acquaintances—reports from the chaos of Paris, the courts in Russia, and the far-off wilds of the young United States.

With ease she trailed after her older brother, Piers, without detection and, to his horror, submitted reports to their father as to his transgressions. And when he complained about Roselie's high-handed ways, she would argue that their sister Margaret hardly counted as a worthy adversary and, that perhaps Piers and his friend, Poldie, ought to try harder if they wanted to avoid detection.

And no one argued with that point.

But despite Roselie's natural talents that should all but guarantee her entry into the shadowy side of the diplomatic agents her father inhabited with ease, there were two words that Roselie heard over and over.

Never, and that other hated utterance, *Impossible*.

So when her beloved father, the man who asked her opinions on world events and had given her free rein, died suddenly, those two words became the fence around her life.

Never. Impossible.

They rose like a solid barricade, set into place by her mother, her sister, her governesses, even Piers, who had eventually forgiven her for always being such an incorrigible tattletale.

So eventually Roselie stopped asking.

Stopped dreaming.

That is, until her first Season in London. In the very first week she'd taken her place in the *ton* as a newly minted debutante.

In one fated night, everything changed.

And Roselie had no choice but to stop listening to what was considered *impossible*, to what could *never* happen.

Because, quite frankly, she had a devil to stop and a war to win.

Even if no one wanted her help.

Chapter 1

*"A lady agent? How utterly ridiculous. A woman could never do
what we do."*

Lord Howers

London, 1811

"Smile, my dear Miss Stratton," Lady Essex Marshom advised.
And not for the first time.

So Roselie did her best to smile.

It was a Herculean effort, to say the least.

She glanced around the crowded room at Almack's and wished
she could be more like the other girls. That her only concern was
who might ask her to dance. Or if she should have worn her green
ribbons or her blue ones. Or whether she needed new slippers.

But she wasn't like other girls.

After all, she'd been out in London Society for four long
years—a veritable eternity in the *ton*. Nor in her favor was her
complete lack of interest in frippery or likely candidates.

Actually, she was rather proud of her ability to send suitors
shying for the hills. And she would continue to be too sharp, too
bossy and whatever else it took to maintain her freedom.

Because quite simply, marriage would ruin everything.

Especially when she had work to do.

She checked once again—and yes, the note she'd been slipped by one of the servants was still tucked in the top of her glove. She wouldn't have a spare moment to read it until she got away from this crush, most likely until she got home . . . and *bother* . . . that was still a few hours away.

The note that might be the answer to all her prayers. Years of work. The last bit of evidence she needed to bring down her enemy, the Marquess of Ilford.

For he was *her* enemy, as much as he was England's. And nothing would deter her from seeing him pay for his heinous crimes.

But in the meantime . . .

Her frustration got away from her, and she sighed. More like, groaned. Quite loudly and rather unbecomingly.

"Miss Stratton!" Lady Essex chided. "The company tonight may be thin, but a lady never reveals her boredom. Why look at Miss Taber! How fortunate Lady Muscoates is to have a ward who illuminates every room she enters." Her ladyship tapped her fan against her chin as she examined the fetching girl across the room. "Though I must say, a ward should never be *that* pretty. Rather, indecent, don't you agree, Mariah?"

Her hired companion, Miss Mariah Manx, nodded in agreement. "However, Lady Muscoates is French, is she not?"

Lady Essex huffed a sigh, as if this explanation was not only utterly correct, but also vexing. "Yes, of course. She'd never tolerate having some unfortunate creature foisted into her care, now would she?"

Mariah winked at Roselie, having done her best to change the subject.

But the diversion hardly lasted for Lady Essex was truly a terrier at heart, especially when it came to matchmaking. Not that the dear woman had any hope of seeing the infamous Miss Stratton betrothed on her watch, but if anyone was willing to give it a try, it was Lady Essex.

And so she went back to her earlier refrain. "Miss Stratton, smile."

"I shall endeavor to do my best, my lady," Roselie told her, smiling sweetly.

Mariah smothered a laugh—one her ladyship didn't notice.

Roselie wished she could be like Mariah, who hid her own secrets with enviable ease.

But tonight of all nights, Roselie's slim patience was worn threadbare and got noticeably thinner especially when Lady Essex fluttered to life as a quartet of gentlemen arrived just before the doors closed.

A striking fellow in a captain's uniform stood at the lead. Captain Benedict Hathaway, if Roselie was to hazard a guess, especially given his remarkable resemblance to the man beside him, Mr. Chauncy Hathaway. Though Mr. Hathaway was hardly worthy of note—handsome, but a second son with no prospects, *Captain* Hathaway caused a stir. More so than the man who followed, Lord Budgey—rich, for certain, but such a nobcock hardly anyone of note considered him eligible.

Then came the last fellow. And to Roselie's credit, she kept from groaning out loud.

For the last arrival was none other than Bradwell Garrick, the seventeeth Baron Rimswell.

Her other nemesis. And not because he was a traitor. No far from it. If there was anyone in London who could unmask her, it was her old childhood friend, Brody.

What the devil was *he* doing here?

Not that he didn't belong. Elevated to his brother's title two years earlier, he was considered quite the eligible *parti*. Worse, he'd grown into a handsome devil. Dark hair that gave him the look of a poet, while his reputation for being a bruiser at Gentleman Jim's and his penchant for hard riding could all be seen in the lean lines of his tall, athletic build.

All around them, there were more than a few feminine sighs as he entered the room.

Including the one that Roselie managed to keep tightly bound inside her heart. That he sent this racing desire through her every time she saw him, every time they had to be in the same room, was exactly why she avoided him.

Nor could she do much more than cross her fingers as he made his usual sweeping search of the room, his gaze pausing on her for that slightly too-long second, offering her the slightest of nods—a poor homage to how close they had been growing up.

As his gaze continued on, she did sigh.

Which, of course, Mariah noticed. "Might be time to tell him."

Roselie shook her head, her reply rushing out. "No." For Brody wasn't just a handsome, eligible *parti,* he was also an agent for the Home Office, although that was not well known.

But Roselie knew. As did Mariah. For they'd made it their business to determine who could be trusted and who might interfere with their plans.

With Lady Essex having moved off to have a good coze with one of her friends, Mariah leaned closer to avoid being overheard. "This is all becoming too dangerous."

Roselie agreed, but she wasn't about to admit as much. "You sound as stodgy as Lord Howers."

"Perhaps you should heed his advice," Mariah told her. "For once."

Roselie ignored her. Much as she ignored Lord Howers.

Not that Mariah was done. Good heavens, her friend had worked for Lady Essex for far too long. She was starting to sound like the persistent old gel. "Ask for his help."

"He won't." Roselie turned to her. "The first thing he'll do is to tell me to stop. Immediately. Then he'll lecture me as to the impropriety of it all. And then, I imagine, he'll tell me I don't know what I am doing."

Mariah, on the other hand, did not share that opinion. "He'll surprise you."

"I doubt it." Shaking off her own misgivings, Roselie continued in a different vein. "Abigail will be off tonight. She'll no longer be in danger. We'll have everything she's gathered and have a full report to Howers before the end of the week. And then—"

A matron came by, slanting a glance at the two, and the pair smiled back. Only after she was well out of earshot did Roselie continue. "And then Asteria will quietly retire."

"Yes, of course she will," Mariah said, sounding anything but convinced.

"She, um, *I* will." Roselie straightened and smiled, for here was Lady Essex glancing over at them.

Asteria.

Oh, what a ridiculous nickname those fools in the Home Office had come up with for the mysterious lady who'd often been spotted with some of London's less-polite denizens.

How she'd like to tell them, one and all, that she was certainly no goddess and definitely not immortal. Still, better a fool's moniker than having one of them actually discover her true identity.

Like Brody. She'd eluded him more times than she could count and he'd nearly caught her twice. Nearly.

But more disarming was the very notion that he'd never once recognized her.

Her. Roselie Stratton.

Yes, yes, it was entirely contradictory that she didn't want him to know what she was doing, but oh, good heavens, she'd like to take him by both shoulders and shake him until his teeth rattled. *How can you not see me?*

No, instead he found Asteria entirely fascinating, and her? She knew all too well his opinion of her.

Then again, he hadn't really looked at her, not in years. Not like he had when they'd been children. Not since she'd been trundled off to school in Bath, and he'd been sent away to Eton.

Oh, but truly, the worst of it was that she saw him. And knew.

Knew what it was like to have him kiss her. Thoroughly, recklessly. To have him touch her, and leave her trembling.

Twice now, he'd caught her. Twice, she'd escaped him.

But not without collecting those damned memories of those stolen moments. His lips. His touch. The way he drove her mad until she was trembling and quaking.

Asteria, that is. Proper Roselie Stratton wasn't supposed to have such ruinous experiences.

It was her curse, her punishment, she supposed. Outside, she must appear the demure, innocent miss, while inside blazed a courtesan's heart and desires.

But how she longed to see Brody's gaze filled with desire for her. That dangerous promise in the turn of his lips.

Longed to see him look for her. Roselie.

If Asteria dared to continue, certainly one night, Brody would come to realize the truth. She knew that.

But this would not be that night, she vowed. It was impossible.

Or so she told herself.

"Is it my mistake, or are we completely outnumbered?" Captain Benedict Hathaway asked as he stepped to the front of the line.

"Tonight is Lord John's Folly," Chaunce provided as he took his place beside his brother, glancing with his usual droll disdain and unruffled demeanor at the scene before them that would have sent most men running for the borders of Scotland.

For every man in the room, there were at least five young ladies. And all of them seeking husbands. And they were ably reinforced by their equally determined mothers.

"So are you telling me, that while the rest of London's male company is cavorting with every pretty petticoat and willing Cyprian over at the earl's, we are *here*?" The captain glanced over his shoulder at the third member of their party. "Rimswell, I demand an explanation for this dereliction in duty."

Brody, having inherited his title two years earlier after the untimely death of his brother, was now quite used to such scrutiny, though even he had to admit that tonight offered the added ghastly sense of being tossed into the Coliseum with a pack of hungry lions.

Still, it wouldn't do to show any fear. Instead, he grinned at Chaunce's brother. "For a man who boasts of never having lost a battle, you look rather bilious, Captain," he teased. "Afraid of a few chits?"

"A 'few chits'? Good God, man, I've never faced such odds," the captain admitted. "The French have the decency to shoot at you."

Lord Budgey, bringing up the rear, had stopped behind the captain and was now blinking owlishly around the much taller man. "Devilish odds, you say? I do like them when they are in my favor." The man shouldered his way to the forefront with far more bravado than one would have expected from the rather mild-mannered viscount.

"How is that?" Brody asked, wondering how much Budgey had imbibed before they'd found him at White's to make him so pot valiant. "Have you finally decided to take a bride, Budgey, my good man?"

It was an old joke, but apparently a jest no longer.

"Mother's quite keen I marry, and I suppose if I must, I might as well do it now. After all, tonight I'll actually be in demand." He made—what he probably assumed was—his triumphant march into the very bosom of London's Marriage Mart.

Brody and Chaunce exchanged a glance and followed their friend quickly. It was never a good idea to leave Budgey to his own devices.

"I thought you didn't want to marry," Chaunce reminded him when they caught up with him. Most likely hoping to nudge the man into a hasty retreat.

Budgey blinked. "I don't. But—"

"Mother says—" Brody and Chaunce chimed in at the same time.

Budgey ignored them. "This is no time for your japery. Rather, I'd appreciate your opinions on the present company and then a glowing introduction to the future Lady Budgey."

"I'm not sure you've thought this through, Budgey," Brody told him. "Every chit in this room already knows who you are."

Budgey pursed his lips. "Indeed? Oh, bother, that's rather unfortunate."

"Why is that?" Captain Hathaway whispered in an aside to his brother.

No matter, Budgey heard the question. "If you haven't noticed, I'm a bit of a nobcock."

Captain Hathaway was polite enough to feign surprise. "No, no, not in the least."

Budgey shrugged. "Obviously I'm not trying hard enough tonight." He looked around again and then leaned closer, confiding in a low voice, "You might not have realized it, but my foolish demeanor is a rather clever disguise."

Brody and Chaunce exchanged bemused glances, for this wasn't the first time they had heard this explanation.

Budgey continued confidently, "Yes, well, the more foolish I appear, the less I'm bedeviled by chits scheming to be the next Lady Budgey. A most enviable position, I assure you." He glanced up at Captain Hathaway. "You should try playing the fool, sir, if you want to survive the night."

Chaunce opened his mouth as if to add something, but his brother staved him off with a quick warning.

"Don't you dare—"

"But—" Chaunce continued, for this was such a golden opportunity to bring his puffed-up younger brother down a notch or two.

"Say it," Benedict warned, "and I'll tell that matron over there—the one with the enormous collection of feathers sprouting from her head—"

"Lady Nafferton," Brody supplied.

"Yes, thank you," the captain said before turning his attention back to his brother. "I'll tell this Lady Nafferton that a distant uncle of ours has died and left you a rather large house and tidy fortune to go with it." Benedict winked at Chaunce. "Devilish bit of luck and all."

Chaunce paled at the very suggestion. So much for his reputation as one of the Home Office's most fearless agents. "You wouldn't dare—"

Benedict folded his arms across his chest and rocked on the heels of his boots. His expression was one of pure devilish delight. *Try me.*

But Chaunce always had just one more shot. "Do it, and I'll summon Mother to Town."

The fearless and daring Benedict Hathaway went positively green. "Now that is uncommonly foul."

Brody couldn't help but join in, leaning over to ask, "Captain, who do you fear more, your mother or the French?"

Before the captain could rise to his own defense, Budgey wedged his way into the conversation. "If you don't mind, I'd like to find my bride before eleven so we can head over to St. John's. If we get there after midnight, all the decent lightskirts will be taken."

Now this was a plan Captain Hathaway could endorse. Wholeheartedly. He rubbed his hands together in glee. "Yes, let's." His enthusiasm was most likely due to the fact that he wasn't the one about to be dropped into the parson's trap.

Budgey was more philosophical. "Might as well join in, Brody. There's no hope for either of us. We both must marry eventually."

"Ah, Budgey, don't you recall," Chaunce drawled, "our Lord Rimswell is holding out for *someone else*." Chaunce winked and Budgey barked a laugh.

"Ah, so you have someone in mind," Benedict said with a knowing tip of his head—though he didn't understand the joke. "Is she here tonight?"

"She might be," Chaunce supplied. "If he knew who she was."

"The beguiling Asteria," Budgey waxed. "I daresay, where is something to drink, we should be toasting this rarest of Diamonds."

"Asteria?" Benedict repeated. "Remind me, for my classics are a bit rusty, but isn't she the last immortal to live with a man?"

"Well, done," Chaunce told him. "And here Mother always said our tutor's fees were wasted on you and Benjamin."

Benedict ignored him and turned to Brody. "Who is this Asteria, your mistress?"

"Mistress!" Budgey laughed and nudged Chaunce. "Our Brody is far too respectable and proper to keep a mistress."

"I'm hardly—" Brody protested, not that the others were listening.

"Who is this paragon then?" Benedict persisted.

"No paragon," Chaunce corrected. "She's a myth."

"Marry her myself if she wasn't a figment," Budgey added.

"She's no figment," Brody told them, despite the fact that he'd sworn he wasn't going to get into this argument again. "She's as real as you or I."

"Introduce us, if you will." Chaunce smiled with that aggravating Hathaway superiority.

"Yes, that's right. Would like to meet her," Budgey added like a Greek chorus. "If you can't, I think you owe us all a round of drinks for having to listen to you all these years."

"Leave off," Brody told them. "When I catch her, you'll all owe me."

"What's all this?" Benedict asked, not liking in the least being left out.

Chaunce snorted. "Lord Rimswell believes there is an English lady who works for the Home Office or for—"

"—the Russians," Budgey added quickly. "My money is still on the Russians."

"She isn't Russian," Brody shot back.

"So you say," Budgey replied, completely undeterred.

"The real point is," Chaunce said, "that Old Ironpants would never enlist a woman into the service. Howers has even said as much."

"We have no idea who her master might be," Brody reminded them.

"Yes, but we all know who would like to master her," Budgey replied and the other two laughed.

Brody ignored the jibe. He'd heard it more than once. But then his temper got the better of him. "She was at the Setchfield Ball, just last month," he told them, folding his arms over his chest.

He hadn't seen her in ages, and suddenly, he'd spied her across a ballroom, but the devilish minx had disappeared before he could corner her. "She was there."

"So was Napoleon if you believe Lady Maugham," Chaunce added, for he'd been sent by Lord Howers to reassure the ninety-year-old, half-blind marchioness that, no, the French emperor was not ruining the social circles of London.

Budgey shouldered his way back into the debate with the best argument of all. "Even if she is real, what then, old friend? Take her home to your mother? Explain that her new daughter-in-law has spent most of her time in the worst gaming hells and corners of London? That will never do."

Brody hardly wanted to marry the woman. He just had this unrelenting need to find her. To unmask her. To know her.

One more time.

Two years earlier

Brody had heard all the whispers about the lady roaming the night and didn't believe a word of it.

Until he found himself in the open doorway of Lord Howers's office and saw the slight, hooded figure leaning over his superior's desk, pen in hand as she dashed off a note. There was no mistaking that this was a woman, for a yellow gown peeked out from her dark cloak. The bright color, like a daffodil, stood in stark contrast to the shadowed room.

Just like the woman herself.

He tried to breathe, tried to say something. This was *her*. The one everyone had been speculating about.

Asteria. Standing before him in the shadows of Lord Howers's office.

A rush of questions trampled through his thoughts. *Who the devil is she? What the hell is she doing here? How had she gotten in?*

Truly, how the devil had she gotten in here undetected? Granted it was late at night—more like nearly dawn, but still—someone should have seen her.

Demmit, no wonder the country's secrets were being sold right and left, if just anyone could wander into the heart of the Home Office unaccounted for.

So who the hell was she?

The only light came from the nearly guttered candle atop the desk, and it was beginning to sputter. Not even the rising dawn, which was only now beginning to tease away at the night, offered him a clear view of this enigma.

Not that anything in his world was clear anymore. Look at the past night—he'd spent it searching for an Admiralty clerk who was rumored to be selling secrets to the French. And in the last hour, Brody had found him. Dead in an alleyway. Knifed in the heart.

And the papers? Lost.

England's enemies were at their very doorstep. The entire world being torn apart by the French.

His world at the very least.

And here she was. The mysterious Asteria. Traipsing quite neatly into the middle of it.

Along with the Admiralty's lost papers. For there they sat, all neatly tied up like a bloody Christmas package.

"Who the hell are you?" The words, not so much a question as an order—blurted out.

She jumped a little and then stilled. Apparently she'd thought the building as empty as he had.

Slowly she straightened, her face the last thing to rise to meet him, but to his chagrin, her features were well covered by a black silk mask.

"My lord," she said, tipping her head in acknowledgment, but not before he saw something in her eyes—a sense of sadness and shared understanding—the sort that spoke of grief and anger and frustration.

All the things running rampant through him of late.

Bloody hell, she knew who he was.

Exactly who he was.

For it was there, in her proper address. *My lord.* The title wasn't an honor, more like an open wound.

You are Rimswell now. Your brother is dead.

Brody's unexpected elevation—not a fortnight ago—sat on his shoulders like a festering reminder of all he'd lost.

"My lord, are you well?"

"Don't call me that," he told her, entering the room and closing the door behind him.

Her gaze flicked from the door then back to him. If she was concerned about being trapped, she didn't show it. "I'm sorry about your brother."

Condolences? From a thief? It hardly made sense.

But one thing did. That voice.

He looked up and saw a bit of panic in her eyes. She did know him.

And so, he certainly should know her.

"Don't speak of him." The words came biting out, filled with the bitter anger that had raged inside him since the news had reached London. Even as he spoke, her chin tipped slightly, warily, her eyes narrowed.

Good. She should be nervous.

He wagged his chin a bit. "You might want to take off that mask."

She tipped her head just so, a flirtatious movement. "Why ever would I want to do that? I think you prefer it on."

It wasn't a statement. It was an offer.

One that sent his blood coursing through his veins. Passion that wasn't meant to soothe or to slake, but a means to drain him of this pain he was in.

So if this was how she wanted to play this charade—to tease and tempt him, then it was a game in which he was willing to join in, for he had every intention of winning.

Did she think he couldn't unmask her? That he wouldn't?

But there was a rub to all this—unmasking her would require getting closer. Very close. Touching her.

Not that he was opposed to handling her—she was a bundle of temptation—but he hadn't forgotten there was a dead clerk in the alleyway. One who'd been knifed by someone standing very close to him.

"Did you come to steal those?" he asked, nodding at the papers on the desk, easing closer because the overwhelming need to unmask her went against every bit of his usual common sense.

"Hardly. I'm returning them," she shot back. So she wasn't the only one harboring a raft of anger, for notably in her moment of resentment, her accent disappeared.

That voice. Good God, he knew it. He could place it. At least, he thought he could. And from the set of her jaw and how her eyes widened in alarm, she knew it as well.

He took another step closer to the desk. With steely determination, she held her ground. And then in a soft subtle motion, one that would make a courtesan weep with envy, she straightened and her cloak fell away to reveal a low-cut gown—a yellow silk that practically illuminated the night—clinging to her body and revealing why the other agents had sworn her a goddess fallen to earth.

She certainly had the form of one. Long lines, breasts that threatened to spill out of the low-cut bodice and curves meant for exploration. The mask stopped just above a mouth meant for kissing—full lips and a generous turn.

And turn they did, in a smile that any man knew was meant as an invitation for immeasurable pleasures.

Oh, yes, this Asteria was an intoxicating vision meant to beguile and distract.

And a wry stray thought occurred to him: he could easily eliminate the Nafferton sisters from his list of potential suspects.

So who is she? The question hammered at him.

"I'm here to help," she offered as if answering his silent query and adding a whole list of others. For her words purred in invitation, ruffling down his spine with temptation.

Help . . . Help me out of my gown . . . Help me out of my mask . . . Help me give you what you want.

"I doubt that," he replied, his gaze dipping from her face to her breasts and back up.

No wonder the agents who'd seen her were mad to find her . . . uncover her . . . cover her.

"You're not a fool, my lord," she told him, folding her arms over her chest and giving him the same sort of once-over he'd given her.

From the wry tilt of her lips, he felt every bit of her regard. Scant regard.

Bloody hell. What was wrong with him? After all, he'd caught her.

Brody's body tensed. Now she was just growing tiresome. Toying with him. Tempting him. Pushing him. Leaving him off kilter.

He nodded toward the papers on the desk. "I know what those are," he said, looking up at her. "How did you get them?"

"That is none of your concern." She rolled her shoulders a bit and pushed off the desk as if she was ready to depart.

But perhaps she hadn't noticed, he was between her and the door. The closed door.

"The hell it isn't my concern. I'll have you tried for treason." *After I unmask you. After I . . .*

A bit of laughter bubbled from her lips. "This was treason until *I* stopped it."

"Then murder, I'd say. For the clerk who stole those papers is dead."

That wrenched her gaze up and gone was that smug, mocking light. "De-a-ad?"

He offered a curt, tight nod. "Did you kill him?"

"No!" The word shot out. "I didn't—" Her hand reached for the desk, steadying her.

Brody moved closer, coiling inside. "Why should I believe you?"

She straightened again, her gaze glancing around the room, measuring. "Why is it so hard for you to believe that I'm on your side? I'm here, aren't I? Returning the papers the Admiralty lost."

"Oh, you're here—but whether to help or to steal, I've yet to discover." And then he moved, stalking around the desk. "Whoever you are, you shouldn't be involved."

One of her brows arched loftily above her mask. "Why is that?"

Did he have to state the obvious? Apparently so. "You're a woman."

She chortled a bit. "About demmed time you noticed."

What the devil did that mean? He ignored the familiar niggle that ran down his spine and continued. "This is no business for a lady."

"And what if I wasn't a lady?" she asked quietly, as if testing the waters.

He wasn't about to wade in. "Go home. Leave this—"

"To the men?" She shook her head. "If you haven't noticed, a woman recovered these documents before they got into French hands. My work is necessary. You need me."

You need me.

Oh, the defiance behind those words. The conviction. She was going to get herself killed.

The murderous events of the night merged into his recent loss, his grief, his anger, his frustrations, all of it boiling over. Of late, he'd hardly known himself, bedeviled as he was with a wrenching sort of discontent, rage. He had vowed not to give in to the crushing grief that the news of Poldie's death had wrought . . . but now . . .

This woman, taunting him, daring him. She'd raised his blood, his ire, and demmit, he'd have his answers.

He'd have her.

His arm snaked out and caught hold of her, yanking her close.

She stiffened, and her eyes flashed angrily.

"You shouldn't be doing this," he told her.

That chin tipped up again, all defiant and determined. "No

more than you should be doing this." She nodded at his arms now holding her fast, his body had her pinned to the wall.

"Doing what?" he asked. Two could play this game. But the game was hardly in his favor, for this close, she was as desirable as he'd imagined.

"This is wrong," she whispered.

Soft and round, curves pressed against him. A body that melded to his. In a instant he could well imagine what she would feel like beneath him. He hardened and leaned closer.

"What is it that you find so wrong?" he replied, his lips just a breath away from hers.

Behind her mask, her lashes fluttered slightly. "Holding me," she told him, then gulped a little. "It's highly improper. Ruinous even."

"I disagree," he told her. "Ruin involves something a bit more intimate. And only if you are caught."

She might have been about to reply, but he cut her off, catching her mouth with his.

All of it, a fortnight of pain, bloody ruthless anger over Poldie's death poured out of him as he devoured her, kissed her hard and thoroughly.

His blood pounded, his heart hammering in his chest. And so he continued to kiss her, explore her mouth, let his hand curl around her breast, his other catch hold of her backside and haul her closer, so she rode against him.

Unmask her. See her, his reason clamored.

In time. In good time. For right now only one thing ruled him: the need to pour out his pain.

Pressing her against the wall, he moved against her, cursing his trousers, her silk gown, everything that was in the way.

His own broken heart.

Beneath him, she writhed, pummeling uselessly at his chest.

At first. And then something unforeseen happened. It wasn't anger that she returned, but something else.

Forgiveness. Her fingers curled into the front of his jacket, she opened up to him. As if she understood this onslaught. His pain. She knew and she accepted it. Offered herself as a safe harbor for him to sail toward.

"I'm so sorry about Poldie, my lord," she whispered as he bent his head to nuzzle her neck. "I wish—"

Poldie? Not Leopold. Not Lord Rimswell. But Poldie. Like she was intimately . . .

He pulled himself back for a moment, his blood pounding in his ears, his gaze out of focus.

And in that moment of hesitation, she moved, shoving him hard enough to send him staggering back. As he struggled to regain his footing, all he heard was a solid click of a latch and a heavy creak, then as he righted himself, he watched with disbelief as the panel, where he'd had her pinned, opened, and then once she'd slipped inside, snapped back into place.

In a flash, Asteria was gone. Like a star blinking its last twinkle in the night, she eluded him by taking refuge in the clear light of day—where, he had to guess she would be able to see him quite clearly, while he would still be standing in the dark, at least when it came to unmasking her.

Chapter 2

London, 1811

As if by habit, Brody took another long sweeping glance of Almack's—filled as it was with ladies and misses.

She could be any of them. Well, 'cept the Nafferton sisters, he reasoned.

"See any likely candidates?" Budgey asked.

"Candidates?" he asked.

"For my bride," Budgey reminded him.

Oh, yes, Budgey's bride. Brody straightened and took another look around the room if only to appear as if he was helping.

"What about one of those fetching creatures?" Captain Hathaway suggested, taking a bit too much delight in choosing another man's fate.

Budgey squinted at the pair. "Won't do at all. Those are Lady Nafferton's daughters."

"Pretty, in a way." Benedict mused, appearing to consider the matter, like he was charting a course. "Where is their father's estate?"

"Norwich," Brody supplied.

"And yours, Budgey?"

"Near Plymouth."

"That seems a reasonable distance."

"You haven't met Lady Nafferton," Chaunce provided.

"Besides, you can't tell one from the other. Could be demmed inconvenient," Budgey pointed out.

Benedict went back to scanning the room. "Who is that intriguing minx over there with Lady Essex?" Then he paused, his mouth falling open. "Good heavens, is that Miss Manx?"

Chaunce nodded.

The captain puffed out a breath. "Never known Lady Essex to keep a hired companion *this* long."

"Miss Manx has unknown depths of fortitude," Chaunce replied.

"She'd have to," Benedict remarked. "But who is the chit with them? That dark hair gives her the look of a Spanish *duquesa*."

"How many Spanish *duquesas* do you know?" his brother asked. No, make that scoffed.

"A few," his brother replied defiantly. "And if she isn't a *duquesa*, then she comes from pirate stock. What a splendid looking creature."

"Oh, you've got the pirate part correct," Brody muttered. For he didn't have to look to know who Benedict had spotted. He'd surveyed the room the moment they'd entered, and noted that Roselie was in attendance.

She was devilishly hard to miss. Why was it she was always the first lady in the room to catch his eye—and it wasn't just her dark hair or her lithe figure.

It was because he always had that singular moment of reconciling Miss Roselie Stratton with his childhood memories of his Rosebud.

Chaunce laughed—whether it was at his brother or Brody was yet to be determined. "That's Miss Stratton." He turned to Brody. "Your property abuts her family's holdings, doesn't it?"

Brody nodded. "Yes, we grew up together." Had been thick as thieves as children. And then he'd gone and ruined it all. Now they shared a polite détente.

"Miss Stratton, is it? Fetching, if I do say so," Captain Hathaway repeated.

"Miss Stratton? Oh, yes, Howers likes her," Budgey offered. They all turned and gaped at him. He puffed up a bit, obviously overjoyed that he had information about the head of the Home Office that they didn't already know. "She takes tea with him and his wife every Friday."

"That's hardly a recommendation," Brody noted. "Howers also likes cold mutton stew and orderly reports."

"Doesn't mean she isn't a likely chit for Budgey here," Captain Hathaway noted, warming to his choice. "Come now, you must admit, Miss Stratton is a delight to look upon."

Brody barked a laugh. "Look upon, yes. Marry? Never. Miss Stratton is the last woman on earth I would ever wed. Or wish upon any poor sod."

Budgey, surprisingly, nodded in agreement. "Oh, no, she'd never do. Mother doesn't approve of her."

"I've always suspected your mother was a wise woman, Budgey," Brody told him. For certainly his own mother didn't approve of Miss Stratton. Or any of the Strattons. Blamed them all for Poldie's untimely death in Spain.

Benedict took a step forward. "Well, I don't want to get married, but I think I'm going to ask the chit to dance."

"You keep thinking that," Chaunce told him, nudging him forward. "Go gain an introduction to the girl who's been out for four Seasons."

That give Benedict pause and he took another glance at her. And after making some hasty calculations, he asked, "Four? What's wrong with her?" Then he glanced over at his brother. "No dowry, eh?"

"Oh, no, she'll come with a tidy sum," Brody provided.

The captain's dark brows knit together. "So what is it? Will she tromp all over my poor boots?"

"Not at all, Captain," Brody told him. "Danced with her myself just the other day."

This brought looks of surprise from Budgey and Chaunce.

"I did it as a favor to Rowland," he supplied, if only to stopper their disbelief.

Chaunce shrugged at this and slanted a narrowed glance at his brother. "Go ask her to dance, Benedict. *If you dare.*"

Those three words were enough to light the fire of competition in the captain.

Brody nearly groaned. What was it with these Hathaways? All one had to do was tell another not to do a thing . . .

"I think I shall," Captain Hathaway announced, straightening his jacket. "Come along with me, Rimswell. You seem to know the chit best. Smooth my introduction for me, will you?"

This time Brody did groan, but acquiesced with a curt nod, for it would be far more entertaining to see what Roselie made of the overly confident Captain Hathaway than continuing to point out likely brides for Budgey.

As the two walked away, Budgey clucked a bit. "Your own brother, Chaunce. *Tsk. Tsk.* Not sporting. Not in the least. She'll scuttle him for certain."

Chaunce laughed. "I'm counting on it."

"Lady Essex, I don't know if you remember me—" the man in the captain's uniform began.

"Benedict Hathaway, how could I forget you? You broke my favorite vase when you were six." Lady Essex looked him up and down, utterly unimpressed with the uniform and the medals on his chest. The wily old girl glanced over the captain's shoulder. "And who have you brought with you? Oh, is that you, Rimswell? Yes, I suppose it is."

Now it was Brody's turn to grimace.

Roselie pressed her lips together to keep from laughing. Lady Essex could put the prime minister in his place.

However, the old girl was not one to look a gift horse in the mouth, no matter how dull she thought him. "I suppose it is advantageous you're here, Captain Hathaway—it is captain, isn't it? I believe your mother mentioned your promotion, but there are too many of you Hathaways to keep straight."

"Yes, ma'am, I just thought—"

Lady Essex's fan fluttered in annoyance. "Imagine your mother's joy when I write to her that you are here in Almack's! She'll stop fussing that none of you intend to marry. For I see quite clearly that you've returned to London to enter the Marriage Mart."

"I assure you, my lady, I haven't—" the poor man stammered.

She had already turned to her hired companion. "Mariah, make a note that I must write Lady Hathaway straightaway. Tell her this most excellent news."

"Yes, Lady Essex," Mariah said, digging into the enormous reticule she always carried.

Lady Essex turned back to the man before her. "Is that your older brother as well? Chauncy?"

Captain Hathaway glanced over his shoulder. "Yes, ma'am."

Her fan fluttered with an annoyed flick. "Dull fellow, your brother. Never dances. Don't know why he bothers to gain vouchers."

"He has his moments," Captain Hathaway told her.

"If you say," Lady Essex replied, already looking around for more likely candidates, and her gaze lit on Brody. "What say you, Lord Rimswell? You're being particularly dull this evening, even for you. Why you haven't even asked Miss Stratton to dance."

Roselie coughed a bit. "He needn't—"

"Nonsense, gel." Lady Essex's fan tapped Brody in the chest. "In my day—"

Captain Hathaway leaped into the fray and Roselie gave him credit for being either immensely brave or an utter fool. "Actually, Lady Essex, I came over with the hope that you might introduce me to your fetching friend."

The old girl's brows knit together. "Mariah? You already know her. She was at the Midsummer's Eve ball two years ago when you were in attendance."

He smiled valiantly, his wandering gaze straying over toward Roselie.

"I believe he means Miss Stratton, my lady," Mariah whispered to her employer.

Lady Essex blinked and glanced to her right. "Oh, yes, I suppose he does. Fool that he is. Miss Stratton, may I present Captain Benedict Hathaway."

Roselie smiled and curtsied. All around them, envious glances shot in their direction and she knew why—for she'd already heard the gossip about this particular Hathaway.

Dashing. Handsome. A captain at such a young age. And a fortune in prize money from taking so many enemy ships. Rumors of a title.

She knew she should be over the moon that he had sought out an introduction to her. But she was more piqued that Brody, of all people, had brought the man over to meet her.

Instead of flashing a furious glance at her childhood friend, she smiled at the man before her, and did what she did best. "Ah, yes, Captain Hathaway, how nice to meet you. I am entirely flattered that you sought me out—"

He looked about to say something, probably a gallantry, but she didn't want to hear it.

So she continued, "—especially since I will now be able to supply the other ladies in the room the one piece of information about you that has eluded us all so far."

The captain straightened a bit and glanced around the room, feigning an air of disbelief that he was the subject of speculation.

Bloody peacock!

"And what might that be?" he asked, all smug smiles, even daring a knowing wink at Lady Essex, who in a rare moment, looked a bit charmed and flushed at this masculine attention.

"Whether it is true your fortune is in excess of ten thousand a year, as Miss Pansy Nafferton claims—having gained the information from Lady Damerell's niece, or, is it as Lady Comber says, that you are only worth half that amount, having gambled away a good portion of your shares last week in an ill-advised card game?" She paused and looked him over. "I suppose that obvious tick in your eye confirms the latter. How unfortunate."

She smiled again, because after all, that was what a good debutante did.

Beside her, Miss Manx had already plucked a vial of smelling salts from her reticule, even before Lady Essex began gasping in shock.

"Oh . . . I . . . never—" the old girl managed even as her intrepid companion uncorked the vial and handed it over.

"Well, which is it, Captain Hathaway?" Roselie pressed. "For the moment you step away, I will be inundated with requests for an honest assessment of your character and I would so hate to lead some poor, innocent lady astray by recommending your company."

"Roselie—"

This warning shot came from Brody even as the captain stammered out a "I–I–I—that is—"

Roselie leaned in, as if attempting to keep their conversation from being overheard.

Which, as everyone knew, was impossible at Almack's.

"What I assume is the question everyone will want answered, and pray, allow me to use a nautical metaphor if you don't mind—"

He nodded and smiled, though this time he didn't appear as confident. "No, no, go right ahead, Miss Stratton. I am enchanted by your forthright manner."

Brody rolled his gaze toward the ceiling. A gesture that had one word stamped all over it. *Fool.*

Roselie's fan fluttered delicately. "I'm certain what the ladies here this evening truly want to know is, if you're going to be the sort of husband who shoots off his cannons at the least provocation, or worse, fires them indiscriminately all over town."

Vial or no, Lady Essex swooned.

Roselie paid her no heed. The lady could keep standing in a hurricane, but she had a terrible proclivity for dramatics.

Which was why they got along so famously.

"Yes, well," Captain Hathaway managed, and then gulped a little, before he panicked and bowed and beat—probably for the first time in his life—a hasty retreat.

Brody shook his head. "Roselie, what the devil? Why ever did you have to go and sink that poor man's battleship?"

Chapter 3

$\mathcal{W}$hile Mariah did her best to keep Lady Essex upright, Brody caught Roselie's hand and pulled her toward the dance floor.

"Whatever do you think you're doing?" she demanded, trying to set her heels, but finding no sure footing against a very determined Brody.

"I must dance with someone," he told her over his shoulder.

"Oh, so now I'm just 'someone'?" She yanked her hand free and as she did, the note tucked in her glove fell out.

Immediately he bent over to pick it up for her, turning it over and examining it, looking for clues. Most likely from habit.

"That is mine," she told him, retrieving it and tucking it back into her glove.

She didn't dare look him in the eye. Brody, of all people, would see any hint of panic there.

"From an admirer?" he teased, for certainly her behavior a few moments before would negate such a possibility.

"Hardly," she scoffed, even as a dangerous thread tugged inside her. "I mean, yes. An admirer. An ardent one."

That gave him pause, but only momentarily, for he gave a short shrug.

Much to her chagrin.

"If you say so," he added with a bemused expression. "In the meantime, our dance." Again he began to tow her toward the floor, and again she stubbornly tried to dig her heels in.

"No." It brought back too many memories. Improper ones. Ruinous ones. Impossible ones.

"No?" He stopped just short of where the couples were forming lines. "Would you rather go back and face Lady Essex after that petulant display?"

"I am never—" she began to protest, but then she took a slight peek back where Lady Essex stood with her jaw set and a murderous light in her eyes. "Perhaps dancing is the wisest course."

"Exactly," he agreed and they took their places. As the music began, he grinned at her. "Far cry from the first time we danced. You remember?"

"You would bring that up." How could she forget?

To her further chagrin, he laughed. "Whatever is wrong with that? I was, after all, the one who ended up with the bruised toes."

"You also called me 'awkward' and pointed out all my shortcomings."

He had the audacity to smile. "Well, in comparison to your sister—"

Oh, he'd always known how to blue-devil her. "Yes, yes, compare me to my perfect sister. You called me Rosebud and said I'd never—" She snapped her lips shut, realizing how easily he had baited her.

As he'd always been able to do.

Nor was he done. "Yes, that you'd never bloom like Margaret had."

She glanced away. She hardly needed to be reminded of one of the most mortifying moments of her life. She'd come home from school, eager to see him again, and he'd changed so much. And then . . .

Oh, the sting of it all still hurt.

Until he leaned close. "But haven't you shown me."

She glanced up at him. "Shown you what?"

"How perfectly a late rose can blossom."

Roselie tried to breathe because she couldn't imagine anything Brody could have said that would send her heart racing more. Oh, damn him. She found his gaze searching hers, and as much as she wanted to lean in and smile at him, to tell him what his words did to her heart, she couldn't.

Tell him, Mariah had urged. But she couldn't. He'd be like everyone else.

So she tucked her nose in the air. "About time you noticed."

He ignored her sarcasm. "Oh, I've noticed."

Her gaze flicked back up. What had he noticed? Oh, this conversation was becoming far too dangerous.

As any encounter with Brody did. So she changed the subject.

"I suppose I owe you a debt of gratitude," she conceded. "You could have left me to hang back there."

"Yes, well, as I said, I must dance with someone. Will hardly do to make my appearance here and not dance."

When she glanced up at him, she found him looking down at her with that teasing light in his eyes. The same sense of humor that had dubbed her "Rosebud."

She made a note to step on his foot before the dance ended. "So why me?"

He continued to grin. "For my mother."

"Your mother does not approve of me," Roselie reminded him.

Brody leaned closer and whispered in her ear. "Precisely why I asked *you*."

"You are horrible," Roselie told him, wrenching back, for having him so close left her . . . tangled. Furious. Delirious. "You are the most wretched man in London."

"So you've told me, and more than once," he said, hardly looking penitent. "Now smile and dance. When my mother hears the news, she'll leave me be for at least a fortnight for fear I've suddenly developed a dreadful *tendre* for you if she mentions the subject."

"Oh, so now I'm also dreadful." Roselie glanced away. "I don't know why I should do you any favors."

"Because right now I'm doing one for you," he reminded her.

A glance back found Lady Essex introducing Captain Hathaway to Lady Muscoates and her ward, Miss Taber. She hardly appeared pleased to be offering up such an eligible *parti* to a mere ward.

Yes, Roselie knew exactly what was in store for her when she returned to her chaperone.

"Let's discuss something else," she proposed.

"Perhaps what has you in such a humor?" he teased. "Poor Captain Hathaway."

"Poor Captain Hathaway, indeed!" Roselie shook her head. "And I am not in a humor."

"Does it have anything to do with that note?"

She stilled a little and then feigned indifference. "You never mind about that note."

"I would like to know who he is," Brody said, all serious now.

"Whatever for?"

"Why, I think it is my duty to warn him off."

"I think I've established that I can do that very well all on my own." She tilted her head and smiled.

"You certainly can," he replied, and they both laughed, earning them censorious glances from the decorous couples around them.

"You don't dance enough, Rosebud," he told her after a few moments.

"You don't ask me enough," she replied smartly. Not that she wanted him to ask—oh, it was far too devilish to have Brody close, but it was heavenly to be in his arms.

"You'd dance more," he began, "if you didn't scare everyone off."

"I hardly—"

"You do," he said quite firmly.

"I might," she admitted, wishing she could scare him off. Just a bit. His hand was too warm in hers, his arms too safe.

"Why?"

Oh, yes, he would have to ask that.

"I have my reasons," she told him.

At that, he shook his head. "You are as contrary as ever. But I will say, your reputation leaves you free for me—"

Those words hung between them, the implication like warm temptation.

Free for me.

"To dance with, that is," he added.

Oh, was that all? She trod heavily on his toes.

"Ow! What the devil was that for?" he muttered as he did his best to straighten and not look clumsy as they turned with the other couples.

"What are you doing here this evening, Brody?" Roselie asked, determined to once again change the subject. "For certainly you don't think you will find *her* here."

"Her?"

"The woman you look for."

And from the twitch of his jaw, Roselie knew she had hit the mark. She shouldn't be doing this, provoking him. Tempting fate.

But she couldn't help herself.

Not that Brody was about to concede. "I have no idea—"

Roselie huffed out a breath. "Please. I've known you all my life. You cannot lie to me."

"There is no one." Again there was that twitch. "No more of this, Rosebud."

Rosebud. The name taunted her.

Well, he left her no choice but to do as he asked. But probably not in the way he'd hoped.

"As you wish. If we must discuss something other than your mysterious lady, then tell me why you and your boon companions are here in such a dull place like Almack's, when you could be having such a jolly time at St. John's Folly?"

"Good God," Captain Hathaway complained once Brody had rejoined them. "Next time you cast a man into a squall, have the decency to warn him."

"I rather thought we had," Brody told him, grinning over at Chaunce and Budgey.

"How is it you survive unscathed?" the captain asked.

Who said he was unscathed? Roselie had left him a tangled mess. She'd changed so much over the years—no longer his Rosebud. And who the devil was sending her notes that had her so vexed?

Still, Brody shrugged at the captain's question. "I've known her all my life. I'm rather used to her antics."

"Antics? That woman is a . . . a . . ." Captain Hathaway searched for the right word.

Brody had a few. *A termagant. Bossy. Unbridled.*

But it was Budgey who ended the discussion. "She is the ever-delightful Miss Stratton. I hardly see what the fuss is all about. In fact, I think I shall ask her to dance," he announced. And with that, the viscount set out for the other side of the room.

While Benedict shook his head and licked his wounds, with a fair amount of ribbing from his older brother, Brody watched Roselie as she returned to the dance floor with Budgey.

As she took her place, and Budgey reached for her hand, something inside his gut twinged. If he didn't know better he might think it was jealousy, but that was impossible.

But still, there she was. Roselie Stratton. Properly and modestly gowned. All perfect manners—at least now that she was dancing with Budgey.

And yet . . .

He'd spent the entire dance with the irrational desire to kiss her.

And the odd sense that he already had. That he knew exactly what it would feel like to tease her lips open and explore her mouth, let his hands roam over her.

They'd been thrown together too much of late and he was imagining things. Yet, there was the matter of that note. He glanced up and spotted her immediately—gracefully and graciously dancing with Budgey.

He certainly wouldn't get his toes trod upon.

Oh, Rosebud, what game are you playing? He'd seen her with a number of eligible *partis* over the years, and she'd rebuffed them all, sending them scattering like autumn leaves.

Worse, it pleased him to see them all shying for the hills. But he shouldn't be. Roselie should be married and settled like her sister, Margaret. But she wasn't.

Yet he also knew that such a staid life would never do for her. Still, who the hell was that note from? It wasn't jealousy that had him cross-patched over the whole thing, but demmit, he'd known her all his life and he had the right to be a bit protective of her. As he saw it, it seemed everyone else had given up on her. Her mother. Margaret. Her brother—though granted his injuries from the war had left him incapacitated for some time, but didn't they all see that an idle Roselie was a dangerous notion?

Like take how a proper miss knew anything about a woman like Asteria . . .

Brody huffed a bit. But of course Roselie knew. She had always been too sharp by half. As her own mother often said, she was her father's daughter. And the previous Lord Wakefield had been a master at the game of information, a legend in both the Home and the Foreign Office.

Gads, if Brody was being honest, most of what had kept him alive—and successful—these last few years were the lessons he'd learned from her father and, in some ways, Roselie.

She'd been the boon companion of his childhood, until time and age had separated them.

Not that it wasn't the first time she'd taunted him with rumors of his fascination with Asteria. She'd made a rather pointed taunt at Lady Gourley's just the previous week.

She'd been haranguing him and her cousin, Tuck Rowland, into helping the rather hapless Miss Tempest rise in Society.

And after Tuck had been dispatched, she'd turned to him and said, *When you are ready to find her, Brody, let me know. I'd be more than happy to help.*

Daring him to seek her assistance. As if they were still children and this was all a game.

Well, he wouldn't. Stubborn pride and something else stopped him.

What if something were to happen to her? He would never be able to forgive himself.

He glanced over at the dance floor and realized she was watching him, and when their gazes met—something jarred loose inside him—a jolting sense of recognition. And she felt it as well, he knew it from the way her eyes widened, and then just as quickly, she tore her gaze away.

But in that moment, he saw something else—the tip of her chin, the determined light in her eyes, the way she always seemed to be daring him on to something . . . dangerous.

He blinked and looked again, but she'd already turned and was out of sight.

Demmit, he'd seen that look before. He had.

And why was it, that at that moment her words from earlier echoed with a haunting familiarity. *About time you noticed.* Words all too similar to what Asteria had said that long ago night.

About demmed time you noticed.

It had seemed an odd thing to say then, but now . . .

And there was that glance. The turn of her chin. The defiance in her eyes. He'd seen Asteria look thusly at him just the other week at the Setchfield Ball . . .

He shook his head. Why ever would he think such a thing? He was being as much a nobcock as Budgey. It was all an utterly ridiculous notion, explained quite logically by the fact that he'd been thrown in Roselie's company too much of late.

That was all it was.

He looked over in her direction again and saw not the beguiling lady of his dreams but just the beautiful minx who left him flummoxed.

And yet . . .

Beside him, Chaunce straightened, his gaze fixed on the entrance. "What the devil?!"

Brody looked up and found Lord Howers pushing his way in past one of the patronesses, which was ever so notable since the doors had already been closed—which everyone knew meant no more guests were to be admitted, no matter how many vouchers they held.

Not that the sacrosanct rules of Almack's mattered to the likes of Lord Howers. King and Country were far more important to him than a collection of hare-brained edicts.

Old Ironpants, as the younger agents referred to him (when they were well out of his sharp hearing), barged right past the matron, unsympathetic to her complaints and outrage.

Howers made his way directly to Brody's side and whispered in his ear, "Come along. Immediately." The man turned on one heel and stalked back toward the door.

Brody nodded and turned to his friend. "I fear duty calls."

"Need some help?" Chaunce offered, his proposal most likely born out of a desperation to flee this wretched den of matrimony.

"You wish," Brody replied. He tipped his head toward the opposite side of the room. "Go dance with Miss Stratton when Budgey is done with her. If you dare."

Chaunce barked a laugh. "You forget my golden rule."

Brody paused, though he had his eye on Howers who was departing with the same brusque momentum with which he'd arrived. "Which is?"

"I leave the hazardous duties to you."

"Miss Stratton!" Lady Essex began, extricating herself from an interview with Lady Muscoates once Lord Budgey returned her from the dance floor. "How could you?!" The lady huffed and shook her head. "I don't dare mention this outrage to your poor mother, for fear she'll expire from despair that you've sent yet another eligible young man packing—before you've even danced with him."

"Did Captain Hathaway mention dancing?" Roselie asked, pursing her lips together. "I don't recall him ever asking." She turned to her old school chum. "Mariah, do you recall?"

Her friend was wise enough to appear too preoccupied with the contents of her reticule to answer.

"Why would the poor captain have bothered when you were being so impertinent? And now look at the man! Dancing with Miss Taber. Oh, such a waste of a perfectly excellent prospect." Lady Essex had her hand out and Mariah was already tucking the lady's fan into her grasp.

Roselie was utterly unrepentant. "I daresay a bit of impertinence was good for the captain."

And as for Brody . . . oh, bother him as well. She glanced across the room and couldn't find him anywhere. Which was probably for the best. "In my opinion, Captain Hathaway seems to have a rather lofty impression of himself."

Lady Essex opened her mouth to argue the matter but then apparently changed her mind.

For it was a point that was rather impossible to disagree with.

"Besides, Captain Hathaway is not the man for me," Roselie hoped the lady heard the hard stamp to her words.

Instead, they brought her back to life. "And who is, may I ask? I daresay you've snubbed every man in London over the last three years. For no good reason, I will aver."

"Four," Miss Manx corrected, gaining her glowering glances from both parties. "Well it is four years," she muttered before going back to sorting through her reticule once again.

After a few moments, Roselie drew a deep breath, suddenly feeling the burden of "her reasons."

Good reasons, she would tell the lady.

But when it got down to it, she went with something more akin to the truth, her gaze straying to the spot where Brody had been standing feeling an emptiness in her heart.

"I want a man who isn't cowed by a simple set-down."

"Simple set-down, my word! You cut his anchor loose." Lady Essex turned a bit so neither Roselie nor Miss Manx could see her lips twitch traitorously.

But they saw.

Roselie grinned. "I did, didn't I? Poor man." Though she hardly sounded the penitent.

Before long, all three of them were laughing.

And when they stopped, Roselie looked across the room, searching unsuccessfully for the one man who had captured her heart and now would barely give her notice, and then only when she demanded it. She couldn't help herself, she sighed, confessing what she truly wanted. "Lady Essex, I want a man who appreciates a woman who knows her own mind."

"Oh, you foolish girl!" Lady Essex snorted. "That is the last thing you want to show a man. And never before you marry him."

They all laughed again and the noise caught the attention of the widowed Lady Muscoates, who then joined their party, diverting Lady Essex's attention long enough for Roselie to pluck the note from her glove and read it.

"Where did Lord Rimswell go?" she asked as she scanned the missive.

"Lord Howers came and got him." Mariah paused. "What do you think your godfather wanted with him?"

"I suppose Ilford is making his move—"

"Is that what Abigail says?" she asked, making a pointed glance at the note.

Roselie nodded and sighed, tucking the note back into its hiding spot. "She means to—"

"No, no, don't tell me," Mariah advised. "The less I know the better. Then I shall not have to lie to her ladyship."

Roselie nodded in agreement. For Mariah's help was often the lynchpin in keeping her work secret. Both their fathers had worked in the Foreign Office and she and Mariah had gone to school together at Miss Emery's.

And while circumstances had left Mariah naught but a hired companion and Roselie out in Society, their friendship had never wavered.

Especially when it came to their dear friend, Abigail, the girl Miss Emery had once declared would be the brightest star on the firmament of Society.

A light, Roselie feared, that was in danger of being extinguished. Abigail had come to their cause out of a fire that had been born and lost in love. And now . . .

No, never, she vowed fiercely.

"What do you need?" Mariah asked, sensing Roselie's fears.

"I need to get home. Quickly. I must change and then—"

"Can you not go to Lord Rimswell or even Lord Howers—" Mariah began.

"No," Roselie told her. Her godfather hardly approved, though he had reluctantly agreed to her help. The needs of King and Country outweighing propriety. Especially when she was able to gather information that eluded his male agents. "Tonight will be the last. I'm certain of it."

"Then let me handle this," the capable companion told her. "Luckily, you've gone quite pale, so it won't take much to convince Lady Essex to leave. That, and the company is so lacking in dramatics for her taste."

"Those are yet to come," Roselie said quietly.

Given that hardly anything said at Almack's remained private, Brody knew Howers wouldn't utter a word until they were well away from the gossips and chattering matrons.

And having worked for Howers for some time now, he knew better than to rush the older man or pepper him with questions.

Old Ironpants would come to the point on his own schedule.

But when he spoke with unusual haste, Brody found himself at all points.

Something was very wrong indeed.

"Ilford is on the move," Lord Howers said in a clipped voice. "I need you inside St. John's Folly now."

The Marquess of Ilford. Brody looked up at the man. "What has provoked him? Is it this wager with Rowland?"

"I don't know. Could be." The older man shook his head. "That devil is lashing out—"

"More than usual?" Brody was prompted to say.

"Yes." Howers had no time for quips. "I suspect something or someone has him at sixes and sevens."

The man never liked matters that didn't add up. Neatly and quickly.

"But who? Or why?" Brody kicked at a stone in the street. The marquess was the heir to an old and respected dukedom. He had no reason to commit treason, but of late . . . there had been whispers . . . and along with the sudden reappearance of Asteria, well, it was a mystery for certain. One he was determined to uncover.

Howers looked up and down the street. "If I were to guess, I'd say Ilford is on the edge of going barking mad. This obsession of his with the Tempest sisters is oddly out of character—"

"A diversion?" Brody mused aloud.

Howers nodded in agreement.

Something else occurred to Brody. "Why would he go to St. John's Folly? He certainly wouldn't think to find Miss Tempest there."

He'd met Miss Lavinia Tempest and the gel had a preoccupation with proper that made Howers look reckless. And the fact that his friend, the devil-may-care Tuck Rowland, no less, had fallen in love with the punctilious chit, made it all that much more amusing.

"No, I can't see how this has anything to do with that, but I won't rule out the possibility. The point is, he's at St. John's and he's in a state. He's about to make a mistake. I know it."

Brody nodded. "What do you want me to do?"

"What you do best," Howers told him. "Observe. Watch. And help *her* if you can." Howers slanted a glance at him that suggested he'd be a fool to ask any further questions on that subject.

Her. Brody reeled back a bit. As in Asteria? Howers himself had railed at all of them for years that it was an utterly impossible notion. The chit was a phantom. And now . . .

In that moment, for some unfathomable reason, Brody found himself looking across the street where Roselie and her chaperones for the evening were hurrying down the steps. While Lady Essex was minding the hem of her gown and bullying poor Miss Manx, there was Roselie with her chin tipped just so, taking a measured glance up and down the street.

A chill ran through him.

That tip of her chin. That pause to reconnoiter. The regal way she continued down the steps as if nothing was out of the ordinary—and yet somehow he knew everything in her world was in tumult.

He'd known it when he danced with her.

Why are you here this evening?

He should have asked her the same thing.

For he saw her suddenly in another place, another time. In a jonquil gown and daring him to play her dangerous game.

As the two images intersected, he tried to breathe; he tried to push them apart.

Roselie. Asteria. The two circled each other like wary cats and then merged into a single beguiling image.

Brody tore his gaze away. No, it was ridiculous.

Besides, Roselie wouldn't dare. She was a lady. She was . . .

Her father's daughter.

He shook his head. This is what came of spending too much time with Budgey. He was beginning to reason like the nonsensical viscount.

Folly. Foolish. *Utterly impossible,* he told himself, as he stole another glance at Lady Essex's party.

Beside him, Lord Howers waved for his carriage. "I would give my best hound to know what Ilford is about. That man's secrets go deep I fear."

"We all have secrets, my lord," Brody told him as Roselie took one more glance around the quiet street and this time her gaze fell on them. Him, precisely.

The distance between them narrowed.

When you are ready to find her . . .

Why did he feel like he just had?

"Unearth Ilford's secrets, Rimswell," Howers ordered as his carriage rolled forward. "Stop him before we lose any more ships. Any more lives."

And it was worthy to note that Howers was also watching Roselie as he spoke.

Chapter 4

It is impossible for a lady to maintain her proper reputation if she chooses to associate with rough company.

Miss Emery, Miss Emery's Establishment for the
Education of Genteel Young Ladies

He doesn't know a thing, Roselie told herself for about the hundredth time since Lady Essex's carriage had rolled away from the Assembly Rooms and out from the piercing gaze of Lord Rimswell.

He didn't know a thing. He couldn't.

She shook off the image of him staring at her, and the very notion that his remarkable powers of observation had finally taken note of her.

This was why she'd been avoiding him for months. Though despite her best efforts, he'd managed to spot her at the Setchfield Ball. It was no longer enough to wear different wigs and pad her gowns, especially when they'd been thrown in each other's company too much of late.

It couldn't be helped, at least so she told herself.

Or was it because she needed him? Especially now, as things seemed to have grown so dark, so dangerous.

Just one more time, she told herself as she crossed her room and opened the wardrobe. Reaching all the way to the back, she pressed the panel and opened the secret compartment behind it.

Even in the dim shadows of her room she could see the jonquil silk.

She hadn't dared wear it since, and yet she reached for it all the same.

One last time, she told herself as she glanced in the mirror and began cataloguing what needed to be done. One last time. And tonight will be the end of this.

But she knew that was a lie.

Asteria. She was as captivating to Roselie as she was to half the young agents in the Home Office. And tonight, she must take the risk. Yet again.

Into the fires, as it were. Right into Brody's reach.

"For Abigail," she whispered.

Bernie came in without knocking, carrying the case they kept in her room—the one that held Asteria's makeup and sumptuous, albeit, paste gems, along with the bag that concealed her elaborate blonde wig.

"We'll need everyone tonight," Roselie told her hired companion and coconspirator, explaining the contents of Abigail's note, as well as her own suspicions.

Bernie muttered something unintelligible under her breath as she opened the case and began to deal out the contents.

Roselie reached for a pot of rouge.

"Miss—" Bernie began.

She paused and looked up at the mirror where Bernie's reflection stared back at her. "Yes?"

"You know that gel isn't in her right mind. She might just be leading us all down a rabbit hole of her own making."

She paused. "I know." Then took a deep breath and went back to applying the paint.

Bernie shook her head and continued sorting out the jewelry. Bless her heart, she was a practical soul right down to her sensible boots. "Sometimes a person, when they can't make things right, they just want it to end. She might—"

Roselie shook her head, unwilling to hear more. This wasn't the first time they'd had this argument.

"I promised her I would help."

"Yes, but you had no idea—"

Roselie whirled around. "I could have prevented it all, if I had just screwed up the courage and made someone listen."

"They wouldn't have heard you," Bernie reminded her.

Which was true enough, but still . . .

She paused and glanced at her reflection. Not even Brody would have given her intelligence credit.

Roselie carefully applied a line of kohl around her eyes. Just enough to darken them, but not so much that she couldn't clean the evidence from her face before she had to face her mother and proper Society on the morrow.

"This ain't proper," Bernie told her, handing over the wig.

"Proper?" Roselie wanted to laugh. "Listen to you. When you came to work for me you were—"

"I knows what I know. And I know what is proper." Bernie tucked a few pins in to hold the grand wig in place and then straightened. "And what ain't."

This was getting them nowhere. "I must go," Roselie told her.

"Don't set that jaw of yours at me," Bernie said, shaking a finger at her. "Old Kelly warned you—"

"Bother him. He's an old maid."

Bernie snorted at this. It was rather like mistaking a lion for a mouse. And she had every right, Old Kelly had never steered her wrong.

"It isn't like I haven't been to St. John's before," Roselie pointed out.

Bernie's thick brows rose into sharp arches. "And we all know how *that* turned out."

"I won't make those mistakes again. Nor will I let *him* interfere," Roselie vowed. For she couldn't. Oh, damn, Brody. How she despised him. Despised how he'd made her feel that night in Lord Howers's office and then again a few months later at the earl's Folly.

How'd he'd awakened all those feelings, those wretched, calculating desires tonight as he'd unwittingly and blithely danced with her.

Then again, every encounter with Brody was a dance . . . of sorts.

She looked up to find Bernie studying her. In that unnerving way of hers. "Maybe you ought to—"

"Ought to what?"

"Go to *him*," Bernie urged. "Have him help you."

Not this again. First Mariah, and now . . .

"No." Roselie couldn't make the word more final. "All I have to do is to find Abigail, convince her to follow the plans we have in place, and get her to the docks, as agreed."

Bernie, meanwhile was shaking out the yellow gown. "Is that all?"

She ignored the woman's sarcasm. "Abigail will listen to reason, I'm certain of it."

Bernie said nothing, which made Roselie feel compelled to fill in the void usually well provisioned by her hired companion's unending advice. "Truly, I'll be in and out of the earl's Folly quickly. So long as—" She snapped her lips shut before she said the rest.

—so long as Brody doesn't see me.

"So long as—" Bernie prompted. Bother the woman, she could discern any crack. Any hint of prevarication.

"Nothing," Roselie told her, turning back to the mirror.

"Oh, right, nothing," Bernie said with a huff. "We both know who 'nothing' is."

"He's no concern of mine. He has no idea who I am." Then she remembered with far too much clarity the piercing light in his eyes.

If he doesn't know already.

Bernie crossed her arms over her chest, once again that piercing gaze leaving Roselie shifting in her seat.

So she added, "Besides, I've eluded him twice now. Thrice if you count the Setchfield Ball. And I've learned much in the last two years. I know what I'm doing."

Bernie huffed and turned back to fussing over the gown.

Roselie knew she could escape Brody. She'd been eluding him since childhood. Look how she'd managed the other times . . .

Well, those might not be the best of examples.

For oh, how those encounters had left her in a prison of a different sort. A need to feel his arms around her again. And not in the chaste way like when he'd danced with her earlier.

No, she wanted him to trap her. Pin her against a wall.

His mouth capturing hers. Kissing her. His body hard against hers.

Leaving her . . .

Damn him. Damn him. Damn him.

Once again, Roselie looked up to find Bernie shaking her head.

"If you are set on this course—" Bernie began as she helped Roselie into her gown. "I'll have Patch bring around the carriage, but then I am sending word to the Honorable. You go inside with him."

"You needn't bother Uncle Hero," Roselie protested.

Bernie blew her nose and stuffed her handkerchief into the pocket of her apron. "I'd wake up the bloody prime minister if I thought it would keep you out of harm's way, but I doubt even that would help."

Roselie grinned at her. "Bernie, I'm off to St. John's Folly. The prime minister will most likely be there."

It was meant to be a jest, but Bernie didn't laugh, rather she left the room in a grand huff, like an old hen caught in a sudden gust, all feathers and disgruntled clucks.

Then again, nor did Roselie feel like laughing, for as she looked into the mirror, her face half done up, part Asteria, part London miss, a horrible sense of foreboding filled her chest. Something about the dark expression Brody had been wearing as Lady Essex's carriage pulled away from Almack's that said all too clearly this night would be different.

Dangerously so.

For both of them.

Certainly it couldn't end any more disastrously than the last time she ventured into St. John's Folly.

London, two years earlier

*R*oselie drew a deep breath as she stepped out of the shadows of the alleyway as a grand carriage pulled up to the front of the Earl of St. John's grand London house. While the brightly clad and painted collection of Cyprians and Vestals climbed out, Roselie did her best to surreptitiously slip into their chattering klatch. Oh, she was as brightly clad as the others, but the jonquil gown set her apart from the red and sapphire and emerald shades her counterparts wore.

A solitary daffodil waving loftily over a bouquet of gaudy silk petals.

I am Asteria, she told herself, doing her best to recall all the lessons she'd learned of late from Uncle Hero and Mrs. Rowland.

As long as you believe the lie, no one will have any reason to question you, the Honorable Hero Worth liked to tell her.

So she nonchalantly made her way up the steps—well as nonchalantly as one might in a pair of devilishly high heels.

I am Asteria, she told herself again, trying to still the quaking in her chest as she entered St. John's Folly. After all, she trusted Old Kelly, London's unofficial purveyor of information and he'd sent her the instructions he'd been passed.

Find the man in the puce jacket and domino mask. He'll give you proof of who's selling to the French and names. But caution—he's being followed.

Oh, she'd heard all the rumors that swirled through Society

after one of the Earl of St. John's Follies, the annual bacchanal wherein the most notorious and jaded rakes, gentlemen and questionable ladies cavorted with wild abandon.

But hearing the gossip and striding right into the heart of such revelry was an entirely different matter.

"Come with me, sweetling," a rogue called out, catching her by the arm. "Don't think I've seen you before."

Roselie brought her heel down on the top of his foot and left him howling in pain as she quickly moved deeper into the crowded foyer, checking to ensure her mask was tightly secured.

She knew what she was doing was dangerous, and foolhardy, and a hundred different scandalous things that Bernie had railed on about before she'd left tonight, but Roselie knew what she must do.

Even if Miss Emery's Establishment for the Education of Genteel Young Ladies in Bath had never managed a lecture on this.

This being St. John's Folly.

Couples openly kissing and fondling each other. A magician whose assistant kept losing pieces of her clothing with each trick. A roulette wheel in the parlor.

This was definitely not Lady Oxnam's weekly card party.

Roselie turned down the offer of a cigar from an older woman dressed in a man's jacket and breeches. Ladies smoking? Miss Emery would be in vapors. When she got to the stairwell, to her surprise she spied their neighbor, proper Lord Claxby entwined with a vivacious redhead, who had her hand down his . . .

Roselie quickly glanced away.

The hypocritical old goat! The man sat two pews behind them in church and spent most of his time denouncing vice in the streets.

Apparently vice indoors was the exception.

She shook her head and continued on, for everywhere she looked she saw someone she knew—neighbors, the prime minister, young bucks out to sow their wild oats, lordlings and rakes alike. And Vestals and Cyprians at every turn—all looking for their next champion, wares well displayed, sampling freely offered. It was rather like finding herself in one of those scandalous French picture books Lady Arabella Tremont had smuggled into the school one dreary winter.

Leave it to the daughter of a duke to have the curriculum one really needed in an emergency.

Roselie moved through the rooms—one set aside for cards—where she spied the Marquess of Ilford—the man had a penchant for gambling, with money and lives. Continuing on, she stumbled into a study where glassy-eyed people lounged on grand tuffets, smoking from a long pipe. Wrinkling her nose at the sweet stench, she continued on.

Oh, bother. She couldn't find the slightest sign of her contact—though she could see why he'd been so insistent on meeting here—for with so many people absorbed in their own pleasures—their encounter would hardly attract much notice.

Notice. She stilled for a second, remembering Old Kelly's words.

. . . caution—he's being followed . . .

Followed. Why she'd thought of *that* right then, she didn't know. Perhaps it was the closeness of the room, or just the unrestrained pursuits happening all around her.

The falseness to all of this forced gaiety sent a shiver down her spine. A warning. A sense of trepidation.

That her frightened contact wasn't the only one being followed.

She glanced over her shoulder, and in that instant, spied him.

She recognized the man immediately, for Uncle Hero had pointed him out in a gaming hell a few weeks earlier.

Craddock.

One of the deadliest fellows in London's underbelly.

What was he doing here? The prime minister—of course he'd be here. The Marquess of Ilford? For certain. But Craddock? He was more likely to be found near the docks or in some hell in Seven Dials.

She continued on her course as if she hadn't spied him, and

after a few steps took another careful glance over her shoulder, and sure enough, there he was.

What was it Uncle Hero had told her at the time? Ah, yes, she remembered.

If you ever have the misfortune to encounter Craddock up close, there is only one thing to be done. Run.

That shiver from a few moments ago now returned, rather like a quake. *Run.* She could hardly do that in this crush. And certainly not before she got what she'd been promised.

And decidedly not in these wretched heels Mrs. Rowland had convinced her to buy on their last "Asteria" shopping trip. She glanced down at the satin monstrosities with their enormous paste buckles and shuddered.

I am Asteria, she reminded herself. She had papers to retrieve. Patch was outside in the alleyway with the carriage. If only he was here inside.

If only . . .

If only Brody was here.

Oh, yes that would solve everything, since he'd been quite determined the last time they met to unmask her.

And kiss her. And hold her . . .

She went back to the unmasking part. She needed to keep her wits. And thinking about Brody and his lips always left her wits . . . a bit scrambled.

And if he was here and if he did unmask her, that would be the end of Asteria. Still, better that than disgracing her entire family when it was discovered proper Miss Roselie Stratton had turned up dead in a courtesan's dress at St. John's Folly.

A courtesan's dress.

She looked down at herself and realized why Craddock was studying her. A courtesan who wasn't seeking out a patron. No wonder she stood out.

She needed to appear as any other of the ladies here—a disreputable and licentious courtesan. Perhaps she should have taken that cigar, for the alternative was . . .

A man caught hold of the woman next to her and pulled her into one of the curtained alcoves that lined the back wall of the ballroom. Given the moans and titterings coming from behind those red curtains, Roselie knew exactly what they were for . . .

The "Devil's Alley" the gossips called it.

Yes, well, she rather needed an alley right now if she was to escape Craddock's notice.

But what experience did she have in these matters? For besides Lady Arabella's picture book, the only other experience she had was with . . .

"Ah, my love, there you are." And in an instant, she found herself towed along, a strong hand at her elbow, her shoes skidding all over the marble floor for it was impossible to find any footing.

When she looked up, the protest that rose in her throat stopped, as if tamped down by a cork.

Dark hair. Tall frame. A whisp past her nose of bayberry and rum and something so very masculine, so very familiar.

Brody.

Her heart hammered in recognition, in the sense that everything was going to be all right.

But it was Brody. And everything was suddenly at risk.

Her mission. Her heart.

He tugged her behind one of the red velvet curtains, and suddenly Roselie found herself pinned to the wall—hands over her head and his body against hers.

She tried to breathe, tried to say something, but his lips found hers and he kissed her, hard and fast as if it were his right.

She tried to buck against him, but he continued to kiss her, his tongue teasing her, calling to her.

And worse, her own body betrayed her. Her mouth opened to him, inviting him to explore her, her body curling up against his.

His tongue stroked hers, and she could imagine him stroking her in other ways.

Catching hold of her leg, he hitched it around his hip, and she gasped, as his hand curved around her bare thigh, warm and teasing.

"Please—" she began, trying to push the other word past her lips, *don't*. But she couldn't dislodge it no matter how hard she tried.

Still, she tried to shake herself free, but he shook his head and leaned close to her ear. "Be still, you little fool," he whispered—no, make that warned. Ordered. Commanded. "Craddock will kill us both—"

He had her attention now.

"—if we can't convince him that we aren't just like the rest of this pleasure-seeking mob." Then he went back to nuzzling at her neck, teasing her with his lips until she shivered. He glanced down at her, his gaze—those dark eyes she knew so well—fixed on hers. "Can I let go of your hands?"

She nodded, not daring to speak a word.

And he did. Release her. Immediately her hands went to his jacket, finding steady purchase as she caught hold of his lapels.

Always, it was Brody there to catch her.

His hand now free, it roved over her gown, and she knew what he was finding—the padding beneath, the corset that pushed her breasts deceptively high in her gown. She was naught but layer upon layer of deception and he was determined to undo them all.

Not that she wasn't opposed to the idea when his hand cupped her breast and his touch sent delicious tendrils of desire through her.

"Who are you?" he whispered.

"The woman you want," she teased back.

"How can you be so certain?" he managed.

"You've rescued me, haven't you?"

"Yes, well, we'll see about that."

Something about the denial in his words, the doubt behind them, stirred that dangerous anger inside her.

Girls can't . . .'Tis impossible, Roselie . . .

He might have staved off her enemy for now, but she still had work to do. And she needed to distract Brody long enough to escape him.

There was no panel here. No passageway that she knew of. While her godfather had shown her that doorway in his office long ago, she couldn't say she had the same experience with the Earl of St. John's house.

How ever was she going to get away?

Then she remembered. *I am Asteria.* Certainly that cheeky minx would know what to do.

Roselie stirred to life in Brody's arms—it wasn't all that difficult to do for his kiss had already ignited her imagination. She rocked her hips forward until her very core rode against him, where she found a hard long length to rub, the feeling of him against her filled her with a new madness, a bolt of desire that flamed furiously to life.

A claiming.

Brody sensed the change in her and done with banter, done with words, his mouth crashed down atop hers, kissing her, deeply, thoroughly. Opening her, his tongue explored with a driving hunger, thrusting into her, just as his rigid stalk wanted to be inside her.

With her leg still hitched up around his waist, he began to explore her, teasing past her silken thigh and right to the patch of curls—until he brushed the pads over her sex.

"Ah," she gasped, as her head arched back, and she rose on her toes, awakened in a whole new way. "Oh, yes, yes." She pressed closer, greedy little jade that she was, gathering her desires like scattered coins.

He deepened his kiss, as his body grew harder and her body rubbed against him with more insistence.

Intoxicating desire left her in a whirlwind of passion.

For a moment she forgot who she was. Where she was. What she was supposed to be doing . . .

Then behind them, the curtain rustled. Opened.

Brody whirled first, reacting with the skill and precision of a man who'd been coiling to strike. His hand clenched in a hard fist that drove with blinding fury right at the intruder, connecting with the man's jaw with a solid, satisfying crack.

A woman close by shrieked, even as Roselie reached for her knife, but as the entire scene came into focus, she saw not Craddock on the floor, but a smallish, well-dressed nobleman clutching his jaw.

"Good God!" the fellow exclaimed. "I do say, I didn't think this alcove was taken."

"Georgie—are you hurt?" the man's companion purred—now that she'd stopped her caterwauling, clinging to her lover and glaring daggers at Brody.

"Sir," the man demanded, "I'll have your name. My seconds will call first thing—"

And that was Roselie's cue.

With Brody's back to her, she fled, slipping past him and hurrying headlong through the ballroom without a backward glance. At the foyer she paused for a moment.

"Looking for someone, dearie?"

Roselie nodded to the cigar-smoking lady. "A man in a puce jacket and a domino mask. He owes me money."

"They all owe us, child. They all do," she said in a voice filled with resignation. She tipped her head toward a long hallway. "Last room on the right."

"Thank you," Roselie told her.

The lady caught her by the arm. "I didn't like the look of that one and you seem a bit new at this. Have a care."

Roselie nodded for she could see Brody striding determinedly through the ballroom toward her, so she had to hurry on.

But when she came to the room and opened the door, she realized that the woman's concerns were hardly for naught.

On the carpet, lay a man in a puce jacket, his domino mask askew. His white shirt bloomed with the bright red stain of blood, while his sightless eyes stared past her to another world.

Dead. He was dead.

Frantically she looked around the room, for he obviously hadn't come into the room alone. He'd had company.

The garden doors were open and there was no one in sight.

Dropping to her knees, she gingerly began to search for the papers he'd promised, but as her hand slid into his jacket, his body still warm to the touch, she stifled a sob and reached up to close his eyes instead.

The door opened, and she whirled around, but found only Brody standing there. Like her, he gaped at the scene before him.

"I didn't do this," she blurted out. For indeed, from the murderous expression on his face, it was exactly what he was thinking.

Why wouldn't he? She was still holding her knife.

"Who the devil are you?" He closed the door behind him.

She ignored him, and frantically went back to her search of the man's jacket.

He caught hold of her arm and stopped her. "What are you doing?"

She didn't dare spare him a glance; instead, she yanked her hand free and went to the man's scuffed up boots.

"Stand aside," he ordered, reaching inside his jacket and pulling out a pistol.

She gave his order scant regard. "Hardly. Not until I know for certain—" She huffed a sigh as she plucked a knife out of one of the dead man's boots and tossed it aside. Too bad he hadn't thought to use it.

Whoever he was.

Shaking her head, she finally looked up at Brody. "The papers are gone."

"Who the hell are–"

But before he could finish, the door opened, and a pair of lovers came tumbling into the room, obviously hoping to find a bit of privacy. Locked in an embrace, their mouths fused in a deep kiss, they continued on, oblivious to the scene before them, until after a moment or two, when they finally realized they weren't alone.

The Cyprian glanced around first, a sly smile turning her full red lips. That is, until her gaze fell on the body at her feet.

Pushing her lover out of her arms, she tottered back on unsteady legs and began to stammer.

Which quickly became an unholy shriek.

Her partner, yanked from his passionate stupor, blinked stupidly at the floor. Abandoning any attempt at courage or nobility, he weighed the situation and immediately fled, leaving his screeching paramour behind, and crying out as if the hounds of hell were at his heels. "Murder! I do say! Murder!"

"Oh, bloody hell," Brody sputtered as he went to stop the fellow.

In that moment, Uncle Hero's advice tolled like a giant bell. *Run.*

Yes, well, it seemed as good a time as any. And so she did, out the French doors and with little thought of grace and composure, or even Miss Emery's adamant advice that a lady always thanked one's host before one departed.

She'd send a note to the earl. That would have to do.

Chapter 5

"It is impossible to solve the world's problems in just one night. Humanity has been endeavoring as much for centuries, and will most likely continue doing so . . . All we can do is learn and move forward. Ever forward."

From the journals of George Stratton,
Viscount Wakefield

London, 1811

𝒯his time, Roselie strode bold as brass up the steps of the Earl of St. John's house. She smiled with a coquette's charm at the various rogues and lordlings lolling about the entrance.

She'd learned much in the two years since her first visit, when she'd tentatively climbed these same steps. But as her father had written in his journal, nothing could be decided in one night. *But this night*, she vowed, *this one, I turn the corner.*

"Pretty bird," one of them called to her. "Come sit on my perch."

His friends laughed, as did Roselie.

"I doubt it is sturdy enough," she teased back—to the great amusement of his friends—and passed them quickly to move deeper into the crush.

A hand reached out and caught her by the elbow. "Come love, you must be looking for me," a now-inebriated Budgey said, "I will keep you in splendor and good company." He blinked owlishly at her, and then opened his eyes a little further beyond their rum-fueled haze and for a moment she feared he'd recognized the woman behind the mask.

But this was Budgey, and a Budgey well into his cups, so she smiled and said, "I don't think my benefactor would be pleased by such an arrangement, my lord." Tipping her head slightly, she whispered for his benefit, "I fear my protector has a terrible temper. His affinity for pistols is well known." She sighed and shook herself free of him, and since it was Budgey, he let her go quite willingly.

Pushed along by the press of guests, Roselie couldn't shake the sense that she was being followed—a leftover fear from the first time she'd come to the Folly, she supposed—but still it hastened her pace until she found herself at the entrance to the room set aside for gambling.

She was surprised to find most of the tables abandoned—the hands and wagers scattered across the green baize like children's forgotten playthings.

Everyone in the room had collected around a single table, Lord St. John's own, and their gazes were fixed on the fast play at hand, including someone Roselie recognized.

Lady Muscoates. Masked, but wearing the same richly done gown she'd had on at Almack's.

Oh, wouldn't Lady Essex find that a delicious *on dit*. Not that Roselie could divulge how she came upon such a tidbit. She would have to suffice with sharing it with Mariah.

Around the table were any number of society's glittering jewels all watching the single woman at the table playing for such high stakes. But it was the man across from the mysterious lady who had Roselie drawing back a bit.

Lord Ilford.

So he *was* here. She'd half-hoped Abigail's hurried note had been penned in one of her less lucid moments. But to their benefit, the usually sharp-eyed marquess had his attention fixed entirely on the woman opposite him.

Roselie's brow furrowed, for she couldn't place the beauty.

Like nearly all of the women at St. John's, she wore a mask to conceal her identity—most likely to keep her paramour from finding out about her misadventures. Or she might be a lonely wife seeking a bit of solace outside her marriage.

In any case, Roselie shrugged, for she hardly cared who this Cyprian might be, for thankfully the creature was keeping Ilford entirely engaged.

If anything, this was her first bit of luck in a long time.

She smiled at the darkly clad woman, silently thanking her for her unwitting help, and then paused as she realized something else. That gown . . .

A deep midnight blue velvet with brilliants sewn about it like stars in the night.

Good heavens, Roselie knew that gown.

She'd seen it not a fortnight earlier when she'd been out shopping with Mrs. Rowland. She'd nearly bought it herself, for it was the perfect sort of thing Asteria might wear. Clearly this woman had seen the gown's advantages as well—for she had every man in the room delirious to know her identity.

Including the one studying her from the back of the crowd.

Brody.

Her heart did that odd pattering, a mixture of panic and something she preferred to ignore.

Roselie whirled around and hastened away, but in her headlong flight immediately stumbled into another gentleman, who caught hold of her, if only to keep her from tumbling over—she had never truly managed to learn to walk in a coquette's heels.

"My pardon, madame," he said, and that voice—despite her best instincts—yanked her gaze up to meet his.

Worse, his name almost escaped her lips.

Tuck.

Her cousin by marriage. Mrs. Rowland's knave of a son.

Instead, Roselie spit out the first curse in French she could think of, and escaped his company as quickly as she could, bolting into the adjacent ballroom.

If Brody were to discover her identity that was one thing, but Tuck?

He'd drag her to Piers's and the two of them would have her trundled off to the nearest convent—without a hearing or a jury. Without a moment's hesitation.

And then most certainly everything would be lost.

Stopping inside the ballroom, she pressed her hand to her stomach and willed herself to collect her wits, even as her heart hammered in her chest.

Too much at stake, she told herself, drawing a deep breath. *Too much to be done.*

So much to lose, the image of the dead man rising up like a specter before her. She'd never found out who he was. There had been a few whispers about a murder, but for the most part the scandal had been hushed up and then, as was the course of Society, forgotten.

Not that Roselie had.

That night, the one that had promised to be the end, had instead become a turning point of another sort. She had her own sort of reckoning, tallied her mistakes and made an accounting of what needed to be done—learning a coquette's charms from Mrs. Rowland, picking locks and pockets from Bernie and devouring her father's journals like other misses memorized all the lineages in Debrett's.

Straightening, she moved with fluid grace through the crush of guests, searching for any sign of Abigail, continuing deeper and deeper into the ballroom.

Still, she couldn't shake that feeling in the pit of her gut that this night was going to be different.

Dangerously so.

So why was it that her thoughts went immediately to Brody? She glanced over her shoulder to see if he had followed her, but he was nowhere in sight.

Brody. Watching her as she left Almack's. Kissing her—in this very room.

That was probably why she'd worn this gown. The jonquil silk. One she knew Brody would spot in an instant.

If she needed help . . .

She chided herself for being foolish and sentimental. Frightened was more like it. The closer she got to uncovering the truth, the more she had the strangled sense of a net tightening around her, threatening to stop her by any means.

Like her murdered informant.

Botheration, she might very well need his help tonight if she couldn't find Abigail.

Yet in an instant, her luck changed, for there across the room shone Abigail's fair hair and pale cheeks, like an angel against this dark night of debauchery. She paced about the corner, a nervous habit she'd taken to recently. Back and forth, muttering constantly, nonsensical one moment, then startlingly lucid the next.

Of the three of them, Abigail, Mariah and Roselie, Abby had been the least equipped for the dangerous course to which they were now tied.

But she'd waded in without hesitation.

Because she'd been the one who had lost the most.

Her heart, to be exact. And now, so it seemed, her wits.

Roselie approached her slowly. "Darling, there you are," she said quietly, as she caught hold of her. "I've looked everywhere for you. I don't know how we got separated." This she said for the benefit of anyone who might be listening, all too thankful to have found Abigail before . . .

Before . . . Roselie saw not her friend, but another. With vacant eyes staring up at her. The dark red stain spilling across the white of a shirt.

She paused and blinked, then glanced around, but to her relief, no one appeared to being paying them any heed.

Tonight. Tonight would be different. No one need die.

"He's here," Abigail rushed to tell her, clinging to her like a child.

And with one look at her friend, Roselie knew immediately that the task before her wasn't going to be easy. "He" could mean one of two things.

Neither of which boded well.

Abigail's eyes glowed with the madness that had been slowly stealing her senses, her gaze flitting in one direction and then the next. She wore the plain dark traveling dress Roselie had bought for her and clutched a small satchel to her chest.

Clung to it as if it was the only bit of flotsam that might keep her afloat.

And it probably was, if it contained what Roselie hoped it might. No, must.

But, oh, heavens, how Abigail stood out in this clutch of feathers and lace. She was far too noticeable in her drab costume.

Which meant Roselie needed to get her out quickly.

"He's here, I tell you," the girl whispered, her desperation coming out in a hiss.

"Who, Abby?" she asked, moving her gently and slowly through the crowd. For recently Abby had grown convinced she was being followed. That someone was watching her comings and goings.

Just as someone else had once claimed. And look how that had turned out.

"Laurence. He's looking for me. I must find him," Abby told her, tugging at Roselie's grasp.

"You know he wouldn't be in such a place," Roselie reminded her ever so gently. "Captain Croft was too good to keep such company."

Abigail blinked as she looked around, taking stock of her surroundings. In an instance, the fight seemed to fade from her, even as her eyes widened. "No. He wouldn't. Of course not."

"Now come along, like we discussed. Patch is in the mews and he'll take you to the docks. You'll be safe from harm in Boston. Remember?"

"Safe?" Abigail shook her head, hugging her satchel closer. "There is nowhere safe for me, save with Laurence."

As Roselie smiled at her, trying to comfort her, she mourned the loss of the girl she'd known at Miss Emery's, the frail, but brilliant daughter of a merchant who could manipulate figures beyond their math tutor's poor skills. A girl so smart, it had at times, left her an outcast among the other students—young ladies more keen to learn table settings and where to find a wealthy, landed husband than how to calculate interest, or manage columns of numbers.

But Roselie and Mariah—outcasts in their own ways—had loved Abigail all the more for her brilliance. For her frailties.

And if anyone could puzzle out Ilford's devious plans it was Abigail. And she had. At least, so she claimed.

So Roselie hoped.

But the loss of her husband had taken a toll on Abigail's health. Left her vulnerable to the cruelties of the world. Nor had the world or Society been kind to Abby.

Not when she'd cast aside her father's wishes for an advantageous match and married Captain Croft instead. And the lady's troubles had only continued when the good captain had died not long after the wedding, and her father had completely washed his hands of his eldest daughter.

"This is a terrible place, Roselie," Abigail whispered, as they made their way through the crowd. "The sort of place where the shadows and darkness win."

Roselie hugged her. "Dear, dear, Abby. You will be safe soon enough. My cousin will not let any harm come to you. She's most joyous to have your company. Remember?"

Abigail nodded. But it was an empty gesture and her gaze was once again fixed on that far away place, the one only she could see.

"Cousin Patience was married to a sea captain as well. You will have much in common."

"Yes, I suppose so," Abigail replied absently.

All the time they'd been talking, Roselie had skillfully managed to guide her out of the house, down into the garden at the back and toward the mews.

With every step, Roselie couldn't shake the sense that they were being watched, followed, but everywhere she looked, she couldn't see anything out of the ordinary.

At least nothing beyond the usual bacchanals.

No villains lurking in the shadows, like the one who had greeted her on her first visit.

So, as Uncle Hero had taught her, she kept to the most public routes, like here, out in the garden, where the gates to the mews were flung open—most likely for guests who wanted to make a hasty, albeit discreet, entrance or exit.

"Your work is done, Abby," Roselie told her, glancing at the satchel. She reached for the case, but her friend stepped away, clutching it fiercely.

"It is all here, Roselie," Abigail told her. "Everything you need . . . I should stay and help. Help you make sense of it."

"If it is all there, Mariah and I will be able to puzzle it out," Roselie assured her. "You taught us how."

Abigail trembled a bit. "I did, I suppose. You and Mariah."

"And we are forever in your debt."

Behind them, a carriage pulled into the mews, and Roselie didn't think she'd ever been so relieved to see her faithful driver, Patch, another recruit provided by Uncle Hero.

"All ready, my lady?" Patch asked as he hopped down—as much as a man his size could hop.

My lady. That always made her brow quirk a bit, for she was only the daughter of a viscount, and properly addressed as *miss*.

But Patch, along with his brother, Solly, took their duties as Roselie's guardians quite seriously, thankful for the employment and in many ways, rather awed by the slight and spirited young woman entrusted to their watchful care.

And so, no number of corrections could stop Patch from addressing her so.

My lady she was to him and *my lady* she would always be in his eyes.

"Come, Abigail, it is time for our farewells," Roselie told her, carefully extracting the valise from her friend's grasp and opening it. There, tucked inside was a packet of papers neatly tied up with a red cord, the very ones Abigail had vowed would solve everything. Having retrieved the treasure trove, Roselie gave her friend back the valise and hauled her into a tight hug. "Remember, Mariah and I will always have you in our hearts. And one day we will be together again, I promise."

But for all the heart behind her words, she couldn't shake the wrenching sense that this was the last time she'd ever see Abigail.

"Thank you, Roselie," Abigail whispered back, clinging to her just as tightly. "Finish this for me. For Laurence."

"I will," Roselie vowed. "I promise."

Satisfied, Abigail climbed into the carriage and sank into the seat with a sort of weary resignation.

With her safely ensconced in the carriage and the door closed, Roselie turned to Patch. "Get her to the docks quickly. Before she becomes agitated. See that she is well aboard the *Dancing Scot* and the captain gets underway immediately." She paused for a second and looked again toward the shadowed figure hidden inside the dark carriage, unable to shake free of the nagging premonition that had been worrying her all night. "And tell the captain not to let her out on the decks without someone to watch over her. You understand?"

"Aye, my lady," Patch said, with a glance as well at his solitary passenger. But when his gaze turned back to his mistress, his great bushy brows furrowed together. "And what about you, my lady? I won't leave you here."

She patted his arm and prodded him toward his perch atop the carriage. "You always say that, and you know I will insist. I've haven't come to harm as yet, and I don't plan on finding myself in its path. Besides, this is Mayfair and Lord St. John—for his faults and proclivities—would never let any mishap befall me."

That hardly seemed to reassure the always skeptical Patch. "You should come along with us, my lady," he told her, nodding toward the carriage door. "See to the poor mite yourself." His heavy brows furrowed, telling her what he wasn't saying.

And so I can keep an eye on you, as well.

Oh, she knew full well what Patch was about.

Yet even as she was crafting her refusal, that shiver of fear, of Fate, one might call it, had her stepping back. "No, we should split up."

Besides, she had Abigail's papers now. This was everything her brilliant friend had amassed. The proof to bring Lord Ilford to trial for treason.

She needed to get this home and assemble her case for Lord Howers.

Abigail's dear Captain Croft and his crew—and all the others Ilford had harmed—would finally have their justice.

She looked up to find Patch waiting still, with his hand steady on the latch.

She smiled at him and shook her head. "Bernie has sent for Uncle Hero to fetch me home. He should be here without delay."

"The Honorable!" Patch snorted. "Oh, he's a wily one, but no dab hand in a fight."

"That's why I'll be there," she told him tartly. "Now off with you. Before the tide turns and our luck runs out. Uncle Hero will see me home."

"Uncle Hero," the man muttered under his breath like a curse. But slowly and reluctantly, Patch climbed up into the driver's seat and set off for the docks.

Roselie drew a steadying breath, that is until she heard a crunch of boots on the gravel path behind her.

Someone coming, and coming fast.

She whirled around to find Brody bearing down on her—his jaw set with a murderous twist and his eyes dark with anger. She took an involuntary step back—Roselie never liked to yield an inch, but Brody looked ready to kill someone.

And then as if all her fears came true, his arm swept out and he shoved her hard, sending her flying backward, her wig tumbling off as she hit the ground.

And when she scrambled to right herself, she saw why.

Brody arrived at St. John's with his reason and instincts at war.

Roselie. Asteria.

Once inside the earl's grand house, he found the usual collection of Cyprians and courtesans and ne'er-do-wells, and immediately set aside his earlier conjectures as utter folly.

For looking from one ladybird to another, he immediately dismissed the notion of Miss Roselie Stratton, the daughter of a respected viscount—tart-tongued opinions, aside—traipsing about in such company.

The Marquess of Ilford, as it turned out, was easy to find—settled into a card game with the Earl of St. John and a mysterious woman who was making a run at the table, an ever-growing pile of coins and markers before her.

As the cards changed hands and the play continued, Brody glanced up at the door to the foyer and to his amazement a flicker of jonquil silk caught his eye.

Asteria.

With Ilford well engaged, Brody followed the vision in yellow without hesitation.

And as he did, he almost laughed that he had thought this sauntering bit of coquette was actually a proper miss in disguise.

That walk was hardly something one learned at a Bath school.

His quarry prowled through the foyer and into the ballroom, pausing for a second in the doorway and then as if on instinct, her head swirled, glancing back in his direction.

He'd been half expecting such a maneuver and dodged out of her line of sight. It was just like when he and Roselie had been children and spent hours secretly following their older brothers.

After a few moments, she made a slight shrug and continued into the ballroom.

He counted to three and continued his hunt. Again in the crush, she wasn't easy to spot, even in that bright silk and a tall blonde wig, but eventually he spied her again, this time on the far side of the room, deep in conversation with another woman.

Brody moved slowly, stalking her as a wolf might a vigilant doe, sliding through the room and using the wild goings-on to cover his approach.

Then as he found his vantage point, Asteria moved slightly and he saw who she was with.

"No." The word escaped his lips as his wits once again clamored to be heard.

Mrs. Croft. No, he must be mistaken, yet a second look confirmed it. Abigail. One of Roselie's dearest friends from school.

No. No. No. This had to be a coincidence.

Yes, right. In a long string of coincidences.

Mrs. Croft paced about in front of her companion, looking a bit disheveled, mad almost, until slowly and craftily, Asteria managed the woman from the room toward the doors to the garden.

It was so well done, he barely noticed, and certainly Mrs. Croft didn't seem to realize she was being herded.

But to where and what end?

They were questions he had to answer.

Taking one more glance back toward the gaming room—he hesitated. His instructions were to watch Ilford.

But Howers, in his usually obtuse way, had also ordered him to be of assistance.

And Brody now suspected he knew exactly what that meant.

So he followed Asteria.

As the pair escaped into the garden, he slipped after them into the shadows of an arbor, well out of sight.

The two women spoke quietly, and it was obvious Asteria was trying to convince the captain's widow to take some course of action that the woman was reluctant to follow.

He could only hear snippets, and those he did, hardly sated his curiosity.

Quite the opposite.

He's here.

I must find him.

You'll be safe from harm.

Brody cocked his head and studied the two women. Why the devil did Mrs. Croft need to be safeguarded? Let alone what was this respectable widow doing here?

He leaned closer as the discussion quieted, though he could see it continued in the same way—back and forth, Asteria coaxing and Mrs. Croft distant and distracted.

Distracted. A cold shiver ran down his spine. He wasn't one for fancies. Or premonitions.

Yet something was wrong. Very wrong.

Like Asteria had before, he took a sweeping assessment of their surroundings.

Yet before he'd finished his search, an odd bit of their conversation floated toward him stopping him cold.

It is all here, Roselie.

Roselie.

Brody's world tipped upside down.

He tried to breathe. He tried to deny what he'd so clearly heard. His instincts railed at him to step out of the shadows and unmask this creature in yellow, if only to prove himself wrong. Deny what he now knew.

Probably had always known.

Fool, his senses railed. *You knew all along.* Memories from their encounters—when he'd kissed her. When he'd teased her skirt up and touched her . . .

It had been Roselie all that time.

And as if to confirm it, a carriage rolled up. A hulking figure in the driver's seat—Patch, Roselie's driver.

Despite it all, Brody still floundered for a way to discredit the evidence before him. But how could he when Patch's arrival was like watching the last domino fall into place?

Still, this was nothing short of madness.

His madness. A white hot surge of rage rushed through him. At this woman who had driven him wild with desire for years. Haunted his dreams. The minx he'd spent countless nights searching for . . .

The devil take her, Asteria had been standing right in front of him, taunting him, the entire time.

When you want to find her . . .

Damn you, Roselie. Damn you to hell.

She'd been mocking him. Or had she been?

His anger hardly abated when he looked up again and found Mrs. Croft being bundled into the carriage.

But not Roselie—a point that appeared to be a bone of contention between her and Patch, for they were having a heated discussion. But like any disagreement with Roselie, she eventually prevailed and Patch climbed up onto his perch and drove away, leaving her alone.

What the devil was the man thinking, leaving her behind?

Brody straightened. So what else did Asteria, or rather, Roselie have planned for the evening?

Whatever it was, he vowed to put an end to it, all of it, as he stepped out of his hiding place. That is, until he looked up and over her shoulder.

What he saw in that instant made his blood run cold—someone else just as determined to put an end to Asteria.

*   *   *

Roselie scrambled to her feet, not quite believing the sight before her. Her mask askew, her wig toppled off, she swiped her own hair out of her face, taking her mask as well.

Brody stood, knife in his hand over the man he'd knocked down.

He'd saved her.

Or had he?

Before she could even blink, the man on the ground kicked out his leg, hooking his foot around Brody's ankle and sending him off-balance.

The villain vaulted to his feet, his dark eyes narrow, his teeth gritted together like a terrier after a rat.

Craddock.

Though a good head shorter than Brody, what Craddock lacked in stature, he made up for in agility and cunning. Proved by the fact that he'd already palmed a knife from his boot and was charging at Brody, grunting some sort of savage, murderous noise.

But Brody was up in a flash to meet him, the two quickly locked in battle.

Roselie looked left and right. Surely Brody hadn't come alone.

She shook off that sensible thought. Of course he had.

Leaning over, she reached beneath her skirt and pulled out her own knife.

If this man wanted a fight, he was going to get one.

She went stalking forward, gauging how best to help, when a carriage—a short curricle with a pair of high-strung horses— came careening to a stop in the mews, a man leaping down and rushing toward her.

She whirled around to face him, knife in front of her.

"My dear, that is hardly necessary," the Honorable Hero Worth blurted out, hands raised in surrender.

"Uncle Hero!" she gasped.

"Yes, indeed," he said, catching her by the arm and giving Brody's situation little to no heed. "Appears I've come in time." He tugged her toward the carriage.

Roselie being, well Roselie, dug in her heels.

But Uncle Hero was just as stubborn. "Oh, no, you don't. I won't have all my training going to waste—"

"But Brody—" She pried at his grasp.

"Get her out of here," Brody ordered, then grunted as Craddock landed a fist in the baron's gut.

"I'm trying," Uncle Hero shot back, even as Roselie did her level best to stomp on his foot.

A move he'd taught her, so it was one he easily avoided.

"He needs help," she pleaded. Well, no, ordered. Not that the Honorable Hero Worth was inclined to listen to orders, not when life and limb were in jeopardy.

Especially his.

"We all need you alive," Uncle Hero told her, having managed to drag her to the carriage.

As it was, there was a crashing sound as the pair of men behind them hit the ground. It was impossible to tell which was Brody.

But one thing was certain, she couldn't leave him like this, so she planted her feet and stopped Hero's progress.

Not that Brody seemed to appreciate her help.

"Go! Now!" he shouted, more at Uncle Hero than to her.

Which for some reason, aggravated her more. As if she couldn't be of assistance.

"Did you get what you wanted?" Uncle Hero was asking her. "Did Mrs. Croft come through?"

His question pierced her mad reckless thoughts, diverted her attention.

"Yes," she said rather absently, surprised to discover she'd managed to hold on to the packet in all this melee.

"All I needed to know," Uncle Hero said, signaling his driver, Patch's brother, Solly.

"I'll not leave without—" she began.

Wasted breath. The giant fellow simply caught her by the waist and tossed her into the back seat of the carriage like an upside down sack of flour.

"We must help him!" Roselie rebelled, clawing her way up-right and scrambling to grab the reins from Solly, but he'd already set the horses in motion and the momentum sent her flying back yet again, this time into the seat beside Uncle Hero, who caught hold of her with a vise-like grip around her waist.

"We cannot leave him," she continued as the curricle veered around the corner, leaving Brody alone with Craddock and her anguished protest lost in the night.

As the carriage went clattering down the alley, the drapes from one of the upper floor windows fell back in place.

"Craddock has failed yet again. You should have sent me," the woman complained, glancing over her shoulder at her employer.

When there was no response, she looked again out the window. "He's gone and let her escape. And that demented widow, as well."

A half-hearted wave of a hand dismissed the complaints. "Poor Mrs. Croft's grief has made her unreliable. Sadly, no one will believe whatever it is she thinks she's discovered."

The woman was hardly mollified. "She'll expose us all."

"Not when she's dead." The words held a chill that would have cooled even the reaper's heart.

"And the other one? The one you haven't been able to discover? This Asteria? Are you willing to let her escape as well?"

"Never fear. I suspect Lord Rimswell will lead us right to her."

Roselie argued with Uncle Hero the entire way home. Not that it did any good.

"I don't need an escort into my own home," she told the pair of them loftily. For she had no intention of going inside. She could outrun them both, and St. John's house wasn't *that* far away.

Brody . . . Brody, I will never forgive myself if . . . She couldn't finish that thought. No, she didn't dare . . .

"You can either walk into the house or I'll have Solly cart you in." It was a rare night that Uncle Hero let himself get ruffled, but tonight he sounded uncharacteristically medieval. "It makes no difference to me."

"You wouldn't dare!" She looked from Solly to Uncle Hero and back to Solly.

Given their stony, unforgiving expressions, apparently they would.

Oh, bother both of them for their loyalty.

"*Harrumph*," Roselie marched through the garden gate and slipped into the dining room, the door having been left unlocked by Bernie.

To her chagrin, the Honorable followed, while Solly stood sentry at the door.

She turned to them. "I am inside and well. The two of you can leave."

"Why is that?"

Roselie turned to find Bernie seated in one of the extra chairs kept in the corner. The darkness shrouded her so she appeared more like a shade than the formidable chaperone she'd proven to be.

Bernie rose and looked not at Roselie, but over her shoulder at Uncle Hero and Solly. "What went wrong?"

"There is nothing wrong," Roselie shot back.

"It was a trap," Uncle Hero supplied, ignoring Roselie's scathing glare. "Craddock came after her."

"No!" Bernie gasped. "Is he dead?"

"That is exactly why we need to go back," Roselie burst out. "Brody—I mean, Lord Rimswell—is in danger. He needs us."

"Lord Rimswell was there?" Bernie asked the Honorable, all but ignoring Roselie.

But she answered anyway. "Yes, Lord Rimswell was there. We need to go back and help him."

"Does he know?" Bernie asked Hero.

"I'd imagine so," Hero said, tipping his shoulder slightly, a gesture that suggested a weary note of resignation.

"He doesn't know who I am," Roselie insisted.

"Where's your wig?" Bernie pressed. "Or your mask?"

Her hand went instantly to her head and then her face. Gone. Both of them. Roselie opened her mouth to issue a denial of sorts, but any burgeoning arguments were quickly doused by a sudden pounding on the front door that had all of them turning toward the noise.

Bernie quickly pinched the candle, casting them into darkness, and all of them grew still.

Deep inside the house, a door opened and the heavy tread of footsteps echoed up the servant's stair, announcing the butler's imminent arrival.

As Dinnes passed the dining room, all four held their breath.

The moment the butler turned the corner in the hall, Bernie caught Roselie by the elbow.

"Not a word," her companion whispered, and hauled her in the opposite direction, toward the back stairs, which was the shortest route up to Roselie's bedchamber, and the only way to get there without being seen, now that whoever was at the front door was determined to awaken the entire house.

It certainly had Roselie's full attention. The pounding on the door seemed to reach inside her and catch her heart. A thousand possibilities raced through her and none of them good.

But even as they made the first turn, an unmistakable voice rang through the house.

"I must see Miss Stratton immediately!"

"Brody," she whispered, relief flooding through her. He was alive.

"I'd say he knows," Bernie muttered as she shoved Roselie into the bedchamber and shut the door behind them.

Roselie whirled around. "I need to speak to him. I need to—"

"What? Explain? Apologize? Convince him he's made a mistake?" Bernie shot back, pacing before the door. "No. Better you stay put and let old Dinnes send him packing, while we come up with a plan." She paused for a second. "Do you think that ship has sailed? We could go to Boston. Hide there until—"

"I'm not going to Boston," Roselie told her. She couldn't flee. No more than she could go downstairs—certainly not wearing this gown and with her face painted like a Covent Garden whore—she'd only confirm everything he suspected.

Knew.

"Did you at least get the papers?" Bernie asked.

Roselie held them up for Bernie to see. She got a *huff* of resignation at this slim bit of luck.

"I must get out of this gown," she said, the yellow silk now ruined beyond repair—stained from the grass where she'd fallen—when Brody had shoved her . . .

Saved her life.

No matter that right now. She'd think about that later. Oh, she'd have a devil of a time explaining her current state of *dishabille,* on the very off chance that Dinnes allowed Brody inside the house and she was summoned for an interview.

Bernie nodded, and got to work, helping Roselie out of the gown in a flash, scrubbing her face clean and tucking her into a snowy white night rail, the sort any proper young lady would be wearing at this time of night.

Or make that nearly dawn.

A dawn that promised to be her undoing.

Chapter 6

*B*rody marched up the steps of the house Roselie shared with her mother, the dowager Lady Wakefield, determined to gain entrance.

No matter that it was well before the proper hour for making a social call.

Then again, this was hardly a social call.

He'd come straightaway the previous night—even before making his report to Lord Howers—determined to confront Roselie.

He told himself it was to ensure her safety, but a wild reckless part of him needed to see her.

Both of them. Roselie and Asteria.

Then he'd find out what the devil she was doing . . . And more importantly, put a stop to it.

Yet to his chagrin, the dowager's butler, having been roused from his bed at such a scandalous hour and most put out by this ignominious summoning, had claimed Miss Stratton safely in her bedchamber and that he—Dinnes—would summon not only the constable to remove his lordship, but Lady Wakefield.

Which was, Brody had to admit, a properly sobering threat.

Lady Wakefield made his own mother look positively amenable.

"Unless, that is, you wish to cause further scandal, my lord," Dinnes had intoned, even as lights in the adjoining houses flickered to life.

So he'd had no choice but to leave. For the time being.

Now with some hours between visits, Dinnes showed him into a small parlor—one he suspected was reserved for tradesmen—and left him to cool his heels.

A good three quarters of an hour later, Lady Wakefield appeared at the doorway. "Lord Rimswell."

He turned around and bowed deeply. "My lady."

She took one step into the room. "You are causing a stir in my household, my lord. Whatever is this about?" Her cool regard, her arms crossed over her chest, left him shuffling his feet, like he was seven again and he and Roselie had been hauled in front of the viscountess over some infraction or another.

The woman never yelled or shouted, but oh, how she could manage to pin one in place with merely a glance.

"'Tis about Roselie, ma'am. That is, I—"

And then he stopped. Oh, hell. How did one tell a matron her daughter was an infamous agent?

"Yes?" she prompted. She'd remained on her feet, leaving him at the disadvantage.

He looked past the open door, half hoping to find Roselie here to save him from this interview.

Of course, now of all times, Roselie was nowhere to be found.

"Is she at home?" he managed. "I need to speak with her."

"At this time of day? Whatever could be so urgent that you've come twice in the last few hours to see my daughter?"

He must have flinched at that word. *Twice.*

"Yes, I know about your nocturnal visit," her ladyship continued. "More so, I suspect in a few hours most of Mayfair will know about your visits." With that said, she held her ground and waited.

He shifted again and tapped down the groan rising in his chest. "It is just that . . . Well, I have a question to ask her."

"A question?" Her brows quirked and then her eyes widened. "*Oh!* Is it that sort of question? Am I to assume you've already spoken to Piers?"

It took him a second to realize what she was asking.

Spoken to Piers about what . . . Then it hit him.

"No!" he exclaimed. "Oh good God, no!" he blurted out before he could stop himself. "My lady, you mistake the matter."

Lady Wakefield's brows arched to sharp points.

Oh, demmit this was not going at all how he'd hoped. He took a deep breath and glanced up at the viscountess.

"Yes, well, be that as it may," Lady Wakefield told him, a spark of humor in her eyes. Bother the woman, she was enjoying his discomfiture.

"Even if you were here to propose," she told him, "Roselie is not available."

"I must insist, my lady."

"She's not here," Lady Wakefield said with a finality to her words. She'd brook no more opposition, that was clear. "Our man, Patch—you might have seen him, he drives Roselie about—"

Brody nodded. Yes, he knew the brute. Had last seen him driving away with Mrs. Croft.

Lady Wakefield sighed and finally sat down, and he saw a weariness she'd been holding in check fall upon her shoulders. "I fear Patch was found beaten last night." She glanced over at the windows. "It is rather terrible. Roselie has taken this unfortunate business most hard."

A cold chill surrounded Brody. "But he's alive—" He didn't ask about Mrs. Croft. He knew better than that.

"Yes. He was taken to a nearby inn down by the docks. The surgeon had to be called. Roselie and Mrs. Pratt have gone to retrieve him. Roselie, being Roselie, insisted he recuperate here where he could be seen to properly."

A thousand questions assailed him as she spoke: *What the hell had happened? Was it just chance or had it been . . . ?*

Yet those words "recuperate here" brought up his gaze. Here.

As in this house. Leading whoever had done this to Patch straight to Roselie.

What the devil was Roselie thinking? She was putting her entire household in danger.

And what of Mrs. Croft? Where was she in all this?

The dowager sat perfectly poised, watching him. Intently.

Much like her daughter. Roselie might be her father's daughter, but she was also a good part like her mother.

A daunting mix, if ever there was one. And as such, he tamped down his questions, so the very astute viscountess wouldn't see the conflict in his heart. Instead, he smiled wanly, like any family friend might and expressed his condolences. "I am ever so sorry for your difficulties. If there is anything I can do—"

"No, no," Lady Wakefield said, making a dismissive wave of her hand. "Roselie is most insistent on seeing to poor Patch's care herself. Yet with all her other obligations—"

At this, his ears perked up. "Her other obligations?"

"Of course," Lady Wakefield replied as if Roselie's extraneous activities were common knowledge.

Good God, did the viscountess know what her daughter was doing at night? He couldn't believe any mother would let her daughter gad about the darkest parts of London on her own.

"She dines with Lady Howers every Friday—the poor lady rarely gets out, what with her infirmities and all. Then of course, she's overseen her brother's estates during his difficulties—"

"Indeed." Not that any of it surprised him. Roselie had always had a head for figures and management.

Lady Wakefield glanced at the mantel clock. "And dear heavens, she pours tea for Lady Gosforth every Thursday—which is today." The lady stilled. "I do hope she hasn't forgotten. The marchioness depends on her so."

With that, the lady rose abruptly and Brody bounded to his feet. "Yes, well, if you still have a question for my daughter, I will be more than happy to convey it to her." She looked at him, silently prodding him to reveal the true meaning behind his visit.

"No, no, perhaps I've come in haste."

"Twice?" she pointed out.

This time he did flinch. "No matter, it can wait." Hastily, he made his bow.

"If you say so, my lord," she said, a wry, bemused note to her words as he took his leave.

Even Dinnes seemed to find his departure amusing, the man positively smirking that he'd been thwarted yet again.

You've only delayed the inevitable, he would liked to have told the imperious butler. *Only delayed.*

And while he was to be delayed, he had a raft of questions that needed to be answered and if he couldn't demand them of Roselie, then he'd discover the particulars elsewhere.

Not that he wouldn't corner Roselie before the day was out.

Yet a nagging realization set in

What the hell was he going to do with her once he got to the truth?

An hour or so later, Brody found himself in the narrow hallway of a poor flat, to be exact, in front of the rooms kept by the Honorable Hero Worth. He'd had to bribe Tuck's scurrilous valet for Hero's address, and then Hero's landlady had demanded her own share, just to let him in.

This chasing after Roselie was becoming an expensive venture.

Nor did he want to spend all day at it. He still needed to get to Lady Gosforth's afternoon in, if he wanted to corner Roselie and rattle the truth out of her. So he began pounding on the door. "Mr. Worth, I need to see you."

Inside he could hear someone scrambling about, along with a muttered, "What the devil—"

Brody smiled. Yes, this was the right place.

"Who's there?" The wily old man called out.

Brody leaned closer to the door and could clearly hear a window creak open.

Oh, hell. This was going to cost him. The landlady would probably demand a king's ransom for this, but he was out of choices. Shouldering the door open, he found a half-dressed old man teetering out of the window. "Sir—"

The Honorable turned toward him and blinked. "Oh my, it's only you, my lord. I thought it was . . . No, never mind who I thought it was." He chuckled and pulled his leg in from the window. Straightening what clothes he'd managed to don, he did his best to appear unruffled.

"I apologize for my uninvited and untimely arrival—"

"No, no," the Honorable said, gesturing to a chair in the corner. "Any friend of my dear nephew—" The man paused, his eyes widening. "It isn't Tuck, is it? He hasn't come to some harm, has he?"

For all his bluff and bluster, it was apparent the man held his family close.

"No, not at all," Brody assured him, taking the chair and sitting. The Honorable took the other. "Actually it's about Miss Stratton."

"Miss Stratton?" The Honorable scratched at his chin in puzzlement.

Brody had to hand it to the old humbug, he actually looked convincing. But he was also forgetting one key point.

"The woman you escorted home last night from St. John's Folly?"

The Honorable's chin jutted out. "St. John's Folly? Well, I never! I'll have you know I'm a respectable—"

"Sir, you forget, I was there." Brody lifted his chin and stared him straight in the eyes.

Again the Honorable blinked. "Oh, yes. Right. So you were." Then he stopped, replacing his outrage with a bland expression on his face. "Enjoy yourself, did you?"

So he wasn't going to make this easy. He was also about to discover that Brody hadn't the patience to play this game. Between Dinnes, Lady Wakefield and now Hero Worth, his tolerance for subterfuge had thinned considerably. "There's been an accident."

Now he had the man's attention.

"Not the fair Miss Stratton—"

"No. Her driver. Patch. He was beaten nearly to death. Down by the docks."

If he thought that was enough to get the old man talking, it hardly seemed the case. "Yes, dreadful news that." Again the Honorable sat silently, hands folded in his lap, looking, for all points, the innocent.

But not so much that Brody couldn't see the frisson of worry behind his demeanor. "Patch is being seen to. But I want to ensure that Mrs. Croft is safe."

"Mrs. Croft? Good heavens, poor lady. I'd forgotten all about her. But I daresay she's well out into the Atlantic by now—" He stopped, as if remembering himself.

"The Atlantic?" Brody leaned forward. "Sir, I need to know everything. And if you aren't inclined to talk, I suspect a visit to your nephew will help loosen your tongue."

The Honorable groaned. "Now that will hardly do. Doubt Tuck would approve. Hardly approve of all of it myself. Not profitable in the least. Not that I'm doing it to make a profit, mind you—"

"Sir—" Brody prodded.

"Yes, well . . . Please don't mention this conversation to dear Miss Stratton. Lovely child, but I daresay, she frightens me a bit. I do think she'll have my hide."

"Both of ours, I imagine."

Together they laughed.

Then Brody continued, pressing his point. "Still, I'd like to make certain that Mrs. Croft—"

"Yes, yes, that does seem a good notion." The Honorable got to his feet and began to gather his things. "You'll need my help."

"If you say she sailed last night, I can check with the harbormaster," Brody told him, getting to his feet.

"Him?" The Honorable shook his head. "If you want to know what's happening at the docks, you don't ask him."

Brody paused. "Then who do you ask?"

The Honorable grinned and donned his tall hat. "I know a fellow."

Of course he did.

Some time later, Brody found himself down at the docks, at the exact spot where the cobbles held the scorched outline of a carriage that had been ambushed.

Where Patch had been beaten. But they hadn't any word as to the fate of Mrs. Croft.

"This is a rather unfortunate turn of events," the Honorable declared, pulling Brody away and leading him into a warren of alleyways until they came to a derelict-looking building. "However, I'm quite sure the Constable can help."

Brody looked around. "I assume he isn't a real constable."

The Honorable ruffled. "Don't be a fool and mention that to him. He's quite proud of his position."

They entered the building and found themselves standing before a large desk, covered with receipts and inventories and other shipping records. The man behind it was hardly what Brody had expected. He looked more like a befuddled clerk than a constable, but, Hero had assured him, this was the man who would know everything they needed.

The Honorable coughed slightly to get the fellow's attention.

"Yes?" the man asked, his brows rising slightly.

The Honorable nudged Brody and nodded toward a jar on the desk. A jar, notably filled with coins.

Brody dug into his pocket and made a deposit. Once the coins jangled to a rest in their new home, the man brightened.

"How can I help, gentlemen?"

"I need to know what happened last night. About the carriage that was burned. The man who was beaten."

The Constable shook his head. "Bad business that. Thought that blighter was dead when I got there. Whoever did it probably thought he was."

"It seems he will live," Brody told him.

"That's good. Too many people around here don't." The man shuffled a few papers on his desk. "If you want to look at the carriage, it's out back." He chucked his chin toward a door behind him. "Can't see what you might want with it—picked clean before it was torched, and whatever was left, well, it's good and burnt."

"So I understand," Brody remarked. "Any witnesses?"

The man laughed. "Around here? No. When people see trouble, they go the other way and if they tell you they know who did it, don't you believe them—they're only trying to rob you." The man shrugged. "Sorry I can't be of any more help. I suppose what you really want is the body."

"The wha-a t?" Brody asked, for he certainly hadn't heard the man correctly. *A body?*

"Yes, I thought that was why you were here. What do you want me to do with the body?"

Brody froze. "What body?"

The Constable tipped his head and studied them. "You'll have to pardon me, but you seemed the sort who might come to collect her."

Brody pushed a question past the bile rising in his throat. "Her?"

"The one they found by the carriage." The man rose. "If you don't want the body, I'll send her off to be buried with the paupers. Wash my hands of all of this. Don't like this sort of thing. Bad for business when proper folks start traipsing around here . . ."

"Was this woman, the one found by the carriage, wearing a black traveling gown?" Brody pressed.

"What was left of it. Pretty thing. Well, she was once. Fair headed. Young." The man looked away, for the depth of the crime had rattled even his hardened soul.

Brody glanced back at the Honorable who was wiping his brow and dabbing at his eyes.

What was left of it. Brody knew that could only mean one thing. One he couldn't stomach, couldn't fathom.

Good God, what sort of business was this? Obviously the sort that had sent Mrs. Croft down here to the docks in the middle of the night . . . And the only reason for that was that she'd been compelled to flee London. And not just London, but England.

But why had the widow been willing to take to the war-tossed seas? And why had Roselie sent her?

He glanced over at the Honorable who had risen and was taking one deep breath after another from the only open window in the room.

The Constable was sorting papers again. "So do you want her?"

Brody nodded, a tight jerk of his head. "I'll send someone later today. She should be buried properly."

At this, Hero turned from the window and studied him, and then, if Brody wasn't mistaken, nodded slightly, with what must have been approval.

The Constable pursed his lips. "Bad business all this. Best to stay out of it."

"Bad business indeed," Brody agreed. "But it's my business now."

Chapter 7

"*M*iss Stratton, whatever is the matter with you this afternoon?" Lady Gosforth asked. "You are most inattentive and if I weren't mistaken, you look as if someone has died."

The marchioness had the right of that, and despite the fresh sting of tears threatening to spill down her cheeks, Roselie did her best to brighten even when her heart was being torn apart.

For it was true. Abigail was dead.

"My apologies, my lady, I fear I was woolgathering," she replied.

"About a certain gentleman—" Lady Comber hinted, smiling knowingly at the other ladies gathered for the marchioness's ever-so-popular afternoon in.

"Lord Rimswell, perhaps?" Lady Oxnam suggested. This was met with a fresh bit of chatter as the assembled ladies voiced their opinions on the current collection of eligible young men.

All Roselie could do was smile blandly and get on with the task of pouring tea, her thoughts far from the Marriage Mart.

Whatever had gone wrong?

Everything.

Abigail murdered. Patch left for dead. The carriage torched.

She'd admonished her friend to tell no one of their plans, to keep her intentions close to her heart.

But Abigail hadn't been careful enough. And Roselie had

learned, via the landlady at Mrs. Croft's rooms, that she'd sent a trunk to the docks earlier in the day.

Giving notice to whoever had been watching her. And they had been watching . . . and waiting. So when Patch had pulled the carriage up, the thugs had attacked.

Abigail, I am so sorry. Roselie shivered, for she'd seen her friend's fate with her own eyes. Gone down there, with Solly and Bernie, only after she'd threatened to take a hired hack without them if they did not agree to accompany her.

She'd had to see, didn't they understand that? Just as she had to continue on despite . . .

Despite the challenges she now faced. No carriage. The last of her gold gone.

She hadn't even enough coins to bribe the Constable to have Abigail buried properly. But, oh . . . she couldn't let her friend just be tossed in a pauper's grave.

She'd have to have Bernie pawn her pearl ring—the one Papa have given her. It would bring enough and there was no other way.

Roselie suspected her father, of all people, would understand.

"I believe Lord Rimswell has set his sights elsewhere," Lady Nafferton was saying, smiling over her shoulder at her daughters who were seated behind her.

Lord Rimswell. Dear God, now Brody was entangled in all this. At least Craddock hadn't . . .

Roselie shuddered to think of Brody lost. Ignoring the clench in her heart, there was also a very practical reason.

I may well need him.

For Abigail's rooms had been ransacked as well—the mattress sliced to shreds, holes carved into the walls. And since they hadn't found what they'd been seeking, that could only mean they would keep looking.

She couldn't help herself, she shivered.

"Dear me, Miss Stratton, you aren't taking a cold, are you?" Lady Gosforth asked. Nothing got past the sharp-eyed marchioness.

Worse, now all eyes turned toward Roselie, for here was a new subject.

"I don't believe so," she managed, smiling brightly for all to see. "But it seems I've let my tea grow cold." She set aside the cup she'd been cradling in her hands and poured herself a new one, and glanced around, searching for some topic that might send the conversation in a new direction, any path. But she needn't have bothered, for here was Lady Comber keen to discuss Piers's recent hasty marriage.

"What does your mother think of your brother's choice?" she asked, making a little sniff that showed her opinion of the match.

Before Roselie could manage an answer, the conversation was off and running without any of them noticing that she hadn't replied. Happily she let the subject swirl overhead like wispy clouds—trailing bits of lace that were of little consequence.

She'd learned long ago that the real information was to be found not in the grand *on dit* of the day, but in what was said in the soft whispers, in asides and in the replies that went unanswered.

If the Exchange was the heart of England's financial world, Lady Gosforth's was the beating vessel of the tempestuous undercurrents and riptides of gossip and tattle that were the very supports of Society.

One should never mistake the matter and think it was good manners and connections that ran the *ton*. Roselie knew with a certainty that what made the world turn was gossip.

Gossip she needed desperately if she was to make sense of Abigail's "proof," an album of clippings and hastily scratched notes and seemingly unconnected ephemera and bits and pieces that her friend had been convinced pointed to the one person who was the key to this entire, treasonous scheme.

Yet, in truth, it was as jumbled as Abigail's wits.

How ever was the truth to be found in such clutter?

"Miss Stratton? Woolgathering again?" Lady Oxnam smiled. "Have you finally fallen in love?"

Roselie glanced up and blinked. Oh, bother, she was supposed to be listening to the conversation and here she was lost in thought yet again. "I fear you caught me out—"

"I knew it! A young man," Lady Comber declared. "You've finally found a likely *parti*."

The rest of the ladies trilled with excitement.

"Oh, no, there is no one," she told them, even if, much to her consternation, an image of Brody racing to her rescue came to mind.

No, definitely not him. Good heavens, what knight-in-shining armor shoved a lady on her arse?

One who wants her to live.

"I don't know," Lady Comber told the company. "I thought Lord Rimswell looked quite attentive last night."

"Last night?" she managed, having nearly forgotten about Almack's.

"Oh, yes, I do believe the baron is smitten," Lady Oxnam declared for one and all. "You were, after all, the only lady he danced with last night."

Lady Nafferton's nose pinched at this news. "Indeed she was." She stole another glance at her daughters, unmarried both, and sighed.

"I hardly think he's smitten," Roselie rushed to add. "It is just that—"

The entire company leaned forward. The ladies who came to Lady Gosforth's were the battle-hardened veterans of numerous Seasons, and could pick a rumor into half a dozen pieces and toss away the dishonest bits in just a few exchanges.

They looked like a flock of hungry hens ready to peck at whatever came their way.

But to her relief, a trio of newcomers arrived—none other than Piers's new wife, Louisa and her twin sister, Lavinia, standing in the doorway, along with their chaperone, Lady Aveley.

A murmur ran through the assembled gathering. Now here was a far more interesting subject.

The scandalous Tempest sisters.

Whatever misgivings Society had about Louisa and Lavinia, Roselie heartily approved of them—especially Louisa, for she'd brought Piers back from the brink of desperation and now her brother had rejoined the living.

For that, Roselie would always owe Louisa a debt of gratitude, which extended to Louisa's twin, Lavinia.

With the company diverted and the guests coming and going, Roselie was left to her own devices and she began planning what needed to be done next, until that is, the discussion strayed well out of the usual tattle into the more scandalous subject of the card-playing beauty who'd mysteriously appeared and disappeared at St. John's Folly the previous night. It was Lady Comber, who was vaguely related to the Earl of St. John and therefore had made an appearance at the Folly, who regaled the company with the story of how this unknown beauty had won a high stakes game against Lord Ilford.

Ilford.

That name brought Roselie's gaze up and immediately she spied Lavinia blushing slightly, as if she wanted nothing more than to change the subject.

Not that such a thing was likely, for after a bit more dissection the ladies decided to find this beauty themselves, dividing up to go discover where she'd bought her distinctive gown and thereby gaining her name.

Roselie could have saved them all the trouble and directed them to Madame St. Vincent's shop in Cheapside, but then she would have to explain how she knew . . .

Oh, the trials of a duplicitous life . . .

Still, she had no intention of joining this pursuit, for she had more pressing matters to see to, but got no further than the bottom step of Lady Gosforth's when out of the corner of the servant's stairs came none other than Lord Rimswell.

"Ladies," he said to the matrons and their daughters filing out in a noisy flock.

Roselie did her best to blend into the feathers and silks, but to no avail.

He spotted her like a lurcher after a rabbit, his gaze dark and foreboding. No, make that unforgiving.

Oh, so is that how it is going to be between us, Brody?

"Ah, Miss Stratton, there you are. Your mother said I would find you here."

"Besotted. Didn't I tell you all?" Lady Oxnam whispered to Lady Nafferton.

Roselie tried not to blanch, and worst, found herself cut from the flock, as the ladies parted to let him in, as if they were doing her a favor.

"Lord Rimswell, this is a surprise," she demurred, looking for an escape route and finding none.

He tipped his hat and grinned, before catching hold of her hand and bringing it to his lips. "Oh, but I don't see why it would be when I told you last night I would call."

This evoked a titter of speculation from their audience.

She snatched her hand back, all the while ignoring the spark that ignited at his touch, his proximity.

Always when she got this close to Brody, he made her feel reckless. Dangerous. As if she were his Asteria.

Glancing around to see if anyone noticed her discomfiture, she saw nothing but speculation and whispering behind fans.

Oh, perfect, he was also igniting the fires of gossip.

Bonfires, from the looks of things.

"I fear you've missed Lady Gosforth's afternoon in," she told him as she went to dodge her way around him, but he smoothly stepped in line beside her.

"'Missed' is not the word I would use," he replied, glancing back at the Gosforth town house. "Tattle and tea is not to my liking."

"I never miss it," she replied, tipping her nose up slightly. "You wouldn't believe what a lady can learn by simply listening."

But Brody wasn't the usual gentleman, and he countered quite easily, "Of some matters, a lady should never learn, *Asteria*."

She stumbled a bit, and he caught hold of her elbow.

Now it was her turn to tug him aside—pulling him well out of the earshot of the gathered ladies, who were watching the pair of them as if this was the final act of some much anticipated Covent Garden dramatic.

And in that moment, she remembered something far more important. "I should thank you for last night—"

"Thank me? I shouldn't have to—"

She shook her head. "But you did."

"What else was I to do, Rosebud?"

Oh, those words sent shivers through her. No. No. No. That would never do.

"Oh, dear heavens, what were you thinking? Craddock? He could have killed you," she shot back, refusing to let her heart rule.

"He definitely tried," Brody replied with an ironic laugh.

"Hardly funny." She'd lost one friend, she couldn't lose anyone else.

"No, it wasn't." Brody shrugged. "Howers and the rest of them came along just after you left, and Craddock escaped."

"That's unfortunate," she told him.

"That's not what Howers said."

"I imagine he was rather furious. He doesn't like it when things aren't neatly tied up."

Brody looked over at her. "Howers knows, doesn't he?"

About her. About Asteria.

"Of course he knows." She sniffed and notched her nose in the air.

"I can't believe he'd sanction such a thing," Brody said, more for himself.

Roselie shrugged and glanced over at the clutch of ladies, all leaning forward hoping to catch some bit of gossip. "I wouldn't say he 'sanctioned' anything—"

Brody groaned. "And for good reason. He knows, just as I do, how highly improper all this is. What if you were discovered, Roselie? You'd be ruined."

Again she scoffed. "Brody, I've been out for four Seasons. Do you think being respectably matched is the only thing I desire?"

Desire.

For a moment he stared at her, hard and unforgiving and then, there it was. That flicker of passion, as if he remembered. Him kissing her. How their bodies fit together.

Yet those memories hardly served her purpose, for they seemed to inflame him in a different direction. An unwanted one. He set his jaw and lowered his voice. "Roselie, you know demmed well what I mean, and if you think I am going to let you—"

"La! Miss Stratton!" Pansy Nafferton called out from her mother's carriage. "Oh, there you are!"

Roselie had never been more grateful to see the Naffertons in her life.

And that was saying much.

"Dear Miss Stratton," Lady Nafferton said, "did you forget your promise to Lady Gosforth to ride with us?"

Roselie opened her mouth to protest, but then again, one glance at Brody moved her to action.

"We were so occupied with our plans we nearly forgot you," Patience added.

"Forgot me?" Roselie managed.

"To help us. Don't you recall? We must discover where that mysterious lady got her gown. Oh, you must join us, for I'm certain you'll help us ascertain her identity before anyone else."

If only they knew how much help she could be . . .

"We do understand why you are so distracted," Pansy continued, tilting her fan toward Brody. "My lord," she added with a flutter of her lashes and a knowing smile.

Ah, so that was the way the wind blew. Pansy Nafferton held a *tendre* for Brody and wasn't about to let another steal a march on her. No wonder she was being most insistent.

A trait she'd obviously learned from her mother, who quickly spoke up. "Indeed, Miss Stratton, I would be derelict in my duties if I left you to wander about unaccompanied."

Roselie would point out she had Mrs. Pratt in her wake, but Lady Nafferton was just as eager to cut her loose from Lord Rimswell's attentions as Roselie was to be free of them.

"Lady Nafferton, my mother always says you are the epitome of . . . of . . ."

Boredom, but that would hardly do.

"Kindness," she managed to finish. Turning to Brody, she plucked her arm free. "My apologies, Lord Rimswell, but I had completely forgotten my previous obligation." She turned to Lady Nafferton, if only to cement her position. "And I might know a particular establishment that would be of assistance. A French milliner who has connections with every—"

"Oh, my dear girl, get in," Lady Nafferton declared, shooing Pansy over.

Roselie turned to Brody and grinned, making a quick curtsy and climbing into the carriage without waiting for him to help her up.

For some reason she didn't trust herself to let him touch her, hold her, even that briefly. Nor did she trust, that given the chance, he wouldn't drag her off, if only to finish his scold.

His inquisition.

"We haven't a moment to lose," Lady Nafferton was saying. "I hope you don't mind, Lord Rimswell, but would you be a dear and see Mrs. Pratt home? I feel terrible, but we haven't room for her in the carriage."

"No, no, my lady," Brody told her. "I would be remiss in my manners if I didn't take this opportunity to walk dear Mrs. Pratt home," he replied, and this time it was his turn to smile. "We will finish our conversation very soon, Miss Stratton," he told her, tipping his hat to the carriage.

"I look forward to it," Roselie lied.

For the prospect of such an interview was right up there with spending the rest of her afternoon with Pansy and Patience Nafferton.

"Well, Mrs. Pratt, it looks as if we are being left behind," Brody remarked.

"Wouldn't be the first time, my lord," Roselie's hired companion said, finishing her words with a cluck of her tongue. "Though I don't know which of us has the worst of it." The lady nodded her head toward the Nafferton carriage as it turned the corner. Then she shuddered.

He had to agree. He'd rather go wandering about naked in Seven Dials in the middle of the night than find himself wedged in between Pansy and Patience Nafferton. "Miss Stratton does have a way of finding herself in the most devilish predicaments. Wouldn't you agree?"

The cagey old girl just pursed her lips and shook her head.

No, getting any information out of her was not going to be easy. But . . .

"Mrs. Pratt, while this might sound a bit improper," he began, taking her hand and putting it on his sleeve and beginning to walk along in a friendly fashion, "but I find myself in the mood for a pint. What would you say to a small libation? I do so hate to drink alone."

She glanced over her shoulder in the direction they should be traveling. Back to Lady Wakefield's town house. "It has been a trying afternoon," the hired companion admitted.

"Exactly," Brody agreed. "You have, after all, just come from Lady Gosforth's. All that catlap and tattle would give anyone a thirst, that is, unless you are of the opinion that such activities might compromise your reputation."

"Compromise my reputation!" The old girl barked with a laugh. "You would do well to watch your own, my lord. A drink or two from now, you might find yourself being compromised— handsome devil like you." And then she had the audacity to wink at him and tow him to the closest public house.

*   *   *

Several hours later, Roselie came into her room and collapsed against the closed door. "Those wretched Nafferton twins will be the death of me."

"Ha! Serves you right," Bernie replied from where she sat at Roselie's desk. The cluttered bits from Abigail's papers lay before her. "Leaving me with that lordling. He threatened to have me dismissed."

Roselie made a very unladylike snort. "I'd like to see him try." She came closer to her hired companion and sniffed. "Have you been drinking?"

Bernie's nose wrinkled and she swatted at it unsteadily. "All his fault. Suggested we go have a pint."

Roselie groaned and sat down on her bed, her hand at her forehead. "You didn't!"

Bernie was known to have a bit of a weakness for a pint. Or two.

"Oh, aye, I did," Bernie admitted. "He offered to buy." As if that made it perfectly acceptable. She went to get up, but it was clear the lady had imbibed more than she ought.

Roselie closed her eyes. "Whatever did you tell him?" Though, quite honestly, she might not want to know. She opened one eye and peered at her unorthodox companion.

"Nothing more than he already knows," Bernie replied, swatting again at some point in front of her nose that only she could see.

"And what, pray tell is that?" Roselie asked, sitting up.

"Everything," Bernie confided.

Yes, well that cleared up the situation entirely. Roselie edged closer. "Bernie, you have to tell me exactly what he knows."

"He knows about that poor mite. Seeing to her, he is, did you know that? He's paid to have her put to rest, proper like." She fumbled in her pockets for a handkerchief and blew her nose in a great *honk*.

Roselie shivered as gooseflesh ran up and down her limbs.

Brody. Her heart did that odd patter. Of course he would do the right thing.

And then Bernie told her all he'd done, and at the end, Roselie reached for the handkerchief.

"He's not going to let this go," Bernie told her, sniffing again. "He's part terrier that one. Are you sure he wasn't born in the Dials?"

Roselie laughed. "No. And don't let his mother ever hear you suggest such a thing. She's the daughter of a marquess and feels quite keenly that she rather lowered herself marrying a mere baron. Seven Dials! Oh, horrors, she'd go into apoplexy at such a notion."

"*Your* baron is going to be a problem," Bernie told her, having blinked and seemingly sobered at the very thought.

"Yes, I know," Roselie said with a curt nod. "And he's not mine." Pushing up from the bed, she looked over at her writing desk, where Bernie sat. "Did you have any luck with Abigail's journal?" She crossed the room and looked over the bits of evidence—a scrap of cloth, a lock of hair, a list of ships lost, clippings from the gossip columns, notes about manifests and names of merchants.

Some she recognized, but others she didn't.

"None of this makes sense," Bernie said. "Seems to me Mrs. Croft was—"

Roselie nodded. Yes, yes, she knew. This jumble of nonsensical evidence before her, evidence of nothing, said it all. And Abigail had been so certain.

Bernie yielded her spot and Roselie sat down and began the tedious task of trying to make sense of it.

"She did like her lists," Roselie muttered as she pulled out a scrap of paper. "Whatever could this be about? Trinity, St. Anne's, and, oh, bother the last two are scratched out." She tipped the paper toward the candle. "I think it is Pope and, perhaps Hoxton." She shook her head and sighed. "Why I've never heard of any of these names—certainly not in society. Perhaps they are merchants."

Bernie sat up. "Read those last ones again."

Roselie began anew, "Pope, Hoxton—"

Bernie was on her feet. "Madhouses."

"Pardon." She'd never seen Bernie go so pale.

Bernie caught up the list. "Those last two are madhouses. In Chelsea."

"Are you certain?"

"Aye." Bernie dropped the bit of paper back on the desk as if it suddenly burned. "I gather since these last two are crossed off, your Mrs. Croft couldn't find whatever it was she was looking for."

"Not what . . ." Roselie furrowed her brow. "Perhaps what she was looking for was a whom."

"Oh, yes, that makes it easier," Bernie said with a loud snort. "Shall we knock on the door of every madhouse in England and ask if there is anyone sensible at home?"

"Well, when you put it that way." She looked up at Bernie. "Still, we'll need to go visit these places, at least the ones that aren't crossed out and try to discover who it was Abigail hoped to find."

"And how do you propose to do that? We haven't the carriage, and that lordling of yours—"

"He isn't mine," Roselie repeated.

"Yes, well, tell him that." Bernie sat down. "He said he'd have me fired. And he won't stop until he gets to the bottom of all this."

"Whatever did you tell him in return?"

Bernie winked. "That perhaps he shouldn't drink so early in the day."

Roselie barked a laugh. "And then what?"

"He threatened to come by promptly at seven and have it out with you."

Roselie looked at the clock. It was nearly six. "And then what did you do?"

Bernie reached into her pocket and pulled out a man's pocket watch. "He won't be so prompt now, will he?"

Chapter 8

I assure you, madame, that Roselie Stratton is the last woman on earth I would ever marry. It is an impossible proposition.

Baron Rimswell to his mother

The next morning, Brody came down the stairs expecting to see Peakman standing there with his hat and coat, only to find the man with empty hands and an apologetic expression on his face.

"My lord," he began, "your mother wishes for you to partake in breakfast with her this morning. She says she has a matter of some import to discuss."

He ground his teeth together. This was the last thing he needed—just a half an hour ago, he'd had a note from Tuck that he needed Brody's assistance with an important matter, then he must track down Roselie—for the exasperating minx had eluded him again last night.

His mother could wait.

But when he turned to Peakman to ask the man to fetch his coat forthwith, his mother came fluttering into the foyer.

As usual, she was dressed in an elegant and perfectly fashion-able day gown. His mother never spared expenses—neither on their well-appointed house or on her own trappings. Certainly there was no real need to economize—the Garrick family had always been dab hands at making money.

As ignoble as that ability might be, it came in handy when one had to pay the bills.

Especially his mother's modiste bill. Or rather *bills*.

"Bradwell, there you are," she said, all aflutter. "I thought you would never come down. I've had cook make your favorites and I would hate to see it all go to waste."

Brody looked once more at the door and then back at his mother, reminding himself of what Poldie had always said about the woman who had brought them into the world.

Father loved her, and she only has our best interests at heart.

To which Brody had always silently added, *Even if she is an aggravating, meddlesome* . . .

Oh, the list went on and on.

"Breakfast?" she prodded, turning down the hall and obviously expecting him to follow. And there was no way to escape now, not unless he wanted to endure a week of her aggrieved sighs and pointed questions as to where he was going and exactly whom he was seeing.

She'd never quite gotten over the fact that he was now the master of this house.

Or rather, forgiven him for it. As if it was his fault Poldie had decided to fight for England.

"Yes, madame," he replied, following her toward the dining room unable to shake the gnawing feeling that he was being summoned to atone for some sort of grievance or another.

For certainly, he and his mother had never been close. She had always made it clear that Poldie was her favorite, her golden child.

And when he'd died in Spain and Brody had inherited, he sometimes thought she resented him all the more for having usurped Poldie's place.

So what remained between them was an uneasy truce.

"Yes, well," his mother began as she took her place at the end of the table. She nodded toward the platters. "All your favorites."

Beefsteak. Rolls. Coffee.

All Poldie's favorites, not his.

"There is no easy way to say this," she began, never one to waste an opportunity.

The chill in her voice gave Brody pause. There was only one thing that could have merited this tense meeting.

She'd discovered he was working for the Home Office.

Not that he was about to stop just because she would find it dangerous, unfitting, reckless, or whatever other complaint she'd find to pile on.

So he braced himself for the onslaught.

Which would most likely begin with her favorite refrain, *"You are the last of your line, have you no thought of what would become of your heritage if you were lost? Of me?"*

She drew a deep breath and spit out her newest grievance. "It has come to my attention that of late you've begun to show a marked interest in Miss Stratton."

Brody blinked. Surely he hadn't heard her correctly. "Miss Stratton?"

His mother's nose pinched slightly. "Yes. You danced with her at Almack's. *Only with her.*" She gazed at him, mouth pursed and her head shaking ever so slightly with disapproval. "Bradwell, you know I find her unacceptable."

For a wicked moment, he considered telling his mother about Roselie's other charming traits.

How she traipsed about London as a masked creature, all wiles and daring—and not just in Mayfair, but all over London. That she was embroiled in espionage. Treason. Perhaps even murder.

Would that gain her his mother's approval? He thought not.

"Mother—" he began instead, moving to nip this ridiculous conversation in the bud.

Not that his mother was about to be diverted. "Do not try and cozen me," she scolded. "You know I find the Strattons overly conceited. And Miss Stratton . . ." She shuddered. "Four seasons and no husband. There is something decidedly wrong with that gel."

Brody couldn't argue with any of that.

Nor was her ladyship done. "And her mother! Lady Wakefield is no proper widow, and now that she's a dowager, I can't imagine the improprieties she'll promote."

"Lady Wakefield?" Brody had always found her an elegant and smart woman. That she'd loved her husband with a deep and abiding respect was well known. She'd never remarried, but she was still followed by a bevy of devoted suitors, as she had reportedly been in her youth.

And that made her the subject of envy and malice by others in her circle.

Like his mother. Who had never had a trail of admirers, or poems cast as to her beauty, or even the hint of scandal attached to her.

Hence . . .

"It is unconscionable that you would consider such a gel worthy of—"

He stopped her right there. "Mother, I hardly think one dance—"

His mother was not to be placated. Not on this subject. "One dance! If it had only been that. But you did so at Almack's. One dance with one favored lady and no other is tantamount to an announcement. And at the very least is the predecessor to a maelstrom of gossip."

"I would hardly call Roselie Stratton 'my favorite'," he protested. More like a nail in his boot. And the most bothersome miss in London.

And like no other, some deep voice of longing whispered inside him. *Beguiling. Tempting.*

"No, not in the least," he said aloud without thinking, more for himself than for his mother's benefit, not that she believed him.

Not that he believed himself.

She huffed a sigh and continued, "Then why ever were you accosting her yesterday outside of Lady Gosforth's?"

That brought up his gaze.

"I've been besieged ever since. Besieged." She pushed her plate aside and looked at him, all cold and unforgiving.

Brody went to push away from the table and end this ridiculous interview, when she rushed to continue, "And the worst of all is poor Lady Nafferton. She is quite grief-stricken." She dabbed at her lips with her napkin, then once again pinned him down with that wretched look. The one she'd always reserved for him.

"Lady Nafferton?" This time he didn't have to feign anything. He hadn't the faintest notion why the viscountess might have an interest in all this.

Of course his mother did. And was more than willing to share. Much to his horror.

"Poor Miss Nafferton," she told him. "The dear girl had such hopes, and she is such a perfectly amiable young lady." Then she smiled at him, silently prodding him to make the connection.

The one she wanted.

"Good God!" he said, as he realized what she was suggesting. "Marry one of those feckless fools? You must be mad."

She straightened. "That is uncalled for. But you can make amends for all of this by attending the Gosforth Ball tonight and dancing with Miss Nafferton—"

"Which one?" he managed to ask, suddenly finding some humor in all this.

His mother didn't notice the wry note to his question. "Well either will do. Even that pretty little ward of Lady Muscoates would be an improvement over *her*. Anyone but *her*."

Something about the pinched tones with which his mother avoided saying that one name left a tight knot in Brody's gut. No, make that a growing anger.

"Roselie," he corrected tightly.

Her lashes lifted. "Oh, has it come to *that*? With you using her given name so freely? No wonder the entire town thinks you are about to propose."

"I am hardly about to do any such thing. And she's been Roselie all my life," he reminded her. "You do recall our properties abut each other, the Strattons are our neighbors and our fathers were the best of friends. Good God, mother, at one time Poldie and Margaret had an understanding."

"Don't remind me," his mother averred. "Oh, the shame of all that—look at how that gel behaved. Throwing off your poor brother and marrying another." She shuddered. "How can you consider such a family? When you could have either of the Naffertons! Granted they are a bit dull—"

"A bit?"

"But they come from a long and distinguished line. Why Lady Nafferton is related to the Duke of Wilton. While the Strattons—" His mother shuddered again.

Brody pushed his chair back. He was angry now, furious really. "The previous Lord Wakefield was highly regarded by the Prime Minister for his work on the treaties in Paris. He was a brilliant man."

His mother flushed. "But look no further than his son to see the true nature of that family. How those bloodlines run. Piers Stratton is a drunk and a derelict. And mad to boot. The very same man who led my dearest—"

Yes, yes, he knew the refrain. Piers Stratton, the current Lord Wakefield had tricked, deceived, and lured poor, dear Poldie into buying his commission. And then had the audacity to come home, alive, while Poldie had been left in a cold, unmarked grave somewhere near Corunna.

No matter that Piers had come home gravely injured and torn apart by all he'd seen, Lady Rimswell held him and him alone accountable for Poldie's death, for *her* loss.

Yet Brody would never blame Piers for his brother's impetuous decision to buy a commission and go to war. That had been Poldie's unfettered choice. This he knew for a fact, for he had Poldie's letters to prove it.

Not that their mother would ever believe them. Not that she'd ever be brought to see that her perfect son could have made such a rash decision of his own volition.

Much like Roselie must have done in donning Asteria's guise and doing—well, doing whatever it was she was doing.

Brody looked up and around him. For in that moment, he found his own sense of clarity. His place, as it were.

And he was done playing this wretched game with his mother. Finished for good.

He rose from the breakfast table. Poldie's breakfast, not his. He'd been ignoring the obvious for too long. It was time to make the title, this house, this very table, his.

"I won't hear a word against Piers," he told his mother in no uncertain terms. "Or any of the Strattons. Not in this house. *My* house."

She frowned at this sudden shift. "Have you no care for my feelings? I won't have that gel here, Bradwell. I won't. I forbid you to marry her."

Marry? They'd gone from the impropriety of one dance all the way to marriage?

"Mother, this entire interview is pointless. I can assure you that Roselie Stratton is the last woman on earth I intend to marry."

"You say that now, but I'm warning you, that gel has wiles that will lead you—this family—to ruin."

"And I assure you such a thing is impossible," he said as he marched from the room, intent on finding that very same, impossible miss, wiles and all.

Roselie half listened to her mother's chatter as they drove across Mayfair to the Gosforth Ball. It was hard not to smile as her mother regaled her with yet another story of Piers's improvement and Louisa's promising influence.

"And just this afternoon, Piers mentioned that he will be meeting with his solicitor. He has every intention of taking over the estates, isn't that good news? Why it will free you up considerably," Lady Wakefield said.

"Yes, excellent news," Roselie agreed, trying to suppress the groan bubbling up inside her.

For it was hardly that at all. While Piers had been incapacitated, Roselie had managed everything. Including using the family's assets to finance her work as Asteria. The carriage that had been destroyed? One she'd had sent up from one of her brother's lesser properties. The money to pay bribes and the salaries of the people who assisted her? Pilfered from the profits she'd managed through careful and, if she was being modest, excellent management of Piers's estates.

If he started looking too close, well . . .

So while Roselie agreed that Louisa had turned out to be the perfect bride for her brother, it was also putting another pinch on her ability to continue working as Asteria—when all she needed was another week or two. A fortnight at the most. The opportunity to slip away to Chelsea and . . .

She ground her teeth together, for she couldn't do any of that until she found a way to keep Brody at bay.

Impossible man. He was determined to ruin everything. Calling at the house at all hours. Tracking her whereabouts. He'd made it all but impossible to slip away, even for her weekly luncheon with Lady Howers, as she did every Friday.

Oh, he was beginning to annoy her to no end.

And haunt her. Haunting the street outside her house. Haunting her nights as her dreams filled with memories of his kiss, his touch.

Worse, he was stirring up gossip, leaving all eyes on her . . . Didn't he realize how ruinous this all was?

Of course he did.

Wretched man.

Yet, why ever did the memory of his touch, his kiss continue to make her nights so very long? So very empty.

Then her mother said something that caught her ear, and she found herself pulled from her reveries.

"Tuck marry?" she asked, quite certain she hadn't heard her mother correctly. "Maman, that's madness."

Her mother sat back, a coy smile playing on her lips. "Mark my words, I see the signs. Besides, everyone does eventually, my dear. One day even you will fall in love."

She crossed her arms over her chest and looked out the window, ignoring how smug her mother looked.

For it had never been a question of love between Asteria and Brody. Passion, yes. Forbidden desires, most decidedly. But love?

Utterly impossible.

She shifted in her seat and sighed, her mother glancing over at her in that quizzical way of hers.

"Whatever is amiss, Roselie?" her mother asked.

"Nothing. Oh, everything," she said, shrugging her shoulders. "I do hope tonight isn't a complete bore."

"I doubt it. Lady Gosforth insisted that your brother and his wife attend," her mother said. "I am ever so thankful that the marchioness has taken such a keen interest in Louisa and her sister, bless her heart. Especially for Louisa's sister's sake—"

"Lavinia?"

"Yes, her." Lady Wakefield sighed and shook her head. "What an unfortunately awkward girl, but ever so pretty. I have a feeling Society is about to change their judgment of her."

"I do hope so. I rather like Lavinia," Roselie declared. "And she's a far sight more interesting than Pansy or Patience Nafferton."

Her mother's brow furrowed slightly. "Speaking of them, whatever were you thinking, going shopping with them? You must have been quite low in spirits to agree to such an expedition."

"It was the lesser of two evils," Roselie remarked, thinking she might have been better off being lectured by Brody.

"That explains that perfume you are wearing." Her mother wrinkled her nose. "I daresay you bought that at some shop Lady Nafferton favors. You quite have the air of a . . ." She searched for the right word.

Courtesan, Roselie would have supplied. For tonight she'd dared much. Putting on Asteria's own perfume, if only to remind Brody of who she was. Who she was capable of being.

Brody. She tamped down a sigh. Would he be at Lady Gosforth's tonight? He'd come by twice today to call on her but Dinnes had put him off with the excuses she'd supplied.

There would be no avoiding him tonight if he were at the ball. Not that either of them would have a moment's peace, not with all of Society watching.

Roselie pressed her lips together to keep from grinning.

In front of everyone.

For he could hardly berate her before the entire *ton*. Suddenly the evening didn't seem quite so bad. Yet a second thought quickly followed.

No, he couldn't chide her for being Asteria in the middle of the ballroom. But then again, neither could he kiss her.

Her mother's carriage pulled to a stop before the Gosforth's house and they got down.

As her slippers touched the curb, a chill spread through her. Bernie would have called it "the sight," but Uncle Hero called it "instincts."

A sense that she was being watched. Slowly, and as subtly as she could muster, she glanced around, but couldn't spy anything out of the ordinary.

Another dull evening in the *ton*, by all the markers. But still she shivered as she walked up the stairs, unable to shake the feeling that this night would change everything.

Just as that long ago night in Lord Howers's office had done . . .

Brody took the steps of the Marquess of Gosforth's town house two at a time. The events in the past few hours had made it imperative that Roselie cease her masquerade—immediately.

He had to make her see reason. Or sense. He paused for a moment as he tried to balance those conflicting notions. Roselie and sense.

Oh, yes, of all the impossible tasks . . .

None of this would be happening if he'd just seen past that demmed mask. He should have known.

Pushing into the crowd, Brody saw Piers standing across the

room with his new bride at his side. If all else failed, Brody would take his case to Roselie's brother.

Or, there was always Lady Wakefield, who stood on the other side of the ballroom, surrounded by her usual phalanx of admirers.

So that left only Roselie. Bother the chit, where the hell was she? He let his gaze sweep over the crush of guests again and still there was no sign of her.

Which only made this ill-ease inside him, this sense of foreboding, clamor that much louder.

He wasn't in the mood for games. He'd spent the first part of the evening helping Tuck save Lavinia Tempest from Ilford's hired ne'er-do-wells. But the evening had made a startling shift when one of the knaves captured began nattering on as to the depths of Ilford's crimes.

Finally, the Home Office had the evidence it needed to arrest the Marquess of Ilford for treason. Brody had been more than happy to go along with the officers sent to bring the man in.

Yet to Brody's surprise, Ilford, known for having a viperish tongue, rode to the Home Office in utter silence—not looking at any of his captors, the rattle of his shackles giving the only evidence that this was no normal jaunt about town.

But when Ilford had stepped down from the carriage, he'd finally managed to find his voice, his foul words coming in a black-hearted vow, whispered hastily for Brody's ears, and his alone.

"They'll find her, you know. It is only a matter of time. And then she'll die."

The bastard had smiled after this, undeniably certain that his revenge would be swift and final, and walked up the stairs as confidently as if he were returning to his comfortable home after a profitable night.

But it was those words . . . that vow, that promise . . . *then she'll die.*

There was no need to ask whom the man meant.

She. As in Asteria. Worse, when he did find her, Brody knew Asteria's fate. Roselie's fate.

He'd seen it when he'd looked down at Mrs. Croft's cold, ravaged body.

The only remaining question was whether or not the man actually knew how to find the lady behind the mask.

After depositing Ilford in a basement cell, he'd gone straight to Lady Wakefield's house, and after a bit of haranguing Dinnes, well, perhaps some threatening, he'd discovered her ladyship and Miss Stratton were attending the Gosforth's ball.

As he waded through the crush, he realized he might have come in haste, for his lack of evening wear and tousled clothes made him stand out, garnering more than one glance that said his appearance would be discussed up and down Mayfair.

Perfect. More fodder for his mother to natter on about.

It can't be helped, he reasoned. Then again, given the hurried chatter racing past him—all of it spreading the news of Ilford's arrest—his state of dress would probably barely rate a mention on the morrow.

Not surprising, Ilford's "friends" were abandoning him without a second thought, adding their own whispers and clucks as to his depravity, his vices and hints of staggering debts.

Brody continued deeper into the crowd, until that is, to his horror, he saw one of the Naffertons headed in his direction. Pansy, he suspected. Or Patience. Not that it mattered. Whichever one it was, the chit wore a determined smile on her lips, and her fan fluttered with invitation.

Immediately, Brody turned his search elsewhere—and as luck would have it—he found himself facing his mother, who was, to his great joy on the other side of the room.

Still, she waved at him to come join her and Lady Muscoates. He pretended like he hadn't seen her and beat a hasty course to his left before his mother all but strong-armed him into meeting some *proper* gel.

But his flight had the happy coincidence of turning him directly in Roselie's path, for there she was, not too far away, deep in conversation with Lady Essex's hired companion, Miss Manx.

He moved quickly, catching her unaware—and by the arm to ensure she didn't take flight—then turned and bowed slightly to her friend. "My apologies, Miss Manx, but I must borrow Miss Stratton for a few moments."

"A few moments, a few hours, the rest of her life, I hardly think she'll object," Miss Manx told him.

"I do object. Most readily." Roselie's sputtering indicated she hadn't any use for either of them, and she was digging in the heels of her slippers as he pulled her away.

He ignored her and dragged her. If he must, he'd throw her over his shoulder.

He was in that sort of mood.

So, it seemed was she. "Good heavens, Brody, this is a formal evening. Whatever are you doing here in that terrible coat? I'm surprised Lady Gosforth let you in."

"We need to talk." He looked for somewhere private. His ungentlemanly haste had nothing to do with the fact that Pansy/Patience Nafferton appeared to be actively looking for him.

Hunting would be a more accurate term.

"Talk? Now is hardly the time," Roselie pointed out. And she was correct. This being one of the most popular balls of the Season, the house was brimming with guests. Even the gardens beyond were filled.

They were hemmed in on all sides.

But that didn't mean he was about to give up. He only needed her cooperation. So he got to the point. "Shall I ask your brother if this is a good time? Piers is known for his understanding."

That got her attention. Her full attention. For her brother was more known for his temper.

"Let me go and you can call on me tomorrow," Roselie told him, doing her best to sound reasonable.

Not that he was fooled. Roselie being reasonable was only Roselie looking for more time to be utterly impossible.

"Oh, yes, put this off until tomorrow, by which time you'll have cooked up a bevy of excuses to avoid me for another day or two. A sennight, most likely." He paused and glanced down at her. "Is your butler in league with you as well?"

She turned up her nose. "I don't know what you mean." But the rosy hue on her cheeks said otherwise.

He leaned in close. "Yes, well, the time is now. Go upstairs. I'll follow in a few moments."

"No."

He ground his teeth together. He hated it to come to this, but he wasn't about to let anything happen to her. "Then a few moments of your mother's time ought to do the trick," he said, letting go of her arm and turning toward the corner where Lady Wakefield stood holding court.

"Brody, please don't—"

He stilled. "I must."

"Whatever for? Why now?"

He turned and closed the gap between them. "Because you are in danger."

If he thought those words would move her to reason, he was wrong.

She shrugged as if he were telling her last week's *on dit*. Which apparently he had. "'Tis of no matter."

Brody stilled. "No matter? Do you even know the danger you are in?" Now it was his turn to sputter a bit.

"Of course I do." Again she huffed and looked around them. "But it is what I must do."

What she—Brody had heard enough.

"Well, no longer."

Especially when her "must" would most likely get her killed. He caught her again by the elbow, but she'd anticipated him and shook him loose.

"And what, my lord, do you think you can do?" She was on point now, her elbows jutting out, her mouth set.

At this he smiled. "Stop you."

She laughed as if he had just shared a fine joke. Looking around, she played the debutante and smiled at the curious on-lookers who were watching them far too intently.

Brody hadn't the same care. He leaned forward, but to his credit, lowered his voice. "I won't leave until we come to some sort of agreement, or"—his gaze lifted to the point across the room where Piers and Louisa stood, the happily married pair being congratulated by their hosts—"I suppose such news would ruin their honeymoon, now wouldn't it?"

Roselie's mouth set in a hard line. Because there was one thing Brody knew for certain, she loved her family deeply and with a loyalty that went all the way to her heart. That part of Roselie would never change.

She glanced in the same direction. "A few moments then. At the most."

"That's all I will need." His hand went to her elbow again and he nodded toward the doors. "Go upstairs and I'll find you."

But he shouldn't have touched her. Not that time. For imme-diately she moved closer, letting her perfume curl around his senses.

The one that Asteria had worn that long ago night at St. John's Folly. A courtesan's perfume.

Of course, she'd worn it this night.

In a flash, she was Asteria, all smoky eyes and that wry, dan-gerous smile. "Lord Rimswell, you rakish devil. I take it you've done this before?" She turned on one heel and made her way to the stairs, the sway of her hips flirtatious, but the clip of her heels and the set of her shoulders said she was more than a bit annoyed.

Beautiful, angry and dangerous. He wasn't fool enough not to realize she was relenting far too easily. He'd thought he'd have far more of a fight on his hands just to get her to agree.

And speaking of fights . . .

"Lord Rimswell! Dear me, is that you?"

He glanced over his shoulder and saw Patience or Pansy—did it really matter which one?—trying her best to circumnavigate a rather large baroness.

Taking advantage of the determined miss's circuitous route, he bolted for the doorway and once there, took the stairs two at a time.

At the top, the hall ran to his right and to his left—down to the right, there was the chatter of voices from the room set aside for the ladies, so he turned to the left and only got a few feet into the shadows before he found a knife at his throat.

He glanced slowly and cautiously over his shoulder at his assailant.

"Good God, Roselie, put that thing away!"

She'd come out of the darkness like a shadow, catching him unaware.

As she always did, he realized.

"I'm not as helpless as you seem to think. Besides, I wasn't sure it was you, given the racket you were making."

"Not me? Who else where you expecting?"

She glanced over her shoulder. "Oh, bother, if you must know I've felt as if someone was watching me all night." She paused as she leaned over and tucked her knife back into her garter.

"Where the devil did you learn to do that?" He paused and thought the better of that question. "No, let me guess. The Honorable taught you."

She laughed a bit. "Hardly. Uncle Hero is terrible with a knife. Actually it was Mrs. Pratt who taught me."

"Your hired companion?" He groaned. "Does your mother—" He didn't bother finishing the question. "No, I suppose not."

Roselie smiled. "Definitely not."

Down the hall, a few ladies could be heard returning from the necessary, so Brody caught her by the arm and hauled her into the first room he came to—which, by the looks of it, appeared to be Lord Gosforth's study.

Bookshelves on two walls, a wide desk at the far end and a collection of chairs and a long settee by the fireplace. On one of the side tables sat a half-filled glass of whisky and an open book, as if Lord Gosforth had been called away from a perfectly amiable evening to join the festivities downstairs.

Either a servant or the marquess had left a pair of candles burning on the mantel. The shadows danced on the walls, while Roselie did her best to appear as the aggrieved debutante.

"We shouldn't be alone," she complained, trying to get around him, but he refused to budge. "I have my reputation to think of."

He barked a laugh. "Suddenly you're concerned about your reputation?"

She bristled. "I don't see why you find that funny. After all, if we are determining the status of my reputation, I would point out that you've already ruined me. More. Than. Once."

"I never—" he began, even as her hands fisted to her hips, and she faced him down.

"Never?" And then that smile of Asteria's turned at her lips.

Memories of her kiss, of holding her, touching her, flooded through his veins.

He shook those aside. "Not intentionally—"

"So says every rake in London after he is caught." She smirked at him. "Tell me, Brody, if you had known, would it have made a difference?"

She stood there waiting, lips pursed together. Lips capable of leaving him breathless. And hard. Willing to . . . Well, ruin every last inch of her.

"Of course it would have," he said, almost believing himself, all the while still lost in the fantasy of taking her up against the wall and . . . ruining her.

"So it is perfectly proper to kiss a woman when you think her a—" Her brows arched up as if she actually expected him to finish that sentence.

Like hell he was going to. He wasn't *that* foolish. Besides, he'd seen her knife. Up close and personal.

Instead, he huffed a breath and stepped away from her—although keeping himself between her and the door.

They had a lot of unfinished business to settle and he didn't trust her.

Or himself.

"Must we go over this? I was only doing my duty." He tried to sound bored, but in truth, the subject had rather consumed him for the last few years.

Asteria's lips. Asteria naked. Asteria beneath him writhing with pleasure.

"King and Country commands that you fondle a lady in her nether regions?"

He looked away because he didn't dare look at her. And also because he'd been about to get to that part of his fantasies.

Yes, touching her down there as she made those mewling sounds of pleasure drove him mad with need.

And no, he hadn't been commanded to do that.

He'd done it because he wanted to. Wanted her.

"I didn't hear you protest," he replied as his entire body woke up, memories of holding her sending his blood racing, of kissing her, touching her, devilishly playing havoc with his . . .

No, no, no. He needed to stop. For even though he knew who she was, he still wanted her—the woman who had fallen into his arms and kissed him with abandon.

His gaze strayed to her lips. Still so very kissable. For suddenly she had stopped being Asteria. At least so he told himself.

She'd always been his. His Rosebud. His. He'd just been too foolish not to see it.

As if she followed his line of thought, she wet her lips. "Tell me what you want . . ."

His mouth went dry. What he wanted was becoming as elusive as she was.

Roselie moved closer. "Otherwise, I have some business to attend to—"

In his distraction, she went to slip past him.

Oh, the vexing little minx. His temper—so raw and close tonight—flared in an instant and he caught her by the arm. Why hadn't he learned yet that it was a mistake to touch her? To hold her? Because in that instant it wasn't Roselie who was trapped, but him.

In the silk of her skin. Her perfume coiling around his senses like a snare. And her dark brown eyes, so full and deep. So full of secrets.

They all but begged him to come exploring.

But he couldn't. For he'd made a vow. To save her. To stop her. And he would.

She had matters to attend to? So did he.

"What business?" he demanded.

"None of yours." Her chin notched up. "You have no say over me." But there was a tremor to her voice that said otherwise. A flicker in her eyes. An invitation? A dare? Fear?

Good God, that was it. Fear. Roselie was afraid. And well she should be.

He released her and took a step back. "Go about your 'business' again and I shall inform your mother as to what you've been doing."

If he thought that was enough to stop her, he was very wrong.

For this was Roselie. And he should have known better.

Chapter 9

A lady will never have to marry in haste and disgrace if she avoids impossible situations.

Miss Emery, Miss Emery's Establishment for the
Education of Genteel Young Ladies

"Be my guest," Roselie dared him.

One of Brody's brows rose in an arch. "Your mother knows?"

She laughed. "Of course not. If she did, she'd have sent me to a nunnery in Ireland ages ago."

"Then you'd best pack your bags."

"Hardly. Packing my bags would be a wasteful exercise," she told him.

He truly hated it when she sounded that smug, stood there with her arms crossed over her chest and her bottom lip stuck out in defiance.

"You don't believe I'll tell her, do you?"

She shrugged carelessly. "I absolutely believe you'll tell her— whether you are willing to tell her *everything* is another matter."

Everything. Yes, that was a rather sticky dilemma. Especially if *everything* needed to include her nether regions.

And his exploration thereof.

That gave him pause, though only for a second. She was bluffing, because if everything came to light they'd be in the first hackney to the archbishop's office for a Special License.

Courtesy of her irate brother and his favorite pistol.

So he called her bluff. "I think I can come up with enough of the facts to see you shipped far from London."

She scoffed again. A less-than-ladylike huff that suggested he was playing a few cards short of a full deck.

"Why do you think I won't tell?" He had to ask.

He shouldn't have.

She straightened and looked him in the eye. "Tell my mother, Brody, and I shall tell yours what you've been doing with your nights."

He stumbled back a bit.

Because Roselie had an unbeatable hand.

It was one thing for him to be jaunting about for the Home Office when he had been the spare and his brother Poldie had been alive, but quite another now that he was Rimswell, the very last of his line.

Yes, her mother might ship her off to Ireland, but his mother would lock him away with the first likely bride—even Lady Muscoates's questionable ward—and keep him locked up until he had a houseful of heirs, by which time . . .

He roared back. "You wouldn't dare! I have work to do!"

She stood her ground, her words low and final. "So do I."

For some reason, her quiet determination gave him more concern than if she had shouted at him.

He shook his head. Time for a new hand. "Roselie, can't you see the danger you've placed yourself in? St. John's Folly, for God's sakes. That is no place for you."

She gaped at him for a moment, and then to his shock, began to laugh. So hard, that she turned and stumbled her way over to the settee where she flopped down in a gale of laughter.

"What is so funny?" he demanded.

She looked up at him, swiping at the tears in her eyes. "That you think St. John's Folly is the most scandalous place I've been.

Good heavens, Brody, I've obviously given you more credit than you deserve."

Then he recalled all the rumors he'd heard over the years about Asteria. All the places others had reported seeing her.

Gaming hells. Brothels. The docks.

This time as he looked at her, he saw Asteria curled up on the settee like a well-fed housecat, all confidence, grinning once again with that demmed smug smile of hers.

He shook his head. "I need a drink." He crossed the room and poured a glass from Gosforth's private stock. Then glancing over his shoulder at the woman behind him, poured her one as well.

"Some night, eh?" she asked.

"Yes."

Handing one of the glasses over to her, he drank his own down in one gulp.

Roselie glanced down at the tawny liquid swirling about in her glass. "Is it true—Ilford's been arrested?"

"Yes," he replied. "Arrested and done for." He looked down at his own glass and saw only the bottom, so he went to pour another one.

"Are you certain?" she pressed. There it was again. That unmistakable note.

Fear.

What had she said when he'd come upstairs? Yes, now he remembered.

I've felt as if someone was watching me all night.

His gaze jolted up to meet hers. "Yes. I'm certain." But he'd been too slow in answering.

"You hesitated. Is he in custody?" She sat up, her feet finding the floor and her hands cupping her glass tightly.

So she was worried. Good. Maybe now she'd listen to reason.

"Yes. And very likely to stay that way for the rest of his life," he told her. "Isn't that what you wanted? Ilford arrested."

Now she hesitated. "Yes, but—"

"He's done for, Roselie. The case is closed." He returned to the decanter and poured another glass.

"You think his arrest is the end of it? I'd wager quite differently, my lord." She sighed, then took a large gulp from her glass.

"What does that mean?" he demanded.

"You know exactly what it means," she fired back. "Ilford's arrest isn't the end. Not by a long shot." She emptied her glass and set it down on the side table, then rose to face him. "You need me now more than ever if you are to stop all this."

"I believe I already have," Brody reminded her. "And you are finished, or, God help me, Roselie, I will tell your brother *and* your mother what you've been doing, and damn the consquences."

For he couldn't stop Ilford's haunting refrain from tolling once again.

And then she'll die.

His gut twisted. *No, a hundred times, no.* Without thinking, he reached out and caught hold of her shoulders, drawing her close. "Demmit, Roselie, you must stop!"

His face must have shown the myriad of emotions rushing through him. Fear that Ilford's vile words would come true. Desire to see her safe.

Desires of another sort.

"Stop what?" she asked, moving closer, her hand coming up to cup his chin. "Helping, or being *her*?"

He reached up to cradle the hand pressed to his cheek and as he touched her his heart gave a wary lurch. Hammered oddly as he looked into Roselie's dark eyes. The woman before him, the woman of his fantasies.

Demmit, he'd move heaven and earth before he let anyone harm her.

That is, if she'd let him.

"If you think someone is watching you, then they most likely are. Can't you see, you must stop this nonsense before. . . . before—" That one word—*nonsense*—flared like a match.

And Roselie, the powder keg.

For she exploded just like one. *"Nonsense?!"* She wrenched away from him, spinning around, her skirt whirling about her ankles. "Why you prudish, overly superior, hypocritical—"

After about the seventh insult, Brody stopped cataloguing them.

"It isn't proper," he interjected. Though this time with a little less *prudish* superiority. When her brows cocked up again, he quickly tried another tact. "It would break your mother's heart if something were to happen to you. If you ended up like . . ."

"Like what?" She snapped, and then almost immediately, her lips snapped shut.

Not what. Who.

The name, the images floated between them like an unholy specter.

She blinked, and all of Asteria's bravado took flight.

"Like Abigail." She turned around as if looking for a steady perch and finally found it by sagging down on the settee.

"Yes." He glanced away for he couldn't look at her and not see Mrs. Croft instead. There in that wagon behind the Constable's office. Her body ravaged. Her sightless eyes still holding an echo of the harrowing horror she'd endured.

Roselie turned toward the fireplace and stared at the coals. "I know what you did. Seeing to her. That she was properly buried and all. Thank you."

He shook off her words. "She was your friend. After all she'd lost, she didn't deserve—"

"No, she didn't," Roselie rushed to say, looking away, but not before Brody saw the heavy rush of tears welling up in her brown eyes.

Gads, she blamed herself for Mrs. Croft's death. But from what Mrs. Pratt had told him, Roselie had gone to great lengths to ensure her friend's safety, to get her far from London.

Still, she blamed herself. Like her brother had blamed himself for Poldie's death.

Oh, these Strattons and their high ideals. Their order of things. Holding themselves to such impossible, lofty standards.

"You did everything you could—"

"I didn't do enough." And then the tears fell.

He knelt before her and gathered her shaking body into his arms, her tears now turned to sobs. "Oh, Roselie, no—"

Whatever was he supposed to say? He'd learned early on in this business that life was a fragile thing. Half a dozen of the agents Brody had worked beside were gone. Lost.

In many cases, no one knew what had happened to them. Just vanished.

Was that any better than knowing? Especially when . . .

He tightened his hold on her, a familiarity to having her in his arms that left him off-kilter. She belonged here.

More to point, he needed her as well.

"She left a note . . . in her things," Roselie whispered. "She said what she wanted more than anything was to be reunited with Lawrence."

"Captain Croft?"

She nodded.

"I suppose now she is."

"Yes, she must be." Roselie's words held a fierce hope.

He pulled her to her feet and fished out his handkerchief, dabbing at her spent tears.

"Don't you see now why you must stop? I couldn't live with myself if—"

"I know the risks," she told him, taking the now-damp square of linen from him and finishing the task. "But my work is necessary."

"Necessary?" Now it was his turn to be incredulous. "There is an entire troop of agents at the Home Office dedicated to doing what is *necessary*. I hardly see how one lady . . ." He paused for a moment. "There is only one of you, isn't there?"

She answered him with a short laugh. "How many other masked women have you kissed in the line of duty?"

A stillness fell between them and that irrational desire to kiss her flooded through him. Yet again.

"Only you."

She tipped her head slightly and studied him. "Just me? Surely, there must be others, Brody."

"No, Rosebud. Only you."

His words, his confession stopped her. Her mouth opened to say something, but she must have thought better of it.

Only you.

In the blink of an eye, Roselie was gone and Asteria stood in her place, a hint of whisky on her breath, tawny with all the right notes. She moved closer. "Do you want only her?"

Want? Dangerous question. Asteria. Roselie. Rosebud.

His.

Oh, yes, he wanted her, his gaze flitting of its own volition to the desk, to the carpet before the fireplace, to the wide depth of the settee—anywhere he could take her and find the release he'd longed for.

But what then?

"No," he protested, more to himself. "This isn't proper. Not here. Not ever again. 'Tis absolutely impossible."

She smiled at him, undeterred. Like a cat, she smoothly slid back into his arms. "Hardly impossible. I daresay, if I had my mask on, I know exactly what we'd be doing here." She caught his hand and brought it to her hip, and moved even closer—yes, well, he might have pulled her in a bit—leaving only their clothes between them.

"Something like this," she sighed before she looked up at him. "Only, I think you'd have my skirt up by now."

Oh, how he hated it when Roselie Stratton had the right of things.

Much to Roselie's dismay, instead of accepting her dare, he set her back from him, crossing his arms over his chest. "The only thing kissing you will bring me is ruin and a hasty marriage."

"It hasn't so far," she pointed out.

Brody raked a hand through his hair. "No. Well, yes. Oh, demmit, you know what I mean." He leaned in. "Only because we haven't been caught."

She mocked him by folding her arms across her chest, and her lips—those plump, kissable lips—pursed into a sultry smile. "So lock the door."

Roselie wasn't such a fool that she didn't realize that her time as Asteria was coming to an end. But that would also mean she could no longer play the coquette with him.

This man and his tousled dark hair. His unforgiving gaze. She might have known him all her life, but she had realized how little she actually knew him.

How much she wanted to know him.

This is Brody. He calls you Rosebud, she tried reminding herself.

I know, her heart whispered happily back.

He left her breathless, restless, aching with desires. Maybe it was the whisky. For all her cares had abandoned her.

Much as he had abandoned his that night in Lord Howers's office. She understood now how grief and fear and frustration could curl inside one's gut and come wrenching out in a dangerous coil.

Her voice lowered, took on Asteria's faint accent, and she spoke as she edged closer to him. "Tell me you don't want to kiss me again. Right now."

Kiss me and take this pain away.

He crossed his arms over his chest—a barrier of sorts. "Not at all."

And they both knew it for what it was. A lie.

Indecision flickered through his eyes and that was all she needed. So she moved quickly, without hesitation.

Because she might never have this chance again.

If anything, being Asteria had taught her to seize the moment. And so she did, moving back into his arms, pressing her body to his and tipping up her mouth. "Kiss me, you fool."

"Demmit, Roselie," he muttered, before his mouth crashed down on hers.

She opened up to him, hungry to feel him inside her, for him to explore her.

He kissed her deeply, her tongue twining with his, their breath—all warm with the whisky—joined together.

A sort of madness took over. Need and long-pent-up desires left them both senseless.

He backed her into Lord Gosforth's desk, and catching her by her backside, set her atop it, so her legs could straddle him, leaving her open to him.

And just as she had said, her skirt rose up as his hand traced a trail up her leg, her thigh, and then to her very apex. She gasped when he touched her so intimately, teasing her with his fingers, until she was writhing, twisting, mewling with pleasure.

This was no gentle exploration, no tentative tease, he played with her just as she wanted—pressing into her, driving her mad with a need that twisted up inside her, left her panting on the edge of release.

She was so very close.

He wrenched free of her kiss, and began to explore her, suckling her flesh, leaving a hot trail down her neck, to the top of her breasts. His free hand opened her gown and freed one breast and then took her nipple in his mouth and sucked deeply, while his finger slid inside her, thrusting in, matching the movements of his mouth.

Oh, heavens, it was almost like . . .

She might still be innocent in *that* way, but oh, that didn't mean she didn't know . . . didn't understand this delirious instinct.

For him.

She reached down for the front of his breeches, frantically trying to open them. Beneath the wool, he was thick and hard. Oh, so very hard. Temptation, need, aching to be inside her.

She had to touch him, hold him. Stroke him. Tease him as he was her.

Free him, so he could be inside her.

Suddenly this hot, relentless chase changed. Roselie didn't know how or why, but suddenly the world around them stilled.

Everything slowed down. His kiss became more tender, her hands less demanding. This need wasn't just his and hers, but theirs.

Somewhere in the chase, they'd become entwined and bound together.

"Come for me," he whispered in her ear, his lips hot and moist against her skin.

"I don't know how."

"Let me help you, Rosebud."

His fingers rolled over her sex again, drawing lazy circles that sent rivers of pleasure through her.

His lips nibbled at hers, and this time his kiss was filled with need, tendrils of desire. Tenderness. All the while, his touch was drawing her toward a warm pool of fire, and when she got to the edge, she tumbled into it.

Her breath caught in her throat, her eyes fluttered open for just a second as she found her release.

"Oh, Brody, oh, my," she gasped, as her body burst to life, Brody surrounding her, pulling her close, kissing her thoroughly as she rocked against him.

And just as she began to catch her breath, her eyes opened and she looked at him—seeing someone she didn't quite recognize. He'd changed.

And from his expression, she had as well.

What the devil had just happened to them?

But there was no time to find out, for just then the door behind them burst open and in tumbled a young lady.

And not just any lady, but Miss Patience Nafferton.

She took one look at the couple, entwined and disheveled before her and said the first thing that popped into her head.

"Oh, heavens! This isn't the lady's necessary, is it?"

Ruin and a hasty marriage.

Those words rang through Roselie's thoughts the next day as she looked up at the altar of St. George's and knew that but for the grace of God and her own sharp wit, it might be her and

Brody up there being bound together in holy matrimony rather than her cousin, Tuck Rowland and Miss Lavinia Tempest.

More shocking was that Tuck was actually here of his own free will, having earlier harangued the archbishop for a Special License and was now happily leg shackling himself to Lavinia.

Had the entire world gone mad? She certainly had to question her own sanity. What had she been thinking last night . . . Kissing Brody like that. Letting herself actually . . .

Just then, someone slid into the pew beside her. She took a surreptitious peek and wished she hadn't.

Brody.

Worse was the almost immediate telltale blush that rose on her cheeks at the sight of him.

Good heavens, whatever was she blushing for? It was only Brody and it wasn't like they hadn't kissed before.

And yet this time . . . this time it had been so very different. Whatever had come over them? One moment they'd been devouring each other and then . . .

Oh, that stillness. The sense of being the only two people. Ever.

Her world had turned upside down.

Brody leaned over. "I had to see it for myself," he whispered. "Tuck and Miss Tempest. I knew he was infatuated, but *this?*"

Roselie ignored him. He needn't sound so incredulous. As if there was something wrong about falling in love and getting married. Which anyone could plainly see was the case between Lavinia and Tuck.

Good heavens, the way they gazed at each other was scandal in itself.

Roselie shifted slightly, moving from one foot to another, because there was something all too familiar about that look.

She slanted a glance over at Brody and much to her dismay, her heart pattered so very differently than it ever had before.

Oh, this would never do.

She yanked her gaze back to the happy couple. A deliriously happy, in-love couple and Roselie thought she might have to bolt for the door as the horrible, wrenching realization escaped her heart, invaded her reason.

She wasn't. She couldn't be. No. Absolutely not.

She was not in love with Brody. Not at all.

She took another look at him, and of course he looked every inch the London gentleman—a superfine jacket and buff breeches, while his boots shone with a glossy hue. His cravat fell in a great waterfall, and his coat sported no less than three capes.

Ever the Corinthian, her Lord Rimswell.

Not hers, she told herself emphatically. Not *this* man. This elegant baron, with all his good manners and propriety. He wasn't the same rakish devil she'd come to know in the night.

Then again, neither are you, her heart reminded her.

"Sorry for leaving in such a hurry last night," he whispered over to her.

She stood ramrod straight, her gaze fixed on the couple before them. "I suppose you thought it best."

That earned her a glance. "You only regret not thinking of it first."

Bother the man. She couldn't help herself, she turned slightly and leaned toward him. "Thinking of what?"

He grinned slightly. "A full retreat."

Wretched, smug bastard.

Honestly though, she couldn't fault him for his flight.

Then again, she should be furious with him. He'd left her with Patience Nafferton, after all.

So she straightened a bit, determined to ignore him, turning her attention to the altar where the vicar was going on in a lengthy bit about the virtues of marriage and chastity.

Though as Roselie looked at Lavinia Tempest, something about the way the beautiful miss from Kempton glanced over at Tuck, and how he returned her admiration with a raw, hungry look, suggested that this lecture by the vicar might be a bit late.

She glanced away, for looking at them left an icy pit rocking through her.

If she was being honest, she might admit she was jealous.

As the prayers finished and the collected congregation sat down, Roselie found Brody pressed into her. She could hardly scoot over and not bump into her mother, but sitting like this, next to Brody, with her hip pressed against his, his arm sliding against hers, and the smell of his cologne—all masculine and musky—left her traitorous heart once again hammering that wretched refrain.

Then Brody only added to her dismay.

He leaned over and whispered in her ear, "That could very well be us."

"Hardly," she shot back. She had no intention of being married in haste. Impossible notion. It would ruin everything. Oh bother. Perhaps Miss Emery should have added a lecture on what exactly was "an impossible situation."

Then again, Roselie suspected she knew. Only too well.

But Brody was becoming insistent. "You aren't so naïve not to realize that eventually Miss Nafferton will reveal what she thinks she saw," he told her. "And then what do you think will happen?"

Thinks she saw?

They both knew exactly what Patience had seen. And unfortunately, so did Patience.

Roselie bit back the retort she wanted to utter and considered a new course of action.

First of all, murder Patience Nafferton. Discreetly, of course.

Secondly, get as far away from London as she could. She hoped Bernie didn't mind living in Yorkshire. Or Scotland. Or even the West Indies . . .

"I assure you, I've taken care of the problem," Roselie told him. "If you hadn't run away at the first cannon shot, you would know that she's promised not to say a word."

He snorted a bit and earned a few scathing glances from the other wedding guests.

Including one from Roselie, for she was still furious with him, abandoning her with Patience, of all the hen-hearted things to do.

But she'd done exactly what Asteria always did: turn the situation in her favor.

"Patience, how relieved I am that it is you *who found me!" Roselie had rushed to the girl's side, even as Brody fled out the door as if he had Napoleon's entire army on his heels.*

"Why is that?" the girl asked, turning to look after Brody, but Roselie caught her by the arm and turned her in the other direction.

"Yes, why?" Roselie repeated as she tried to think quickly. Oh, bother she was a muddled mess, but she must gather her wits. And then it came to her. "For you are my dearest friend and would never reveal anything you might think you've seen."

Patience's brow furrowed. "I wouldn't?"

"Of course not! That's what it means to be confidantes." Roselie linked her arm around Patience's and steered her toward the door.

And well away from the scene of the crime.

"It does?" Patience sounded overly disappointed by the prospect of not being able to share such a perfectly delicious on dit.

Roselie nodded. "By every definition. So it is imperative that you mustn't repeat what you think you saw."

"Think? But I know what I saw," she insisted, trying to turn back to the study if only to piece together the now fleeting images she'd witnessed.

Miss Stratton. Lord Rimswell. Oh, goodness, it was all a tangled mess.

"I know what you think you saw, but it was hardly that. Not at all," Roselie assured her as they left the scene of the crime and continued toward the stairs. "Think of how such a lie would wound your sister. She holds such a delicate tendre *for Lord Rimswell."*

"Oh, that she does. Is quite convinced that he'll—" Patience's brow furrowed again as it mostly likely dawned on her that her sister's hopes of a lofty marriage weren't all that certain.

Roselie smiled encouragingly. "Poor Pansy, she'd be devastated if she thought the baron's affections were ill-placed—which I assure you they are not. Most of all, I would so hate to lose her friendship—and yours— over what is nothing more than a terrible misunderstanding."

At this, Patience stopped. "It was terrible?" Her eyes widened and her mouth fell open. "He didn't—"

"Of course not," Roselie rushed to assure her as they began to descend to the ballroom. "I can hardly remember what happened—I must have tripped and Brody—that is Lord Rimswell—caught me—"

She wisely ignored the fact that she shouldn't have been alone with the baron under any circumstances, but she hoped Patience hadn't gotten that far.

"I must say your timing was perfect, Patience, my dear, dear friend." Far too perfect. "You quite saved me from a dreadful misunderstanding and a most undeserved ruin—and think of it! You've quite saved poor Pansy from terrible heartbreak. We'll both be in your debt forever."

"In my debt?" Patience brightened at this. "Oh, my!" Then the girl, who had never had much of an original thought in her life had to ask, "Whatever does that mean?"

Roselie had a sudden vision of endless afternoons in the company of the Nafferton sisters. Shopping. Going for ices. Sharing confidences.

She did her best not to shudder. At least, outwardly. For the alternative—ruin and banishment from Society—wasn't much better. "That this must remain our secret. For that's what it means to be boon companions."

"Oh, yes, of course," Patience promised most faithfully then glanced down the stairs where her twin was doing her best to corner Lord Rimswell. "For Pansy's sake."

"Exactly," Roselie had told her before excusing herself and going to find her mother and beg a terrible megrim.

Roselie sat up in the pew and after a moment, leaned over and told him in all confidence, "You'll be pleased to know that Miss Nafferton has vowed never to reveal what she thinks she witnessed. I impressed upon her how important it is that she doesn't say a word."

At the front of the church, Tuck slid a ring onto his bride's finger and the entire congregation murmured with approval.

Then he kissed his glowing bride and everyone rose to their feet and began to applaud.

"Yes, well, if she does, we'd have to get married," Brody pointed out, even as he was smiling down the pew at Lady Wakefield, who had stopped watching the proceedings at the altar and was now looking at the pair beside her with an expression of unparalleled curiosity.

"It won't come to that," Roselie whispered back as everyone moved forward to congratulate the happy couple. "Patience has promised. I'm certain she'll keep her word."

And Patience did. Keep her word. For an entire day.

Until, that is, Pansy had made some boast about being the next Lady Rimswell and how sad it was that Patience would spend the remainder of her days as an old, unwanted spinster living in the attic.

Not at all happy with that turn of events, Patience blurted out the words that ensured they would both be sharing that attic together.

The news that greeted Brody that evening when he arrived at the Home Office did nothing to lift his spirits. He'd made it a habit to visit the marquess in his cell each day—if only to reassure himself the man was still locked up.

As much as he told himself that Ilford's vow to find "her," was hardly worthy of note now that he was locked up, he couldn't stop Roselie's words from haunting him.

You think his arrest is the end of it? I'd wager quite differently, my lord.
Wasn't it?

But this night, he hadn't gone more than a few steps inside the office to know that something had gone terribly wrong.

Howers stood near a knot of agents, issuing orders right and left.

One of the fellows turned to Brody. "Dead, Rimswell. Can you believe it?"

No, he couldn't. The main witness against the Marquess of

Ilford, Charlie Bludger, had been found lifeless in his cell in Newgate.

"How the devil did that happen?" he asked the man.

"No one knows," he replied. "But Old Ironpants wants answers now."

He wasn't the only one who wanted answers. Brody hurried down the stairs to check on Ilford, where he found the marquess gloating over his apparent victory.

He lay on his back on the narrow cot, hands behind his head, hardly looking the worse for wear, despite having been locked up for the last few days.

"I understand that Mr. Bludger has met an unfortunate ending. *Tsk. Tsk,*" he clucked. "How tragic, but not unexpected for a man of his predilections. From what I hear, he had a number of enemies."

Brody's gut clenched. "How the—"

"Do you honestly think I don't hear the news? Even in here?" Ilford sighed, his gaze still fixed on the ceiling. "I know everything, you trifling boy."

Roselie's prediction began to appear more like a sure bet.

Brody stepped closer to the cell. "You're done, Ilford. You can't harm anyone from here."

His head turned slowly, like a lizard in the sun. "Can't I? Is that your wager?"

"Given your luck with wagers of late, I'd be a bit more hesitant to put your blunt at risk. The last wager you made put you in here."

That got the man's attention. Right in the bull's eye. His face flashed with rage.

"I'll see her—" he began to rant.

"Yes, yes, I know," Brody replied, doing his best to sound bored. "Dead." He heaved a sigh and turned to leave.

Make him angry. Prod him to make a mistake. Never before had Brody been driven with such a need to discover the truth. Untangle this mystery.

There was too much at stake. Especially now.

They'll find her you know. It's only a matter of time.

No, they won't, he vowed. He glanced over his shoulder and found Ilford watching him, his eyes narrowed into two slits.

"I wager you'll hang," he continued, feigning bravado he didn't feel, turning back to the cell.

Because if anything were to happen to her . . .

Ilford sat up. "You honestly think *I'll* be tried for treason? Without that sewer rat's lies, you have nothing. Nothing." He spat out the last word, his eyes darting about. "The man was venal, wanted by the navy for desertion, you know, would have said anything to avoid the rope. It was always his word against mine, and now, unfortunately for you, Mr. Bludger's gone rather silent on the subject, hasn't he?"

Brody snorted.

Oh, but Ilford was hardly done. "My father will have me out of here by the end of the week."

Brody latched onto that. "Where is your father, Ilford? Howers sent word to the duke right after you were arrested and what have we heard—" He paused, hand cupped to his ear. "Yes, just like I thought, *nothing.* He's as silent as your friend Bludger. Perhaps he's more than happy to wash his hands of you. Or is he the one who's been pulling your strings?"

For a moment, the man's eyes flickered with resentment, but just as quickly he sat up and laughed. "My father? He's a fool," the marquess said, chortling. "Can't even manage a hand of whist, let alone whatever mad scheme you think I've been a part of. No, Rimswell, this is only a temporary setback for me—especially now that there is no evidence. No one to testify."

"Isn't there?" Brody asked, taking a lesson from Roselie. It was a dangerous bluff, but he was running out of choices. "I wouldn't be so sure."

And besides, he had a nagging suspicion she had the right of it. There was more to all this.

The mad flicker returned as Ilford's angry gaze strafed the bars between them. "I never let an enemy escape—that is where you and I are different, Rimswell." Then as if remembering himself, he lay back down and resumed his insolent pose. With a flick of his hand, he dismissed his visitor, and Brody knew from previous chats that Ilford wouldn't say another word.

At least not now.

Brody turned and left, but when he was halfway up the stairs, he paused.

Why *hadn't* the old duke come to London?

Chapter 10

$\mathscr{M}$onday morning, Roselie bounded up early. For all Brody's dire warnings, Patience had kept her word and now it was time for Roselie to get back to work. Specifically, she needed to visit the remaining madhouses in Abigail's notes and try to discover whatever Abigail had been seeking. Or rather, whom.

It hadn't been easy making the arrangements. With the plain carriage lost, Patch still on the mend and her brother now in command of his estates, she'd sent a note around to Mrs. Rowland to help her find another carriage.

Which would most likely come at a pretty penny. Roselie smiled a bit as she jangled the new coins in her purse—all courtesy of Brody's pocket watch which Bernie had gotten a fair price for when she'd pawned it.

If she felt guilty about it, she had also sold her pearl ring. She knew it would take every bit of gold she could get her hands on to finish her work.

And finish it, she would. No matter what Brody said or threatened.

Roselie was just tucking the last strand of hair back up into her bonnet, when Bernie came bolting through the door, closing it behind her and leaning against it as if she were hoping to stop some unexpected hordes from gaining entry.

The woman's usually rosy cheeks were drained of color and her eyes held a frantic light.

"Dear heavens, Bernie! Whatever is it?"

"Didn't you hear the bell?"

"Yes, I did," Roselie replied. The bell rang often. Her mother was a popular guest and had numerous admirers—invitations and tributes poured in regularly.

"There's quite the hullabaloo down there." Bernie looked over her shoulder and drew a fortifying breath.

"What now?" Roselie asked as she dug around in her bureau for her favorite reticule. The one that held her small pistol. As she checked it, she asked, "Did *Maman* misplace her gloves again?" That usually had the entire staff running about.

Bernie shook her head, and leaving her post at the door, she went to the clothespress and pulled out the small valise they used for Asteria. "No. Your brother and his wife are here."

"Piers and Louisa?" That was rather noteworthy, for Piers never called on anyone, but now that he'd taken a wife . . . and it seemed Louisa had been the perfect tonic for his despair. But that was hardly worthy of such obvious panic. Then again . . . "At this hour? How odd."

Bernie opened the valise. "It's no social call."

Roselie paused and glanced at her usually calm companion. Nothing ruffled Bernie. "No?"

"No." Bernie glanced around the room. "And it's not just him and his lady wife."

"It isn't?"

"No. He's got that lordling of yours in tow."

Roselie froze. "Which lordling?" She only asked, because she hoped she was wrong.

Very wrong.

As it was, she wasn't.

"Lord Rimswell," Bernie replied impatiently as she began to empty the bag. "And the mother as well."

Roselie's mouth fell open. But she needed to be certain. "Lady

Rimswell? No, you must be wrong." Goodness, she hoped Bernie was wrong.

Her companion paused. "Sour-looking bird? Mouth set like she's been dropped into Sodom and Gomorrah?"

Roselie groaned. Yes, that could only be Lady Rimswell. She had no love for the Strattons, so it would have to be the devil's own errand that would force her though their door.

But what? Roselie did the math and quickly came to one conclusion.

Patience.

The room closed in around her and now it was her turn to panic.

"Whatever are you waiting for?" Roselie blurted out, unholy fear blinding her usual good sense. She bolted from her seat and pushed Bernie toward the clothespress, while she pulled a few essentials out of the drawers of her dressing table. "We must pack quickly. We'll take the back stairs. Mrs. Rowland can help us . . . We could—"

Bernie caught her by the arm, and slowly removed the hairbrush and comb she was clutching, settling them back on the dressing table. "'Tis too late for that, child."

"But—" Plans tumbled rapidly through her thoughts, but she had to discard one after another.

And it seemed that Bernie knew it as well. She shook her head, and bid her to sit down. "Sometimes the cards don't fall in your favor, even when you're the one shuffling them."

"Then whatever do I do?"

"Bluff," Bernie told her, as she gently pulled the pins holding Roselie's bonnet in place. "And if it comes to it, you'll just have to pay the piper."

A scratch on the door brought both Roselie and Bernie to attention.

"Miss?" Dinnes called out. "Your mother has requested that I bring you downstairs. She is in the large salon." There was a hint of Scottish burr to his voice, which only came out when one of the footmen showed up inebriated, or a tradesman became cheeky.

Roselie glanced at Bernie, for they both knew it was as bad as they suspected.

"Good luck," Bernie said, reaching out and squeezing her hand.

"You aren't coming with me?"

"And get sacked?" The older woman shook her head. "Better that I let her ladyship cool down a bit before we cross paths."

"Coward."

"I prefer cautious. Pragmatic. Of sound mind." Her implication was that Roselie was anything but.

Well, certainly, Bernie had a point there. Especially when it came to Brody.

"Bluff," Bernie whispered to her as she opened the door.

"Yes, well, it's what I do best," Roselie said, smiling graciously at Dinnes.

She held on to the hope that Patience Nafferton had held her tongue and this was all some trifle over conflicting invitations, or some slight problem that could be easily managed, though none of those theories explained Lady Rimswell's arrival in their midst.

But she wasn't consoled when she entered the room. No, rather her heart sank.

Oh, yes, Piers and his new wife, Louisa, were in attendance just as Bernie had said. But her companion had left out the inclusion of Lady Gamston.

Otherwise known as the elder Stratton sister. The proper one who had made an excellent match in her first Season.

Margaret was here? No, this didn't bode well. Not at all.

Oh, and the farther Roselie waded into the room, the depth of the tragedy unfolding before her became all too clear.

For here was Brody's mother, severe black gown and all. Since the death of her son, Poldie, she'd refused to wear anything other than black. Her way of railing against the cruel fates that had taken her darling son from her.

As for the lady's remaining son, he stood looking out the far window.

Notably, he didn't turn to greet her.

As bad as all that, is it, Brody? She chose to ignore him, smiling at the others sitting stiffly about the room.

"Ah, Roselie darling, there you are." Her mother rose from her chair, the one that commanded a view of the room, and came forward to pull her into the very heart of the stage.

One Roselie wanted no part of—clearly, for her slippers dragged against the carpet.

She dared another glance at her brother, but the murderous glare on his face—the one she hadn't seen since he'd become enchanted by Louisa—was enough to send a frisson of fear through her.

He looked ready to blurt something out, explode really, but his wife laid a steadying hand over his, then she looked up and smiled at Roselie, a wistful glance that offered her support.

Or something more akin to, *I'm ever so sorry.*

As Roselie sank into the only empty chair, her mother immediately began. "My dear, we need you to help us clear up what seems to be a most grievous misunderstanding."

Lady Rimswell snorted. "Misunderstanding, indeed!" She wasn't a woman for sugarcoating or mincing about.

But she was going up against Lady Wakefield—a diplomat's wife and the daughter of a politician—who always managed difficulties with a modicum of tact. "Yes, well—"

However, her son had not inherited that inclination and, impatient as ever, he jumped in. "There are rumors about town that you and . . ." Piers's gaze flicked toward Brody, who had turned around from the window, a bland expression on his face.

But it was the details that told the entire story. Brody hadn't shaved. Looked as if he'd been rousted from his bed. Or hadn't ever been there.

What the devil had gone wrong that had him looking as if the entire world had run amuck? Besides this audience . . .

"Rumors?" Roselie did her best to appear puzzled. "You've taken to listening to rumors? Piers, how unlike you." Smiling innocently, she looked around the room and hoped this bluff, the most important one of her life, was convincing.

Far from it.

"Roselie, this isn't one of your games," Piers informed her, all clear-eyed and angry.

Which was far more dangerous than if he'd been in his old state—angry and drunk, wherein he wouldn't have bothered with any of this.

It was Margaret who finally got to the point. Clearly and succinctly. "You were seen with Lord Rimswell."

"Seen?" Roselie shook her head, and grasped at the dwindling threads of hope, the ones she prayed would help her escape this tangle. "I've been seen with Lord Rimswell any number of times—why we danced together at Almack's just last week, I can hardly see how that—"

Her sister had little patience for subterfuge. "You were seen in Lord Gosforth's private study with Lord Rimswell *in flagrante delicto* by no less than Patience Nafferton." Margaret shook her head. "Does that make it clear enough?"

She couldn't tell if her sister's disdain was over the fact that Roselie had been acting in such a scandalous fashion, or that she'd been foolish enough to do so in front of such a feather-witted gossip like Patience.

Roselie would guess it was a little bit of both.

"Yes, well, I do recollect I was there, but it was hardly as bad as all that. It was my . . . necklace . . . yes, that was it, my necklace had come loose. And Brody was kind enough to try to fix the clasp. And, truly, Patience Nafferton is such a goose. And so horribly nearsighted." She turned to her sister, pleading. "Don't you remember, Margaret, how she once mistook Lady Sandison for the Prince of Wales? Why she can't see past her nose, and whatever she thought she saw—"

"Don't play coy with us, you bold jade!" Apparently it was

Lady Rimswell's turn to erupt. "You've ruined my son's life with your calculated wiles!"

"*Wiles?*" This came from Lady Wakefield, who, for all her manners and gracious nature, was not one to stand idly by while one of her children was being maligned.

It was rather like poking a sleeping lioness with a sharp stick.

But it was Brody who surprised her most.

"Enough!" His sudden eruption caught everyone by surprise. Well, nearly everyone.

"I will have my say. I won't stand for—" his mother continued.

"Not another word or I will remove you from this house myself. Then I will remove you from mine." Brody's words rang through the room, leaving it silent. Uncomfortably so.

His mother's mouth opened and then closed, as if she wasn't too sure what had just happened. But that didn't mean she was about to stop.

"Your brother never would have—"

"He's not here, madame. I am. A fact you would do well to remember more often."

It was a cold, private moment, one that ached with all the division and rancor that existed between the baron and his mother.

Oh, what have I wrought, Roselie thought, guilt tugging at her heart that Brody must have his private pain so publicly aired.

Brody turned to her and Roselie had to admit, she had the same bit of trepidation as Lady Rimswell. "Roselie, you are making a valiant effort, but it is all for naught. Patience hasn't left a single stone unturned. Everyone knows."

"Oh, that horrible little—"

"Roselie, no," he said as he knelt in front of her and took her hands in his. The warmth of his touch took some of the chill out of the air, though his appearance was hardly reassuring.

From the haunted look to his eyes, to his unkempt and disheveled arrival here this morning. Moreover, he looked her up and down, as if reassuring himself of something.

Brody, what have you been doing? What have you discovered? Questions she could hardly ask in such company. Besides, it appeared they had a more pressing problem.

"Roselie, it is done." His words sounded so final.

Despite that, she pressed on. "But she promised!"

He shook his head. "We all make promises we cannot keep."

"Brody, no," she managed. "'Tis impossible—"

He smiled wanly. "Impossible, indeed. But it is what we must do."

She glanced up at the others in the room. Was he suggesting . . .

No.

Roselie suddenly realized this wasn't a drama she'd entered, but a court, one where the jury had reached their verdict well before she'd climbed into the docket.

Except for one holdout who seemed more opposed to the idea than Roselie herself.

"I will not sanction this," Lady Rimswell declared. She rose to her feet, shaking her black silk gown out like a crow might ruffle its feathers on a rainy day. "I had such high hopes for you, Bradwell. That you might make a decent match, an advantageous match. Now this horrid gel has ruined all my aspirations for you!"

"Cease this!" Brody let go of Roselie and got back up to his feet. "Stop before you say something you will regret."

Lady Rimswell was past the point of caring. "But how could you? And with *her*? Why, I'll have to move to the Dower house to hide my undying shame."

"As I said before, enough." He straightened his coat and rose to his full height, towering over her. "I will not hear another word from you on this subject. I kissed Miss Stratton. Quite thoroughly, if you must know."

"No!" his mother wailed, stuffing her handkerchief to her mouth. She turned from her son and sniffled loudly.

"So the story is true," Margaret remarked into the shocked silence. Margaret did love her facts unencumbered.

"Yes," Roselie admitted.

"Well, with that said, there is nothing left to do but plan the wedding breakfast," Lady Wakefield declared, sounding surprisingly pleased. Then again, she'd never been one to cry over spilled milk, or apparently, ruined daughters. "Margaret, Louisa, I could use your help. And Lady Rimswell, if you would like to be of assistance—"

"I will not!" the soon-to-be-dowager spat back. "I will not sanction this farce. Your daughter is nothing more than—"

"—your future daughter-in-law," Lady Wakefield told her sharply. She stepped in front of the baroness and said, in no uncertain terms, "You will hold a civil tongue regarding Roselie, and for that matter, my entire family, or you being tossed from this house by Dinnes will be the least of your social woes."

Lady Rimswell made a loud *harrumph* and stalked out of the room. Of her own volition.

After the front door closed, there was a moment when everyone seemed to take a breath and realize they needed to get on with the problem at hand.

Which was just the way Strattons did things.

"Margaret, Louisa, you are with me," Lady Wakefield said, brushing her hands over her skirt. She glanced at her son. "Piers, go see the rector at St. George's and explain that we have need of the chapel again." He looked to protest but his mother didn't give him the opportunity. "Do I have to have Dinnes escort you out as well?"

Her son laughed, but fell in step behind his mother. He paused in front of Brody, looking him eye to eye. "My congratulations." He smiled, but it was more a feral look.

And then Roselie knew why.

Piers leaned closer. "Break my little sister's heart, let any harm come to her, and I'll put a bullet through your chest." Then he grinned, slapped him on the back. "When you're finished proposing—for knowing Roselie, she'll want bended knee and a sincere expression of fidelity—I'll go with you to see the archbishop about a Special License. I've become a bit of an expert on hasty marriages of late."

He laughed again and left, abandoning Roselie.

At least that was how it felt.

After a few uncomfortable moments of silence, Roselie began her own protest. "I see no reason why we must—"

But apparently Brody had as much tolerance for her complaints as he'd had with his mother's. "There is every reason why we must."

She glanced up at him. "Such a lovely proposal. 'We must.'" Shaking her head, she got to her feet. She'd never been one to sit idly. "I don't care a fig about my reputation . . . Or if I ever marry. I won't do this."

"You are many things, Roselie Stratton, but selfish is not one of them."

That stopped her in her tracks. "Selfish? How ever am I being selfish?"

"You might not care a fig about your reputation but what about your family's? For Piers and Louisa? They've enough strikes against them, without you adding to the fire. And Margaret? Lord Gamston is rising in politics, she's immensely proud of him—will you have their reputations tarnished by your indiscretions?"

She pursed her lips together. *Oh, bother.*

Damn Brody and his sensibilities.

"Not to mention my reputation," he added with a devilish grin.

"Yours?" Now Roselie laughed.

"I do have a reputation," he told her, grinning.

Crossing her arms over her chest, she shook her head. "Yes, as a rather dull, proper and respectable gentleman."

"Can't have everyone finding out that I'm actually quite a bit of a rake."

Roselie barked a laugh. "A wha-a-at?"

He struck a pose. "A rake."

There was nothing to do but laugh. And she did. But then he proved his point, coming close, hauling her to her feet and up against him so she hadn't any room to wiggle free.

That is if she had wanted to.

He was ever so warm, so hard against her. Her body woke

quickly, as if the embers from the other night had been well-banked and merely slumbering.

Especially when he leaned close and whispered in her ear, "You weren't laughing the other night when you asked me, no make that pled with me to take you and—"

Oh, yes, that stopped her laughter and she playfully slapped his arm. "Don't you dare repeat that."

"Yes, well, you did," he replied, and if she wasn't mistaken, he was preening a bit.

Hadn't she wanted him to do just that—toss her skirt up and ravish her—for far too long?

Hadn't she wanted him to explore her, let her explore him until there was nothing but passion and bliss between them?

But this . . . marriage. It was so . . . well, sensible. Impossible, really.

Wasn't it?

He must have seen the conflict in her eyes. "We must, Rosebud. Not just for ourselves, but for them as well," he said, nodding toward the closed door.

We must.

"It doesn't seem fair," she said, flouncing petulantly back down on the sofa. Doing her best to ignore him.

Ignore the odd rattling of her heart.

"It isn't," he agreed as he sat beside her.

"Your mother certainly doesn't want you to marry me."

He leaned back and grinned. "Actually this is quite the boon. She did threaten to move to the Dower house, didn't she?"

"Yes," Roselie said, "but how is that a boon?"

"Good God, I've been trying to get her there since Poldie died. If I'd known that marrying you would do the trick, I would have proposed years ago."

"Oh, thank you," she replied. "That's the most flattering thing you've said yet."

"You aren't an easy woman to flatter."

No, she supposed she wasn't.

They sat there in silence for a few long moments before Brody spoke again. "Roselie, you know you must stop."

She turned to protest but the look on his face, his haunted expression gave her pause.

"No more Asteria," he told her, sounding weary and determined. Before she could even take a breath, he added, "No more jaunting about town, no more gaming hells, no more follies."

She started to laugh, but stopped when she saw that he was hardly joking. "You're serious—"

"Deadly so."

Something was horribly wrong. She'd sensed it before but now she could see it so clearly.

Brody was afraid. And knowing the man as she did, that left her with a chill running down her spine.

"What has happened?" she asked. "What aren't you telling me?"

He turned toward her and reached out, letting one of the loose curls of her hair slide through his fingers. His dark gaze settled on hers. "Why don't you tell me why you think Ilford isn't alone in his crimes?"

Her mouth set stubbornly, refusing to speak.

So Brody did, but first he got to his feet. "So be it. Hear me well, Roselie Stratton, soon-to-be-my-wife, you are done. And that is the end of the matter."

Oh, that was just too much, but even as she opened her mouth to protest, she closed it.

Hadn't Lord Howers said much the same thing all those years ago. Forbidding her to help and yet relenting when he realized her value.

Brody would just have to learn the same lesson. And once she discovered the identity of Ilford's master, then he'd see how wrong he was.

"Then it is settled," he declared, as if her silence was hearty agreement. "Oh, and do let Piers know I'll be around his house at quarter past three to go see the archbishop." He leaned over and placed a chaste kiss on her forehead and left.

Just like that.

Roselie groaned and kicked at the tea table, earning herself a sore toe. And in her pain and frustration, she realized she was still waiting for one thing.

For him to propose.

Which he hadn't. Well, not properly.

But as she sat there, wishing she wasn't so rash, and rubbing her aching toe, two questions continued to prod her.

Why ever had Brody acquiesced to their marriage so easily?

And more importantly, what was he so afraid of?

Chapter 11

*B*rody could forbid her all he wanted, Roselie fumed, but he wasn't her husband yet.

She'd hurried upstairs—avoiding her mother who was issuing instructions to Margaret and Louisa—only to find her loyal companion packing her own belongings.

"Bernie! I never thought of you as a turncoat."

"If your mother doesn't send me packing, do you think that almost husband of yours is going to let me in his house?" She huffed and went back to stuffing her meager things into an old, battered valise.

Roselie reached over and caught her hands. "No! We are together in this and together we will stay."

"I don't see how—"

"I'm not finished yet," Roselie told her. "I'm not. But I can't do it without your help. Besides, Lord Rimswell is quite wealthy. I'll see to it you get a raise—"

Bernie's face brightened. "How much?"

"Enough." Roselie began to unpack the bag, continuing by saying, "I—We must find out who, or what, Abigail was looking for before—"

"Before you are shackled?" Bernie teased, regaining some of her all-too-useful sensibility.

"Exactly," she agreed. "So we had best get cracking, before Brody returns with . . . with . . ." She couldn't say it. *A Special License*. Instead she went to the clothespress and collected her old bonnet, quickly donning it. It was a plain affair, one she preferred when she went on these sort of errands.

"I suppose he'll be in a hellfire hurry to get you into his bed now."

Roselie's fingers froze in the middle of tying the ribbons.

Oh, goodness gracious. She and Brody were to be married, then they would . . .

She blushed just thinking of it.

"Finally realized that, didn't you?" Bernie laughed. "Wondered when you were going to get around to *that*."

"Oh, heavens, I hadn't," she admitted.

Bernie snorted. "First thing I thought of. He's a handsome devil. And it isn't like you haven't—"

Roselie held up her hand. "Stop! I don't want to think about it."

Hadn't she been thinking of it far more than she should have since the first time he'd kissed her?

Dreaming about a thing and facing it coming true—very true— were two different things.

Why it was conceivable that by this very evening she would be in his bed. Roselie panicked, shuddering right down to the soles of her plain boots. "Oh, Bernie. I can't!"

It was one thing to be in Brody's arms when she was masked, when she was Asteria, but she was going to have to face him, in his bedchamber, wearing . . .

Well, nothing. Not even her mask.

"Yes, you can and you will," Bernie told her. "So I suppose we must hurry if we are to finish all this."

Roselie nodded in agreement and collected her reticule. She opened her door and was about to step out into the hall—well, more like flee from the house—when she realized her way was blocked.

"Maman!" Roselie quickly put a smile on her face. "Mrs. Pratt and I were just going out. Um, to do some shopping. For the wedding." Her words tumbled out and sounded more rushed than convincing.

"Excellent!" her mother declared. "I'd just come up to collect you for the very same thing. We have so much to do."

"Perhaps we could divide and conquer, as they say," Roselie suggested, trying to sound more helpful than she was actually feeling. "We could cover so much more if we . . ."

She faltered to a stop because her mother had *that* look on her face. The one Margaret, Piers and Roselie had learned at an early age not to argue with . . . under any circumstances.

"Yes, well, I suppose we can all go together," Roselie agreed, trying to sound delighted when she felt anything but.

"Oh, what an excellent idea," Lady Wakefield declared, twining her arm around her daughter's elbow and drawing her toward the front stairs.

She turned and looked longingly toward her favorite route of escape: the servant's stairs, even as her mother continued on, coming up with a shopping list that would most likely take not only today, but most of a week.

". . . how unfortunate there isn't time for a new dress—I had promised Madame Conde that she could make your wedding gown—especially after she did such an excellent job with Margaret's—but time being of the essence, we will have to improvise. Then again, I always say a new hat can do the trick quite nicely. It draws the eyes upwards and no one will notice you're wearing an older gown especially when . . ."

Roselie nearly groaned, for she doubted there was any hat that would help her escape this mess.

As it turned out, Lady Wakefield had no objections to a hasty wedding, but not one done in an *unseemly* hurry.

"A proper bride and a proper wedding breakfast," she'd declared. So it was to be, and two days later Roselie found herself in the antechamber of St. George's waiting to be joined in holy and respectable matrimony.

Not that her mother had given her a moment's peace.

"Ah, how lovely you look," Mrs. Rowland said, poking her head into the small room reserved for the altar servers and apparently unwilling brides. "Madame St. Vincent outdid herself."

"Yes, quite," Roselie said glancing down at the gown that Tuck's mother had hastily procured from Asteria's favorite modiste. The pale yellow silk seemed the perfect choice—modest enough for a London miss and just a hint of Asteria.

For a moment, she wondered if Brody would notice the color, thinking of the jonquil gown.

"Yes, yes," Uncle Hero declared, pushing past his niece, and coming to stand before Roselie, his admiring glance leaving her blushing. "You do look perfect, by jingle! Marry you myself if you had a better dowry."

Roselie laughed, for it was the perfectly outrageous sort of thing Uncle Hero might say.

"Go get us a decent pew, Jenny," he bid his niece. "I've a word for our dear girl."

Mrs. Rowland shook her head, her gaze rolling upward, but she left nonetheless.

"Third wedding in as many weeks," he mused, settling down at the small table in the corner. "This is becoming overly familiar." He pulled a worn deck of cards from the pocket inside his jacket. His emergency cards, he liked to call them. He nodded for her to take the seat opposite his.

She did, of course. She had no argument with Uncle Hero. "Were you sent to make sure I didn't bolt for the docks?"

"No," he laughed. Then he paused his shuffling and looked up at her. "Are you planning to bolt for the docks?"

"Of course not," she lied. Then she remembered who she was talking to. "Perhaps. If the opportunity arose."

He dealt the cards. "Might I point out that if you are planning an escape, the docks will be the first place they'd look."

Roselie sighed as she looked over her hand. "I rather thought they'd check the mail coaches first."

He shook his head. "You are too fetching for the mail coaches. Someone would recall you."

That shiver of panic ran through her yet again. The one that had been plaguing her for the last two days. "Then help me, Uncle Hero," she pleaded as she set her cards facedown on the table. "Help me out of this."

He shook his head. "Can't do that."

"Can't?"

He looked up and studied her. "Won't." He sighed and leaned over and caught her hand. "And why would I? Your Lord Rimswell seems an excellent young man. Title. Fortune. Not a bad wager, not in the least." He squeezed her fingers and went back to looking over his hand.

Roselie did the same. "Now you sound like Bernie."

Uncle Hero smiled and leaned back in his chair. "Ah, Berenthia Pratt. You should heed her advice. Such a remarkable, practical woman."

"I don't want to get married." Considering that she was seated in the church, with the ceremony about to begin, it seemed a moot point, but she was just mulish enough to continue to hold out.

That was also a Stratton trait.

Not that the Honorable agreed. "Why ever not? You like the man. I would daresay you're terribly fond of him." He glanced up from his cards, his brows at a jaunty tip. "Make the best of this, my dear girl. You've been playing a dangerous game. Wouldn't be able to live with myself if you ended up like—"

A haunted look crossed his face, and he immediately went back to studying his hand.

Abigail. He didn't need to say her name. Roselie's heart clenched. "I never meant—"

"Yes, I know," he hurried to tell her. "Lest you forget, we all entered into this venture with our eyes wide open, even poor Mrs. Croft. All of us, with the only exception being you, my dear."

"I've always understood—"

He laid down a card and looked her directly in the eyes. "No, I don't think you have. Not until now." He paused then nodded for her to play. "Listen well, the winds are changing out there. You need a safe harbor right now, and this man is your best hope."

"Safe harbor," she repeated. "Listen to you."

But the Honorable wouldn't relent. "I haven't lived this long by not knowing when it is time to fold my hand and run." He reached again for her hand, forcing her to look up at him. "Listen to me, you must stop. At least for the time being. It is too dangerous."

"I cannot . . . I must—" She pulled her hand free.

"No, you mustn't," he insisted. "Not now."

"You and Brody. He's quite insistent I stop."

"Smart man. Do as he tells you." He retrieved the deck and played the next round, clucking a bit at the cards he'd dealt himself and rearranging them back and forth.

Roselie was not fooled. He always clucked like this before he laid down a perfect hand.

"Why?" she asked.

"Why what?" he feigned.

"Why is the danger so different now?"

He pursed his lips and considered his words. "You've managed to step into a hornet's nest," he said, dodging around the question. "And the only choice is to retreat. Hide. At least until the storm passes."

"So I'm close to discovering the truth—"

"The truth?" Uncle Hero huffed a great sigh. "How I deplore the truth. It might seem like a new shilling, all bright and shiny, but the path to collect it is always full of hazards."

Such as Abigail's life. Patch's well-being. Of course he was correct, but . . .

They went back to their game and played on, until he spoke up again.

"Does he play cards?" When confronted, Uncle Hero could always be counted on to change the subject.

Roselie looked up. "Who?"

"Your Lord Rimswell. Does he play?"

"No."

"Shame." Uncle Hero looked over at the card she'd laid down, and added his own. "Perhaps I could teach him."

"No." She played another card. "He'd most likely ban you from his house if he realized—"

"Ban me?" Uncle Hero ruffled a bit. "Why, I'm family."

She smiled at this. Uncle Hero was no more related to her than he was to her cousin, Tuck, whom the Honorable claimed as his dearest nephew. But to her, he was a beloved part of her circle.

"Well, nearly family," he conceded. "But I've always said the family we choose is so much better suited to our own temperament than the ones we are provided by chance."

"You won't get any arguments from me, but the Garricks are a little more particular about these things." Roselie laid down her hand. "Bloodlines and all."

The door opened and Piers poked his head in. The sight of his little sister playing cards with the Honorable was hardly the sight he expected. "Roselie! Have some decorum. You're in church."

"Not by choice," she pointed out as she smirked at Uncle Hero, having beaten him quite handily.

The man sat back in his chair and rubbed his chin, unable to fathom quite how that had happened—especially since he had not only dealt, but used his emergency cards.

"Then you shouldn't choose to let a man ravish you," Piers muttered as he came in, closing the door behind him, lest someone else noticed and added this bit of scandal to the long list she was gathering about her.

Roselie stood and shook out her gown, the pale yellow silk shimmering in the bit of sunlight coming in from the high window above. "Is it time?"

"Yes," Piers said. "Brody just got here. Looks like hell. Like he hasn't been to bed in a month."

"Yes, well, I know how he feels."

And before she knew it, Roselie found herself led down the

aisle and standing beside Brody, and the vicar was saying the words that would bind them together.

For better or worse.

She glanced over at him and found his jaw set in a determined line. And now that she could see him close up, Piers had been correct, he did look terrible. Dark shadows under his eyes, hastily shaved and his hair barely combed.

One thing was for certain, whatever had been driving him the other day had only gotten worse.

You've stepped into a hornet's nest.

So had he, it appeared. And suddenly she saw Brody, as lost as Abigail, and that image left her unable to breathe.

He was in as much danger as she was.

And while Uncle Hero might be right (*might* was probably not the correct word, more like *spot-on*) about the danger getting too close, there was no way Roselie was going to lose anyone else.

Especially not Brody.

Becoming Brody's wife because of her recklessness was one thing, but ending up as his widow because of her mistakes would be unforgivable.

Lady Muscoates got into her carriage and settled down into the comfortable seat. It wasn't until they'd turned the corner that she acknowledged the man sitting across from her.

"So he married her?" he asked.

"He did indeed," she replied, glancing down at her gloves. She tugged at them a bit and then examined them again. "I can't say that I'm surprised."

"What, that he married her?"

"No, not that," she said. "Rimswell is far too honorable not to marry her. Rather, I'm not surprised Miss Stratton is *her.*" She tipped her head slightly and looked out the window.

"As in Asteria?" The man laughed. "You think that spoilt chit is her?"

"I do indeed," Lady Muscoates replied.

"And how have you come to that clever assumption?"

She turned back toward him. "She was wearing a gown from Madame St. Vincent's shop."

"So?"

"Proper young ladies don't frequent Madame St. Vincent's," Mrs. Muscoates pointed out.

"So she ain't that proper," he replied. "You might recall why that wedding was such a hasty affair."

"No, no, you misunderstand. It is also the same shop where Asteria buys her gowns," her ladyship said, looking out the window and then back at the man who was far too dangerous to be contained, but made a most ruthless and efficient lover.

Rough enough to please her, and rough enough to know what needed to be done.

He rapped on the roof of the carriage. "Madame St. Vincent's," he told the driver.

Chapter 12

*H*is wedding night.

Brody glanced in his dressing room mirror as he tugged off his cravat.

And while this wasn't his first choice—to be married in haste and under a cloud of scandal—a reluctant part of him was almost willing to admit that marriage to Roselie, to Asteria, had him on edge . . .

And not with trepidation.

But with a relentless desire to have her.

He'd imagined this woman in his bed too many times to count, and now she would be in his bed always.

He glanced into the mirror again, and scratched at the rough stubble on his chin.

If she didn't murder him in his sleep.

Oh, God, what was he going to do? For knowing Roselie as he did, she'd find trouble without even looking. It was just her nature.

Something he'd always loved about her.

That realization gave him pause. All these years, he'd loved her. Roselie Stratton. Not Asteria. Roselie.

And even after he'd met Asteria, thought himself in love

with her, how many times had he stolen glances at Roselie and wondered.

Ridiculous notions. Like what she'd look like in a yellow gown. And now he knew.

As he also knew she was a passionate handful. This reckoning, this moment, had been simmering between them for years now. This desire, this passion.

God, he wanted her.

Moving beneath him, making that mew of pleasure that ignited his desires.

He wanted to see her face as he entered her for the first time, brought her to her completion and then he wanted to find his.

And then he wanted to do it again. And again. Until daylight pierced the night.

He glanced at the door that led to his bedchamber and found himself caught.

Because he wanted her in his bed.

But if he did that, if he gave into his desire, his passion for her, how ever would he do what needed to be done.

Send her far from London. Far from harm. Far from his bed.

They'll find her you know.

No, no they won't, he silently vowed yet again. *Never.*

Roselie stood in Brody's bedchamber and looked around. She didn't know what she'd expected, but this opulent den was not what she'd thought she'd find.

The large mahogany bed featured a grand canopy with gold velvet curtains and ornately carved posts.

The rest of the room was done in the same fashion—rich coverings on the chairs, gilded cornices over the doorway and richly framed mirrors.

She reached up and flicked one of the tassels that hung from the end of the canopy and shook her head.

"Yes, rather overstated, don't you agree?"

She whirled around and found Brody standing in the corner. How had she not noticed the doorway hidden there?

But there he was. In his breeches and shirt. And his boots.

His boots?

That said something. He wasn't staying.

He wasn't staying?

"My mother had this room decorated for Poldie. She thought it befit his station."

"Perhaps if he'd been a duke. One with very bad taste," she replied, moving slowly around the bed, suddenly feeling wary. Trapped. Unsure.

None of which she liked.

"We need to talk."

That she liked even less. Talk? What the devil for? Nor did his dark countenance reassure her. Quite frankly, the gleam in his eyes frightened her.

Desire. Fear. Anger.

Whatever was he mad about? She wasn't the one who wanted to talk.

Roselie moved closer, and went to reach out and cup his jaw with her hand.

To feel him. His heat. The rough stubble of his chin.

To let him know, in no uncertain terms, she wanted him. She wanted this. After all, they had no choice now, but to make the best of things.

But her hand only managed to brush against him for he very quickly sidestepped her, her hand fluttering for a moment in the air and then dropping awkwardly.

What was wrong?

To her chagrin, he told her. "I have something to say which I don't think you'll like." He walked over and studied the soft flicker of the coals in the grate. "So I'll just say it: I'm sending you away."

She couldn't have heard him correctly. "Away?"

"For your own good. For your safety."

Of all the things she'd imagined the two of them discussing this evening, this was not one of them.

Roselie straightened. "I can take care of myself."

He flinched sort of, and then his shoulders drew into a taut line, as if he were preparing for battle.

And he was.

She moved toward him again, quickly, and caught hold of him, her fingers twining with his, her other hand catching hold of his shirt and tugging him close. "I won't go."

He shook his head. "Yes, you will."

Oh, yes, he was determined. Bother Brody and his stubborn hide.

"We can do this together."

"No, we will not." He shook her off and stepped away.

The cool of the room hit her, much as his words, his accusation, had earlier.

She hadn't realized until then how much heat had encircled them. How much desire. For certainly that *want* had her trembling, shivering.

She didn't know what was worse: how much she wanted him or that he knew it.

"Roselie, if you stay, you'll do something foolish and end up like Mrs. Croft—"

He couldn't have said anything worse.

Yet instead of instilling a sensible note of fear in her, he made her mad. For his warning tolled in her ears like the warning bell she'd heard all her life.

No, Roselie, girls can't . . .

Desire and fury, she realized, were far closer than she'd ever suspected.

Brody prosed on, having not an inkling of the rebellion he was stoking. "You'll leave in the morning."

She certainly hadn't heard *that* right. Why didn't he just lock her in the cell next to Ilford's?

"You will go to Barwick House."

"Barwick?" Roselie shook her head. She'd never heard of it. Garrick Hall was the family seat.

"It is in Yorkshire."

"Yorkshire?" How much further could he send her before she fell off the edge of England? Why not just send her to Ireland and be done with the matter.

Of course she didn't say *that* out loud because he might just consider it as a better alternative.

"I won't go." The flames inside her again burst free.

"You will."

She reached for him again, and he sidestepped her. Determinedly.

"Brody, I'm your wife. You can't send me away," But the moment she said those words, she regretted them.

Saw the folly in them.

"I can send you away because you are my wife. Before, I couldn't have protected you, but now I can. I will."

She didn't know whether to be outraged or let that possessive statement creep into her heart.

It wasn't just a matter of masculine prerogative, but something more. Another word, that left the air in her chest whooshing out.

No. She wasn't ready to face *that*.

Worse, if Brody loved her, then she would have to admit her own feelings. She might even be willing to do as he asked.

For if she let him seduce her, edge her over that precipice, take her all the way, make her his wife in name and deed, she'd be under his spell for the rest of her life.

And right now that just wasn't possible.

Roselie awoke alone in Brody's bed. There was no sign of her husband.

Her husband. *Before, I couldn't have protected you, but now I will.*

Husband, indeed! Her jailer was more like it.

Protect her . . . She'd see about that. Throwing off the counterpane, she got up, determined to continue this discussion.

Did Brody think she would be so easily deported?

Just then there was a scratch at the door, and a maid peeked her head in. "Your ladyship," she murmured as she bobbed a quick curtsy. "I was sent up to help you pack."

"I'm not packing."

The girl flinched slightly. "Yes, but his lordship said—"

"Can you help me get dressed?"

This question brightened the girl's mood considerably. "Yes, my lady, but—"

"No buts, just help me get dressed," Roselie told her. She was a baroness now. And the mistress of this house.

That, she decided would serve her purposes nicely.

The girl proved to be a dab hand, getting Roselie's unruly mop of hair into a neat semblance of order and quickly discovering the perfect day gown in one of the trunks that had been sent over the day before.

"Unpack those, please," she told the maid, nodding at the collection of trunks and valises stacked in the corner.

"Yes, my lady, but his lordship said—"

"Unpack them," Roselie told her, imitating her own mother's firm tones.

The girl nodded and scurried off to do as she was bid, while Roselie made her way downstairs, where the front door was open and out at the curb sat not one, but two elegant traveling barouches.

Two? That seemed rather ostentatious.

They could be sent back as far as she was concerned. Turning on one heel, she marched toward the back of the house determined to find where the dining room was situated.

By the time she did find it, she had her arguments at the ready. "Brody, if you think you can pack me away like some delicate bit of—"

She stopped right there. For there was only one other occupant in the dining room, and not the one she'd been expecting. For here was the other Lady Rimswell gaping at her, and apparently no happier to have her breakfast interrupted by her unwanted daughter-in-law than Roselie was to find herself facing the woman.

"I thought—" Roselie glanced around the empty room hoping that she had just missed where Brody was sitting. "That is, I was expecting to find—" She looked around and felt rather foolish, for the room wasn't that large, so unless the dowager had murdered him and stuffed him under the table, it was obvious the master of the house was not here.

"My son is out. I would have thought his wife would know *that.*"

"I forgot," Roselie lied, glancing over at the sideboard, and deciding she might as well fortify herself for battle. The one with Brody and the one brewing at the opposite end of the table.

She filled a plate and sat down at the other end of the table. It was most likely Brody's spot, but she feigned innocence and began to eat.

What did the Honorable like to say? *A pot boiled over best when ignored.* It didn't take long for the dowager to do just that, boil over.

"I blame you," she sputtered, flinging her napkin down on the table like a gauntlet.

"Blame me?" Roselie looked up from her meal and blinked.

"For all of this," the woman huffed. "For thirty-five years I've been mistress of this house and now I'm to be sent off like some—"

Sent off? "What do you mean? I'm the one being trundled off like some dottering—" Roselie was about to say *dottering dowager"* but stopped herself just in time.

Or rather the dowager stopped her, when she interrupted with an outraged, "*You*? He's sending me off with *you*? Oh, of all the insults, of all the degradations—"

"Just a moment," Roselie said, rising from her seat, "Does this mean he thinks to send us both away?"

"Apparently," her ladyship said, getting to her feet as well.

Ignoring the obvious horror of being shuttled off with the dowager, Roselie knew that without a doubt something was very wrong if he thought to send both of them away.

"You may choose to do what you will, but I'm not going," Roselie told her.

Lady Rimswell, a harridan if ever there was one, but also one who had never brooked her husband, gaped. It quite possibly had never occurred to her that she didn't have to do what was demanded of her.

And the look of astonishment on her face, and that spark of rebellion in her eyes, gave Roselie a flicker of hope. But it didn't last long. For it was hardly female solidarity that had the dowager raising a flag and calling for the charge.

Rather, it was the notion of abandoning her house—for certainly the lady would think of it as her house until the day she died—that was behind her turnabout. Apparently, leaving the care and management of it to Roselie was enough to send a shaft of iron through her spine.

"Then I'm not going either." There was something about the set of the dowager's shoulders that gave Roselie pause—for certainly she was going to be a challenge for some time to come, but for today, she had other problems.

"Good," Roselie told her, "I plan on giving dear Rimswell a wide berth for a few hours before I inform him. I'd advise you to do the same, madame."

"Yes, that might be wise," the dowager agreed, looking nonetoo-pleased to have to agree with anything her daughter-in-law said, but willing to concede for the moment. "I had planned on going shopping. And what, may I ask, do you have in mind?"

"Going someplace my husband would never set foot," she replied.

This gave the dowager pause and she tipped her head to one side, eyeing Roselie with suspicion. "And where might that be?"

"It is Thursday, isn't it?" Roselie asked.

"Yes." Lady Rimswell only needed a moment to realize what

Roselie was suggesting and when she did, she shuddered. "Oh, how dreadful! You can't possibly think to . . ."

"I do," Roselie told her as she sailed past the lady, not waiting to hear the woman's further opinions of her choice. Nor could she help adding, "Besides, your son once told me it was impossible to imagine himself ever setting foot in such a place—which makes it the perfect place to hide."

Brody returned from his solicitor's, where he'd gone to make the necessary changes to his estate now that he was married. The man had wished him hearty congratulations and felicitations on this blessed event, but Brody hardly felt blessed.

Not with the threat of Ilford hanging over them.

Perhaps, once he had both Roselie and his mother safely out of London, he would breathe a bit easier.

But he soon discovered that relief would have to wait a bit longer.

"My lord," Peakman greeted him as he entered a quiet house with hardly a flutter of activity.

Excellent. Most excellent. He tipped his head and listened a little more intently, for he could hardly believe that Roselie had gone without incident.

"My mother and my"—he paused for a second before he finished his sentence—"my wife," he finally managed, "got under way without—"

Without murdering each other. Which was exactly why he'd ordered separate coaches.

Peakman flinched. Actually flinched.

He'd never seen the man look so uncomfortable. And he'd worked for Brody's mother for all these years, so that was saying much.

"Peakman, what is it?" A frisson of alarm ran down his spine.

"It's just that—"

"Out with it man, what has happened?"

"Oh, nothing to worry yourself about, my lord, it is just that her ladyship, and well, her ladyship," the man said, faltering over how best to address the two mistresses in the house. "They didn't depart."

Roselie. Brody ground his teeth together. She'd brooked his order. Of course she had. Whatever had he expected?

"Where are they?"

"Gone, my lord."

Brody paused. "I thought you said they didn't leave."

"They didn't, that is to say, they haven't left London. As it is, they haven't left Mayfair."

"Where are they, Peakman?"

And then his butler told him, that his mother was shopping on Bond Street, and then the man told him where the new Lady Rimswell had taken herself off to.

And Brody realized he was about to face his worst nightmare.

Chapter 13

The most impossible feats can be accomplished if one exhibits perfect posture.

Miss Emery

ℒady Gosforth's afternoon in was all a twitter with the news of Miss Roselie Stratton and Lord Rimswell's hasty marriage.

"The dowager is most displeased with the match," Lady Oxnam advised the gathering of gossips and matrons.

"Wouldn't you be aghast to have that shameless creature as your daughter-in-law?" Lady Blaxhall shuddered.

This earned her a sharp glance from their hostess, the indomitable Marchioness of Gosforth. "I think it an excellent match for both," she declared. "There are any number of us who were married with a Special License and we have proved all the naysayers wrong."

This quieted the assembled gossips—at least for a moment—for to continue on would be to insult their hostess, who had made her own indelicate dash to Gretna Green all those years ago—but then again, such an *on dit* could hardly be quelled, even by her ladyship.

Lady Essex nodded in agreement. "I noticed his fondness for her the other night at Almack's. Why, I said straightaway that evening, that a wedding wouldn't be long to follow, didn't I, Lady Muscoates?"

The baroness smiled. "You did indeed, and his passion for Miss Stratton, and she for him was on display for one and all—"

There were a few gasps in the audience, for *passion* was not a word the matrons liked, especially not linked to a young lady. But then again, Lady Muscoates was French by birth and she had to be excused for her occasional lapses into such licentious notions.

"—but that is what it is to be so young and full of desires," she finished, for even after forty some years in England, the woman still hadn't grasped the notion of "proper reserve."

Lady Nafferton shot a disapproving glance toward her daughters, as if to say, *Do not listen to a word that dreadful baroness is saying.*

"I thought Miss Stratton looked very lovely. Radiant even," Mariah Manx offered, surprising everyone in the room, for Lady Essex's hired companion rarely, if ever, spoke up.

"I agree," the newly minted Viscountess Wakefield—and former Louisa Tempest—chimed in. "I am firmly convinced my dear sister-in-law has made a perfect match."

Her childhood friend, Harriet Hathaway, now the Countess of Roxley, agreed. "From what I've heard it is a definite love match, which will serve them both well." She glanced over toward the corner of the room where her own husband was standing and smiled, a soft warm light in her eyes.

"A love match!" Lady Nafferton scoffed. "That gel trapped poor Rimswell with her—" Her words abruptly ended as every head turned to the newest arrival standing in the doorway.

None other than the very subject of their gossip.

"Lady Gosforth," the new Lady Rimswell said, making an elegant curtsy to her favorite hostess. "I fear I'm late."

"I honestly didn't expect—" the marchioness began, lifting her quizzing glass to get a better look.

Roselie, well aware that all eyes were on her, smiled and moved into the room, settling down on the sofa next to Piers's wife.

"Louisa, you are a dear. How nice of you to help Lady Gosforth with the tea in my place. You must have thought I'd forgotten."

"But of course, we hardly expected you to be out—" Even Louisa seemed at a loss for words.

As was everyone else, save one.

"Yes, indeed. Out so soon!" Lady Nafferton made a significant glance about the room. "One doesn't know what to think."

"I merely got married," Roselie replied fearlessly. After all, this was Lady Gosforth's afternoon in and no place for a shrinking violet. But oh, heavens, it seemed every single gossipy matron in London had come by today.

And she could well imagine what the conversation had been before she arrived. Doing her best to still her hammering heart, she calmly poured a cup of tea and passed it over to a gaping Lady Rushbury.

"Yes, my dear, but a wedding night can prove to be quite taxing for those of a delicate nature." Lady Rushbury looked from the saucer and cup in her hands, back up at the lady who'd offered them. "How is it that you aren't resting today?"

A few of the ladies tittered at this. The married ones, that is.

"It isn't as if I've come down with dropsy or the plague," Roselie replied, filling Lady Essex's cup and earning herself a wink from the old girl—who definitely loved being part of a *scene*. "Anyone else?"

Lady Muscoates's ward, Miss Taber, held out her cup and smiled. But it wasn't the sort of friendly expression one might expect from an unmarried miss, but something almost feral.

Something that took Roselie aback. The teapot rattled in her hands and she straightened quickly.

"Is something amiss, Lady Rimswell?" Lady Muscoates asked, looking from her ward and then to Roselie.

"No, nothing," Roselie assured the lady, pouring a cup for herself and straightening her posture.

Though it hardly was. There was a reason why the dowager

Lady Rimswell had shuddered. This was rather like volunteering to be cast to the lions.

"Yes, well, out so soon." The thwarted Lady Nafferton sniffed, glancing over at her unwed daughters. "How highly irregular you are, Miss Stratton—oh, I mean Lady Rimswell. Trouble at home, perhaps? Married in haste and all—"

"So many hasty marriages of late." Lady Blaxhall shook her head disapprovingly, glancing over at Louisa and Harriet who had both married quickly, the countess already showing signs of being with child. "Shall we be bracing next Season for the arrival of another horde of you Kipple spinsters—"

"Kempton," Harriet corrected, quite proud of her little village and its reputation. "Kempton spinsters."

"Yes, yes, Kempton," she said, waving her hand at the matter. "But are there more of you?"

"No, I can't think of anyone else," Louisa said, glancing at Harriet.

Harriet tapped her fan to her chin as she considered the matter. "A few, I warrant, though I imagine most of my un-married brothers should be in Town. Perhaps even all five."

"Five?" Lady Nafferton gasped as if she had just discovered a cache of gold under her seat cushion. She glanced again at her daughters, this time with renewed hope. "You mean there are more than just Captain Hathaway and Mr. Hathaway?"

There was a sort of happy sigh around the room and the conversation began anew as to the various Hathaways and their prospects, until Lady Blaxhall, perhaps bored that the talk was not focused on her new hat—a fetching creation of ostrich feathers and lavender ribbons—changed the subject abruptly.

"Have you heard the news of poor Ilford?"

That stopped nearly every wagging tongue.

"I would hardly call the man 'poor,'" Lady Essex sniffed.

"How else would you describe the situation?" Lady Blaxhall held out one hand and examined the embroidery on her new gloves before she glanced up again, "I hardly believe the accusations against him and now . . ." Her lip trembled a bit, a move that might have worked better on a male audience than a room full of seasoned matrons, but nonetheless, she continued with her Haymarket dramatics. "Why, despite all the pleas, his father has remained silent as to any assistance."

Everyone had something to say on that note.

"And why shouldn't he?"

"I've always thought the marquess a terrible menace."

"Hardly surprising," their hostess noted.

"No perhaps not," Lady Blaxhall agreed. "But it has destroyed Ilford—to be cut off from everything. I fear he'll go mad."

"That would hardly be surprising," Lady Oxnam said, with a wry shake of her head.

"Yes, just like his mother. Poor soul," Lady Rushbury said with a solemn sigh.

Others nodded in agreement.

Roselie sat still as the talk swirled around, keeping her gaze fixed on the teapot if only to hide the interest and shock she knew were lighting her eyes.

Mad.

Why ever did that word continue to haunt her? Drawing her closer. Calling to her. As if it held the keys to all this.

Still she bit her lower lip and wished she could . . . say something. Yet it would hardly be proper for her to—

Suddenly she sat up, brightened actually. She wasn't Miss Roselie Stratton any longer. And as Lady Rimswell her choice of subjects wasn't regulated to the weather or gown colors, or the proper amount of lace on a hem.

As a married woman, no subject was taboo.

Not a one.

"His mother?" she asked, testing this new world with an air of feigned innocence.

And no one batted an eye. Just like that, one night as a married woman and she was one of the matrons. And off they went, leaving Roselie to wonder why she hadn't gotten married years ago.

The chatter was like a flurry of falling leaves.

"Oh, yes, the poor duchess."

"Such a frail, dear creature."

"Her death was such a shock—"

"—and all hushed up. As if no one would notice."

"Never understood why His Grace married her, but ah, love?"

Lady Nafferton sighed. "Her Grace was—" She faltered to a stop and looked around for help. After all, she hadn't forgotten that there were innocent ears in the room.

"Troubled," Lady Gosforth said in her usual decisive manner.

"How ever did she die?" This came from Pansy Nafferton, who had never mastered the boundaries of polite conversation. It also earned her a sharp glance from her mother.

"Truly, the woman is gone. I've never understood the fashion for speaking ill of the dead," Lady Nafferton announced, as if such a reminder would stop the conversation.

"What can one say," Lady Comber said to no one in particular, "when the entire business was all so questionable." Her gaze flitted in the direction of Lady Muscoates and stayed there for a measured moment.

"One knows exactly what to think," Lady Essex huffed. "Dear heavens, let us be plain about this. The duchess was mad as a hatter and her death a blessing for His Grace."

"Poor, poor dear," Lady Rushbury whispered.

"But you knew her best, didn't you, Lady Muscoates?" Lady Blaxhall sat back a bit as her question brought an uneasy stillness to the room.

Roselie's gaze swiveled up. Any bit of caution left her in that moment.

That revelation.

"I did." If the woman thought that was going to be enough of an answer, she was very wrong. A roomful of expectant gazes pinned her in place and Lady Muscoates had no choice but to continue. "Her Grace was most kind to me when I first came to England." Then she shrugged, in that French way that suggested she'd said enough.

But this was England, more specifically, Mayfair, and such a thin answer would never work for this audience.

Not even if they knew the story, for there might be some new detail to be unearthed, and pecked over endlessly.

And Roselie couldn't help but sense that she'd happened upon the very thing she'd been seeking all this time.

Ilford's mother had gone mad?

Then she went right back to that list from Abigail's papers. Pope, Hoxton, Beaufort, St. Anne's. All madhouses. What had Abigail found . . . or thought to find?

Or rather, whom?

A chill ran down her spine, and when she looked up, Lady Muscoates was staring at her. No, studying her with an icy air.

Brazening a polite smile, she quickly reached for the warmth of the teapot, absently filling Louisa's cup, to give herself something to do while her thoughts ran wild.

Lady Muscoates and Ilford's mother had been friends?

Roselie was just about to ask another question when once again Lady Blaxhall blocked any hope of discovery with her vain and unwitting interference. "Such a sad subject. Shall we find something else, something more appropriate for innocent ears? How ever did such an unsuitable conversation begin?" She preened a bit and cast a disapproving smirk at Roselie.

Beside Roselie, Harriet leaned over. "Whatever did you do to earn her ire?"

"My brother. He was to marry her," Roselie noted, ever so thankful that the vain woman had cast her brother aside when he'd come home from Spain wounded. "I'm so glad he didn't."

"As am I," Louisa added.

The three of them laughed quietly, as the conversation—now changed to a debate as to the proper subjects for young ladies—continued.

Harriet paused and glanced around, a thoughtful expression on her face. "You are one of us now," she said, again quietly enough that no one else could hear.

When Roselie glanced at her, the Countess of Roxley smiled. "Our husbands. They share a mutual pursuit and a friend. Lord Howers?"

"Yes, indeed," Roselie said. So Harriet knew of her husband's work for the Home Office.

They shared another glance and in that moment, a bond formed.

Harriet sat up a bit and held out her cup for Roselie. "I've found that sometimes it is up to us to fill in the missing details." Then she smiled at the company around them.

Roselie could hardly believe it. Harriet was here for the same reasons? To distill from the day's gossip information that might be of use to her husband.

Then the lady said, "If I may be of assistance—"

"No," she said, sharper than she meant to, but a sudden vision of Abigail had come rising up like a specter and she certainly wasn't going to let another—especially a lady with child—risk her life.

Not even for England.

"If you say so," Harriet said, still smiling and selecting a biscuit from the tea tray. "It was just that you looked rather surprised, and eager to discover more about the duchess."

Roselie pressed her lips together. Bother! She been too obvious.

Nor was Harriet done. "Still, if you need an extra set of ears, or a hand—"

"No, I think I am well on my way," Roselie assured her.

"Seems so—" Harriet nodded toward the door.

Roselie looked up and there in the doorway—make that filling the doorway—towered Brody.

All resplendent in his perfectly cut jacket, a grand waterfall cravat that would make any valet envious, and a polish to his boots that made the entire room a little brighter.

He stopped every conversation, save one.

"Impossible," Roselie uttered, unable to look away. And here she would have wagered her unwanted virginity that he'd never set foot in Lady Gosforth's.

Oh, bother Brody. One look at the set of his jaw and she just knew he intended to ruin everything.

And then he did his level best to do just that.

Brody schooled his features not to reveal the murderous rage he felt inside.

Of course seeing Roselie here safe and sound helped, but demmit, she shouldn't be here. He'd dispatched Peakman and several footmen to go fetch his mother home.

Oh, there would be a terrible row when they were all assembled back at home, but he was determined that his wife and mother should both be well and away from London.

But since they weren't—and he had no doubts who had instigated this rebellion in his household—he enlisted all the skills he'd accumulated over the years and grinned with delight at his traitorous wife. "There you are, my dear."

He bowed to their hostess and then entered, crossing the room and brushing a kiss atop Roselie's forehead. He shouldn't have done that. For the moment his lips touched her silky skin, need raced through him, filled with frustrated regrets from the previous night.

For a moment they shared a glance, and he could see she was furious with him. Deadly so. Those dark eyes of hers boiling with fire, like the very gates of hell. But she'd been furious with him before and then that fury had turned to—

Visions of the night in Howers's office, in the alcove at St. John's . . .

No, no, he couldn't go there. He needed to stay calm and reserved if he was to keep her safe.

Instead, he took her hand and brought it to his lips, smiling at her as a reminder that she had a role to play as well. "I was bereft when I came home and found you gone," he said more for the benefit of their audience. Then he winked at Lady Gosforth and the old girl laughed wickedly.

"Of course you were, Lord Rimswell. We all chastened your bride for running away the day after her wedding," the marchioness declared.

"She is turning out to be a headstrong wife," he laughed. There were nods of agreement around the room as he went to stand next to his old friend, the Earl of Roxley.

At least he didn't have to face this horror alone. And, he'd survived the worst of it.

Or so he thought.

"Dangerous shoals," Roxley said in a quiet aside.

"First time," Brody replied. "Does it show?"

"Only around the edges," Roxley replied with his usual droll humor.

The conversation resumed, and Brody watched, as if observing some odd foreign ritual for the first time.

Of course he knew the rules of Society, but this was an entirely different world—a strange dance of accusations, insults and recriminations, all said with smiles and the flutter of fans.

And that was just Lady Nafferton's opening salvo.

"How do they do this?" he whispered to the earl.

"With grace and elegance," Roxley told him, casting a smile at his countess, who sat beside Roselie. "And a healthy measure of fortitude that we men do not possess."

"Whatever have they been discussing?" Or rather, dissecting.

"Why you, of course."

Brody blanched a bit. *Of course.*

"Never fear, the subject diverted quite perfectly into a discussion regarding Lord Ilford and his mother."

"His mother? Whatever for?"

"You might want to ask your wife. She found the subject most captivating."

Brody ground his teeth together. Of course she had. Nor would it seem that she'd ended her forays.

"She won't, you know," Roxley told him, shifting his stance slightly, crossing his arms over his chest.

"Won't what?"

"Stop."

Brody turned sharply to look at him. How much did Roxley know?

Probably everything, given this was Roxley.

"I do hope she doesn't draw Harry in," the earl said, nodding toward his wife, the former Miss Harriet Hathaway.

"She won't. I'll see to it," Brody promised.

Roxley began to laugh, but managed a more choking, coughing sound, that brought a few glances in their direction. He pulled out his handkerchief and politely coughed into it. Once it was over and no one was bothering with them, he said, "I doubt either of us could do that."

"Stop them?"

"Heavens, yes. A more defiant pair you'll never meet, and now that they've joined forces, we'll have our hands full."

How frustratingly true.

As the conversation ebbed and flowed, Brody found that Roxley's spot, here in the corner afforded them the perfect vantage point to follow the varied subjects.

And the ability to watch Roselie. The curve of her neck, that nape so fair, so very kissable.

He shook off that dangerous line of thought and got back to business, which was watching his wife. And if he didn't know better, he'd say the little minx was eavesdropping on Lady Essex and Lady Muscoates, but he couldn't imagine what those two could have to say that was so riveting.

Then again, the look on Roselie's face, the furrow in her brow suggested she was none-too-pleased with what she was hearing.

Then something drew his attention. The miss next to Lady Muscoates. Her ward. For he'd only met the pretty chit once. But to his shock, Miss Taber flashed a glance at him from over the top of her fan that was unmistakable.

An offer, of sorts.

Brody wrenched his gaze away from the flirtatious minx.

Bloody hell! For there was Roselie, sharp-eyed as ever, having seen the lady's invitation and looked ready to answer it.

With a pistol.

Thankfully, the ladies began to rise, as if some unheard bell had tolled, ending their gossipy dance.

Several of them spoke to their hostess, while others continued to chat with their companions as they gathered their things and began to make their way to the door.

Brody stepped forward and quickly caught his wife by the elbow, for she had the look of a cat about to slip out an open door, that or look for an opportunity to slip that wretched knife of hers into Miss Taber's back.

Roselie might be dressed like the perfect Mayfair lady this morning, but Brody had no doubt that Asteria was never too far away.

"Roselie, dear, I wouldn't think of having you return home unescorted," he announced.

"How kind of you," she replied, sounding neither grateful or thankful to have such a thoughtful husband.

"I asked Peakman to send over the carriage so you could ride home in comfort."

"It isn't going to whisk me off to Yorkshire, is it?" she whispered, even as she smiled at several of the matrons passing them.

"Don't tempt me," he shot back, making a great show of carefully escorting his wife out to the curb, where indeed, the carriage sat waiting.

"I am not going to leave. Not until—"

"You are most decidedly done here," he told her. "Nor will you escape me easily."

"If I wanted to escape, I would already be gone," Roselie told him as she climbed into the carriage.

He looked his wife straight in the eyes. "And I would find you."

* * *

There was no mistaking the vow in Brody's words.

I would find you. Roselie clenched her teeth together. Oh, damn him, he would.

"Whatever do you think you are doing?" she began, taking a different tack. "I have shopping to do. You cannot trail after me while I choose my new wardrobe."

Brody glanced over at her. "A new wardrobe?" Suspicion marked each word.

"I'm a married woman now. I can hardly go about Society looking like a miss fresh out of school."

"You stopped looking like that some time ago," he shot back.

"Very funny," Roselie replied. "Perhaps, you would prefer Miss Taber?" Oh, it was a waspish, wretched thing to say, but she'd seen the look that gel had been casting Brody and something inside her had snapped. "She's young enough."

It wasn't jealousy. It just wasn't.

"Honestly, how long has it been since you've seen the inside of a schoolroom? I suspect Pansy Nafferton or even that Miss Taber could give a better account of what one looks like."

Not to be outdone, she replied hotly, "Then you should have kissed one of them."

Then he spoke, just as warm, but in a different sort of heat—all smoky and full of passion. "I didn't want either of them."

Damn him! Why did he have to say such things? The sort of statements that left her insides aquiver. Left her breasts all tight, that spot between her legs aching to have him touch her.

Leave her thinking that he wanted her . . .

After a bit, he spoke up again, doing his best to sound all innocent, as if he didn't know he'd just interrupted whatever she'd been planning. "So where do we begin this shopping of yours?"

Roselie wanted to groan. She had planned on going to collect Bernie and heading for the first house on Abigail's list while she still had a chance. Especially now that she had the most tantalizing kernel that needed to be examined.

The Duchess of Ranworth. She'd taken her own life. And yet, somehow she was the key to all this. That, and the other bit Lady Essex had said to Lady Muscoates.

Oh, yes, *that* needed to be examined. Thoroughly.

But she could hardly tell Brody what she'd unearthed. He'd have her locked up if he suspected she was going to wade deeper into this mystery.

So there was nothing left to do but call her own bluff.

"Where else but Bond Street, my lord?"

Brody stood at the doorway of the parlor surveying the very domestic scene before him. His mother, seated in her favorite chair, doing needlework, while Roselie sat quietly reading the latest issue of *The Lady's Magazine*.

The entire tableaux left him a bit queasy.

And entirely suspicious.

"I want both of you to stay home tonight." By the time they'd returned from shopping, it had been too late to send them off. He'd have to do everything in his power to see the pair packed off at first light.

But right now . . . Well, right now, he'd been summoned to meet with Lord Howers.

"No dallying about. Do you hear me?"

"Indeed," his mother replied, poking her needle into the fabric and looking up. "Why would I want to go out? There is nothing of interest happening tonight. Other than Lady Oxnam's card party." She sniffed at such a low gathering.

"I fear it is to be a rather dull evening," Roselie agreed. "And where are you going, my lord?" She smiled sweetly at him and again, Brody thought he should not only keep an eye on her, but also take a glance behind him to make sure she hadn't hired one of her nefarious friends to take him by surprise.

"I have some business at White's I need to conclude."

"Yes, well, I suppose you must," his mother said, waving her hand at him. "Your brother kept his business dealings to daylight hours, but you have your own way of doing things." She sniffed again.

Roselie's brow furrowed for a moment, as if she was going to give his mother a set-down, but instead she shook her head slightly and sent him a look that said much.

Be careful.

Brody stood there for a few more seconds, not entirely certain he should trust the pair. Trust his own heart.

Especially after this morning. But his mother was being honest about one thing: there wasn't much to do this evening. The only invitation in the salver was to the aforementioned card party at Lady Oxnam's.

A gathering that promised to be about as much fun as an evening spent reading a treatise on proper field drainage.

He glanced at the front door. Certainly he didn't trust them, but he must go out. He could only hope his suspicions were wrong and that the pair of them would do as they were told and stay put.

Unfortunately, he wasn't. And they didn't.

Wrong, that is. Or stay put, as promised.

Chapter 14

The front door had hardly closed when Lady Rimswell threw off the large, cozy shawl she was wearing.

The one that concealed the evening gown she had on.

She immediately rang for Peakman. "Bring my carriage around now," she told the butler.

"But his lordship said—"

"Bring it around now, Peakman," the dowager ordered, standing her ground.

The man set his jaw, but nodded and did as he was bid.

Then she turned to Roselie. "I suppose you are going to object as well."

"Far from it," she told her as she set aside her magazine and got up. "As it is, I plan on retiring early. The past few days have taken a toll on me. Besides, Lady Rushbury was most specific in her advice for the newly married: rest as often as one can." That wasn't precisely what the viscountess had said, but Roselie wasn't going to worry about those details, not when Lady Rimswell's eyes widened at the implication, and her nose pinched a bit.

"Indeed!" was all the lady could manage as she turned on one heel and left in a huff, obviously having no wish to discover any more particulars regarding Roselie's need for respite.

Once the front door closed, Roselie hurried up the stairs, happy to find that Bernie had finally arrived, and in her very Bernie-ish fashion, had brought everything she needed.

For there on the bed lay another of her favorite Asteria gowns, the red silk.

She hadn't dared send any of her extravagant costumes over in her trunks, if only for fear one of the maids would find them. So instead, Bernie had brought them over in one of her trunks.

"Since," as Bernie pointed out, "the maids around here will hardly be in a rush to unpack my poor belongings."

Nor had they.

"The duchess committed suicide," Roselie said over her shoulder as she stepped in front of the mirror and adjusted her gown, tugging down the bodice so her breasts nearly came right out.

"According to who?" Bernie asked as she did up the hooks in the back of the gown.

" 'Tis what Lady Essex and Lady Muscoates were discussing. If I want to know more about the Duchess of Ranworth, then I need to find—"

"*Him.*" Bernie frowned. "Couldn't you find some yappy sort here in Mayfair? Heaven knows these fools spend most of their time nattering on about this and that."

"That's just it," Roselie said, pulling on a pair of plain slippers. No high heels tonight. Not where she was going. "I need someone with wits—who hears all the tidings, high and low." Besides, there was another point she'd overheard—one she needed someone low indeed to help her ferret out the truth.

Bernie was already shaking her head. "But why him?"

"He's the perfect choice." Roselie set her hands on her hips. "And don't look like that. I've asked the Honorable to go with me—though he's late."

Bernie muttered a rather salty curse under her breath. She didn't swear often, but when she did . . . "I won't have you leaving until that old fraud arrives. Not to go down *there.*"

Roselie shook her head, and continued to gird herself for the evening ahead. Her reticule. Her gloves. Her pistol. Yes, all in order. She looked up at Bernie. "I cannot wait all night for the man. What if Brody comes home?" She shook her head. It was now or never. "Besides, I'll have Solly with me."

Yet the recrimination floated there between them as if Bernie had offered it up instead of holding it in check.

That Roselie was no more safe with Solly than Abigail had been with Patch.

Roselie ignored her and hastened to add, "When Uncle Hero gets here, send him after me. He knows where to go."

"And what am I to say to Himself if he comes home before you?"

Oh, yes, there was Brody to consider.

"You'll think of something," Roselie told her. "Tell him I went to discuss some estate matters with Piers."

Bernie heaved a sigh. "At this time of night?"

Yes, well it wasn't the most believable excuse. "It might keep him occupied until I can return."

"I can think of better ways for you to keep that man occupied," Bernie told her as they made their way down the back stairs.

Brody got as far as the front steps of White's and had one of those moments of frightening clarity.

He shouldn't be here.

It wasn't the bright lights from inside or the sounds of raucous male laughter, but the slim figure down the street who slipped into an alleyway to avoid detection when Brody turned his head slightly.

The man had been following him the entire way. And if he was being followed, then he had to assume . . .

Brody stilled, filled with only one thought.

Get home.

He spun around and walked crisply and quickly down the block, before he ducked into an alley. The man followed with some skill, but Brody wasn't entirely a novice. He slipped through the back door of a local public house. When he exited out a side door—one reserved for particular patrons—and then hurried into the night, he knew he'd managed to elude the fellow.

From there, he hastened home. Not that he was relieved by what he found there—which was nothing. Both his mother and wife were gone.

In his mother's place sat Mrs. Pratt.

Never mind that his mother would be furious that a hired companion was seated in her favorite chair, but the woman was actually smoking one of Brody's cigars and reading a novel.

In French, no less.

He had truly underestimated Roselie's companion.

"Where are they?" he demanded from the doorway.

Instead of acting the guilty party, Mrs. Pratt reluctantly stubbed out the cigar and set aside the book. "Who?"

"My wife." And after a moment. "And my mother."

Mrs. Pratt heaved a sigh and glanced longingly at her cigar before she looked back up at the master of the house. "Your mother has gone to that wretched card party. According to Peakman, she said something to the effect that even that dull company was better than sitting around here with a common—"

"Yes, yes, I can imagine what she said," he replied.

Mrs. Pratt smiled, a sort of enigmatic turn of the lips. "Yes, but still, Lady Oxnam's? Dull business, that. Ha'penny stakes and all. A supper that should have been fed to the cat a week ago. She'll regret it."

Brody was going to regret not firing the lot of Roselie's compatriots the moment he married her. And he said as much.

"Pack your bags. You are let go, Mrs. Pratt."

The woman shook her head and settled deeper into the chair. Even had the cheek to pick up the cigar. "No I'm not. I'm family. You can't cast out family."

"Family?" He had no idea if that was true or not. He knew Roselie had some far-flung shirttale relations, but Mrs. Pratt?

The woman was bluffing.

"I can and I will. Now, where is Roselie?" He rather hoped she'd gone with his mother. Serve her right, for Mrs. Pratt hadn't lied about one thing: the supper at Lady Oxnam's would be off.

"Roselie?" Mrs. Pratt asked, rubbing her chin as if she had never heard the name. And if he wasn't mistaken, playing for time.

He tapped his boot to the parquet floor.

"How would I know?" Mrs. Pratt told him. "I don't work here."

Brody ground his teeth together. "And if you did?"

"Then I might know," she told him, bartering like a fishwife. Which he suspected she came from a long line of.

So he got down to business. "Mrs. Pratt, I just spent the last twenty minutes eluding some fellow who was most determined to follow me. So I suggest you stop playing coy and tell me where my wife has gone."

This prodded the woman along. Only slightly. "Yes, yes, she's off playing cards as well."

For just a fraction of a moment, Brody breathed a little easier, for no harm could come to either of them at Lady Oxnam's, but then he realized Mrs. Pratt had only said that Roselie was off playing cards.

And secondly, the likelihood of his mother going to a party in Roselie's company was about as likely as Napoleon showing up Lady Oxnam's.

"*Where* has my wife gone to play cards?"

"That's the problem, my lord. I don't rightly know." Mrs. Pratt glanced around the room. Notably, anywhere but in his direction.

Brody straightened, his temper starting to boil. "And who would?"

"Now that would be me," came a voice from behind him.

And there, in the open doorway stood the Honorable Hero Worth.

What the devil was Tuck's rapscallion uncle doing here?

The man bowed and gave a great flourish of his hand in greeting. "*Tut tut*, my lord, didn't expect to see you here—"

Brody stood his ground, brows at high points and his arms crossed over his chest. "In my own house?"

The Honorable looked around. "Well, yes, I suppose this is. And a fine one it is, indeed."

"And if you didn't expect to find me here, sir, to what do I owe the pleasure of your unexpected company?"

For probably the first time in his disreputable life, the Honorable appeared to be out of words.

His lips flapped a bit and he looked helplessly over at Mrs. Pratt for a bit of direction. "I've come to . . . That is to say . . ." After a few more floundering attempts he suddenly found the right words. "Come to bestow my most sincere felicitations on the happy couple." He smiled as he rocked on his heels, hands folded behind his back.

"Most people send a note," Brody told him.

"Rather impersonal," the Honorable replied, unruffled now that he'd found his footing and he even had the cheek to come in.

As if he had been invited. Which he probably had been.

"Well, rather than your felicitations," Brody began, "I would prefer your company. And a bit of information."

"Indeed?" His brows rose slightly and again he looked over Brody's shoulder toward Mrs. Pratt.

Brody glanced at Mrs. Pratt as well, and the woman—he had to give her credit—held her own, with a stony expression and not a waver to her features. But Brody would bet his mother's favorite Bow porcelain figurine—the very one the Honorable was currently examining—that this pair knew exactly what was going on and that they were going to help him.

The Honorable looked up just then and found Brody watching him. The shepherdess went back to her resting place on the mantel and he said, all nonchalant and mannerly, "What do you have in mind, my lord?"

"A bit of gambling, I think," Brody proposed. "Could I coax you into joining me?"

Behind him, Mrs. Pratt groaned.

And with good reason.

"Gambling you say? I don't often . . . But, well, ‚ I might. What harm is there in a friendly game amc men?"

"Yes, exactly my thinking," Brody said, throwing a ⟍ ionable arm around the man's shoulder. "But I had in something a little less mannerly. Starting with whatever hel. intended to take my wife to."

"My star! My rose! Always a delight to see you," Captain Reddick enthused, pushing himself up from the table where he'd been playing cards. His ruffled lace shirt was open, his coat hanging on the back of his chair and he had a bit of a shadow on his chin. Obviously, he'd been playing for some time.

Roselie smiled at him, deigning him with a gracious nod of her head, but at the same time gauging the crowded room for likely problems.

This particular gaming hell had no name. It wasn't the usual sort of place that the fast set in the *ton* liked to sport about—far too dangerous for their blood.

This was the place where the kingpins, the robber barons, the bosses came to gamble. The true underbelly of the London docks filled the place, and they preferred that it had no name, no gawkers.

So the captain might spend most nights playing in Mayfair, in more reputable establishments frequented by the wealthy and the titled, but when he needed to lay low, the docks welcomed him into its dark corners with a mother's love.

And like Uncle Hero, he was no more a captain than Hero Worth was an Honorable. A pair of self-invented rogues who had risen out of the dregs of London, but had never forgotten the lessons of their youth.

Nor did the thieves and reprobates turn their back on their own. Especially when it might be profitable.

And via Captain Reddick, Asteria had found her way into these shadowy dens—with Patch or Solly at her back. Since no one was o certain where she'd come from, or why she hid her identity, she was given a cautious welcome and ample berth.

The captain parted the crowd as he came to take her hand and bring it to his lips. Then his gaze flicked over her shoulder. "And Silent Solly, my good fellow, wise beyond your years. When you speak, I can only hope I am close enough to hear your words, for what a tale you'll have to tell."

Solly crossed his arms over his chest and flicked his gaze down to where the captain still had Roselie's hand in his grasp.

The captain glanced down as well, his eyes widening a bit. "A ring? What is this?"

Roselie pulled her hand free. Bother. She'd forgotten to remove Brody's ring.

Forgotten or had no desire to do so? She hadn't time to consider which.

"You've wed?" he pressed.

"I've always been a bit of a romantic," she told him.

"And here I had such hopes—" The man's eyes flickered with suggestion, but with a huff from Solly, any thoughts of indiscretion were quickly doused.

"Yes, well, I suppose you've come on business, which I can accommodate as well, that is unless . . ."

"It is business, I assure you," she told the devilish rogue.

He shrugged and led them both to the back of the room, catching up his coat as he went. "To what do I owe this pleasure?" he asked as he shrugged it back on.

"I have need of information." Roselie glanced around. "Regarding a woman."

"And you thought of me. I'm flattered."

"You might not be. I want to know more about the Duchess of Ranworth and Lady Muscoates."

The man stilled, as if he hadn't heard her correctly, but then he moved quickly, glancing around to see if anyone else had heard her question. Flipping a coin to the man at the bar, one which the fellow caught with a deft movement, Reddick took her by the elbow and led her to a heavy door—which an enormous fellow opened for them—and then led her down a set of stairs toward the rooms where cards and deals were done in private.

Solly followed right on their heels.

It wasn't like she hadn't been to this part of the place before, but something about Reddick's haste told her this was hardly their usual business. And at the bottom of the stairs, a pale and hurried Reddick opened the first door they came to and nodded to Solly to stand watch.

Solly looked to Roselie for confirmation, and she tipped her head in agreement.

A chill that had nothing to do with this dank basement ran down her spine. She'd never seen Reddick look like this. Frightened. No, make that terrified.

And that in itself set her on edge, coursing with the thrill of the hunt. She was finally on the right course. But her momentary triumph came to a quick halt as the captain pushed her into the room and closed the door behind them.

A single candle burned on the table. He huffed a breath and turned on her. "What the devil are you thinking? Mentioning *her* name like that? Do you want to get us both murdered before daylight?"

Brody listened to the Honorable's instructions with half an ear as the carriage moved deeper and deeper into the docklands.

Certainly he'd been to his fair share of the less-than-reputable corners of London, but this . . . "Where the devil are we going?"

"As I said, it has no name." The Honorable looked around and shook his head. "This is why I insisted we take on a more austere appearance. Never ends well if one turns up looking like an overstuffed Christmas goose, plump and ripe for the trimming."

Brody looked out the window again, at the tumbledown buildings, the shadowy residents lurking about the corners, the stench from the gutters and the nearby Thames rising with a pungent bite.

"You mean to tell me my wife is here?"

"Yes," came the direct answer. The carriage stopped and Brody went to rush out and the Honorable caught him by the elbow. "Caution, my good man. This is not your world. And I would remind you that they do not play by your rules, by your notions of nobility and honor down here."

"Then what are the rules?"

"Don't get yourself killed." The Honorable climbed out of the carriage and walked confidently toward the door.

Brody wished he felt the same ease, but then again for some reason he remembered Poldie, and something his brother had written him from Spain.

If ever the odds seemed stacked against you, my dear brother, wade in as if you have a pocket full of gold and nothing to lose.

"Impossible," he muttered. For he had everything to lose.

"What was that?" the Honorable asked as he rapped on the door and was granted entrance.

"Nothing."

"Good. Better not to speak. Allow me to handle matters from here on out."

The close-packed room took him aback. They were greeted with silence and then a murmur of speculation. And here he'd thought he'd seen everything just because he'd been to St. John's Folly.

The Honorable forged ahead, greeting a fellow, a one-eyed man by the moniker of Poxy, who stood behind the bar, picking his teeth with a long knife, when he wasn't wiping mugs with a filthy rag.

The weasely slip of a man merely nodded at the Honorable's greeting, his gaze lingering on Brody as if he were taking a tally, an inventory of sorts.

He most likely was.

"Ah, Poxy, you grand fellow! How is the missus?"

"Ran off with the Ratter."

"No, you don't say?" The Honorable shook his head. "Poor fellow. Did you warn him?"

Poxy laughed. "Why would I? Well rid of her now."

"I suppose you are," the Honorable laughed and glanced around the room. "Have you seen the Captain tonight?"

"Didn't quite make that out," the man said, holding out his hand.

Hero looked over his shoulder at Brody. "Do you mind?"

Brody dug out a coin and flipped it to the man.

The fellow's hand flicked into the air and snatched the coin before it barely had a chance to turn.

With his prize caught and secured, he ignored Brody and looked at Hero. "Aye."

Then the man had the audacity to return to his vague attempts at cleaning a cracked mug.

"That's it? Aye?" Brody began to elbow his way forward. "Where the devil is—"

Hero shoved his way between Brody and the bar. "Caution, my friend," he said quietly over his shoulder, tapping his forehead with a finger. "Remember? Rules." He huffed a bit and then straightened his jacket. "And the next time, don't give him any more than ha'penny to begin with."

Hero shook his head and turned back to Poxy. "The Captain is expecting us."

"Doubt it," the man replied, then leered a bit as he leaned forward. "Got a ripe, pretty one who came in afore you. Cap'n not the sort to let a bird pass 'im by, if you know what I mean. Especially when she came looking for 'im." Then he winked and went back to his cleaning.

Not for long.

Brody elbowed the Honorable out of the way, forgot every notion of caution and good sense he'd learned over the years.

That *bird* was his wife.

He caught the whip-thin fellow by the neck and half pulled him across the bar. "Where is this captain? Tell me now or I'll wring your neck and get my money back."

The rattle of conversations behind them came to a sudden stop and the room fell silent. A pause that was quickly ended by the scrape of chairs as nearly everyone in the place got to their feet.

Ready for whatever came next.

"Oh, now, this is hardly productive—" the Honorable advised.

Not that Brody was listening. He shook the fellow like his gamekeeper did a rabbit pulled live from a snare. "Tell. Me. Now."

He punctuated his request with the knife he'd pulled, tucking it under the man's chin until it nicked a drop of blood.

The fellow went a bit bug-eyed with fear, but it was the enormous fellow at a nearby door, who finally broke the silence.

"Hey, there. Now that's enough." His thick, heavy voice bounced off the walls. It held the sort of warning that every man in that room understood.

Not that Brody was listening. "Is it?" he said, challenging even this giant of a fellow. He'd ransack the place if he must to find Roselie.

"Aye, it is." This time the fellow sort of smiled a bit. As if he held a measure of respect for anyone willing to challenge his authority.

That, or he was simply plotting how he was going to rip Brody from limb to limb.

"The captain and his bird are down here," he said, opening the door behind him.

Brody released Poxy, who immediately scrambled out of his way, all the while rubbing his neck and cursing.

The tension in the room ebbed and then flowed back into the corners as play resumed, and the hum of cards and wagers continued.

"Sorry about that," Brody told the doorkeeper.

The man frowned, but none the same, opened the door, his disapproving gaze fixed on the Honorable. "Can't have him killing my bartender. Sets a bad precedent."

"My apologies, Smiley," the Honorable said with a slight bow. "He's new to these parts."

"You don't say? Stinks of Mayfair."

"Ah, but it is a pleasant and profitable stench," the Honorable replied as he handed the man a coin. As they went down the stairs, he leaned toward Brody and added, "I'll need to be repaid for that."

But Brody was barely listening, he marched down the dark staircase, the poor boards groaning with each thud of his boots. Even as the darkness engulfed him, Brody had only one thing in mind.

Find Roselie.

He barreled toward the only bit of visible light and came to a stop when he found Solly guarding a door.

"Where the hell is she?" He didn't wait for a reply—not that one from Solly would be forthcoming—just shoved the door open.

Chapter 15

*R*oselie had listened to all Captain Reddick had to say about Lady Muscoates and knew she'd come to the right place.

"My lady," he said, "what sort of trouble have you been stirring of late?"

She glanced away. "I got married, that's all."

"I hardly think that's the cause of all this," the captain replied.

This brought her gaze back up. "All of what?"

"The word is that anyone who knows you—well, knows Asteria—is being visited."

That hardly sounded good. She suspected "being visited" didn't mean tea and cakes. "Who?"

"Madame St. Vincent," he said, lowering his voice. "I'm afraid she had a rather ruthless time of it just a day ago. I hear she packed what she could carry and disappeared."

"No," Roselie said, the word rushing out. "Poor lady. I'm ever so—"

"Don't be," he told her. "She'll manage. I daresay, we all will."

But they all hadn't. And Roselie couldn't help but think of Abigail.

Clearly, so was Reddick. He paused for a moment and crossed himself and after a bit, straightened, returning to his cool gambler's façade. "Yes, well, it is clearly time to move along. Lady

Josephine Tremont taught me that. You should meet her. She could teach you a thing or two about knowing when to make a well-timed exit. Which is exactly why I've spent the last fourteen hours trying to gain a stake."

Roselie reached out and caught hold of his arm. "That bad?"

"Unfortunately."

Now they were all in danger. Some more than others.

Roselie shivered. Hadn't she felt much the same ill-ease for days now? So apparently had Brody. No wonder he was in such a hellfire rush to have her and his mother out of London.

But before she could make any further inquiries, the stillness of the room was invaded by the heavy trod of boots pounding down the stairs, and then the door flying open.

She and the captain pulled apart—they'd been standing close so that no one—not even someone trying to listen in from one of the adjoining rooms—could hear them—so the sight that greeted this new arrival looked more damning than it actually was.

"Get away from my wife."

That guttural order ran like a chill through Roselie. Oh, the devil take her, here was Brody, crossing the room like lightning and crashing into the captain and carrying the man to the far wall, hauling him up until his boots dangled in the air.

The captain was no small man, tall and lithe, but he had nothing on Brody's muscular build, and now he helplessly flailed in the air.

"Put him down, Brody. What the devil!" Roselie tugged uselessly at his elbow as her irate husband continued to strangle her informant. Her long-time friend.

"Good God, I need him alive," she continued, wedging herself between Brody and Reddick. Catching hold of Brody's chin, she turned his head so their gazes met.

She couldn't quite believe what she saw there. Jealousy. Raging, burning fury.

Roselie almost laughed. Brody was jealous? Oh, of all the times. But then she remembered she was quite furious with him. "He's on our side, you daft fool."

For a long moment he continued to glare at her, a feral light in his eyes that signaled he was well beyond reason. But slowly, he finally released Reddick and turned his ire on her. "What the hell are you doing here?"

His gaze flicked toward Reddick for a moment, adding the damning implication of *with him*?

She ignored his masculine posturing. "You idiot. Did you mean to wake up everyone down here with your blundering about or just intend to get us all killed?"

That is, if what the captain had warned her of didn't happen first.

"Yes, yes, listen to her, my lord," Uncle Hero advised, having made his late entrance to the party. "Caution, my good man. Caution."

Behind them, Reddick was straightening his clothes and fixing his cravat. "The husband, I gather?" He'd stepped out of reach and moved so he had an open path to the door.

Roselie should have known. Of course, Reddick would have experience with angry, wild-eyed spouses. "This is Lord Rimswell," she told him, not really answering his question.

Reddick took another look and nodded. "Oh, yes, I recognize you now. Captain Reddick, at your service, sir." He bowed, but only slightly, keeping his gaze fixed on Brody. "You, my lord, are out of your element."

"Perhaps," Brody acknowledged. "But you have something of mine and I don't share well." He glanced at Roselie, a look that was full of some sort of medieval possession.

And as much as she had always deplored the notion of being any man's chattel, that look in Brody's eyes sent a rather dangerous thrill down her spine.

He wanted her.

Roselie took a deep breath to counter the way her heart came hammering to life.

Brody *wanted* her. That she was his, and woe be it to any man who thought differently.

Oh, she hardly needed to be thinking like *that* right now. Of Brody possessing her. Taking her. Carrying her off.

As he bloody well ought to have the previous night.

Certainly, as much as Brody's anger was utterly thrilling, it was also a double-edged sword, a cutlass through her plans.

"What the devil do you think you are doing here?" he asked. No, make that demanded.

Demanded. Of her. Oh, it was time they had this out.

"What am I doing here?" Roselie shot back. "None. Of. Your. Business."

"*Cherie*, do as he says," Reddick said stepping closer to her, and nudging her slightly with an infuriating air of familiarity.

"Stay out of this!" Brody and Roselie snapped in unison.

Hands up, Reddick backed away, but rather than chastened, the rogue grinned, utterly bemused by the scene before him.

Bother the man, he rather liked his role in all this.

Brody put himself between her and the others and leaned close. "I need to know what you are doing here."

She huffed a sigh. "Trying to uncover the real evidence against Ilford."

His jaw set. Mulishly. "How many times do I have to tell you, Ilford is done for. You need to stop. You must."

"Must?" she repeated, hands fisting to her hips.

"I forbid it," he told her, coming closer—and ignoring the low whistle of warning from Reddick. He towered over her, but Roselie was hardly cowed.

Rather, she wondered how one arranged a murder. And every man in the room, with the possible exception of Brody, knew it.

"My lord," the Honorable began in his usual conciliatory tones, "I wouldn't—"

Upstairs, there was a faint rustle of chairs scraping against the floor and an odd stillness settled over the denizens above them. It gave them all pause, save for one.

"I will not have you—" Brody continued.

"Not now," Roselie shot back, as upstairs the quiet had turned into a commotion of boots hitting the floor with sharp *thuds*, the thick boards groaning back in protest.

Something was wrong. Very wrong. Roselie glanced over at Reddick, who had gone still as a cat, while Uncle Hero had done something more alarming.

Paled to the color of her mother's best sheets.

So it was as bad as she suspected—and as if to punctuate that thought, there was a hard, *thud, thud, thud*.

Someone banging on the stairwell door.

They all glanced in that direction.

"What the devil is going on?" Brody asked, looking more at the other occupants of the room—as all of them, Solly included, had begun to move.

"I'll tell you what's going on—" Roselie snapped.

"We need to leave," Reddick interjected as another crash shook the rafters. "*Now.*"

"Bloody hell," Brody muttered, catching hold of Roselie and hauling her after Reddick. "I still have questions."

"Ah, my lord, now is not the time," Uncle Hero advised as he hurried along behind them. "For what use are answers if we are all dead?"

"Excellent point," Reddick agreed.

The commotion upstairs grew louder. Chairs being broken. Shouts and curses turning into a cacophony.

"Is this a common occurrence?" Brody asked as they turned a corner and went down another rickety flight of stairs.

"Depends. This has all the markings of your wife stirring the pot, as it were," Reddick told him as he paused at the bottom, catching up the candle in the sconce and holding it aloft like a beacon, then racing to the right as another crash echoed through the dark halls above them.

"Dear God, my dear girl," Uncle Hero said in a long exhale. "You've really annoyed someone this time."

"I daresay I have," she admitted, glancing sideways at Brody, who still held her arm.

As they made their escape, Solly brought up the rear, blowing out the few candles that lit the passageways, leaving their pursuers in the dark.

"What is this place?" Brody asked.

"A smuggler's warren," she told him.

"A wha-a-t?"

"You heard her," Reddick replied as they came to a stop in front of a large door. "Not all the business in London is done by the respectable, milord."

There was a bit of insolence to that last part. Reddick handed his candle to Roselie and tried to pull the door open. "Some of us weren't born to wealth and privilege. We've had to find our way by our wits." He tried to yank it again, but it remained fast.

"Together?" Brody suggested.

Reddick nodded, and they both got hold of the latch and pulled, the hinges complained, but the door finally opened, revealing a narrow, dank tunnel before them.

"A wise man always has an additional way to make a hasty departure," Uncle Hero said in approval, and not wasting any time, led them into the darkness.

Then again, the Honorable never saw anything ignoble about a respectable and hasty retreat.

The shouts and curses behind them grew louder, and they shoved the heavy door back into place, Reddick sliding a thick beam into the iron slots to hold it shut behind them.

"That ought to keep them at bay for a bit," the captain said, reaching for the candle. "But that doesn't mean we shouldn't hurry."

"How ever did they discover—" Roselie stopped for she already knew the answer.

As I said, we're all being watched . . .

And so it seemed did Brody.

"There was a man following me earlier," he told Reddick. "I would guess they've been watching my house. But why—" Even as he asked that last bit, they all knew.

And they all looked at her.

The air in her chest left in a giant *whoosh*. "I've been discovered." Her realization came out in a quiet rush. "We're done for. We all are. I'm so very sorry—"

"Oh, hardly as bad as all that, my dear," Uncle Hero told her. "Well, sink me, I do love my country. And we're hardly finished yet. Always fancied I'd look quite dashing with a medal. For King and Country. For now we've just got a bit of a problem—"

Behind them there was a loud crash.

"Mayhap more than a bit," he conceded.

Roselie's heart clenched. She'd truly gone and entangled Brody in all this. She'd never meant to bring him this far into her dangerous game.

I would find you.

And he had. One look at the determined set of his jaw said something else. *He wouldn't let her go.*

They had to get out of here. If it was the last thing she ever did.

Behind them the shouts grew closer.

"You certainly have a way about you," Brody told her. They'd come again to another door.

"She does, doesn't she?" the captain said with a laugh.

Both men grinned, apparently having found common ground.

"I'm right here," she reminded them.

Brody squeezed her hand. "Yes. Yes, you are."

Reddick muttered something under his breath as he reached for the bar that held the door fast.

Roselie suspected it was a prayer.

Brody reached out and stopped the captain. "Where are we?"

"Hopefully where we should be," Reddick told him, slowly pressing down on the latch.

"Tell me you're the only one who knows about this little byway of yours," Brody asked.

The captain shook his head. "I wish I was."

* * *

The cool night air that greeted them was a welcome relief from the oppressive tomb-like confines of the tunnel. Even if that breeze was filled with the dank ambience of the Thames, Brody didn't care.

Anything was better than being inside that trap.

Captain Reddick stepped out first, and Brody followed with Roselie still in tow. Uncle Hero and Solly brought up the rear. Following the captain's example, Brody had retrieved his pistol from his jacket. He wasn't alone, for he found Solly holding a cudgel with easy familiarity, while Uncle Hero also sported a pistol.

Much to his dismay, here was Roselie pulling a small pistol out of a pocket hidden inside her pelisse.

"What the devil?" Brody sputtered when he spotted it in her grasp. "Do you even know how to shoot that thing?"

Then she showed him as a man came lurching out of the shadows, knife in hand. Brody saw only the hulking figure rising out of the darkness, the meager flash of the knife's blade aimed straight for him, when a shot erupted, cleaving the restless din of the docks in half.

The man reeled back, clutching his shoulder, his knife clattering useless to the cobbles.

Reddick moved fast, past the man on the ground, kicking the fellow's knife well out of reach, barely breaking his pace or sparing a glance. "He'll live," he said in answer to Roselie's paled expression.

She nodded, and her features shifted, taking on a resolute air and he was struck yet again by her mother's words.

Too much like her father.

Brody had heard all kinds of tales about the former Viscount Wakefield—his daring deeds, reports filled with facts, and some that seemed more fiction than truth.

But looking at the man's daughter, Brody wondered if there was more truth to those reports than he'd dared imagine.

Though now was not the time to find out.

"My carriage and horses are waiting on the main road," he told Reddick, and the man nodded, turning in that direction.

But the sharp retort of Roselie's pistol had awakened their surroundings, the devils coming crawling out of their various nooks and crannies, using the darkness for cover.

Wary and ready to take what they might.

Reddick looked over his shoulder at Roselie. "Should have sent you back the moment you uttered that name."

"What name?" Brody asked.

Notably neither replied. However, there was no time to press the matter for they'd come to the main road, where Brody's carriage should've been sitting.

Should have been.

"Well, this is unfortunate," the Honorable remarked.

And as if to underscore that sentiment, another villain came reeling out of the darkness toward Reddick. This time Brody fired, sending the man pitching face-first to the cobbles.

"We need to make a run for it," Reddick urged.

Brody nodded in agreement. "Together we stand out," he said, recalling a chilling flight from Paris detailed in one of Wakefield's old field reports.

"So we split up," Roselie said, most likely having read the very same report. As it was, her suggestion quickly moved among them and silently they all nodded in agreement.

Reddick was the first to move, sliding into the shadows without a word. In an instant he was gone.

Hero leaned over and bussed a kiss onto Roselie's cheek. "Must get to Jenny."

He turned to leave, but Roselie caught his hand, her gaze fixed on Solly who stood silently behind the Honorable.

"Go with him," she pleaded.

Solly's expression turned murderous.

Even Brody knew what the silent fellow wanted desperately to say.

No.

Roselie moved into the giant man's shadow, taking his large paw of a hand in hers. "Yes. You must. For Tuck and Mrs. Rowland's sake. They need Uncle Hero. Besides, I have his lordship."

The fellow turned a stern gaze toward Brody, a look filled with promise, a rather dark one. *If you let any harm come to her . . .*

"I'll see her safely home," Brody vowed.

With that the Honorable and Solly fled down another alley.

"Yes, well, Rosebud, that was a fool's promise," Brody told her quietly, taking her by the hand.

"How is that?"

"I have no idea where we are," he confessed, as it seemed the shadows around them lengthened, reached out toward them.

Roselie, his Rosebud always, grinned. "But I do."

It was well past midnight, but that hardly mattered around the docks, ships came and went at all hours, slaves to the vagaries of the tide, so there were plenty of people milling about, looking for quick employment.

Roselie could feel their greedy eyes as she and Brody made their hurried flight.

"We stand out," she muttered, glancing down at her red satin and then over at Brody, done up for an evening at White's. They had come to a stop on a corner to catch their breath. "This will never do."

"What do you propose?" Brody teased. "We go naked?" He nodded down the street where a half-dressed dolly mop and her customer were loudly arguing over the terms of their transaction. The woman had hiked up her gown showing off her bare leg in an effort to get more coins.

Over on the next block, shouts could be heard, urging on their pursuers.

"This requires," Roselie said, "what my mother calls the trick of a new hat."

"The trick of a what?"

She pulled her befeathered and beribboned monstrosity of a hat free off its perch and plucked his top hat off his head.

"Hey, that's my new—"

"Exactly my point," she said, her gaze fitted on the couple down the way.

Roselie sauntered boldly down the street toward them, ignoring the fact that they'd already begun their transaction. "Excuse me," she said in a rolling broad accent of a country lass, albeit one who'd been in London for a bit.

The whore looked around her customer. "Bugger off. We're busy."

The man turned and took an appraising glance at Roselie. "Well dearie, if I had seen you first—" That earned him a swat in the arm from his current paramour. "But once I get my money's worth here . . ." He leered and winked at her.

Roselie turned and shot Brody a warning glance. She didn't need him going all jealous husband on her right now.

"All I want to do is make a trade," she told them, holding up her hat and pelisse. "These, for your cloak and hat." She chucked her chin toward Brody. "That one likes it a bit rough and it would be a shame if they were to be ruined, if you know what I mean."

They both blinked at her as if they hadn't the vaguest idea what she meant. Hells bells, she would have to find the dimmest pair in London.

So she tried another tack.

"And you, sir, this—" She held up the grand beaver and the man's eyes widened with greed. *Yes, that was more like it.* "For your trouble, and for your fine cap."

The man's hand went up and doffed his hat, already willing.

But his companion turned out to be a bit more canny. "Don't see why I'd want that—" She sneered at Roselie's fine offerings as if they had just been plucked out of a trash bin.

Further down the street a new commotion erupted.

"Roselie—" Brody urged.

"Yes, yes, I know," she told him.

Worse, the savvy whore smiled. "Now I see what this is all about. Don't know if I want such finery. Especially if it's been pinched." But the glitter in her eyes told another story.

The woman was merely playing hard to get, driving for a better offer . . . Especially as the telltale clamor drew closer. "Nicked it from some toff's trunks, didn't you? Constable don't like that."

"Roselie—" Brody nudged her in the back. There was no time left.

"Do you want them or not?" Roselie asked, turning as if to leave. Because if they couldn't gain their trade now, they needed to make a run for it.

"I'll take them," the woman huffed, stepping down from the steps. "But I want the bobs as well." She thrust her hand out, lips pursed and one brow arched up.

"Now see here—" Brody began to complain.

However, Roselie was already pulling the pearls from her ears. "Take 'em."

Once the goods were passed back and forth, Roselie caught hold of Brody's hand and pulled him down the street, all the while tossing the woman's dark cloak over her bright dress and plopping her small, tawdry hat atop her head.

She could tell the poor thing tilted to one side, but there was nothing to be done, save stick her hat pin in it and hope it stayed on. She glanced over at Brody. "Put that cap on low over your ears."

"Oh, God! Must I?" he said, looking askance at the filthy cap in his hands.

She didn't blame him—it looked rather loathsome and she doubted his valet would approve, but there was no choice in the matter.

Still, she let out an exasperated sigh. "Put the damn thing on so we can get out of here." He did, but it was hardly enough, for his shirt was far too white, and the red satin of her gown sparkled where it poked out from beneath the large cloak.

"Bother this gown." There was no choice but to take advantage of a nearby coal bin, and she shoved her hands into the dust and then rubbed them over her satin gown. Almost instantly the red was replaced with a grimy hue.

She turned to Brody and his expression grew horrified. "No one wears anything so pristine down here."

"Don't tell that to Wicks," Brody remarked as she wiped her hands down the front of his shirt, ignoring the muscled planes beneath. "He has an utter horror of even the least little spot."

Roselie stepped back and admired her work. "Yes, that ought to do the trick."

He groaned. "It should, but remember, Wicks will most likely quit when he sees this. You'll owe me a valet."

"I'll ask the Honorable if he knows a less discerning replacement for you," she quipped.

He was about to reply when at both ends of the block clusters of men appeared, closing in on them like a knot being tightened.

"This doesn't look good," Roselie whispered, reaching unconsciously for Brody's hand.

As her fingers intertwined with his—his strength and warmth filling her veins—she knew exactly what needed to be done.

"Kiss me."

Brody glanced down at her. "What? Now?"

"Like St. John's Folly," she whispered.

His eyes widened for just a flicker and then he moved—catching her by the waist and hauling her into the dark shadows of a doorway. He pressed himself against her, covering her. "Like this?"

"Oh, yes," she managed before his lips crashed down on hers. *Exactly like this.*

Taking a lesson from that long-ago night at St. John's Folly, he kissed her.

No, make that, he devoured her. Apparently doing his best to make it look like he was getting every penny's worth of the time he'd just purchased.

Roselie ignited under his kiss, his touch. Whether it was her pent-up anger over his untimely arrival, or her fear that something could happen to him—her desires, her needs, her own starving passions responded in kind.

More like burst free.

His mouth covered hers, his tongue danced over hers, and his hands—oh, his damn, bloody hands, knew exactly how to touch her, teasing her nipples into tight peaks, leaving her legs quaking beneath her.

So when she moaned—rather loudly, it was no act. No deception.

As the men drew closer, Brody pulled away and they shared a glance.

Hot, dangerous unanswered need burned between them. That, and a mutual vow to stop at nothing.

She knew his instincts urged him to turn around and challenge the entire lot of them—but it would be five against two. And while she wasn't a bad shot, Roselie always preferred a bluff.

And so it seemed, did Brody, picking up the lesson learned just minutes before.

"Bugger off," he growled using a bit of local vernacular and rough flavor. "You can have a go when I'm done." He spat on the ground and nodded toward the largest fellow. "Not that I recommend her. She's an expensive bit and likes to bite."

Playing her part, she trod heavily on his boot and earned herself a shake.

"She's all yours," one of the other fellows laughed roughly. "I don't like 'em that scrawny." He nudged the man Roselie assumed was their leader, the one giving them a good once-over. "Let's be off," the man complained, sending a sniff of dismay toward her. "Craddock's money will buy us a house of whores, and I don't want to see old Billy nabbing 'em 'afore we do."

The men moved on, taking different routes, while Brody went back to getting his money's worth, catching her lips with his, and kissing her deeply.

After a few moments, well perhaps a few more than that, Roselie tipped her head back. "I think they're gone."

Brody continued to nuzzle her neck. "Are you certain?"

"Not in the least," she whispered, lost in a haze of desire. And to make sure, she tipped her lips to his and he kissed her thoroughly once more, leaving her aquiver with need.

Much more, and she'd be begging him to take her. Right here. In this dirty, dank doorway.

She reached out and drew his hand off her breast—much to her regret—then tugged him out of the shadows—to her even greater regret. "We need to go now."

"Yes, I suppose we must." He squeezed her fingers and grinned at her. "Which way, Rosebud?"

For a nickname she'd deplored before, she was beginning to find it endearing. Especially when he teased her so. "That depends," she told him, leading him down the street.

"On what?"

She paused and glanced back behind them. "Do you still row?"

"If it gets us out of this mess, then yes, I do." As they continued to make their way in stealth toward the river banks, he leaned forward. "Don't tell me you keep an emergency boat down here?"

She couldn't help herself, she laughed. "Like the Honorable's emergency cards?"

"Something like that. On the way here he tried to engage me in a few rounds—to pass the time."

"Never pass the time with the Honorable, unless you know how to cheat."

"I would never—"

"That is why you shouldn't—"

"About this boat—" he prodded.

"I haven't one." They'd come to the riverside, and Roselie looked up and down the embankment. "At least not yet." She spied a sturdy looking specimen tied up and hurried toward it.

Brody followed in her wake. "You mean you intend to—"

"Yes, steal one." She glanced around and nodded for him to climb down, even as she was beginning to untie it.

He looked ready to balk at such a dishonorable notion, but not far away the mob searching for them was raising the hue and cry, gathering more forces.

"Yes, well, there is honorable, and then there is saving one's hide," he agreed as he hurried down the ladder. Once he'd gotten himself situated, Roselie yanked the rope free and scrambled in after him.

Brody pulled at the oars and just like that the small boat caught the current and they were being pulled along.

"We'll have the tide for another hour or so," she said. "So we'd best hurry."

"Thus says the lady in the stern," he shot back, pulling hard on the oars.

"Oh, no," she said, shaking her head. "Don't make it look like we are in a hurry."

"Row casually?"

Roselie ignored that hint of sarcasm. "Yes, exactly." She settled back into her seat and watched their progress over his shoulder. "Pretend this is one of Lady Oxnam's water parties."

At that, he groaned.

"So I take that to mean you've been to one," she replied.

"I have."

"Dreadful notion," Roselie said. "Whatever was she thinking?"

"Yes, this is so much better," he teased back. "You did bring cakes and tea, didn't you?"

"I fear I forgot those."

"Lady Oxnam never did."

"Then perhaps you should follow her about," Roselie replied. "Instead of me."

He shrugged a bit and pulled hard on the oars. For a time it was just them and the soft slap of the water against the oars as he continued to row.

Clutching the sides of the boat as it rocked slightly, Roselie leaned forward. "Why, Brody? Why did you follow me?"

He never broke his steady pace. "You know why."

"You shouldn't have," she told him, turning to watch the passing shoreline, all shadows but for a lamp here and there to guide them, like a haphazard string of stars.

"Neither should you."

And she knew exactly what he meant. She shouldn't have gone off to the docks. She should have stayed home.

"You left me no choice, and you know it," he continued.

"We always have choices."

"When it comes to you, no, I don't."

They passed under the bridge, and on the other side moved through a shaft of light. Her heart twisted as she looked at him— his expression so clear, so full of desire, of fears of what was to come.

What had she done? What had she brought him to?

Finally, they bumped into the dock near the Beaufort Wharves, just a stone's throw from Covent Garden, and Roselie scrambled up, carrying the rope with her and tying off their purloined boat.

When Brody followed, the first thing he did was catch hold of her and kiss her. Slowly, tenderly, like he had at the Gosforth's Ball. If she had any doubts as to why he'd followed her, he answered each one with his kiss.

And when he let her go, Roselie wavered for a moment. *No, damn you, you cannot love me.*

For it was as if he had whispered the words into her heart.

You are mine, Rosebud. Mine forever. Mine to love. Mine to protect.

He tugged her along, as if nothing had passed between them, when in fact, everything had. Roselie followed almost blindly. For she couldn't shake off that terrible fear—that in his determination to protect her, he would get himself killed.

"If the house is being watched," Brody began as they finally stole their way into the borders of Mayfair, "we need to approach it cautiously."

They meandered their way through the alleyways and mews, until they slipped into the garden behind the house and they got to the door.

"I daresay it's locked," he told her.

"I daresay it isn't," she replied, opening it.

"Bloody hell," he muttered. "I'll have a word or two for Peakman in the morning."

"It's not his fault," Roselie whispered as they made for the back stairs. "'Tis Bernie. She always unlocks the door for me."

"Yes, well," he huffed, "she'll have no need to do that any longer."

"If you think I am going to stop just because—"

Brody opened the door to his bedchamber and tugged her inside, closing it behind them. "You will stop because you are my wife, and I say so."

"Your wife? Bah! I'm barely your wife."

"You wear my ring."

She held up her hand, the emerald flashing. "You put more store in this ring than you do in me." She made an attempt to tug it off her hand, but it stayed where he'd put it.

He smiled with what looked like a bit of triumph, a possessive bit of passion. *You are mine.*

When the ring wouldn't come off, Roselie growled in frustration. "Doesn't matter. I am not your wife."

He stalked over to her and hauled her close. Gone was the tenderness from earlier.

This Brody was far too dangerous, raging with pent-up anger, and from the dark flicker in his eyes, passion.

"We are married." He glared down at her. "You had best not forget it."

"No marriage is binding unless it has been—" Roselie snapped her mouth shut for she didn't dare finish that sentence.

. . . unless it has been consummated.

"Then let it be done," he told her, catching her up and hauling her to his bed.

Chapter 16

$\mathscr{B}$rody's blood had never raged so hot. This woman, this vexing, impossible woman drove him to this madness.

He pinned her to the bed, covering her. Ignoring her complaints, ignoring her threats.

She was his wife. His wife now and forever. And if this was what it took, then so be it.

His mouth crashed down on hers, maybe to stopper her protests, but maybe it was so he could breathe in her scent, fill himself with the taste of her.

With hands pinned over her head, and his lips locked with hers, she was his. His to take.

But oh, that was the devilish part of all this . . . because even when he thought he had her mastered, the tide shifted—just like the Thames. One moment the waters pushed and rose, and the next, they began that inevitable drift back toward the sea.

It started with her kiss—for she was no longer fighting him, her tongue matching his with the same hunger. Hot, and teasing, moving over his as seductively as a cat. Tempting him to stroke her, to twine with her.

Her hips no longer bucked at him, but were arching up, rubbing against his erection. Teasing him. Tormenting him.

He reached down and yanked up the hem of her gown, his

hand running slowly up her leg, up her calf, along her thigh, right to that spot where his fingers found her wet and slick, ready for him, her breath coming in a tattoo of gasps as he began to tease her.

She moaned, softly at first, then a bit louder as he found her cleft and dipped his finger inside her. God, she was hot and wet. How he wanted . . .

He released her hands and they came to his shoulders, immediately tugging him close. Close was good, for it allowed him to tease her nipples into hard points until her lashes fluttered and her mouth opened in a wide moue as she tried to find her breath.

"Oh, ooooh," she gasped.

And so he went lower still, and tasted her—the very core of her, teasing her now with his fingers, his tongue. Earthy and raw, she was his and he was going to have every bit of her. And the deeper he kissed her there, the more she rocked against his mouth, greedy puss looking for every bit of passion she could catch hold of, and just before she was about to tumble into that hot abyss, he stopped.

Pulling back and letting his breath blow over her quaking sex. He looked up at her, this tumbled mess that was his wife, her dark hair falling free from its pins, her eyes wide and smoky, her lips swollen from his kisses and in a moue of need.

This was his wife. His Rosebud and she was ready to blossom.

Oh, she was furious with him, of that he had no doubt, but her eyes flashed with unanswered need—something he understood, for he was aching with it—he'd never been so hard, so ready to thrust himself inside a woman and find his release.

"Brody, you wretch," she whispered. "Don't you dare stop."

"You are my wife," he told her, feeling stubborn over the fact.

"Yes, I am," she told him. "Now make me so."

Roselie was past the point of caring. She'd never been afraid of his rough handling—for she knew the man beneath the unrestrained passions.

Brody. Her Brody. She wanted him to take her like this. She was furious with him, and yet, how she needed him. It was as if she would never be whole until he came to her.

"Demmit, Brody," she told him, her fingers twining in his hair. "Please. Now."

And he did, rising up from between her legs, all that a man ought to be—for here he was pulling off his coat and his shirt, and her breath caught at the sight before her. He was a masculine devil to behold, muscled and lean. Her gaze strayed to the long, hard bulge in his pants, and he grinned at her, slowly opening the buttons.

She scrambled up to help him, brushing aside his hands. Bother the man, he was taking too long. And then his pants opened and she moaned as she found what she wanted. It was as if some innate need in her had come to life. She wanted him, this.

Her thumb rolled over the tip and now it was his turn to groan.

"Does this feel good?" she asked, as she ran her hand over him, cupped his balls and brought her lips to tease a kiss onto the tip. A dot of moisture lay there and she licked at it. Tasted him.

Her body clenched, her breasts tightened. And from the way he groaned as she continued to run her tongue over him, he was in much the same straits.

He began to tremble, groan and he pulled back from her and they faced each other, surrounded by shadows.

It was as if the entire world had come down to this place, this moment. It was just them. This man. This woman. And so much unanswered need between them.

Roselie shook her hair back, out of her face, and began to pull at her gown. She wanted out of it. She wanted to be naked. Naked with him. Beneath him. The chill in the air had no power over the heat this man brought to life inside her.

She couldn't think of anything but the way her heart pounded, her body ached. Oh, how she needed him.

To *feel* him. *All* of him.

Clothes fell all around them like wedding petals, and then he was above her, climbing into the bed, storming over her, his chest hard against her breasts, his knee nudging her legs apart even as she opened herself to him.

And then he was. Inside her. She'd stroked that length, and had imagined more times than she could count what it would feel like inside her. But to her consternation, he entered her only slightly and paused as if full of hesitations. Doubts.

Roselie rebelled, her fury, her desires clamoring for answers.

"Fill me," she begged, her hands curled around his shoulders pulling him closer, her hips rising, jutting up to meet him. Wild with need, so very close to her own release, a madness, a blindness had taken over. "Don't stop."

And so he thrust inside her, sweeping away her barrier in one quick movement. She gasped for a moment and then, oh he needed no other urging, he drove into her, pinning her to the bed, and pumping and thrusting, as she tried to breathe, tried to think, but there was only her release, waves of passion that carried her away.

She called to him, clung to him, and very quickly, he followed, gasping, crying out and driving himself inside her, right up to his hilt, for he couldn't go any farther as he poured himself into her.

"Mine," he gasped into her ear as he made his last thrust. "Mine always."

She arched up, grinning. *His.*

Some time later

*B*rody reached out and played with a loose curl of her dark hair. Her eyes lay half closed and a dreamy smile flitted at her lips.

After their first frantic joining, they'd made love again. And then again. And now, exhausted and somewhat sated, they'd collapsed together in a burrow of tangled sheets.

He nibbled at her neck. "Sorry about your ear bobs."

"Paste," she said, arching so he could continue.

"Pardon?" He was drowsy and not really listening. Besides her skin was so warm, so soft. So very kissable.

"They were paste. I sold the real ones years ago." She made her confession so nonchalantly as if a young miss selling her jewelry was hardly worthy of note. "I could only take so much from Piers's estate without . . ."

Brody sat up. "You stole money from your brother's estate?"

She stretched and glanced at him. "'Stole' is such a harsh word. I much prefer *'redirected.'*"

"And just how much have you *redirected*?" But even as he said the words he was shaking his head. "No. No. Never mind. I don't think I want to know."

"No, I think it's better that you don't." She snuggled closer, then as if prodded toward confession added, "It was only the profits. The ones I managed."

"Yes, well that makes it all so much better," he replied. "Far less shocking."

His sarcasm had no effect. In fact, she preened. "I'm rather good at it."

"Stealing or profiting?"

"Both."

He shook his head. "I've only one more question—"

"Only one?" She laughed and rolled toward him. "I doubt that."

He pulled her close, her warm skin against his. "Yes, well, perhaps more than one. But let me ask the most important one: Why?"

"Why what?" she teased back, fluttering her lashes at him.

It was overly distracting but he meant to discover the truth, so he did what was nearly impossible and set her at a distance. "Help me to understand. Why?"

She reeled back a little, her eyes widening, and in that moment, he saw something he'd never seen on Roselie's features. Not as the unflappable debutante, not as the impossibly dangerous Asteria.

Regret.

With a deep breath, she exhaled one word. "Abigail." And with that word, that name, came a rush of emotions: guilt, pain, loss.

Shaking her head, she rolled away. "Does it really matter?" She glanced over her shoulder at him. "You have your reasons. I have mine. I suppose they aren't so different."

"Perhaps. Though mine are rather obvious." He didn't need to state it though, they both knew.

His brother.

"Are you certain there weren't other reasons," she said, reaching out and cupping his chin, smiling at him. "I daresay you wanted to vex your mother a bit."

He laughed. "It might not have helped that after Poldie bought his commission my mother told me, lectured really, 'If you ever do something as foolhardy as your brother, I will never speak to you again.'"

"I fear she didn't see the likely consequences of such a tempting offer," Roselie remarked.

"Quite." Brody grinned.

"Yes, well, I suppose Piers inspired me—in a sense." She sighed again. "He left the year before my first Season, and he was so dashing. I followed his exploits avidly—through his letters and newspaper accounts—since that is all a lady is allowed to do— and even that little is frowned upon." She huffed a sigh. "And when we have something we can do, must do, can really help, save lives, we are ignored. Patted on the head and sent on the way."

"Is that what happened?" Brody asked quietly.

She nodded. "I failed Abigail. I failed them all."

"All of who?"

"The crew of the *Intrepid*."

"You've lost me now. How ever did you fail them?"

"It began at Almack's," she told him.

His eyes widened. "That was the last thing I ever thought you'd say. Truly? Almack's?"

"Sadly, the world begins and ends there, as impossible as it seems."

He laughed.

"Oh, you find that amusing? So did the Lord Admiral and Lord Howers. If they had just listened to me, the French would never have sunk the *Intrepid*, or taken so many other ships. Captain Croft might still be alive . . . and Abigail . . ." Her voice quaked and trailed.

Now she had his full attention. "Go on," he urged, kissing her brow. "Take me back to this momentous Wednesday evening."

"I thought you didn't like Almack's?"

"I don't," he said, "but for you, I'll make an exception."

"You were there, you know."

"I was?"

"Yes, but you were ignoring me—"

"I would never—"

"Oh, please—"

"Perhaps it was because you are too pretty and had too many suitors—"

"Too pretty—" She snorted.

"I have to confess that when you returned from school, I barely recognized you. You weren't my Rosebud. You'd quite blossomed."

'Twas how she'd gotten her hated nickname—because she'd been such a late bloomer. All long limbs and no curves. He'd teased her mercilessly one summer and the name had stuck.

But now . . .

"Tell me about Almack's," he prompted.

"I was waiting for you to ask me to dance and I ended up near Lord Ilford."

"You see, perhaps it was most fortuitous that I was ignoring you."

She shook her head. "Well, you were dancing with Miss Fox–"

"I never—"

"You did. You were like all the rest of the fools that year, traipsing after her."

"She did come with five thousand a year," he noted.

"You hardly need it," she shot back.

"A few thousand more never hurts," he teased.

"Yes, well while you were having your toes trod upon by that ungainly bit of baggage–"

"Jealous?"

"Not in the least. Though she is a marchioness now. With a rather lovely coronet." Roselie tipped her head as if imagining such a fetching crown atop her own head.

He poked her. "Now who's the baggage?"

"Not at all. As I was saying, I was waiting for you—"

"And I apologized for that."

"Yes, so there I was wedged in by Lady Trumbel—"

"There! No wonder I couldn't see you," he teased her again.

"There is that, but the point is Lord Ilford didn't notice me and obviously had no concerns regarding Lady Trumbel hearing him."

"She's rather deaf," he noted.

"Most likely why he was using her for cover," Roselie acknowledged. "So he was talking with Sir Walter—"

"Poor sod."

"Not really. Sir Walter was making a tidy profit from shipments of munitions and arms to Portugal." She huffed a sigh. "Lord Ilford was prodding him a bit as to when the next shipment was to sail and wasn't Sir Walter worried about the French snatching his profits away from him."

"And he fell right into Ilford's trap," Brody said, shaking his head woefully.

"Like a greedy fish after a worm on the hook. He boasted that the Navy was sending the *Parnell* and the *Intrepid* along to ensure Sir Walter's ships made it to Lisbon. And Ilford applauded the forethought."

"Always the patriot our Ilford," Brody replied.

"Yes, quite," she agreed just as sardonically. "But there was something about the entire exchange that didn't seem right."

"How so?"

Roselie's nose wrinkled. "The way Ilford pressed him—and when Sir Walter became hesitant, Ilford whispered something to him that left poor Sir Walter looking as if he was about to succumb to apoplexy."

"Wonder what he said?" Brody mused.

"Does it matter? Sir Walter laid out the shipping schedule. That the *Torquil* was to sail ahead, escorting a ship of no value, and thereby drawing off the French, while the *Intrepid* and the *Parnell* slipped out just before dark with the real ships." She closed her eyes as if she might be able to blot out the memory. But it was so ingrained so unforgettable. "I knew that with that information, the French could send a single ship to give chase after the *Torquil*, if only enough to make it appear as if they were taking the bait—"

"While the rest of their contingent sat out at sea waiting like wolves." Brody drew a deep breath at the thought of it.

Roselie nodded. "I knew it was a bad bit of business and went the next day to see the Lord Admiral."

"Oh, I imagine that went well."

"He laughed at me. Sent me packing, and that was after he made me wait for hours. He said he only saw me out of respect for my father. Then he patted me on the head like I was still a child and sent me home. Even offered me a peppermint."

"What did you do next?"

"I went to see Lord Howers—he's my godfather, you know—"

No, Brody didn't know that, but it explained much.

"—and he sent me on my way in much the same manner."

"I'm ever so sorry."

"Not as sorry as I was when the news came. I hadn't realized at the time that Captain Croft had been assigned the *Intrepid*. He and Abigail had only been married for such a short time. And I knew. I knew, Brody. And no one would listen to me."

She turned away from him and he caught hold of her pulling

her around and shaking her just a little. "What could you have done differently?"

"I don't know. I've asked myself that question a thousand times since. Then Sir Walter turned up dead." Roselie closed her eyes and sighed, but after a few moments, continued, "I began to watch and listen. Digging at rumors and doing my best to unearth as much of the truth as I could find. But to stop it? I had no idea how."

"So what did you do?"

"This might surprise you, but I confided in Mrs. Rowland one night and she offered to help."

"Tuck's mother." He didn't sound surprised.

"Yes, she's remarkably resourceful."

"So I've learned of late."

"She found Bernie for me, and then Uncle Hero offered to help, well, more like insisted. Then I tried to learn as much as I could so I could get the answers I needed to stop Ilford."

"Which brings me to my next question," Brody began, "how ever did you convince Lord Howers to go along with this madness?"

"I was persistent—"

"I can imagine," he laughed.

"And in the end it was Lady Howers who insisted I be allowed to help and so truly his lordship had no choice."

"Lady Howers?"

"Oh yes, she quite rules the roost."

"Wouldn't I like to nose that about the Home Office."

"Don't you dare! He'll know exactly how you found out."

Brody leaned back on his pillow. "Don't worry, I have no desire to spend the rest of my life inspecting mail."

"Then I would suggest never crossing Lady Howers."

"Duly noted." He looked her over, the furrowed brow, the set of her jaw and knew she was still at odds. "Whatever is it, Roselie? Ilford is done for."

"Is he? I know you think you've found the answers, that with him arrested he's finished, but there's a missing piece out there, one that rises beyond Ilford." She paused for a moment. "Brody, he isn't the ringleader. I'm certain of it."

"Well, certainly you've annoyed someone."

"Other than you?"

He laughed, and weighed all that she'd said. It made sense. "Perhaps," he began, grudgingly, "we can puzzle this out together. Work together."

Her eyes lit up. *Work together.* Words she most likely thought he'd never use. An impossibility.

She leaned back on a pillow and shook her head, a wry smile on her lips. "How can I work with you tagging along?"

It was an old line, one Piers and Poldie had often used on Brody when he been young and they hadn't wanted a mere child dogging their heels.

He liked hearing it now about as much as he had then.

Still with Roselie grinning at him, it was hard to stay mad at her.

"Actually, I could use your help with one thing," she told him.

He didn't know if he dared to ask just what she had in mind.

And she whispered into his ear exactly what she needed. Wanted from him.

Brody readily agreed by pulling her beneath him, kissing her deeply, and burying himself inside her.

It was well into the next day when Brody woke up. Exhausted and contented. They'd come to an understanding that they would work together and now it was time . . .

He stirred and rolled over. What a mad night. How many times had they made love? He'd lost count.

No one could dispute now that they weren't properly man and wife. Especially Roselie. He smiled as he began to dig through the tangled sheets looking for her. His magnificent bride.

But as he rolled over he discovered there was nothing but a cold, empty space beside him.

Knowing Roselie, she'd probably gone to get something to eat. Come to think of it, he was famished as well.

He got out of bed and tugged on his trousers and a shirt. As he went downstairs it seemed the entire house was abandoned. There was no one about, that is until he got to the breakfast room.

"Ah, my lord, would you prefer breakfast or luncheon?" Peakman asked.

"That late?" Brody asked.

"So it seems, my lord," Peakman replied.

"Where is her ladyship?"

"Her ladyship is out."

"No, I was referring to my wife not my mother."

"As was I, my lord."

"Out?!" He got to his feet. "Where the devil has she gone?"

"I'm not certain, my lord." The man considered the question for a moment, and then said, "She did however mention something about it being Friday."

Friday. Something rose like a flag in his memory. And then he recalled what her mother had once said about Roselie's many obligations.

The baron looked his butler straight in the eye. "Call for Wicks. I need to go out immediately."

Chapter 17

A woman hasn't the keen faculties for deduction and discernment.

Lord Howers, outside of his wife's hearing

"𝒥 am so pleased you could come by, Roselie." Lady Howers's warm greeting was full of enthusiasm. "Or should I say, Lady Rimswell?"

"Oh, please don't," Roselie told the matron, knowing that she was blushing even as she protested. A hue she knew the lady had spied—given her knowing smile.

So, Roselie caught hold of the back of her wheeled chair and pushed her toward the dining room.

"I must admit I hardly expected you today," Lady Howers said up over her shoulder.

Roselie refused to look her in the eye. "Why ever wouldn't I be here? It is Friday after all."

"But you are married now. I'm shocked you have time for an old woman's gossip."

She leaned down and whispered in a conspiratorial tone, "Yours is my favorite sort of gossip. Besides this is also my favorite meal of the week."

"The food or the chatter?" Lady Howers laughed.

"Decidedly both." Roselie grinned at her. "I fear Lord Rimswell's cook is nowhere as good as my mother's, or yours for that matter. He's impossibly dull."

Lady Howers shrugged. "I've always found that one's cook reflects the personality of the lady of the house. And since that has now changed, may I suggest a change in the kitchen as well?"

"Such a suggestion would cause quite a row with the new dowager."

"Send the horrible fellow along with her when she decamps to Garrick House as she's complained from one end of town to the other."

That stopped Roselie in her tracks. "She's what?"

Lady Howers chuckled. "Been telling one and all that you are demanding that Lord Rimswell banish her."

They'd arrived in the small, elegant dining room, where the table was already set for their usual luncheon. For all her protests that she hadn't expected Roselie, her ladyship had clearly hoped she'd be here.

"If I could, I would send her packing," Roselie admitted. "She's terribly dreadful."

"I would," her ladyship told her. "And there isn't a single soul in town who would blame you."

At that, they both laughed.

The servants brought out the simple luncheon that her ladyship preferred and Roselie adored. The two of them ate and shared the current tattle floating about town—avoiding the most obvious subject, Roselie's hasty marriage to Lord Rimswell.

But eventually, as was always the case, they got down to business. "I have something to ask you, Lady Howers," Roselie began.

"You always do," her ladyship noted, settling her napkin on the table.

"What can you tell me about the Duchess of Ranworth?"

Brody was still furious with Roselie, though he did concede, at the very least, that she'd had the good sense to have Solly drive her.

Though he couldn't help but remember that Patch's presence hadn't been enough to save Mrs. Croft.

So it was, he was right in the middle of drafting a stern lecture for the pair of them—Roselie and Solly—when he nearly bumped into Old Ironpants himself going up the steps of the Howerses' residence.

"I do say," the older man huffed, blinking owlishly at Brody as he came out of whatever course of thought he'd been pondering. "Rimswell! Didn't think you'd get my message so soon." Howers continued up the steps—for it was rare he paused for anyone or anything.

"Message, sir?"

"Never mind that now. You're here. Best you come along. Though these matters will have to wait until after luncheon."

Brody followed his superior. He'd never been to Howers's residence, never been invited to dine. "I believe my wife is here."

"Your wife?" The man looked positively puzzled—but only for a second. "Ah, yes, I did hear some nonsense about you and Miss Stratton."

The door opened, and the butler greeted them. The servants took their coats, hats, and accoutrements quickly—moving with efficiency and all due haste.

They obviously understood their mercurial and impatient master.

"Sir, about Roselie, er Lady Rimswell—"

"She's a fine woman, Rimswell," Lord Howers told him as he set off into the house.

Not knowing what else to do, Brody followed. "Yes, well, I daresay she's been afforded a shocking amount of, shall we say, leniency."

"If you say—"

"I do," Brody told the man. "And if you don't mind me saying, I blame you."

Howers came to an abrupt halt. "I do mind, you impertinent pup!" He huffed a bit and scratched at his chin. "But she's your wife now, and you are allowed your opinions." He continued down the hall.

Brody set his jaw and jogged after him. "Sir, it is my considered opinion that she is a raft of trouble, and has been left to her own devices for far too long." He didn't realize this, but he'd said this as the two of them had turned into a small dining room.

And of course, there was Roselie, nose tipped defiantly in the air. "I'm sitting right here."

"Good," Brody shot back. "So one might hope you'll listen."

He couldn't help himself, but as angry as he was with her, what with her chin jutted out as if daring him to contradict her, he found himself wishing he could gather her up and spend the entire day as they had the previous night.

Well, the later part of the evening.

As it was the two of them glared at each other.

Lady Howers looked from one to the other and laughed. "Ah, young love! Now if you two are done sparring, I imagine poor Lord Howers is famished—he gets so devilishly peckish." She paused and smiled at Brody. "Sir, I'd be most honored if you would join us." She nodded toward the chair opposite Roselie's.

Lord Howers, having already settled into his place, smiled at his wife, acknowledged Roselie with an indulgent grin, as if her spot at his table was a common enough occurrence.

"Am I to assume, Everard, that this is Lord Rimswell?" her ladyship asked her husband, nodding toward Brody who still hovered in the doorway.

Howers looked up and blinked. "Why I suppose it is." He waved his hand at the empty chair. "What are you waiting for, my boy, sit. Seems everyone is here today." He huffed a bit as he was wont to do, and nodded to the footman to begin serving.

"Lord Rimswell, I don't believe we've ever been properly introduced, though dear Roselie has told me much of you," Lady Howers said, holding out her hand.

With the introductions made, Brody found himself seated across from his wife.

Roselie, he would note, was doing her best to look everywhere but at him. Avoiding the inevitable.

Though Howers was never one to suffer silence when there was work to be done. "Whatever were you two discussing?" he asked as he accepted a well laden plate from the footman.

"The Duchess of Ranworth," Lady Howers informed him.

"You don't say," he noted as he cut into a slice of pork pie. "Such an enchanting lady in her day. Well, before—" The man stopped, as if remembering himself, and took a renewed interest in his luncheon.

Not that Roselie had any such restraint. "Before what, my lord?"

"I suspect you already know," Howers remarked dryly.

"What you might not know, is how the duke put such grand expectations on her," Lady Howers told her.

"Expectations?" Brody asked, taking his cue from Roselie, who appeared right at home between these two.

Besides, wherever this line of query was going, he suspected Roselie had her reasons.

Ones he wanted to know about as well.

"Of an heir," Lady Howers told him.

An uncomfortable silence surrounded them. For Lord and Lady Howers had lost their only child in an assignment for the Home Office ten years earlier. The young man had disappeared in France after the peace of '01 had collapsed and he'd never been heard from.

"Yes well, it does seem when one has Ilford for a son—" Brody remarked.

"Oh, that was well before he was born. They had been married for years without any hope of a child." Lady Howers sighed and glanced about the table as if she thought something might be missing. "The longer the duchess's ordeal went on, the more she despaired."

"There was even talk of the duke setting her aside. That is until *that* woman came along." Lord Howers's great bushy brows burrowed together.

It was an expression Brody knew well. Every new agent in the Home Office had had *that* look cast at them at one time or another and learned quickly to run for the north rather than continue making their report.

"Who was she? This woman?" Roselie asked.

"Why Lady Muscoates, of course," Lady Howers told her. "But back then she was known as Madame Aufroy."

Brody could see Roselie adding these pieces one by one to her grand puzzle, even as Lady Howers continued, "She came to England with her husband," she said. "He was an attaché of some sort to the French ambassador and most unfortunately died within a few weeks of arriving."

"Why didn't she go back to France?" Brody asked, earning a hot glance from Roselie. He smiled at her. *Two can play this game of yours.*

"Why didn't she go back?" Lady Howers remarked. "She wasn't wanted there."

"Ellie!" Lord Howers interjected, his wife having obviously strayed into something confidential.

Lady Howers hardly appeared quelled. "Well, it's the truth and rather common knowledge," she said, turning her nose up, much like Roselie did when someone rebuked her. "His family certainly didn't want the responsibility of such a young widow. Not to mention they'd opposed the match to begin with."

"Why was that?" Roselie asked.

Lord Howers barged back into the conversation. "The usual reasons. I believe the lady's family was in trade."

"And not the respectable sort," Lady Howers added.

But that comment—*not the respectable sort*—left Brody thinking of the warren of tunnels he'd toured the previous night.

Not all the business in London is done by the respectable.

Apparently not.

"So she stayed in England—" Roselie nudged, trying to sound innocent, but about as subtle as a cat threading her way through one's legs in an effort to be fed.

"And why wouldn't she? She was such a fetching creature—" Lord Howers said with some youthful gusto.

"Everard!" his wife chided.

"Well, she was. She was also flirtatious and quite engaging." Lord Howers smiled and waggled his brows at Roselie. In return, she laughed.

Brody closed his mouth which had fallen open. For here was Old Ironpants, shamelessly flirting like some old roué.

No one in the Home Office was ever going to believe him.

"She was flirtatious because she was in search of a new husband." Lady Howers remarked, as if that made all the difference in the world. "Then, she made friends with the duchess."

"Preyed on her," Lord Howers corrected, waving his fork for emphasis.

His wife nodded in agreement. "Yes, the duchess had always been prone to melancholy, and here was Madame Aufroy so filled with charm and exuberance. Soon, she and the duchess were inseparable. And not long after that, Madame Aufroy was living with them." Her lips pinched together in a disapproving line.

"*With* the duke and duchess?" Roselie asked.

"Oh, yes, *with*," Lord Howers told them, again with that waggle of his brows.

"Oh mind you, it was ever such a scandal but the duke and duchess seemed to have found a new happiness."

"Yes, and one can only wonder why—" Lord Howers muttered.

"Everard! Remember yourself!"

"What? Roselie's married now." He looked over at Brody and added, "I've always said there was more going on in that household—"

Lady Howers put down her fork with more than a clatter. "This is luncheon."

Lord Howers nodded to his wife, as if remorseful, however his acquiescence didn't last for long. He set down his silverware and looked his wife square in the face. "You can't say that having a young widow in that household, and the old duke, being as he was—so fond of pretty young things—that something untoward wasn't happening."

Lady Howers opened her mouth to protest, and when the words failed her, reached for the teapot instead, poured herself a cup and ignored him.

Brody glanced up and found Roselie with her quivering lips pressed together. He winked at her and she grinned back.

"Then what happened?" Roselie prompted.

"Like all affairs of the *ton*, it simply ran its course," Lord Howers supplied. "Eventually that French bit married Lord Skidby—"

Lady Howers shook her head, furiously so. "No, no, she married Lord Farcet."

"I'm quite certain it was Skidby," he told her.

"Never. It was Farcet, then Bramber, then Muscoates," Lady Howers told Roselie, as if that was the last and final word on the subject.

It wasn't. "Skidby, not Farcet," Lord Howers persisted.

"So Madame Aufroy got her match—" Brody added, nudging the conversation out of this apparent rut.

"Yes, in a manner of speaking," Howers agreed.

"It was inevitable, especially when Her Grace had borne an heir," Lady Howers added.

"Ilford," Brody remarked with no small amount of animosity.

"Yes, well, he certainly hasn't turned out as they'd hoped," Lady Howers said a bit more diplomatically.

"I hardly think a bad heir is a reason to drown oneself," Roselie remarked.

"That is a foul lie!" Lady Howers told her. "The Duchess of Ranworth did not kill herself. Quite plainly, she was murdered."

Lord Howers shook his head. "Not this again, I have it on good authority—"

"Yes, yes, 'good authority.'" Lady Howers turned to Roselie. "I saw the poor dear just before, well, *before*, and while she looked haunted, I can't believe she would have done such a thing. Not *that*."

"She'd always been a bit delicate." Lord Howers shook his head. "There had been rumors for months that she wasn't well. But murder? Absolutely not."

"*She* was there—"

"She?" Roselie ventured.

"Lady Muscoates," the matron said in a bit of a huff. "She was at Chessington when Her Grace—" She stopped there and shook her head. "I still maintain there was never a proper investigation."

Lord Howers sighed. "There was an investigation."

"Not a proper one."

Brody wondered if this is what he and Roselie were going to look like in forty years.

Lady Howers looked ready to continue the matter—stubbornly so—but it was Roselie who ended it, for the most part, by taking a side. "Your lordship is right. Her Grace wasn't murdered. Not in the least."

Lord Howers gloated, but only for a moment.

"The Duchess of Ranworth wasn't murdered, nor did she kill herself," Roselie told one then the other. And then she introduced her true line of reasoning, laid down a new piece to the puzzle.

"I don't think the duchess died. Not at all."

As Roselie was making her farewells to Lady Howers, Lord Howers pulled Brody aside. "Get her out of town, my boy. As soon as possible."

"I've tried. She refuses to budge. She's determined to winkle out this entire miserable business." Brody shrugged.

"And I say this nonsense about the duchess is going to get her killed. That woman is dead."

"Try convincing Roselie of that."

"If the duchess is alive, I'll give your wife the office next to mine."

At this Brody barked a laugh, drawing the attention of his wife and Lady Howers. Roselie's eyes narrowed and from the set of her jaw, the line of her brows, she did not approve of whatever it was he and Howers were discussing.

Not in the least.

"Now listen clearly, young man," Howers told him. "That headstrong bit of muslin is like a daughter to me—and I don't even want to consider how much she means to Lady Howers. So I am going to make this an order. Your wife must leave London immediately."

His lordship had Brody's full attention now. "You know Roselie. She doesn't take orders well."

The older man made a loud *harrumph.* "No, that she doesn't. Like her father. Too much like her father, if I do say so."

"She won't go," Brody told him, looking over at Roselie, who had that stubborn set to her.

"You'll both go," Howers told him, looking as well at Roselie. "And that's an order."

Brody's gaze swung up, and he began to protest. "I can't go—"

Which also explained why Howers had sent around a note and was now glaring daggers at him. "Let me be blunt. Your wife is in terrible danger—if half the reports I heard this morning are true . . . and now this impossible theory of hers." He shook his head. "If she doesn't leave today, you'll be a widower before the week is out."

Brody shook his head as they left Lord Howers's home. "You must admit, it seems a bit mad to think that the Duchess of Ranworth didn't die." He'd sent Solly on home with quiet instructions to have their belongings packed and the carriage prepared. It was time to leave London.

"I know this entire thing sounds far-fetched—" Roselie began.

"Far-fetched? It's preposterous." Brody took her hand and slid it onto his arm, giving her fingers a reassuring squeeze. "You heard Howers, they pulled the duchess's body from the lake."

"They pulled a body," she agreed. "But I ask you, have you ever seen someone after they've been in the water for a time?"

He grimaced, then nodded.

"So you know, there could be some questions as to who exactly it was they pulled from the water."

They continued walking, this time in silence. For a bit . . .

"But still—" Brody began.

"No, hear me out," she insisted. "In Abigail's papers there is a list of madhouses—"

"The packet she gave you the night of St. John's Folly—"

"Yes—"

"When were you planning to share that with me? With Howers?"

Her lips pursed together. "When it became relevant." She glanced away, her nose tipped stubbornly upward.

"I think it is very relevant now, Lady Rimswell," he told her. "I do recall you promising me that we would do this together."

Together. The word tugged her gaze back to meet his.

"Yes, I suppose so," she replied, but he could hear the hesitation in her voice. Then with a deep breath, she continued, the words coming slowly. "As I was saying, there is a list, but some of the houses have been crossed out—"

"So Mrs. Croft had determined those weren't the ones."

"I suspect so." Roselie shrugged. "But there are three remaining. Three places I was going to visit before—"

"Before what?"

She held up her hand, the one that bore his ring.

"Yes, before," he noted. "But the most pressing question to me still seems to be: Why ever would the duke fake his wife's death?"

"Who said it was the duke? Perhaps it was the duchess. Or someone else." Roselie glanced at him, her eyes full of challenge. "Oh, bother! There are too many pieces and they are such a jumble."

Brody nodded. "Tell me."

"If we find the duchess, I suspect we will answer all these questions, starting with who it is that's behind all this."

Find the duchess. An idea began to take hold of him. Still he couldn't help himself, Brody huffed a bit. For he had a solid opinion on who was behind all this. "That's easy. Ilford."

Now it was Roselie's turn to scoff.

Yet Brody persisted with his evidence. "Howers agrees with me."

"Lord Howers is wrong, as are you."

Brody laughed a little. "Yes, Old Ironpants certainly appreciated you telling him that."

Roselie grinned. "He never does."

"But the fact remains, Ilford is behind all this. We have evidence, Roselie."

"You had evidence," she told him, giving him that smug look that always made him cringe.

"So you heard about Charlie Bludger?"

Her gaze rolled upward. So, yes, of course she had.

"Ilford is up to his ears in debts," Brody pointed out.

Again, she scoffed. "That's hardly evidence. Most noblemen have debts. But they don't commit multiple acts of treason to pay them off."

"Yes, well, there is that," he conceded. Grudgingly. Then he admitted the one fact that had been eluding him. "What I've never understood is why? Why is he in debt? He stands to inherit a dukedom, he has no reason to worry about money."

"Doesn't he?" she said, that sly smile teasing him.

"What do you know?"

"His father hasn't supported him for the last four years. Cut him off without a penny about the time the duchess supposedly died. Nor is the duke as solvent as the world might think."

Brody's head spun. "How the hell do you know that?"

"Do you remember my friend, Miss Sutton?"

"The one who married Sir Denys last year?"

"Yes—"

"I always wondered why you were sponsoring her." He paused.

"After all, isn't her father merely a . . ." Brody stopped. *A solicitor.* Then it occurred to him. "Let me guess—she's the daughter of Ranworth's solicitor."

He hoped like hell he was wrong.

He wasn't.

Roselie shrugged a little. "Now that you mention it, he does happen to be the duke's personal solicitor. Fancy that."

"Yes, what a strange coincidence," Brody remarked.

Nor did Roselie's confessions stop there. "And I might have gone through Mr. Sutton's papers during Miss Sutton's wedding breakfast."

"Roselie!" he groaned.

"What?" she protested. "You've never read someone's private files?"

He took a deep breath. "Of course. I'm an agent of the Crown."

"So am I."

"Not officially."

Completely unrepentant, she fired back. "Well, do you know that the Duke of Ranworth is throwing away his estate, leaving a bankrupt tangle of debts and bad investments? It's as if he's doing it deliberately."

"Deliberately? That makes no sense."

"It does if Ilford's father doesn't want to leave him a single shilling."

"That still doesn't prove that Ilford isn't the mastermind," Brody pointed out. "What next? You'll tell me we're holding an innocent man?"

"Oh, he's guilty, but not for the reasons you think. There is someone else who is the master of it all."

"You keep saying as much—" Brody began. Then he pulled to a stop and turned to face her. "So who is this grand mastermind?"

"I think it might be Lady Muscoates."

Brody barked a laugh. "Now I'm certain you have gone mad. That poor, little widow is trying to overthrow Britain?"

"She's French," Roselie shot back. "And she's a schemer. You heard Lady Howers say as much."

"You don't like her because her ward is too pretty."

"That's exactly why I suspect her," Roselie told him, as if that was proof enough.

Brody shook his head and started walking again; after a few moments, Roselie hurried after him. "Mark my words, Miss Taber is not who she appears to be."

"A fetching heiress?" Brody paused. "Oh, yes, I'll take that to Howers immediately—I'm sure he'll agree that being pretty and rich is treason. Will stand up in court without a doubt."

"You don't understand. She doesn't pour properly."

Of all the foolhardy reasons . . . "Roselie—"

"No, hear me out. Miss Taber is no lady. She's not a proper miss. I wager she's no heiress."

"How do you know?"

"She flirts."

Brody glanced over at her. "So does Patience Nafferton."

Roselie groaned. "That's different. Patience is utterly horrible at it. She hasn't the vaguest notion as to what she's doing."

"You'll get no argument from me in that regard."

"But Miss Taber does. She knows."

"Knows what?"

"Exactly what she's doing. It was like she was born to be a coquette. She's beguiling. Utterly so. And don't tell me you haven't noticed."

He had, but hadn't the least intention of admitting as much to Roselie. She'd consider it more evidence in her favor.

But he did have one argument to make. "And my fine, beguiling Asteria, who taught you? By your own reasoning, that makes you an imposter as well."

"Mrs. Rowland and the Honorable taught me all I needed to know. As you might have guessed, I'm a quick study."

Well, he had no arguments there. Then she surprised him.

"The rest, I learned from you."

"Me?"

She smiled up at him, that wistful, one might even say, beguiling glance, that had driven him mad with desire for his mysterious Asteria.

"Glad to hear I helped. I think," he said, pulling his gaze away from her, for she was ever-so-distracting. And being distracted left them . . . left them . . .

Surreptitiously, he glanced around, weighing the crowded streets around them and looking for that someone who didn't quite fit in. For suddenly, he couldn't shake the sense that they weren't alone, that someone was watching them.

Even as Roselie blithely went on about her theories regarding Lady Muscoates, he spotted a fellow winding his way toward them. A quick glance suggested he fit in with the Mayfair denizens, but as a gentleman with the punctilious Wicks as his valet, Brody could see this man's cravat was sloppily tied and more yellow than white. Worse, was the dull sheen to his boots.

This fellow was no Mayfair toff, just poorly done up to appear like one.

And as he drew closer to Brody and Roselie, his hand shifted slowly into his jacket.

Brody's muscles tensed as the *thud* of booted feet came pounding up from behind—belonging, he guessed, to more than one troublemaker.

Demmit. They were about to be attacked from both sides.

When the first man came level with them, he pulled out a knife, his narrow gaze fixed on Roselie. But he hadn't anticipated that Brody was well aware of his intentions.

Brody slammed his fist into the man's jaw, a hard blow that sent the man toppling over. But it wasn't fast enough, for he heard the scuffle before Roselie's cry sent a chill through his blood.

"Brody!"

He whirled around to find her being dragged toward a waiting carriage, but her assailants were having a time of it. His determined bride was fighting the henchmen every step of the way—kicking at their shins and biting one of the thugs until he released her, howling in pain.

The other man redoubled his efforts, nearly getting her to the carriage, but Roselie had dug her heels in—for once her demmed stubbornness worked in her favor—and with her free hand began to pummel the bastard.

Then to Brody's shock, the absolutely unimaginable happened. The man turned and clouted Roselie across the chin. She stilled and slumped over immediately.

Brody's entire world narrowed to a murderous red haze, and all his fury fixed on the bastard holding his wife. He hurled himself into the fellow sending them both crashing to the cobbles.

Uncle Hero's words from the other night rang in Brody's ears. . . . *there are no formal rules, no studied blows, no thought of restraint.*

They'd been cautionary then, but now they cut loose every demon inside him. Restraint?

Forgotten.

He hit the man over and over again with a bloody refusal to stop, until he felt a sharp tug on his arm.

He whirled around, about to give hell to whoever dared interfere, when his blurred vision came into focus and he heard the words that reached through his raw anger.

"Brody, no! It's me!"

Roselie.

It was enough to get him to stop. He blinked and then caught hold of her with the same determination with which he'd gone after her assailant. He hauled her into his arms, holding her, pulling her against him, if only to bring his raging anger down to a mere boil.

Roselie pulled back, catching hold of his jaw and meeting his wild gaze. "We must get out of here. Now!"

She tipped her head in the direction of the sidewalk, where a crowd of shocked and upright citizens stood clustered in knots, appalled to see brawling in the middle of Mayfair.

It wouldn't be long before the constable arrived.

Brody caught his breath. Yes, she was right. This would be hard to explain, and impossible to escape the inevitable gossip if they didn't get away.

Thankfully, he didn't see anyone he recognized and hoped no one—not the servants milling about or the ladies in the crowd—knew Roselie.

The driver also sensed the changing tide and scrambled back up onto his perch, shaking the reins and getting away as quickly as possible, leaving his cohorts to their fate.

"We must go," she insisted.

Brody looked at the telltale red mark on her face and couldn't forgive himself. *This is all my fault. I should've sent her away. Immediately.*

Roselie must have sensed his remorse. "Yes, yes, he hit me. Come along. It barely stings."

She had used that excuse any number of times when they were children—after she'd fallen from her horse while racing him across the meadow, tumbling off a rock wall, or once when he'd had to fetch her out of a brawl with the stable lads.

It barely stings.

Brody didn't believe her now anymore than he had then. Instead he hurried her along the street, wrapping his arm around her and shielding her from the curious glances of the surrounding bystanders. "I think it is time we left London."

"I agree."

His gaze wrenched away from surveying the route before them. "You do?"

She nodded. Emphatically so. "Absolutely."

They rushed across the street and turned a corner. "You aren't going to argue?"

She shook her head. "Heavens no. We're closer than we think. First last night, now this? Someone wants me dead."

"You needn't sound so pleased."

"But don't you see, we are so very close to the answers. Besides, Howers ordered you to get me out of London, didn't he?"

Brody flinched. How had she known? The better question was, how could she not have known?

"No," he tried bluffing anyway.

"Truly? I'd be shocked if he hadn't—" She studied him again. "Besides, it is only logical. You would never voluntarily leave London unless you were ordered."

Brody shook his head. Not after the last few moments. Not when he'd seen Roselie being dragged away from him.

The depths of that moment, the harrowing emotions. He couldn't explain them. Couldn't fathom where they'd come from.

But they were there now. In his heart, in his gut. And he wouldn't rest easy until all of this was settled.

And Roselie was safe.

"I suppose he thought if the two of you indulged me in my mad plan, I'd go along."

"Roselie—"

"Never mind," she said, shaking her head, shaking off him. "I don't care what either of you think."

"You would if you knew what Howers said—" Brody told her as he opened the garden gate for her.

"Do I dare ask?"

"He said that if the duchess is alive, he'd give you the office next to his."

She grinned. "I shall like that one. It has a lovely view of the river."

"How ever do you know that?" Brody asked.

"Because my father always wanted that office."

Chapter 18

The next day, the dowager Lady Rimswell was well aware that every eye was turned on her when she entered Lady Rushbury's afternoon in.

Well, she did love to be the center of attention—it happened ever so rarely—though she wasn't too certain she wanted the attention now. For it had nothing to do with her and everything to do with her wretched daughter-in-law.

A point proved by Lady Rushbury's eager question. "How is the happy couple?"

"Oh, yes, how is the *new* Lady Rimswell?" came the chorus.

The now "old" Lady Rimswell blanched at the mention of her usurper, nor could she help herself, she sniffed at the very mention of Roselie Stratton. "Rather too happy, if you know what I mean."

A few of the matrons and the younger married ladies laughed behind their fans.

"Oh yes, young love, so very passionate," Lady Muscoates mused.

"So very noisy," Lady Rimswell replied. Oh heavens, had she just said that out loud? Gauging from the titters around the room, apparently she had.

"I think that was the origin of the Dower House," Lady Oxnam declared. "To spare one from such embarrassing and uncouth situations."

There was a round of knowing nods.

"Well, it will be quiet enough for the time being, thankfully," Lady Rimswell declared.

"How is that?" Lady Rushbury asked, tipping her head at Miss Taber to pour the new dowager a cup of tea.

Lady Rimswell took it gratefully, and straightened. But when she stole a glance at the saucer in her hand, she frowned. Dear heavens, the girl couldn't pour a proper cup. There was tea all over the saucer.

Wherever had Lady Muscoates found her?

She glanced up and realized she'd been asked another question. "Pardon?"

"How is it that you find yourself with a peaceful home again?" Lady Muscoates asked.

She sighed, and set aside her cup of tea. It was quite spoilt now. "Lord Rimswell came home yesterday and announced they were going on a honeymoon."

"A honeymoon?" Lady Oxnam shook her head. "I'm not all that fond of these foreign notions."

"I think it sounds quite romantic," Lady Muscoates told her.

"That all depends entirely on where they've gone," Lady Nafferton added with her usual authority. "Lord Nafferton was quite convinced that a shooting expedition in Scotland was the most romantic notion ever conceived." She huffed a bit. "I spent a fortnight scratching at midges."

There was a spate of laughter from around the room, and comparisons as to the most dreadful places in England where the various lords had dragged their lady wives on "romantic" wedding tours.

When a lull in the conversation arose, Miss Taber spoke up. "I don't think you ever said, Lady Rimswell, where the happy couple went?"

Certainly Lady Rimswell had never approved of Miss Taber.

She held a general horror of this fashion for *wards*, young ladies of questionable breeding and origins being paraded about good Society as if they belonged.

Where had the *happy couple* gone? Of all the impertinent questions. Well, it was none of her business, and so Lady Rimswell ignored her.

But even in that moment, she saw Lady Muscoates turn her gaze toward her, an intense interest there that sent an odd chill down her spine.

For some reason, the bruises on Roselie's wrists and the mark on her face flitted through the dowager's thoughts. It was merely an accident. At least that was what Bradwell had told her. Clumsy of them, what with Roselie being brushed by a passing carriage. Terribly careless of him not to be watching more carefully.

But it hadn't been that.

Lady Rimswell wasn't one for such things, but for some odd reason she knew Roselie's bruises hadn't come from an accident, an errant carriage.

Nor did she feel comfortable with the way Lady Muscoates kept watching her. Especially considering all the rumors about her and the Duchess of Ranworth's terrible *accident*.

Don't tell her a thing.

"Oh, yes, Lady Rimswell," one of the Nafferton sisters pleaded. Heavens, she could never tell those two nits apart. "Do tell," her twin added.

"I hardly know," she lied looking anywhere but at Lady Muscoates or that creature of hers.

"Lord Rimswell is such a sensible fellow," Lady Nafferton declared. "He is most likely taking his new bride on a tour of his estates so she can see what needs to be done to them."

At this Lady Rimswell flinched, for all the houses were perfectly appointed. She'd seen to it herself.

"Or the seaside perhaps," one of the unmarried young ladies suggested.

"Or perhaps Scotland, it is said to be quite nice this time of year."

"Oh no, the midges are dreadful!" Unwittingly, Lady Nafferton scratched at a long forgotten memento from her own honeymoon.

"You do know how to choose your honeymoons, Lady Rimswell," Brody told his wife as they stepped down from the carriage.

Before them rose the dark and imposing stones of St. Anne's Asylum, the front gates already tightly locked for the night, though the long summer day was just barely coming to a close.

This was the third and last of the remaining madhouses on Abigail's list. The first two places had turned out to be unlikely choices. Squalid, horrible houses.

"I believe it's too late to investigate this one," Brody told her. "At least for today."

Roselie shuddered as she looked beyond the cold, iron gates. "I don't think I'd want to venture inside there in the dark."

"Neither would I," he said with a laugh. Then he looked down the road toward the small village that had sprung up around the old abbey.

They walked in that direction while Solly followed them with the carriage. It felt good to stretch their legs after a long day of traveling. To be certain they weren't followed, Brody had instructed Solly to take as many turns as he could—and so they'd spent the last few days mostly ambling and roaming about the countryside.

He glanced back at St. Anne's and pursed his lips. Once they'd eliminated this one, how ever was he going to keep Roselie out of London? He supposed he'd come up with something then.

Once inside the local public house, Brody made arrangements with the landlord for rooms, while Roselie spoke to the landlady about having supper sent up and a meal for Solly.

When Brody came back to fetch her, she leaned close to him, "There is something you must do."

He grinned. "Remember we are in a public house. You can't be as loud as you like."

It took her a moment, but then it dawned on her what he was

suggesting and she elbowed him in the ribs. "Not that. Not yet. Not unless you do as I ask."

"Ask away, my love. My Rosebud," he teased, planting a kiss on her forehead.

"Do you see those three men over in the corner?"

"You want them to join us?" That earned him another jab in the ribs. He supposed if he didn't want to end up with a spate of bruises, he'd best stop teasing her.

"They work at St. Anne's." Roselie glanced back in that direction.

He saw immediately what she wanted. "I do believe their tankards need refilling."

Roselie smiled at him. "That is exactly why I married you, Lord Rimswell."

"My prestigious generosity?"

"Hardly that," she replied, her gaze fixed doggedly on the trio in the corner. Oh, it was like watching the inner workings of a clock, ever ticking away as the gears fit perfectly together. "I want you to get information from them."

"Yes, my dear, I know," he told her and signaled to the serving girl, and instructed her to fill the men's drinks including one for him. Once she'd gone to fill a pitcher, he turned to Roselie. "Go on upstairs and wait for me. This is decidedly a man's job."

She huffed out a breath, most likely at the rank unfairness of it all, but she could hardly argue with him. "If it is mentioned—" she began, unable to leave her fingers out of the pie.

He put another kiss on her forehead and nudged her slightly toward the stairs. "Go on. Upstairs." He felt it necessary to make sure she did just that. Didn't circle around the inn and try to listen in at the window or crease some other wrinkle into their plans. "I'll join you soon."

"And make sure to ask if—"

"Roselie, I know what I'm doing." When her brow furrowed, he leaned close and whispered in her ear. "Do you think I would return without a full accounting? Gads, you're worse than Howers."

"I'll consider that a compliment," she told him, still casting envious looks over at the trio. This was exactly the sort of task that Asteria had done so well, but now . . . "A full accounting, Brody, or you shall be sleeping in the water closet."

"Then I shall exceed your expectations," he promised, "for I am ever so fond of having you in my bed."

And if he wasn't mistaken, he thought for a moment that Roselie was blushing as she turned to retreat up the stairs.

Impossible minx.

Roselie climbed her way upstairs, glancing every few steps down at Brody as he made his way over to the trio of men.

Oh, bother! If only she had one of her Asteria gowns, she'd have the information she wanted in a thrice.

The serving girl was waiting upstairs by an open door. "This way, ma'am," she said. "'Tis the best room, just as your husband asked."

And surprisingly it was a lovely room with a grand bed.

She smiled at the girl, indicating that the room was to her taste, and the girl flitted quickly about, lighting a few candles to chase away the growing shadows of night, bobbed her head and said that if she needed anything to just call for her.

Roselie nodded absently, for she couldn't wrench her gaze away from the bed.

Everything was different now.

Very different.

It was one thing to go dashing through the streets of Seven Dials unscathed, but when she couldn't even walk the streets of Mayfair—in broad daylight. She huffed a sigh, her fingers going to her cheek where that lout had struck her.

She winced a bit as she touched the tender spot—but her hesitation was more for Brody.

What if he'd been hurt? Or worse . . .

It was one thing to risk her own life—but now her masquerade had put far more people in danger than she'd ever considered.

Captain Reddick. The Honorable. Madame St. Vincent.

Abigail.

Brody.

She sank into a nearby chair. "No."

Blowing out the candle next to her, Roselie wanted nothing more than to sit in the shadows. She felt safer there.

For she'd never been so exposed, so full of fear as she watched Brody launch himself at that tough.

He could have been killed.

It's why she'd agreed so readily to leave town—he thought it was to keep her safe, but as far as she was concerned, it was to keep him far from the danger closing in around her. *Around them.*

Besides, she was beginning to see that they were stronger together.

She wound her shawl tighter around her shoulders and glanced over at the bed again, then glanced down at her hand.

Where Brody's emerald ring sat. And the sight of it did something odd to her insides.

To her heart.

Oh, she hadn't expected this . . . How much he . . . well . . . what he meant to her.

Certainly she'd loved him from afar for years. Since childhood if she was being honest.

Been mesmerized by his kiss, enchanted by his touch. The way he'd looked at Asteria—with that hot, powerful need for possession—he'd turned that into an inferno the other night.

Yet as much as they were now good and bound together, their union felt all the more fragile.

There was so much more to lose. So much more that needed to be said.

Words that didn't come easily to her.

Like love.

She shook her head. She just couldn't love him. Not like that.

The cards you are dealt, the Honorable liked to say.

Of course, he always carried a spare or two up his sleeve to change what the Fates had handed him if necessary.

There was no changing this. How much she loved . . .

There was a scratching at the door.

She turned toward it. "Yes?"

The serving girl came in with a large tray. "Supper, ma'am. But I fear you might be eating alone. The mister, he appears to have found some new friends."

"Has he?" Roselie got up, the smell of beef luring her from her musings. Nor was she disappointed when she peeked under the covers. "Then it will be his loss."

The girl smiled and left, and Roselie sat down to eat, and did what she did best.

Puzzle out how one stopped oneself from falling in love.

But the only answer she could find was the most obvious.

You can't.

Roselie awoke with a start when she heard the door to the room open.

Her hand slid under the pillow, then swung out with her pistol, demanding, "Who goes there?"

A familiar chuckle greeted her.

Brody staggered into the room, closing the door behind him. "Some greeting." He tossed his hat on the chair, however it bounced off the cushion landed on the floor. He shrugged and continued toward her.

"What did you find out?"

He wandered past the tray and paused to lift one of the covers. *Tsk. Tsk.* "You, my dear Rosebud, are not a proper wife. I'm famished, and here, you've eaten my supper."

"It appears you drank yours."

Brody spun around and winked at her. "Not enough."

"Not enough, what?"

He took an unsteady step. "Not enough to make me forget how beautiful you are."

She pushed aside the quiet thrill that ran through her. Apparently words were quite easy for Brody right now. But still she had to know. "What did you discover?"

He heaved a sigh and circled around the bed. "That you will most likely have the office with the view before I will." He fumbled with his cravat for a moment and then gave up, his hands fisting to his sides.

She scrambled across the top of the bed to help him, swatting away his floundering attempts and unwound the elaborately tied silk herself. He smelled of brandy and ale and smoke, and grinned with a boyish delight as if he had found an untold treasure.

"You are much prettier than Wicks," he said, reaching up to brush aside the wayward strands of her hair.

"I am certain Wicks will be pleased to hear that." She paused and looked up at him, and oh, how her heart hammered, pressed at her to say the words, but she couldn't. Not now.

He seemed to sense her indecision. "Don't stop."

"Stop what?"

"Undressing me—"

Roselie shook her head. "Not until you tell me what you found out."

"Take off my coat," he told her taking a step back.

"What?"

"Take off my coat, and I'll tell you what you want to know."

Oh of all the wretchedly devious, wickedly charming things he could have said.

"That's blackmail," she shot back. "Hardly ethical for an agent of the Crown."

"I've been taking lessons." He nodded again at his coat. "Help me out of this or I won't tell you a thing."

Setting her jaw, Roselie climbed out of the bed, her hair tumbling around her shoulders, while her night rail fell like a whisper to her bare feet. "If I must."

And so she did, schooling him in his own game.

She slid his coat slowly from his shoulders, her hands lingering over the muscles in his shoulders, down his arms, while she laid her head against his chest, and just breathed in the scent of him. All too soon, his coat found the same fate as his hat. She took a step back, and looked at the fire in his eyes. "Tell me what I want to know."

"My newfound friends assure me that their establishment is genteel enough for my mother." For this was the ruse that they had come up with, that they were looking for a place to settle Brody's failing mother. He crossed his arms over his chest and grinned in that cheeky way of his.

"And?"

"Take off your night rail."

"*That* was not our deal." She crossed her arms over her chest. The devil take him.

"You simply asked what I discovered. You didn't ask for a full accounting." He winked at her. "If you want to hear more, take off your night rail."

So this was the game. He was playing with fire. Then again, so was she.

She slowly wound her hair up, and turned so her back faced him. "I'll need help."

He quickly obliged her, bending over and catching up the gossamer hem and slowly bringing it up over her head, his hands lingering over the curves of her bottom, rounding the fullness of her breasts, stealing kisses on her neck behind her ear as he lifted it up and over her head.

"I'm quite good at this, aren't I?"

Roselie wasn't quite sure she could breathe. "Yes, most skilled. I don't want to know where you learned these tricks."

He reached out, toying with another strand of her hair. "All part of the Home Office training."

"I hardly think Lord Howers would approve—"

"Can we not discuss Old Ironpants?" He teetered over to a

chair, and sat down, sticking his long legs out in front of him and crossing his boots. "Be a love and tug those off while I tell you about the duchess of St. Anne's."

"She's there? The Duchess of Ranworth?" Roselie hadn't quite believed it herself that they would actually find her, so she hurried over and knelt before him.

"Be a love." He nodded at his feet. "The boots?"

She grit her teeth, but got to work pulling the first one off.

"According to a rather singular fellow by the name of Mr. Ronald Jones, an attendant at St. Anne's, there is an elderly woman who the matron on rare occasions calls "Her Grace.""

Roselie stilled and looked up. "So we've have found her."

"We've found an old woman who thinks she's a duchess. And I would make a note that none of my new compatriots have ever met a duchess, so the lady in question could be a laundress for all we know."

Roselie tugged off the second boot. "What else did they say?"

"Only if you help me out of my shirt," he said rising again. She pulled it off in haste, but he caught her hand and pulled her close. "Come to me and I'll make it worth your while."

Now she definitely couldn't breathe—not with their bodies entwined so. As much as she wanted to know everything that had happened downstairs, she wanted nothing more than to fall back into the warm comforts of that bed and let Brody make love to her.

"Rosebud, come with me."

Oh, the way he whispered those words in her ear left her shivering with need. She didn't care what had transpired downstairs, not anymore, not in this fragile delicate moment.

"I never imagined this," he told her softly, pulling her closer still, and kissing her with some urgency.

The sort of quickly fired passion that spoke of need and want. And so much more.

The heat of his kiss rippled like lightning down to the tip of her toes—and he must have felt the same. For he caught her in his arms and carried her to the bed, where they fell into a pile of tangled limbs and kisses, and desires.

She helped him out of his pants, and pulled him atop her, opening up for him, which he obliged quickly, entering her and then pausing.

"Not like this, not tonight," he whispered in her ear, and then proceeded to slowly stroke her. His lips teased her and gently explored her. There was a poetry in the way he moved inside her, as if he were trying to say the words, that, like her, seemed stuck in their hearts.

Some time later, after the second or third time they'd teased each other to completion, she curled up to him and took his face in her hands.

"Thank you," she whispered, tracing her finger down the line of his jaw.

"For what?"

"For saving me the other day."

He shuddered. "If something had—"

"Nothing is going to happen to us," she told him, shivering happily and then drifting off to sleep.

But Brody felt a different sort of shiver. *No one can promise that.*

Chapter 19

𝒯he next morning, Brody and Roselie presented themselves to the matron of St. Anne's as Mr. and Mrs. Longton, who were looking for a place where Mr. Longton's mother might reside.

"For her own well-being," Roselie confided, as they followed the matron to the woman's office. While the previous night, the looming stone edifice of St. Anne's had seemed formidable, in the light of day, the old abbey was quite lovely, and the insides surprisingly well appointed and tidy.

The sort of place that might suit a duchess.

"We are newly married and my dear mother is having difficulties with the situation," Brody added. "During my father's life, she was quite amiable and manageable, even with her frailties and infirmities, but since his death last year, she's become a bit of a—"

"Burden?" the matron supplied, closing the door of her office and waving at them to take seats on the chairs before her grand desk.

Roselie sighed, trying to fold her hands in her lap and not look overly eager—but based on the information Brody had gleaned from his new friends, the duchess could be very close at hand. "Exactly." She hardly knew what to do with her hands, so she tugged at her gloves. "But we wouldn't want her to be placed close

to people who aren't . . . Oh, dear, how do I say this delicately?"
She looked toward Brody with a flutter of lashes and then back at
the matron. "Genteel. Yes, that's it. Genteel. Quality."

"I assure you, Mrs. Longton," the matron said, "the residents of
St. Anne's are of the highest order. They come from some of the
most respectable, dare I say, noble families in England. Though
we do like to keep those matters private." Her lips pursed together in a tight, uncompromising smile.

"Of course," Brody agreed. "We came here on a recommendation from one of my wife's relatives—a Lady Essex Marshom?
Perhaps you've heard of her?"

At this, the matron brightened, for here were clear signs that
Mr. and Mrs. Longton had prospects.

As in income and position.

Quickly, the woman launched into a long speech of how welcome the elder Mrs. Longton would be at St. Anne's.

Only half listening, Roselie's gaze strayed toward the windows
where outside a pair of servants carried a table and chairs out into
the garden. A maid followed with a cloth folded over her arm and
a basket. Quickly the table was set, and the tea tray placed just so.

And then to her delight, an older woman, leaning on her
cane, slowly ambled across the lawn. She carried herself with a
dignified grace. One might even say, like a duchess.

Roselie could barely contain herself.

"Mrs. Longton? Is there something the matter?" the matron
asked.

"I fear all this talk is giving me a terrible megrim," Roselie replied, pressing her fingers to her brow. She did her best to look
utterly forlorn.

"How you suffer, my poor dear," Brody told her, patting her
hand like the most concerned of husbands.

"Perhaps if I were to take some air," Roselie said. "Your garden
seems quite the refreshing spot."

"Indeed, please be my guest," the matron told her, nodding
toward the French doors that opened into the bowery.

And after Roselie had left, the matron looked at Brody, a know-ing tilt to her thick brows. She took off her spectacles and cleaned them carefully with a handkerchief. "Perhaps, Mr. Longton, it isn't your mother who needs a place to reside?"

"Yes, indeed, madame," Brody told her. "You see my predica-ment so clearly."

Roselie walked out into the garden, pretending to admire the roses in their first blush of bloom.

"Lovely, aren't they?" The older woman at the tea table asked her.

She smiled in return. "Yes, quite."

"Are you new here?" the woman asked. "You must be, for that gown is perfectly lovely, and most likely the latest stare."

"Yes, it is new, and thank you," Roselie said, glancing not at her new gown but around the gardens. "If you don't mind me saying, you've a lovely spot for tea."

The lady smiled, a hint of wistful regret to the turn of her mouth. "I suppose it is. I do hate to be so terribly informal, but might you join me? I don't often receive visitors."

"I most certainly will. Thank you for offering." Roselie sat down at the chair opposite the lady.

"All these years, I've had them bring me a second chair and now finally, it is going to be used," the lady confided. "I've always liked the potential it represented."

"Such a lovely notion," Roselie agreed. She itched to ask the woman who she was but she recalled every bit of advice she'd ever received.

'Tis a long game you're playing, my dear, the Honorable would often tell her. *Patience will always deal the perfect hand in the end.*

Roselie glanced back at the abbey where, inside the office, Brody appeared to be going over paperwork with the matron.

Bless his heart, he had the woman utterly engaged.

Roselie reached for the teapot and then glanced across the table at the woman. "Do you mind if I pour?"

"I'd be delighted," the woman said. "I always say there is much that can be learned about a young lady in the manner in which she pours tea."

"Agreed," Roselie told her. "It is said, 'A lady is defined by the manner in which she can pour tea with grace and dignity—'"

"'—and such a lady will never be turned away,'" her hostess finished, a delighted expression on her face. "Oh, I haven't heard Miss Emery quoted in ages."

"You went to Miss Emery's?" Roselie slanted a smile at the woman as she filled the lady's cup.

The woman nodded in approval at Roselie's skill. "I did indeed. Though it was the younger Miss Emery in my time." She held out the plate with the cakes, and Roselie took one.

Leaning across the table, Roselie told her, much as she would with Lady Howers, "Your Miss Emery is still keeping the place *up to the most exacting standards*," in the same lofty tones as their former teacher might use, earning her a bark of laughter from the lady. "While her niece, Miss Gemina Emery, is being trained in her place. You'll be pleased to know that Miss Gemina is a holy terror when it comes to seating charts and the proper folding of napkins."

The lady sighed with delight. "It is ever so good to know that some things never change."

"Indeed," Roselie agreed. "Oh, where are my manners? Both the Miss Emerys would have me cleaning silver for a week if they saw me now. Dear lady, I am Lady Rimswell."

This brought a furrow to the woman's brows. "Rimswell . . . Rimswell . . . Oh, I knew a Lady Rimswell once. But it was such a long time ago. And far be it from me to criticize others, considering my own grave sins, but she was, if I remember correctly, a most disagreeable creature."

Roselie grinned and reached for another cake. "She still is."

They both laughed.

From the garden walkway, several attendants had gathered, looking over at the pair as if they didn't know what to make of the situation. And when one of them left and went toward the matron's office, Roselie knew she didn't have much more time.

Her hostess seemed to hold the same understanding. She set down her tea cup and leaned across the table. "They will tell you that I am not in the full control of my faculties. But I am. I came here of my own volition and your arrival is a godsend, dear Lady Rimswell. We Miss Emery graduates must see to each other, no matter the situation. Don't you agree?"

Roselie nodded, her heart trembling with excitement.

"I would like to go home. Could I trouble you for your assistance to see me taken there?"

"But of course," Roselie asked her. "And where would that be?"

"Chessington."

The ancestral home of the Duke of Ranworth.

Roselie and Brody hurried down the front steps of Saint Anne's toward their waiting carriage, where inside the duchess sat happily ensconced.

"This is impossible. Utterly impossible," Brody told his wife, glancing back behind them. They'd had a terrible row with the matron when she discovered the true reason for their visit. And when the duchess had announced her intention to leave with Lord and Lady Rimswell, the matron had summoned her largest attendants.

"Do you have your pistol handy?" he asked as they got to the back of the carriage, where Solly was loading the last of Her Grace's trunks. The matron appeared to be formulating a plan, and her attendants looked more than happy to carry it out.

Brody's drinking companions, to be exact. They weren't any more pleased than the matron that they'd been duped.

"My pistol? Always," Roselie told him.

"We may have need of it," he advised.

Roselie glanced back at the door. "And here I thought your threat of summoning the magistrate had done the trick."

"Still, I suspect our dear duchess is taking a rather large stipend with her."

"We could send your mother as a replacement," Roselie offered.

"I doubt they would keep her."

"Now see here," one of the fellows called out as he began to muscle his way down the steps.

Solly came around from the back, small club in his hand and grinned, like he'd appreciate nothing more than an opportunity to break a few skulls—which worked to stall the man's forward progress. Yet after some urging from the matron, the other two joined their friend and seemed ready to risk the odds, until that is, Roselie heaved an irritated sigh, and just simply pulled her pistol out and pointed it at the first man.

"I fear I'm ever so clumsy with this," she said, smiling apologetically. "But I am not opposed to using it."

It was enough to send them all scurrying back inside the asylum.

"Have you considered that we might be taking the wrong woman?" Brody asked as she tucked her pistol away. "That your new friend is as mad as the matron says and isn't really the Duchess of Ranworth?"

"I believe she is the duchess."

Of course she would. "How?"

"She went to Miss Emery's," Roselie explained.

"So she says," he shot back, wagging his chin at the new occupant of their carriage.

"You weren't there. She complimented me on how I pour tea. And she knew about the back stairwell."

Brody was afraid to ask, but given the circumstances . . . "What has that got to do with anything?"

"Anyone who went to Miss Emery's knows about the back stairwell." Roselie paused for a second, before continuing her explanation. "The third step from the bottom creaks something terrible."

"And that's important because?"

"How ever does one sneak out if they don't know which step

to avoid?" She said this as both a matter of fact and as if he were a complete simpleton.

Of course Roselie would know how to sneak out of her Bath school. And apparently so did the Duchess of Ranworth.

The only thing that proved is that both ladies were lifelong troublemakers.

"Yes. Yes. But that doesn't prove she's the duchess." Brody was like Lord Howers in that respect. The word of a possible mad-woman was hardly something to rest his reputation upon.

"You want proof? She gave me this." Roselie thrust out her hand and opened it to reveal a small signet ring. It bore a familiar lion on the crest.

"That could be a fake," he persisted.

"You know whose crest that is. And it is her wedding ring. From the duke." Roselie glanced down at it. "This will gain us entrance."

Brody pulled off his hat and raked his fingers through his hair. "So you truly think you can beard the lion in his own den?"

"It is the only way." Roselie nodded to Solly and went toward the carriage door, but Brody reached out and caught her by the arm.

"He'll never go along with this. You are talking about treason. What makes you think he'll help us?"

Roselie straightened her shoulders. "He must. It is his duty."

"I should point out that most dukes consider their primary duty is to see to themselves, first and foremost."

"I think he's been doing that for long enough."

"Madness," Brody repeated two days later when they found themselves standing like beggars on the Duke of Ranworth's front steps. It had seemed like an eternity had passed since Brody had first rung the bell. He glanced back at the carriage where the duchess had decided to wait, then gave the bell a second hard tug so that it jangled loudly on the other side.

After another interminable wait, the sound of footsteps coming closer at an agonizingly slow pace could be heard, and finally the portal slowly opened a crack.

"Yes?" an ancient-looking butler intoned.

"Lord and Lady Rimswell to see His Grace," Brody told him.

"His Grace is not at home," the butler replied, with an air of resignation as if he had said as much to the hundred or so previous inquiries.

"Of course he is at home," Brody replied, tapping his walking stick to the hard stone of the front steps. "Now tell the duke we are here on a very pressing matter, my good man."

The butler straightened. "His Grace is not receiving guests."

"So the duke is at home," Roselie prompted as she stepped forward.

The butler's brows arched, becoming more imperious than cowed by this cheeky interloper. It was a scathing glance that had probably turned back more than one party.

But this was Roselie.

"So, if I am correct, your first statement about him not being home wasn't true," she pressed, glancing first at Brody, as if for confirmation, and then back at the butler.

The man's entire face puckered. Apparently he wasn't used to being questioned. Or countermanded.

"So I must conclude your second statement—that he is not receiving guests is also false. Now if you would, please tell the duke we are here to see him." Roselie dug into her reticule and pulled out a single object, then held it up for the man to see.

Her calling card of sorts. Or as the Honorable would say, *An ace up your sleeve, eh, gel?*

The man blinked and gaped. "Where did you get *that*?"

Brody made an impatient *tut tut*. "You know precisely where we got it," he told the butler. "Now tell the duke we request an audience."

The butler, bless his determined heart, reached out to take the ring, but Roselie was too quick for him and snatched her hand back. "Not until we see His Grace. I was instructed to give this to no one but him."

"But—"

Brody tapped his walking stick in a sharp tattoo. "My good man, we haven't got all day. Hurry along." And with that he pushed his way inside, towing Roselie along with him.

The butler, realizing that he wasn't going to be able to shoo them off with his usual haughty disdain, nodded for them to wait in the foyer.

After he left, Roselie glanced around and shook her head. "It's a tomb."

Brody nodded in agreement. "Damn horrible one now."

For indeed there were Holland covers on what furnishings there were. Dust coated everything. And in the rooms beyond there was nothing but bare walls and unpolished floors. Where were the gilded furnishings, the flotilla of servants, any signs of great wealth and position?

"It is as if the house has been whittled down to nothing," Brody said quietly.

"Blackmail perhaps?"

"Leave it to you to come to the most heinous conclusions," Brody teased. "But it would seem the Duke of Ranworth has not had an easy time of it as of late. And here we are, only to add to his troubles."

Again, Roselie glanced around and then shook her head. "You know, my father never liked him."

"My father wasn't overly fond of him either," Brody added. "Too proud. Dreadfully arrogant. Rather like his son."

Roselie shook her head. "Still, it is rather sad to see a noble family brought so low."

"They aren't the first," Brody said. "Nor probably the last." He leaned on his walking stick and nodded to her. "Even with that ace up your sleeve, how ever do you think you'll be able to convince him to help us?"

But before Roselie could reply, or even speculate for that matter, the answer came from behind them, by none other than the duke himself.

"What? And bring my family name any lower than I've already done? Never!"

Chapter 20

$\mathscr{B}$rody and Roselie followed the duke to what appeared to be the only furnished room left in the house. Leaning heavily on his cane, Ranworth took what must be his usual chair close to the grate.

Notably, he did not offer them seats, so they found themselves standing, while the butler fussed over the duke, laying a heavy shawl around the man's thin shoulders, and going to get a lap robe, but the old man waved him away and bid the butler to leave and close the door behind him.

Nor did Ranworth waste any time with them, getting directly to the point. "Well, you've intruded on my privacy, but since Bertram went to the trouble to let you in, I'll ask this once and then be done with you: what do you want?"

"Your Grace." Brody bowed and continued with his introduction, "I'm Lord Rimswell and this is my wife—"

"Rimswell?" The man huffed. "Never liked your mother." He wagged his chin at Roselie. "I know who you are. You're Wakefield's daughter. Must be."

"I am, Your Grace."

"You have your mother's features."

"Thank you—"

The man turned back to watching the coals in the grate. "But unfortunately it appears you've inherited your father's manners."

Brody couldn't help himself, he grinned at her. Roselie smirked back.

Nor was Ranworth done. "Half the fools in London wanted to marry your mother, you know. They all offered for her, but your rapscallion father seduced her with a basket of tulip bulbs, no less." The old man snorted. "Undone by tulip bulbs!"

"And they still bloom without fail every year," she told him, completely unfazed by his tone and manners.

The duke looked them both over and turned again to Roselie. "And all you managed was him? A baron. Your mother, at least, had the sense to hold out for a viscount—even if he was unworthy of her."

"I'm rather fond of him." Roselie rocked on her heels, hands folded behind her back.

The duke shrugged. "Women. Foolish creatures, the lot of you." When he was done with his mutterings, he turned back to Brody. "You haven't come here simply to harangue my poor butler and barge into my house just to exchange pleasantries. So let's get on with this." He coughed for some time, as if the expense of words had cost him, a rattle that spoke of the coming shadow.

It wasn't only the estate that was dying, but the duke as well. Once Ranworth had gathered himself together again, he continued, "What do you want? Money? Is that why you've come? If you think you'll gain anything from me, you've come to the wrong place. She's already taken everything."

"We have no desire for money, Your Grace," Roselie told him, moving closer and speaking in quiet tones. "We've come for the truth—"

"The truth?!" The old man exploded to life, pounding his cane to the floor, his knuckles white as he held it in a tight grasp. "You tell that blackmailing bitch I'll have no more of her. She's already taken enough from me."

Blackmail. There it was.

Roselie smiled slightly at her husband. *I told you so.*

But the duke's anger wasn't going to get them what they

needed, so Brody stepped forward. "Your Grace—" He tried to sound as calm as possible, for he was starting to wonder if the wrong Ranworth had been committed to St. Anne's. "We haven't come to blackmail you."

"Bah! You think you're the first pair to arrive on my doorstep and claim to have found him?"

"Him?" Brody and Roselie said at the same time. Roselie appeared as confused as he felt. Good God, was there yet another piece to this impossible puzzle of Roselie's?

"Well, whatever you think you've discovered, I won't hear it." And then suddenly the fire inside the man grew cold. He shuddered and tugged the shawl tighter around his shoulders. "Besides, I know she's behind all this. How I wish we'd never met—" He faltered to a stop and turned to gaze at the fire.

Roselie picked up the thread, quietly persistent. "Lady Muscoates. You wish you and the duchess had never met her."

The duke turned a cold gaze on Roselie. "Lady Muscoates . . . Is that what she calls herself now? That whore is no lady."

"I agree. But it is up to you to stop her." Roselie's firm, moral conviction prodded at the man.

And not in a good way.

He spared her another glance. "Oh, you think you're a smart one, Lady Rimswell, don't you? Probably are too smart for your own good. This business you've waded into will get you killed. You and your baron."

Roselie stepped closer. "Then it is your duty to help us."

"Duty?" It was probably the first time the duke had ever been told what he must do.

"Yes, your duty," she insisted.

"And why must I help you, you presumptive slip of muslin?"

"Your Grace, you are speaking to my wife," Brody told him, pulling Roselie aside and putting himself between her and the duke. "Remember yourself."

Ranworth wagged his finger at Brody. "Your wife is a meddling—" He glanced over at Roselie and huffed, shaking his head. After a moment, he pushed up from his chair and hobbled toward the door. "I'll have no part of this madness."

But Roselie wasn't finished. Hardly defeated. She followed after the duke with the tenacity of a terrier. "Like how your son's meddling sank the *Intrepid*? Killed every last man and boy on board."

The duke stilled. "No, I won't hear it."

"You shall," she told him with just as much arrogance as the duke. "And so will all of England if you don't do the honorable thing."

So much for not blackmailing the man, Brody mused as he watched Roselie fearlessly go after the Duke of Ranworth.

"You can't prove a word of this," the duke shot back. "Besides, this has nothing to do with me."

Roselie bristled. "Nothing to do with you? I beg to differ. Your son's treachery sank the *Intrepid* and countless other ships. Good British lives lost because he sold information to the French. Your heir, Your Grace. Your family's legacy."

"Ilford is not my heir," the duke shot back, and then, as if remembering himself, he clamped his lips shut.

Not his heir? Brody and Roselie gaped at each other. What the devil had they discovered?

The duke looked away from them, his cane shaking with the effort to keep him upright. "I won't help you. I can't." He stumbled back to his chair, waving off the silent help Brody and Roselie offered. His pride bruised, but unwilling to admit defeat.

As the duke sank back into his chair, the door opened, and Brody fully expected to see the butler arriving with some scavenged footmen, ready to toss them out.

But it was someone else. Someone who had obviously been listening at the door.

"You can and you will, Gordon," the Duchess of Ranworth told her husband. "It is time to do what we should have done years ago. Stop her. Stop them both."

*   *   *

With the arrival of the duke's long-lost wife, Roselie and Brody backed away while the duchess knelt before her husband, hers hands clasped in his, eyes wet with tears.

Both hers, and his.

"How can this be? What treachery is this?" Ranworth asked as his shaking hand reached out and touched his wife's hair as if he didn't quite believe she was real, as if this was more villainy. "I saw them pull you from the lake. I *buried* you."

The duchess tipped her head into his hand and smiled at him. "I fear I played a terrible deceit upon you. But believe me, I did it to save you. Restore you. I had hoped . . . that it might be enough . . . to save even Ilford."

And for a time the two stared at each other, silently letting the years that had separated them fall away.

"I suppose you have told them all," Ranworth said to his wife, wagging his chin at Brody and Roselie.

"No, not everything," she replied, trying to rise to her feet. Brody rushed over to assist her and when she finally stood on her own, she patted his hand fondly. "But they deserve to know the truth."

"Do I? Do I deserve to know how is it you are alive?" the duke asked in a weary voice.

"Yes. But the entire story needs to be heard so they will understand as well," she told him.

Brody had retrieved a comfortable chair from across the room and set it alongside Ranworth's so that the duchess might sit beside him. She sank into the cushions gratefully.

After a long pause, she began.

"We met Lady Muscoates when we were still quite young. Simone was new to London—her husband was an attaché to the French ambassador. There had been some scandal about her back in Paris, so when her husband died suddenly, she wasn't in a position to return home. Then I made my first mistake by ignoring the gossip swirling about her and invited her to come live with us."

The duke picked up the tale. "It is my fault as well," he said. "At first, I saw no harm. She made you happy, and when the two of you became inseparable I didn't have the heart to send her away. Then again, she was a pretty thing, witty, charming, a bit risqué, well, French, I suppose, and so it was to be expected." He looked away for a moment. "It made the disappointment in our union more bearable."

Roselie could see the flash of confusion on Brody's face. She leaned over and whispered, "No children, remember?"

He nodded as the duchess continued, "We'd been married for fifteen years and had no issue to show for it. Not even a bit of hope."

"Not for a lack of trying," the duke said with a rare bark of humor. But just as quickly he turned somber again. "We'd sought the help of doctors, midwives, chemists . . . a more horrid collection of charlatans you'll never find. We despaired of ever having a child, let alone an heir."

The duchess sighed. "So you might understand why Simone became the light in our darkness and for a time, she brought great joy to our lives."

"For a time." The duke huffed a bit. "I should have seen how she was the most devious one of them all. Oh, she was never completely disgraceful, but you could always imagine how she might be . . ." He paused and looked away. "Then one night, I found out how far she was willing to go. I'd consumed a bit more brandy than I should've, and then I imagined too much."

The duchess nodded and glanced away as well, but the slight turn of her lips and the sadness to her eyes spoke of forgiveness.

"You took her to your bed." Roselie said in her usual straightforward manner.

"The only one taking was her. She came into my bedchamber, knowing full well I was tanglefooted and top heavy." The duke heaved a sigh. "But I shouldn't make excuses. It was my fault."

They all sat in silence for a time, weighing this terrible confession. After a few moments, Brody's hand reached for Roselie's and he squeezed her fingers.

Only you, my love. Always.

She slanted a thankful glance at him.

Eventually the duke continued, "I wasn't the best of husbands, as you might imagine, but I never . . . well, never had done *that*. It was rather a point of pride. At least until that devious cat came crawling into my bed."

The duchess rose to his defense. "Simone knew exactly what she was doing."

"Then—" Ranworth tried but couldn't continue.

"She was pregnant," Brody said, even as the pieces fell together for Roselie.

What had the duke said before? *Ilford is not my heir.*

The whole ugly truth rose before her. Oh, heavens, this was far worse than she'd ever imagined.

Ranworth snorted again. "Yes, full of my child, and full of plans as well. A grand deception."

"An opportune solution to our failure. My failure," the duchess added.

Roselie reached out and patted the lady's hand.

The duke picked up the story again. "What else was there to do? Here was the child we'd longed for. The heir to take away my younger brother's smug hopes. For you see, he was my heir apparent, and standing behind him were his four healthy sons. He'd always been my father's favorite, and he made no bones about it that one day the title and line would pass through him. It had been a dagger in my heart for years. And here was an heir to finish those hopes—not that time didn't do that anyway."

"What do you mean?" Roselie asked.

"My brother died, and one by one, so did all his sons."

"Save for Edmund," the duchess added.

"Yes, Edmund. His second son. He went to sea ages ago, and I've never been able to find him. If he were found, he would be my heir."

"Instead, Lady Muscoates bore your child," Roselie said to the duke, nudging him back to the story that needed completing. For here were all the missing pieces, and now that she was so close to finding the answers, she was determined to put in place every fact.

The duke huffed a bit. "And a son, to boot. And for all appearances, my heir. At the time, it was the perfect solution."

The duchess tipped her head in concession. "Yes, Simone and I had gone to a small village in the north, where no one knew us. I posed as her sister, and she a widow. After the baby was born, Simone returned to London and married Lord Farcet, and I returned here to Chessington with the baby. For a time, all was well, until Farcet died, his brother inherited and sent her packing."

"So she returned," Roselie said, charting the line of events.

"Oh yes, she came back," Ranworth said, bitterness and venom chilling his words. "Bad pennies always do. She made her threats, demanded money. And to my unending shame, I gave it to her."

"She was briefly married to Lord Bramber, but he perished rather quickly as well, just as all his money had." The duchess cast a significant look at them.

"You think she—" Roselie couldn't say the words—*murdered them.*

"I have no doubts," the duchess said with utter conviction.

Roselie sat back in her chair, shaking her head. So many lives lost to this woman's villainy—but why?

The duchess continued. "When she married Muscoates we thought that would be the end of her. He had enough money to satisfy her greed, and he gave her an utterly lofty and respectable position in Society. So if in the rare instance that she decided to reveal the truth, as she'd threatened to do in the past, she'd be ruined as well."

The duke nodded in agreement. "Muscoates was a terrible stickler. He'd cozen no such scandal attached to his name, and if a word of it came to light, he'd have cast her aside without a second thought. Her scheming days appeared to be at an end."

"So we thought ourselves quite safe," the duchess said. "Or

so we believed, until Muscoates died and it was discovered his estate was bankrupt. A series of bad investments."

"Am I the only one who sees a theme here?" Brody asked. "I can see one husband dying unexpectedly, but three?"

"Yes, quite," the duke said in agreement.

Both men shuddered.

"So after Lord Muscoates died, what happened then?" Roselie prodded.

"Here she came, arriving on our doorstep, trunks and bills for expenses in hand," the duke told her.

"Not that this was a surprise," the duchess said with resignation. "She was well past an age to trap another husband."

"That, and given her record—" Brody added.

"Exactly," the duke said with a nod. "No one would have been fool enough to enter into such a bargain with her." He paused. "And she knew it as well, so she'd devised a new plan—claimed she'd found the midwife and nursemaid from up north, that she had signed affidavits from them, capable of exposing Ilford as illegitmate. She'd ruin my only heir, my very name, the future of my line."

"Ilford," Roselie and Brody said together.

"Yes. Ilford," the duke said, spitting out the name, his gaze narrowing. "She knew I'd go to any length to avoid the title going into abeyance. But then she went too far. She threatened the duchess." He looked away and said quietly, "I thought she'd killed you." He looked away. "At least until a few minutes ago."

"Yes, well, I had rather hoped that with me gone it would be enough to stop her."

"So you faked your death?" Roselie grappled for the one thing. "*Why?*"

"Insurance, of sorts," the duchess replied. "With me gone, she'd have no leverage. She could tell her tale, but without me there, her story would sound like nothing more than jealous, vile lies. There had always been gossip about her place in our household—I wasn't such a fool that I didn't know that. So I thought that if it

appeared that I had taken my own life, committed such a grievous act while she was here at Chessington, there would be enough
questions, and better yet, rampant speculations as to her part in
it." She turned to her husband. "I am so sorry for what I did. But I
thought without me, at least you would be free of her. Especially
after Ilford—" The duchess choked up and looked away.

"What did Ilford do?" Brody asked.

"He followed Simone here. Confronted us," the duke replied.
"It was evident she'd wormed her way into his confidence, so
I told him the truth. Warned him of what she had planned. I
thought it would keep him safe. That he'd see her for what she
was. To my shock, he already knew. Then he dared to call me
an old fool. He knew his value, his place and just like her, took
advantage of the opportunity." Ranworth shook his head. "He
even had the audacity to demand an increase in his quarterlies.
The very nerve!"

The duchess reached over and caught hold of her husband's
hand, as if to anchor him to her. "As it happens, there was an old
beggar woman who had died in the woods that week. Bertram
asked me what was to be done with her body, and I seized my opportunity. We filled her coffin with rocks and had it buried, and
then dressed that poor woman in my gown, weighted the pockets
down with rocks, and late that night, I deliberately had a desper-
ate row with Simone and Ilford—a loud row, then went out for a
walk, and never came back. Meanwhile, Bertram threw that poor
woman's body over the bridge. I knew that by the time anyone
found her, or rather thought they had found me, she would be
unrecognizable, only identifiable by the dress."

"It worked." The duke gazed at her again as if he wasn't even
still sure that she was truly here. His eyes shone with regrets.
Anger. But mostly, regrets.

"Not the way I hoped," the duchess mused.

"I wouldn't say that," the duke told her. "With you gone, I had
nothing else to lose. I grew determined to find Edmund, and used
every last shilling I had in that endeavor. To see the title pass to

the true heir and foil every single one of Simone's schemes. But I fear that is a lost cause as well."

"How so?" Roselie asked.

"He cannot be found. He sailed to India and hasn't been heard of since. Not a single agent or solicitor has been able to locate him."

Roselie sat up. "What if we were to help you?"

"Help? How?" The duke asked, once again wary.

Even the duchess appeared to be at a loss as to what could be done.

"Find your heir," Roselie told him firmly, with the sort of conviction that made one believe she could actually do it. "We shall see to it all, Your Grace. You have my word."

"Your word, Lady Rimswell?" The duke shook his head.

"Upon my father's grave," Roselie told him. "Assist us with our endeavor now, and in return once the war is over, we shall use all the resources of the Home Office and my father's contacts in the Foreign Office to find your heir."

The duke barked a laugh. "You have some cheek, Lady Rimswell! For all you are your father's daughter, what do you think you can do when the best men in London have failed?"

Hardly cowed, Roselie smiled at the man. "I managed to find your duchess."

Now it was the duchess's turn to laugh. "She has you there, Gordon."

Ranworth's jaw worked back and forth. Then he turned to Brody. "Rimswell, help me to my writing desk. Then tell Bertram to fetch the vicar. I want the man to witness something, so there will be no question of its authenticity. Ever."

"You've just added to our obligations," Brody said as they walked down the front steps of Chessington to their waiting carriage. Solly sat in the driver's box frowning like a gargoyle. "How are we to ever find Ranworth's long-lost heir?" he asked as he helped her inside the carriage.

Roselie grinned at him. "We found the duchess. How hard can

one heir be to discover? Besides, we still have a traitor to catch and a war to win." She settled into the seat. "As the Honorable always says, *One card at a time.*"

Brody shook his head and followed her inside, taking the seat beside her. "I agree with the duke—you are impossible, Lady Rimswell."

"Thank you." She hardly thought it an insult.

"Now that we have all this," he said, patting the packet of papers the duke had entrusted to them, "what are we to do next?"

"I haven't the least notion," she confessed.

"That's hardly the answer I thought I'd get," he told her, as they rolled down the driveway. Almost immediately they came to the bridge and Brody glanced over at her. "Do you think this is—"

"The spot? I do indeed." Roselie felt a chill run down her spine. For this must be where Bertram had carried out the duchess's grisly plan.

"Hardly looks so tragic today," Brody remarked.

No, not in the least. It was almost disappointing that the duchess had chosen such a bucolic scene. Trees lined the lake, the sunlight sparkled across the water, and a pair of local lads stood at the edge fishing.

One of the boys had just cast out his hook and when it hit the placid water, it sent ripples across the surface in ever-widening circles, and almost immediately he began to pull at his line—for he'd quickly hooked an eager fish.

"Should ask him what he's using for bait," Brody muttered, more to himself.

Bait. Roselie sat up. In that instant, she knew exactly what needed to be done.

"Do you still fish?" she asked him. For they had spent many hours in their childhood trying to catch trout in his father's lake.

"On occasion," he answered, glancing over at her. One brow rose with a bevy of questions she suspected he had no desire to ask.

Bother, he knew her too well, for he could see she was concocting a plan. A mad one, even she would concede.

Roselie smiled. "And what is the best way to catch a wily trout?"

"The right fly," Brody replied slowly, suspicion wiggling in his words like a worm on the hook. "The right bait."

"All we need is to find the most irresistible bait in London," Roselie told him leaning back in her seat. "I'm thinking a packet ship full of gold and a rather dashing captain, which we already have."

"I highly doubt the navy is going to give us a packet ship or loan us the gold to go in it," he pointed out.

"But we do have a very handsome captain."

His expression went from wary to horrified as he realized where this was going. He twisted so he faced her. "You mean to use Captain Hathaway as bait?"

"Miss Taber has shown a particular fondness for the captain," Roselie pointed out.

"Have you considered that the captain may be their next target?"

"I have high hopes that he is," Roselie replied. "Why, he's the perfect sort of braggart who might unwittingly be seduced by a pretty lady."

"I doubt Hathaway would find your description very flattering," Brody said with a laugh, leaning back in his seat. "Though I imagine his brother Chaunce would agree with you utterly."

"Given the captain's excessive amount of pomposity, I do believe he'll recover quite quickly."

"If this mad plan of yours doesn't get him killed in the process."

"I have no intention of seeing the captain harmed," Roselie told him in all certitude.

Brody perked up. "Why is that? Do you harbor a certain fondness for him?"

Roselie laughed. "Hardly! But I have grown rather fond of his dear sister, Harriet, and I would so hate to lose her regard over the matter. I have every hope that we shall become the best of friends in the years to come."

Chapter 21

"My lady," Peakman intoned, "you asked to be notified when his lordship returned and I do believe the carriage has just arrived."

The dowager Lady Rimswell set aside her embroidery and hurried to the front door. She stood front and center when Peakman opened it to admit her son and that woman.

She just couldn't think of Roselie Stratton as her son's bride. His wife. The new Lady Rimswell. And look at her! All blushing cheeks and smart looks cast about the entryway—just calculating how she was going to change everything.

The dowager just knew it. But right now, she had a more pressing matter.

"There you are!" She caught her son by the arm and hauled him away from that strumpet's side. "I was beginning to think you'd never return. I am at my wit's end." She paused and turned her cheek just so.

It was ever so with Bradwell. Leopold had always known how to greet her properly and promptly.

"Where else would we go?" Bradwell teased as he placed a hasty peck upon her cheek. "And whatever has you in such a coil?"

Besides having to tolerate that creature in my house, she resisted saying. Instead, she went directly to the most pressing matter.

"You know, Bradwell, that I am never one to complain, but that dreadful Lady Muscoates has been here every day inquiring as to your welfare. I have had to make her welcome because"—she turned a wry eye on Roselie—"that dreadful woman claims to be a particular friend of your wife."

The dowager sniffed and raised her nose.

"I'm hardly that," Roselie said, all blithe and unapologetic, as she handed her hat and gloves to Peakman.

"And you say she's called every day?" Bradwell asked, his gaze narrowing with concern.

At least he had the good sense to see the impropriety of such company. Too bad he hadn't shown more sense when it came to taking a wife.

"When do you think she'll return?" Roselie asked.

"She and that dreadful ward of hers expressed their intentions of returning tomorrow for my afternoon in, with the express hopes you would be returned by then. I tried to make it clear they weren't welcome, as if one can discourage such people to stay away. I have been deluged by riffraff and low company ever since—" She didn't finish the sentence. She was too much of a lady for that.

Ever since you came into this house.

But what did one expect of a Stratton? Oh, she'd seen the sorts they gathered around themselves—foreigners and country people. And their servants! Starting with that dreadful Mrs. Pratt. *La!*

The dowager shuddered. She'd have to pull her son aside and have a word with him about seeing that woman removed from the house. Why, she suspected the dreadful creature was smoking his cigars.

But in the meantime . . .

"I won't have it, Bradwell. I won't have such persons in this house. Leopold would never have tolerated such low associations."

Bradwell turned and faced her. "Then it is a good thing he isn't here, for I fear you will have to bear her company one more time," he told her. He turned back to his wife. "Tomorrow? Do you think that is enough time?"

"It has to be. Do you think you can get Captain Hathaway here?"

"I'll do my best."

Captain Hathaway? The dowager pressed her lips together. Oh, this was going too far. And she told him so.

"The Hathaways?" The dowager shook her head. "I've never approved of them. I don't know what to make of the company you are keeping, Bradwell." His mother sniffed again, shot a censoring glance at Roselie, as if this was all her fault, hoping he would finally see the truth.

Behind him, Roselie was fidgeting and muttering. "—there is always St. Anne's."

Whatever that meant!

But to her dismay, Bradwell remained unmoved. Instead he quite lectured *her*.

"It is very important, madame," he began, "that Lady Muscoates is made to feel welcome just this once more. And then I promise you, she shall never set foot in this house again."

That was hardly good enough, but she supposed she had no choice in the matter.

Too bad she couldn't convince him to say the same about his wife.

For the first time ever, the dowager's afternoon in could be called a stunning success. The news that Lord and Lady Rimswell had returned from their hasty honeymoon had swept through Mayfair like a winter gale and brought all the necessary players to Roselie's carefully set stage.

She stood in the doorway and looked over the crush of ladies who had arrived early—if only to get the best seats. Lady Nafferton and both her daughters, Lady Essex, Miss Manx and Lady Roxley. On the far side of the room sat Mrs. Rowland, Roselie's mother, and several others, including and most importantly, Lady Muscoates and Miss Taber.

"For Abigail," she whispered to herself, before she swept into the room with a grand smile on her face.

"There you are, Lady Rimswell," the Countess of Roxley said, patting a chair next to hers.

The others in the room extended their greetings, including Lady Muscoates and her ward. Their polite salutations sent a chill down her spine.

She'd barely settled into her chair when the conversation began anew. The dowager sniffed, nose in the air, lips set in a disapproving line.

Roselie soon found out why.

"As I was saying," Lady Muscoates announced, "I fear I've heard some terrible news from . . ." Her hand fluttered about a bit as if trying to retrieve a name from thin air, and when that failed, she shrugged as if the purveyor of this news was hardly worth noting. "Well, I had it directly from a very respectable source that Lord Rimswell was in an altercation the other day—right here in Mayfair." She shook her head. "Whatever do you make of such a thing? I never thought one would find gentlemen brawling in the streets."

This last part was posed toward Roselie, but it was the dowager who waded in first.

"My Bradwell?" the dowager said in an icy voice. "As in my son? Impossible." Her tone said very clearly the subject was not to be continued.

So of course it was.

"An altercation? How alarming!" Lady Nafferton declared. "I was just saying this very morning to Lord Nafferton that one hardly dares to go out anymore."

"And yet she continues to dare . . ." Lady Roxley muttered under her breath.

Roselie coughed to keep from laughing.

"I do hope dear Lord Rimswell was not harmed," Pansy Nafferton said to Roselie. It was both an inquiry and a hook tugging for more information.

"I don't really recall—" Roselie began, trying to demure, however she was undone by her nemesis all too easily.

"You should, for it was reported that you were there as well," Lady Muscoates continued.

All eyes turned toward her, and Patience Nafferton, ever her dearest friend, said, "Oh my, Roselie! Is that a bruise on your face?"

Without thinking, her hand went to her cheek. Bernie had done her best to cover the purple hues with cream and powder, but it was still faintly discernible.

Forcing a smile on her face, she turned to Lady Muscoates. "Oh! You must be speaking of that terrible misunderstanding. Goodness, it was nothing but a trifle. I am ever so clumsy. I got brushed by a coach. I was so lost in telling Lord Rimswell the most enchanting *on dit*—I don't even recall what it was I was telling him—but in my distraction, I failed to realize there was a carriage coming. I fear his lordship and the driver had words, but it was no brawl." She smiled at everyone. "How these things become far more than they ever were, I can't imagine."

"But I distinctly heard—" Lady Muscoates pressed, but she was interrupted by the arrival of another pair of guests. Brody and Captain Benedict Hathaway.

Right on schedule.

The captain came in with a flourish, making a beeline for his sister, Lady Roxley, and giving her a kiss on her cheek, and then giving a flirtatious greeting to Lady Essex, who both flushed and gave the man a good rap on his arm with her fan.

"Benedict Hathaway, you are ever a rogue!" she declared, though it was obvious she was tremendously fond of him.

Then the good captain made a grand show of taking up one lady's hand. "My dear Miss Taber, I had so hoped, so desired to see you again."

As his lips brushed against the tip of her gloved fingers, both the Nafferton sisters sighed loudly with envy.

Brody chuckled slightly, earning him a wry glance from his mother. Still, he continued, "I fear, my good captain, that I must leave you in the company of my mother and her guests—"

"What is this, Bradwell? You cannot leave," his mother protested.

"I fear I must," he told her, told all of them. "I would stay in such graceful and lovely company but I have an errand of the utmost importance to see to."

Brody bowed and was about to make his leave, when Roselie stopped him, saying, "Oh yes, must you go?" After all, she had a part to play as well.

"Yes, indeed," the dowager added. "Bradwell, can't you see we have guests? I'm certain your errand can wait."

Brody went to his mother and bussed her on the cheek. "No, I fear not. Mr. Sutton is expecting me, and I did promise the duke, when we took our leave of him, that I would deliver his papers promptly after I returned to London."

Brody's announcement did exactly as they had suspected, for the mention of "Mr. Sutton" and "the duke" caught the attention of every pair of ears in the room.

"Mr. Sutton?" Lady Wakefield asked. She paused for a moment and glanced around the room, "Roselie, isn't that Miss Sutton's father?"

"Oh yes, I'd almost forgotten Miss Sutton," Lady Nafferton exclaimed. "That's the solicitor's daughter you helped marry above her station." She glanced around the room, her nose pinched with dismay. "From Lincoln's Inn Fields to Mayfair. I for one never approve of such matches."

Mostly because they left far fewer choices for her own unmarriageable daughters.

"My apologies, but I mustn't keep the man waiting," Brody told them. He pressed a kiss to his wife's brow, and whispered for only her to hear, "Good luck."

After Brody had left, it was Lady Essex who paved the way for Roselie to drop her *on dit.*

"Isn't Mr. Sutton the Duke of Ranworth's solicitor?" Lady Essex asked.

"Indeed," Roselie told her. Picking up the teapot and pouring tea for Captain Hathaway as if Brody's visit to the solicitor on the duke's behest was a normal course of business.

"Why ever is Lord Rimswell visiting him?" Lady Essex pressed. "I thought he used Mr. Hardell's services. He isn't thinking of changing solicitors, is he? Not to question Mr. Sutton's skills, but I've always found Mr. Hardell to be a most excellent source of assistance."

"Oh, no, nothing like that!" Roselie told her, shaking her head slightly. "It is only that His Grace asked Lord Rimswell to carry some very important documents to London and to see them placed by his own hand directly into Mr. Sutton's care." She leaned forward a bit, as if about to impart something she shouldn't, something very confidential. "It is actually a rather sad business."

Lady Nafferton made a *tsk tsk*. "Of course it is a sad business when one's heir turns out to be a common criminal."

"That would be true indeed, if Lord Ilford was actually the duke's heir." Roselie sipped her tea and let that little hook drop into the room.

The fish bit quickly.

"Not his heir? How ever is Ilford not the duke's heir?" Lady Nafferton asked, as if she'd never heard anything so foolish in her life.

Roselie sat back in her chair, saucer and cup cradled in her hand, and smiled. "I abhor gossip, simply abhor it, but it isn't like this isn't going to be nosed about soon enough." She sighed, then said, "The duke has disavowed and disinherited Ilford. Well, Ilford no more. Heavens, I don't know what to call him, since apparently he is not legitimate."

"Not . . ." Lady Nafferton sputtered, glancing first at her innocent daughters, then at the rest of the company. She was caught between her need to know every detail and propriety. It was obvious which was going to win out.

"How ever can that be?" Lady Essex demanded. "How ever can that be proved?" She had none of Lady Nafferton's concerns.

Roselie peered over her cup. "Well, by the duchess of course."

Given the shocked expressions around the room, Roselie suspected that by next week, her mother-in-law's afternoon in would rival Lady Gosforth's Thursday gatherings in notoriety.

"Lady Rimswell, that can hardly be. Her Grace is no longer with us." Lady Muscoates smiled gently at Roselie as if she were merely reminding her that she only wanted one lump of sugar in her tea, and not two.

"Is she not?" Roselie tipped her head just so, glancing about the room. "She seemed quite in the pink when Rimswell and I took our leave of her at Chessington." She smiled as she looked about the room, at the collection of shocked expressions, no one more shocked than Lady Muscoates, who shifted back and forth and looked ready to bolt for the door.

Only the Countess of Roxley grinned back at Roselie, as if to say, *Well done, well done.*

"But she is dead," Lady Nafferton insisted, most stubbornly. "Her obituary was in *The Lady's Magazine.*" Which apparently made it as indelible as scripture, for heads nodded around the room. "Why it brought a tear to my eye when I read those lines . . . *lost so tragically.*"

Then the matron shot a disapproving glance toward Lady Muscoates, for everyone in the room had heard the suspicions about her part in the duchess's accident.

The lady sat up straighter, her dark gaze fixed on Roselie, as if calculating both her exit and her revenge.

"Hardly a tragedy for Her Grace," Roselie told one and all, "simply a case of mistaken identity."

Lady Essex rapped her cane to the floor. "*Harrumph!* How ever can a lady's demise be a mistake? I will have my answers."

Most likely so she could spread this amazing *on dit* from one side of Mayfair to the other.

Roselie proceeded to explain how the Duchess of Ranworth's illness had forced the poor lady to seek sanctuary at St. Anne's, seeing it as a kindness to let everyone think her dead.

"And now the duke has enlisted Lord Rimswell to find his true heir, which shouldn't be a problem, since he did such an excellent job of locating Her Grace for him." Roselie glanced up at Captain Hathaway. "It is so fortunate that Captain Hathaway is leaving so soon and can carry Lord Rimswell's entreaties far afield."

Now all eyes turned toward the handsome naval officer.

"You're leaving?" Pansy Nafferton pouted.

Patience wasn't about to be left out. "But certainly you will return very soon?"

"I don't know when I'll return," the captain replied. "I'm not even supposed to be nosing it about that I'm leaving. Shame on you, Lady Rimswell." He wagged a finger at her, and then shrugged at his audience.

"Oh my, I forgot that your departure was supposed to be a secret." Roselie pressed her lips together and hoped she appeared as if she wished with all her heart that she could take those words back.

Which she wouldn't, not for all the tea in China, for it appeared she had caught the attention of Miss Taber.

"Ah! I was reading in the papers something about a gold shipment . . ." Lady Roxley said in her usual forthright manner.

"And as my sister, you should know that I cannot speak of such matters," Captain Hathaway scolded.

"I hope it isn't too presumptuous of me to ask when you are leaving, Captain?" This question came from Miss Taber, a flutter of lashes and flash of interest. "I had rather hoped to dance with you tonight at Almack's."

Not to be outdone, Pansy Nafferton hastened to add, "And I as well."

He glanced around the room. "Since there hardly seem to be any French agents about, I can assure you both that I will be happy to oblige you, for I do not set sail until just before dawn—so it seems I will have time for a dance or two." His gaze strayed from the sofa where the Nafferton sisters sat to the spot held by Miss Taber.

"That is most excellent news, Captain Hathaway," Lady Nafferton said, smiling at her daughters, not seeing in the least that the man's attentions had wandered elsewhere. "Do you mean to go out and harry the French, sir?" The lady paused for a moment and glanced over at Lady Muscoates. "No offense meant, my dear lady."

"None taken," Lady Muscoates replied. "But I believe there will be little harrying done by Captain Hathaway, for don't you sir, sail a packet ship?" She glanced about the room. "As I understand it, while a packet is a fast ship, it is not meant for battle, so the captain is hardly in danger of fighting."

Captain Hathaway straightened and smiled, a devil-may-care glance. "As it is, I sail far too fast for any ship to catch me, madam. But never fear, I'll fight if I must—especially with a hold full of the King's gold beneath my feet."

Chapter 22

"I have this well in hand, gentlemen," Captain Hathaway told them as he straightened, rocking on his boot heels, and surveying the crush of ladies and matrons and Corinthians streaming into another Wednesday evening at Almack's.

They—Brody, Chaunce and Captain Hathaway—had gathered in the alleyway across the street from Almack's to finalize their plans. Meanwhile, Roselie and Miss Manx had taken their places in the grand ballroom, while the Honorable and Solly waited with the horses and carriage on a nearby street.

Now it was all up to Captain Hathaway, who seemed a little too confident as to what needed to be done. Especially when Lady Muscoates and Miss Taber arrived.

Chaunce tried to give him a bit more advice, but his younger brother brushed him aside.

"I know what I'm supposed to do," Benedict told him, taking an arrogant stance. "I'm to let that little bundle of ribbons over there"—he nodded at Miss Taber, a perfect vision of feminine frailty in a pale pink gown—"seduce me into telling her all my secrets."

"Yes, but—" his brother began.

This was met with a hasty wave. "No buts about it. Leading ladies astray is my specialty." Then he paused and looked from

Brody to Chaunce. "Just to be clear, there won't be any hue and cry over this. Demands from her guardian that I actually marry the chit?" The captain's gaze narrowed.

Apparently Benedict wanted to be very clear on that point.

"No, no," his brother said, shaking his head. "Even if she cried foul, no one would hold you accountable. We'd reveal her to be a fraud and she'd be cast out. Just remember, we don't even know who she is—the real Miss Taber died five years ago."

A fact Roselie had discovered during a quick visit to Lady Howers. Where she'd found out such a fact, Roselie hadn't been able to determine, but one never questioned Lady Howers's information—it was more infallible than her husband's.

Chaunce got straight to the point. "Don't be an idiot, Benedict. We have no idea who that *Miss Taber* might be. Dallying with that bit of muslin over there might be worse than marrying a girl from home. She could be Agnes Stakes all over again."

Brody had no idea who Agnes might be, or what the devil the woman had done—though he'd once heard some nonsense about a curse that hung over Chaunce's home village of Kempton, but obviously it was enough to get his younger brother to see his quarry more clearly—for here was Captain Hathaway, the hero of His Majesty's Royal Navy, turning quite green, his hand going protectively, instinctively, to his gut.

"Yes, well, when you put it that way . . ." Benedict said, his wary expression evidence that he'd finally gained a proper appreciation for the task at hand. But then again, he was a Hathaway, and unfortunately, he rallied quickly and rashly.

"Never fear, gentlemen," he told them, bluff and bluster freshly inflated, "I have this well in hand. I've faced rougher seas than this petite devil of yours."

Without waiting for any further cautions or advice, the captain strode across the street, rakishly greeting all he met.

More than one lady's head turned as he passed by.

Chaunce shook his head. "I wager a pony we'll find him gutted before midnight."

Brody nodded in agreement. "Most likely. Though I'd wager another that he won't last to eleven."

With that, Chaunce raked his hand through his hair. "Oh, demmit, what have I gotten that fool into? I suppose I'll have to keep a close eye on him." He and Brody hurried across the street and followed the captain into Almack's.

When he got inside, Brody looked around until his gaze fixed on his wife. *His.* It was such a strange notion, but once he found Roselie, chatting with Lady Roxley as if nothing were amiss, he let out a quick sigh of relief. She glanced up, spotted him and smiled.

A bit of light and hope, something he'd never fathomed before rushed through him. A feeling he didn't dare name.

Oh, good heavens, he'd be lost without her. How ever had this happened so quickly?

"There's Mariah," Chaunce said, nodding to one side of the room. "Now where the devil is Benedict?" There was a hint of annoyance to his voice. Or perhaps worry.

"Your favorite brother, aye?" Brody asked, nodding in the direction of the captain. A dashing figure in his uniform, he had bowed first to Lady Muscoates and then Miss Taber. Now he finished his greeting by taking her hand and bringing her fingers to his lips in a very gallant and public show of affection and favor. Then he led her out onto the dance floor.

Chaunce groaned. "My favorite? Benedict? Oh, good God, no. Not at all." He shook his head. Emphatically, it should be noted. "But he's my mother's favorite. And I fear her wrath far more than God's."

Brody chuckled. For he had met the indomitable Lady Hathaway more than once.

And he had to say, all of England should fear her wrath.

"What has you so captivated, my dear Sparrow?"

Mariah Manx knew better than to turn around. If she did, the man behind her would most likely slip back into the shadows as he always did. And as much as she wanted him to do just that—disappear, she couldn't help herself, she waded into his ocean of temptation.

"Nothing of import, my lord," she replied with a feigned air of nonchalance.

Not that it fooled him.

"Mariah, anything that holds your attention so avidly is not 'nothing of import'."

She felt him shift behind her, and knew all too well he was using his keen gaze to sweep through the room, that he was all too quickly making his own assessments. "You're helping that foolish friend of yours again, aren't you?"

Tamping down the urge to bristle with indignation, she once again played this game of theirs with an air of indifference. "And what if I am?"

Apparently he wasn't in the mood. "You shouldn't be," he huffed. "'Tis a dangerous game Lady Rimswell plays. Which you should very well know by now."

"And of what import is it to you?"

He said nothing. Instead his fingers grazed over the inside of her palm. It was a movement no one would see, but it sent her heart hammering. And worse, his hand closed around hers, and he pulled her ever so slightly backward, into the shadows with him, closer to him.

"You are everything to me." And then he let go of her hand, and she felt nothing but bereft at the loss of his warmth and strength.

It had been the briefest of contact, yet left her adrift with emotions . . . and desires.

"I know what happened to your friend, Mrs. Croft." Again, his words came out gruff and possessive and full of an anger held barely in check.

His fingers caressed her hand again, but this time she pulled it away.

"My lord, please . . ." She should be finishing her plea with an emphatic *don't!*

Yet the word escaped her.

As it always did around him.

"If you won't listen to reason, then let me wager what is happening here tonight. You've baited your trap with Captain Hathaway and are dangling him before Lady Muscoates's ward."

She said nothing.

Which it turned out was confirmation enough for him. "It won't work."

Mariah tipped her nose in the air. "From my vantage point, the chit appears quite willing to do whatever it takes to gain the captain's confidence."

For indeed, there was Miss Taber, flirting shamelessly with Captain Hathaway.

"Yes, before she slits his throat."

Mariah stilled. "I hardly think—"

"I am told that in the Dials she is referred to as *Belle Chates*."

"'Beautiful gallows'," she translated quickly, both the French and the cant.

"This is a bad business. That little bit of muslin has sent more men to hell than Tyburn. From what I've heard, she gutted her first victim at the tender age of ten."

Mariah didn't bother debating the issue. If he said that was who Miss Taber was, then she wasn't about to doubt it. But there was one thing for certain. She needed to warn the others. She glanced around the room for the one person who would believe her.

And, as if he knew where her thoughts were straying, he caught her by the hand. "You cannot. If you tell them, warn them, this plan will fail in the worst of ways. Nor will there be another opportunity."

"I thought you said this plan didn't stand a chance," Mariah reminded him.

"Perhaps I've underestimated Hathaway's charms."

Whether he was speaking of the captain or the other Hathaway in the room, Mariah wasn't sure. But he was correct, across the way, Miss Taber was leaning into the captain, whispering to him from behind her fan, while the captain was playing a very eager and willing rake.

Then again, for Benedict Hathaway, being an eager and charming ne'er-do-well was rather second nature.

Roselie and Lord Rimswell had chosen their lure perfectly.

"I cannot let Captain Hathaway or any of the others—"

"Don't you mean that pup, Chaunce Hathaway. You would warn *him*."

When she remained stubbornly silent, he changed his tactic. Or rather resorted to an old one. "Come away with me, Sparrow. Tonight. We'll take a ship, we'll go anywhere you want to go. Just leave this business now before . . ."

"I'm well aware of what this is. But I won't abandon Roselie." Or Abigail, for that matter.

She knew what he was thinking. *Sparrow, you will end up the same way. I won't have it.*

Mariah straightened and focused on the task before her. Which meant she needed to ignore the man behind her.

Which, it turned out, was utterly impossible.

Especially when he was one step ahead of her.

Then again, he always was.

He'd leaned closer still and whispered for her ears only, "It appears the object of your attention is about to make her move."

She looked up and found Miss Taber at one of the servants' doors. The girl stood smiling over her shoulder at Captain Hathaway, enticing him to follow her, and indeed he did, tagging after the dangerous miss as she slipped through the open doorway and disappeared from sight.

Oh, bother, where was Chaunce? He was supposed to follow. To her horror, she found him waylaid by the Nafferton sisters, their overbearing mother bringing up the rear offensive.

Ghengis Khan would have been easier to dispatch.

As she continued to watch their plan dismantle, to her horror, Roselie stepped into the works and followed Miss Taber and the captain through the door into the unknown.

Alone.

"Your friend is a fool. She'll end up dead . . . or worse . . ."

Mariah's gaze frantically searched the room for someone to help. Why wasn't Lord Rimswell intervening? Why wasn't he following his wife?

But to her dismay, Lord Rimswell had been engaged by none other than Lady Muscoates. Expertly so, for he wasn't so much engaged but had been maneuvered by the lady so his back was to the doorway.

And when Mariah looked again there was no sign that Roselie had returned. Oh, dear heavens!

Mariah's insides twisted with panic. *No!*

She went to step forward but found herself stopped yet again. This time his grasp was unforgiving.

"I forbid it." Oh, those words, so full of authority and privilege. Full of his lofty status. He was rarely if ever brooked. No one dared.

Save her. His Sparrow. The lady's companion who wasn't supposed to hold such lofty aspirations.

Instead of thanking him for his gallantry, she yanked her arm free. "You have no right to tell me what to do."

And as she pushed her way into the crowd, his parting words haunted her yet again.

"Only because you deny me."

Brody turned around for no other reason than a shiver that ran down his spine, the Honorable's previous advice echoing his feelings of unease.

Always trust your instincts, Lord Rimswell.

And his instincts were clanging like the bells of St. Paul's.

He finally managed to extract himself from Lady Muscoates's clutches—she'd been asking all sorts of questions as to Captain Hathaway's prospects, having brought along Lady Essex to help her in this seemingly respectable interrogation. For what sort of chaperone would she be if she didn't see to her ward's prospects?

Lies, all lies, Brody had thought with every question the woman muttered, and it seemed she knew it as well, for all of a sudden, she'd made her excuses and left.

After breathing a sigh of relief, Brody turned, his gaze sweeping from one side of the crowded ballroom to the other. *Roselie, where the hell are you?*

He couldn't find her. Oh, the devil take him. Something was wrong. Very wrong.

"Benedict's gone." Chaunce said as he rejoined him. "I had a run in with the Naffertons and lost sight of him." He took a look around the room and shook his head. "And so is Miss Manx."

Suddenly there was a grand commotion at the front door. It had been forced open and a small figure darted into the room. A cry was raised at this interloper and servants began chasing the urchin through the room.

The small slight child moved with amazing agility and speed, dodging and darting away from his pursuers, all the while calling out, "Lord Rimswell! Lord Rimswell!"

Brody caught the lad by the arm. "I'm Rimswell."

"The Honorable sent me. Supposed to tell you, that they took 'em, milord."

"Took them?" Brody managed.

"The ladies, milord. The Honorable said they took 'em."

Of course it didn't help, that Lady Essex rejoined them just in time to hear the child's tale and come to her own dire conclusion.

"Who's taken Mariah? She has my smelling salts. And my best fan. I demand she be returned at once." Lady Essex looked from one to another, a murderous expression on her face, but it became overly imperious when it landed on the boy.

"Was yer Mariah in the blue dress?" the little boy asked.

Lady Essex blinked as if she wasn't quite sure what she was seeing or hearing. "Yes, Mariah is wearing a blue silk tonight."

The grubby little urchin nodded. "'Fraid she got 'erself snatched."

"Snatched?" Lady Essex looked up and glared at the pair of men before her.

If ever there was murder in the lady's heart, Brody suspected she'd kill them all right where they stood. In the middle of Almack's and damn the consequences. Apparently she considered hampering or impeding a lady's companion a higher sin than treason.

So much so, she immediately turned her disdain on Chaunce. "I have every suspicion you have had a hand in this, sir. Explain yourself."

"I-I-I, that is—" He looked to Brody for help.

"Mr. Hathaway," Lady Essex continued, "am I correct in assuming that you've lured Mariah into this folly?"

"I assure you, my lady, that Miss Manx's safety is—"

"*Harrumph!* Your mother will not be amused," Lady Essex told him sharply.

Chaunce sighed. "She never is, my lady."

"Oh bother you all!" Lady Essex glared at the pair. "I don't care what it takes: Get my Mariah back."

"We intend to, my lady. Besides, she isn't the only one missing," Brody told her. "They took my wife as well."

"Wives! What are wives?" Lady Essex huffed. "You men replace them like snuff boxes. But do you know how difficult it is to find an excellent companion? Nigh on impossible!" She turned back to Chaunce. "Get my Mariah back, or your mother will hear of this."

"Yes, my lady," Chaunce said with a slight gulp.

"Where the devil would she take them?" Brody said, raking a hand through his hair and doing his best to ignore the curious glances being tossed in their direction. The crowded street in front of Almack's was no place to have this discussion.

But there was no time to waste.

They'd found Captain Hathaway behind the building, half-conscious, with a large rap to the back of his head. All he'd seen was the enticing Miss Taber offering him . . . Well, it hardly mattered now *what* she'd offered, but he had managed to let slip the particulars about the gold, then he'd been hit from behind. But not before he'd seen Lady Rimswell coming around the corner of the alleyway.

Then it all went blank.

"You weren't supposed to leave with her," Chaunce said. Well, more like scolded as he paced back and forth in front of his younger sibling. "Just give her the information and let us do the rest."

"She's a mere slip of muslin. Hardly an object of fear," the captain protested. "And she'd offered to—" He looked around and huffed. "How was I supposed to know—"

Know that she'd have help. Waiting for her.

Chaunce groaned and folded his arms tightly across his chest. "You're lucky she didn't murder you." The elder Hathaway looked ready to finish the task himself. "You got Lady Rimswell and Miss Manx taken. Bloody hell, you're an arrogant fool, I should toss you down the deepest hole—"

Captain Hathaway looked ready to argue the point—honestly, when weren't the Hathaways arguing?—so Brody intervened. Besides, Chaunce's threat had given him an idea.

"This isn't helping," he told them. "We need to find where they went." And he had a notion of where, pieces of the puzzle falling together.

What was it Roselie said? *If you dig long enough, gather the facts . . .*

"Lady Muscoates probably has some bolt hole in the Dials, or even the docks," Brody began, piecing together what the duchess had said about the Frenchwoman's past.

"The docks?" Chaunce paused his restless pacing about and stared at him. "Why it's the devil's own knot down there."

Brody turned to the Honorable. "Do you think he'll help us?"

"He will," the Honorable said, "if we aren't too late."

* * *

"Caution, my lord," the Honorable complained an hour later as he huffed and puffed after Brody up yet another flight of stairs, into the darkness of the rooming house stairwell. "He's most likely to bolt before we even reach his floor considering the hullabaloo you're creating."

"I'm in a hurry," Brody shot back, taking the stairs two at a time, his boots pounding against the creaky treads.

"How can you be so certain he'll bolt?" Captain Hathaway asked, trailing behind the Honorable and watching their rear.

"It's what I would do," the Honorable said over his shoulder.

"How can you be so certain, Brody, that this man will know where they are? That he'll help us?" Chaunce asked, skeptical of this entire venture.

"A wild goose chase" as he called it.

"I am." Besides, Brody suspected the man had more than a professional interest in Asteria. In Roselie.

God help him, he hoped the man carried a torch for her. For while Brody might not like another man holding a *tendre* for his wife, if he could help get Roselie back, Brody wouldn't begrudge him his unrequited desires.

They'd gotten to the top of the stairs and Brody looked left and right. "Which door?" he asked the Honorable.

"The second one from the end . . . on the right."

Brody stormed down the hall and didn't bother to knock. He kicked the door open in one great burst of anger.

"So much for stealth," Chaunce muttered to no one in particular.

Brody had lost his usual cool reserve, the methodical demeanor Asteria had teased him about. Perhaps he was taking a page from her, perhaps he'd finally learned to follow his heart.

A heart that was torn in half, wounded, lashing out. Nor would he stray from this course until he had Roselie back.

"Reddick!" Brody demanded as he came to a stop in the middle of the room.

That's all it was—a single room—the narrow bed pushed

against the wall, a rickety nightstand, and a small table. A solitary chair. Apparently the captain didn't entertain much.

It was a poor, lean place, that said quite clearly that living by his wits hadn't been all that good to Captain Reddick of late.

The captain, looking as poor and disheveled as his room, stood beside the bed, shoving his meager belongings into a battered valise. He spared them a glance before he went back to his packing.

"I've got no time for your games, Rimswell. I'm a marked man and I have you to thank for it," he told them as he shoved the last few items into the valise and snapped the bag shut. "Now if you don't mind, I'm leaving."

Brody moved forward a few steps. "Not yet. I need your help."

"My help? You need—" His eyes narrowed. "The hell with you. Because of you I've got to run. That bitch has put a price on my head."

"That bitch has my wife."

Icy words that slammed into the captain. Stopped him cold.

"She's taken Roselie," Brody said into the stillness of the room.

Reddick glanced over his shoulder. "You lost her?"

Brody winced. Then he nodded.

Reddick blinked once and then exploded into a fury of movement. Like a shot of lightning he dove across the room, grabbed Brody by the lapels of his jacket and shoved him against the far wall next to the door.

Brody hit with a loud *thud* that shook the room, nearly rattled the building.

"How the hell did you let that happen?" Reddick's hands went to Brody's throat. "You don't deserve her. You never did."

The two men wrestled back and forth, accusations flying as furiously as their fists.

That is, until Chaunce and Benedict intervened. With five Hathaway brothers, they had no small amount of experience in dispatching a row.

Deftly and quickly.

Reddick shook himself free of Chaunce, ruffling like a wet hen, all indignation and ire. "How the hell did you let this happen?" he shot over Chaunce's shoulder. He might not be able to hit Brody, but he could still wound.

Brody tugged his jacket back in place and pulled at his lop-sided cravat. He felt the weight of the world suddenly come crashing down on him. He had let this happen. This was all his fault. He sank into the chair.

"Have you considered how impossible it is to tell her *no*?" Brody heaved a sigh, and looked the man directly in the eyes.

Reddick paused, and then suddenly barked a short laugh. "Yes, well, there is that." He crossed the room and held out his hand. Brody took it and the captain tugged him to his feet. "How do we get her back?"

Brody laid out what they did know and finished by asking, "Where would Lady Muscoates take her?"

Reddick's brow furrowed as he considered the question. "The docks, I suppose. She's done for here. Rumor had it she had her eye on one last prize."

"The docks? That's a rather broad swath of London," Captain Hathaway said. "Can you be a bit more specific?"

"Not likely." Captain Reddick shook his head. "There's no telling where on the docks she might be."

"Yes there is."

They all turned to Brody.

He straightened as Roselie's words seemed to ring with a clarion truth. Every and any piece can lead you to the right conclusion.

So it seemed that this entire mire had given him exactly the piece he needed. "I know just the fellow."

Chapter 23

Roselie stirred awake, her head aching. She was sitting, but as she opened her eyes and blinked, it was a muffled darkness that greeted her. A hood. There was a hood on her head. She reached for it but found her hands bound behind her.

A temporary problem, she told herself, if only to quell the growing panic inside her. It would take some time to manage, but she was quite certain she could get herself free . . .

As she twisted her hands to and fro, she searched her memory to recall what had happened.

She'd been at Almack's. Captain Hathaway was following Miss Taber out the door. He wasn't supposed to do that. So she'd gone after him, and then . . . Well, it all got a little hazy after that. One thing was for certain, she hadn't fared well. And now . . .

She struggled a bit against her bindings which were tightly wrapped around her wrists and . . .

At least her feet weren't tied. But the ropes around her wrist, well, they were a devilish inconvenience. She twisted her hands, testing them. Whoever had done this certainly didn't want her to escape.

And if they weren't going to let her go . . .

She stilled, for she didn't want to consider what might come next.

Oh, Brody. I've made a dreadful mess of things.

And she hadn't even had a chance to tell him . . . To say those words . . . The ones that had been lodged in her heart for far too long.

There was a stirring just off to her left, followed by footsteps, then the hood yanked from her head.

She closed her eyes and then blinked again, the grim room coming into focus. Certainly this wasn't Mayfair.

And given the sharp, ripe smell, she would guess they were near the docks.

"Lady Rimswell," her captor said in greeting.

Roselie looked up. "Miss Taber," she said politely, as if they had just run into each other at Lady Gosforth's afternoon in. "Would you be so kind to loosen my bindings? I daresay they are chafing a bit."

Miss Taber laughed, and not the polite and ladylike way Roselie had grown used to hearing. It was a rough sound, full of hate and, worst of all, victory.

Oh, this hardly boded well.

There was a groan beside her and Roselie twisted toward it, as well as her bindings would allow.

The person next to her was hooded as well, but the blue silk gown told her everything she needed to know.

"Mariah!" she gasped. *No!* Roselie shook her head, turning back toward Miss Taber. "Let her go. She has naught to do with any of this."

Miss Taber sauntered over toward Mariah and yanked off her hood.

Mariah was wide awake, but she'd chosen not to speak. Mariah was never one to speak out of turn—more inclined to taking everything in before making her opinions known.

She met Roselie's gaze with a flicker of determination.

"You're a bit long in the tooth," Miss Taber said, catching Mariah by the chin and yanking her head up so she was forced to look her captor in the eyes. "But her ladyship has assured me you're a virgin. Fetch a pretty penny, you will. 'Specially, if you show the same sort of spirit that you did when we caught you. For a quiet one, you can put up a hell of a fight."

Mariah jerked her head out of the woman's grasp and looked away.

"As for you, my fine Asteria," she said to Roselie, "You'll make me a fortune. Seems like there are a lot of buggers who want to see you beneath them and getting what you deserve." The girl laughed and took a step back to admire her prizes.

"You'll not get away with this, Miss Taber. You'll hang, you'll—" Roselie began, if only to take the woman's attentions away from Mariah.

"Shut up!" she snapped back. Gone were the purring tones of a lady, and in their place, all the markings of a Seven Dials thief. And as if she knew what Roselie was thinking, she added, "And my name is Belle." She hiked up her skirt and pulled a knife out from her garter. "Belle Chates, they call me."

"Lovely to meet you, I'm certain," Roselie said back. "But your neck will stretch just the same no matter what pretty name you call yourself."

A snarling, furious Belle came at Roselie like a rabid dog, snapping and wild-eyed, and yet just as she reeled back to strike, the door opened.

"Enough!"

And that word, that command, was enough to stop the girl in her mad tracks.

"We haven't time for this," Lady Muscoates told her as she strode into the room. A man followed her and Roselie realized she'd seen the fellow before.

Twice now. At St. John's Folly.

"Craddock," she whispered.

He smiled at her, a feral look that sent shivers of fear down Roselie's spine. "The elusive Asteria," he said, sweeping a glance over her. "Not so pretty without that mask, my lady. Rather disappointing actually. I had hoped one day that I might get to—"

"They are already at the Constable's office, and they'll be here soon enough," Lady Muscoates snapped at him.

Roselie heard all this and came to a quick conclusion. They? The Constable? Brody!

Her heart pattered that he was so close, and yet . . . the closer he came, the closer he came to being in danger.

"The Constable will never talk, not if he knows what's good for him," Craddock told her, almost bragging.

"Oh, he'll talk," Lady Muscoates said, her hand flutter in a dismissive wave. "All men do eventually." Then she turned her ire at Belle. "Why is she still alive?" She jerked her head toward Mariah. "We need to move now if we are to catch the tide ahead of anyone else. I want no loose ends behind me."

"But you said I could sell her—" Belle protested.

The door of the warehouse swung open and all of them turned in unison. Roselie held a momentary flicker of hope that she was about to see Brody come charging in, but it was only one of Craddock's rats. "The cap'n wants to know which trunks you want, my lady. There ain't room for all of them."

Lady Muscoates heaved a sigh, and glanced over at Belle. "Kill her. Quickly."

"Leave Mariah out of this," Roselie pleaded, and earned a clout for her trouble.

"Now, now, Craddock," Lady Muscoates purred. "Poor Lady Rimswell hasn't lost enough friends and family yet to understand that sometimes, the Fates, well, they have other plans."

"What did the Fates do to you that made you so cruel? So evil?" Roselie shot back.

"You know nothing about what I've suffered. What was taken from me—" she shot back. Then as if remembering herself, she stilled.

"I don't see how you've lost anything—other than a string of husbands, ones I'd venture you murdered," Roselie continued, if only to stall.

"And what if I did? Men! They've lied to me all my life. Starting with Aufroy. That bastard promised me the marriage was legal, but as it turned out it wasn't. By the time we'd arrived in England, he'd tired of me and was going to cast me out, so I killed him, and tried to force his noble family to accept me—which of course they wouldn't. Called me a common whore, and refused to acknowledge me. Left me stranded here—to fend for myself."

"Stranded!" Roselie scoffed. She knew she only needed time. For either Brody to find them or for her to find a way to work her hands free. "You were hardly suffering when you cast yourself into the duke's household."

"Ranworth and his pathetic wife," she spat back. "What a dreadfully dull pair. How I hated them. Especially when it was obvious they were growing tired of me as well, no matter that I gave them everything they'd always wanted."

"You used them—"

"Shut up, bitch," Craddock snarled.

"Indeed, Lady Rimswell, Craddock is right," Lady Muscoates said in cold tones. "You should have learned your place years ago. Kept your mouth shut."

"As you should have, before you sold out to the French."

"I am French," she shot back. "Something you arrogant, dull English nitwits have reminded me of every day I've been stuck on this wretched island. But the revolution gave me hope and when Napoleon's agents contacted me, offered me gold, how was I to refuse?"

"Those are the sons of people you know. Your friends."

"I've never had friends," Lady Muscoates told her. "And with the Aufroys dead, the new government offered me their properties in return for a little help. And so I helped. And helped myself. And now I will go back to France, and live the life that was stolen from me."

"And what about my life?" This protest came from Belle. "You promised me I'd get my due after having to endure all those months of mincing around with that dull lot." She jerked her head at Mariah. "I know what she'll fetch in the Dials and I'm taking her with me."

Craddock turned to Belle. "Shut up and do as you're told."

Belle's face curled into a silent fury, her knife twisting in her hands, the sharp blade glinting in the meager light.

"Ah, Lady Rimswell, I am so sorry about your friend here." Lady Muscoates circled behind Mariah and then caught her by the head, tipping her neck just so, as if testing to see what it would take to snap it. "Unfortunately as long as she's alive, she can talk."

Mariah's eyes widened slightly, but then, having served Lady Essex all this time, she took on a stubborn resolve.

But Roselie felt none of her friend's resolute calm. Horror and panic rippled through her. "You cannot do this. You will not. I will not help you if you harm Mariah."

"Oh, but I don't need your help," Lady Muscoates said in a purr, twisting Mariah's head further and then, when it seemed she would do the worst, she let go.

The woman stalked across the space between them and tipped Roselie's chin up with a single finger. "All I need from you, my dear lady, is your presence for a few more hours, then you shall share your friend's fate. Though I daresay drowning at sea is a bit more of a struggle, and I suppose will take far longer than an encounter with my dearest Belle." She pulled back and smiled. "Why it is said her knife is the quickest in all the Dials. One moment you're alive, and the next—" She cringed slightly, then shrugged.

"This is all well and good, but what about the trunks?" the rough fellow repeated.

Roselie had almost forgotten he was there. "Please sir, help us."

She earned another clout from Craddock and it split her lip. Nor did her plea do anything to aid their cause, but it did give her an extra distraction. A few more moments to work at her bindings.

Nearly there . . .

"The trunks?" the man repeated, looking positively bored. He wasn't being paid to rescue anyone, just get the ship loaded.

"Oh, yes, my trunks. And with the tide turning." Lady Muscoates sighed. "Such are the hardships of hasty travel—" She nodded again at Mariah. "One can't take everything, now can you? And unfortunately, the indispensable Miss Manx is rather unnecessary."

"I was promised—" Belle protested.

"Enough!" Lady Muscoates snapped, even as Craddock eased forward and looked ready to do the job himself, starting with the former Miss Taber.

Lady Muscoates huffed a bit. "With me," she said to Craddock as she moved to the door. Then she turned to Belle. "Kill that girl and gag Lady Rimswell. She talks too much."

Everything was going to shit. Craddock knew it. He could smell it. And while Lady Muscoates cursed thoroughly—lady, indeed, he mused, having bedded her enough times to know differently.

Still all her ranting might be in French, but it meant the same bloody thing in English: their entire scheme was falling apart.

The gold that Hathaway had boasted of wasn't to be—no ship, no gold. All of it a fine lure, one he hadn't been able to talk her out of dangling after.

Not that she'd had a sensible notion since she'd learned about that duchess coming back from the dead, or that the duke had publicly disavowed Ilford. He wasn't such a fool that he didn't know that the money and wealth that would have come their way with Ilford's inheritance had gone up in smoke as well.

All her fine plans, lost. Not that she hadn't squirreled away her fair share. What with all she'd collected over the years, blackmailing Ilford and his fool of a father, her cut of the ships that had been taken and all she'd pilfered from her husbands.

But she had hungered for one last take, one large enough to keep her in grand style for some years to come.

It was always like that with her. Greedy, thieving bitch. But it was also why he liked her. Still . . . he'd warned her and she hadn't listened.

And now agents of the Crown were on their heels. Or so his spies told him.

Craddock cursed his own luck for throwing himself in with her. At least they still had *her*. Asteria. Like Belle had said, she was worth much.

He'd get his equal share out of this mess. Take his revenge on that Asteria bitch and then sell her to the highest bidder.

After what seemed forever sorting out the trunks, they got back to the room, only to find Belle gone. And where there should be a dead gel, an empty spot.

So Belle had taken her reward and fled. Craddock had to admire her nerve.

Lady Muscoates was of a different opinion. "Deceitful little bitch."

Craddock shrugged, since he knew full well the woman had planned to eliminate Belle at the first opportunity. No loose ends, after all.

Lady Muscoates cursed and nodded toward the chair where Lady Rimswell sat, hooded and tied up, and obviously gagged, for her complaints and protests were all garbled.

At least Belle had taken the time to do that. Mighty considerate of her.

"Get Lady Rimswell. Bring her," Lady Muscoates told him. She sniffed at her surroundings and retreated to the door. "It is finally time to go home."

Brody had taken them straight to the Constable. And faced with two government agents, and one very irate naval captain of some repute, the man had finally dropped all his pretenses that he maintained law and order around the docks and talked.

To be fair, Captain Hathaway and his brother sped things along by explaining to the Constable—in enthusiastic detail—the finer points of being keelhauled.

The Constable had quickly named which warehouse Lady Muscoates and her associates used, and then had gone back to his paperwork—only after extracting a bribe and a faithful promise that his part in this venture would not be shared.

After all, he had a reputation to maintain.

Meanwhile, the Honorable dispatched several guttersnipes out into the docklands—with the help of a handful of shillings courtesy of Brody—to see what they might gather. In the interim, Reddick had sought out a public house he was familiar with— one inhabited by sailors and smugglers alike—to discover which ships were planning to set sail when the tide shifted.

Brody glanced at the sky, where the first hints of dawn were starting to climb over the horizon. They had an hour, at the most, before the tide turned and Lady Muscoates would be down the Thames on any number of the waiting ships.

He could only hope they had arrived at the warehouse in time. Pistols drawn, they went in, but to their dismay, the place was abandoned.

"Look over here," Chaunce called out. He stood by two chairs. Empty chairs.

"What is it?" Brody asked.

"Mariah was here," he said with enough certainty that Brody didn't even question him.

"How so?" the Honorable asked.

"She left this behind for us to find," Chaunce said, holding out a small garnet ring for all to see.

"We'd have been better served if they'd penned us a note with some directions," the Honorable muttered.

"Sir?" One of the urchins called out, coming into the warehouse dragging along another equally dirty gutter rat. "'E says they left not long ago. The fine lady, Mr. Craddock and another one—but he couldn't tell who she was—on account of she was wearing a hood."

"What color was her gown, lad?" Brody asked, shoving his

hand in his pocket and pulling out a gold piece for the boy to see.

His eyes lit up as if he didn't quite believe it was real. "Yellow, my lord. Her gown was yellow, like that there guinea."

"Indeed," Brody nodded. "And where did they take her?"

"To a ship. Not far. I can show you," he said, his gaze fixed on such a tempting prize.

"Get us there before it sails, and this is yours," Brody promised.

They arrived at the docks just in time to see a small ship slipping into the current of the Thames. On the deck stood Lady Muscoates, and beside her, of all people, Craddock. He didn't know why he was surprised. Of course she'd align herself with someone of his ilk.

But the sight that stopped his heart was of the woman Craddock had a tight grasp upon.

Roselie.

Hooded, but he'd know that yellow gown anywhere.

"Demmit," he cursed, looking down at the dark, dank water and along the banks for something, anything that floated so he could give chase. He'd row all the way to France if he must.

He couldn't lose her. Not before . . .

Before he told her the words that had been locked in his heart.

Brody looked over at Chaunce and his brother, both of them grasping the railing as well. Chaunce looked as if he'd been gutted, for suddenly he realized something else.

There was no sign of Mariah.

He looked again and a foreboding sense of disaster hit him.

If they'd already done away with Mariah . . .

Oh, God. No.

"Lad," Captain Hathaway caught hold of the boy who'd brought them here. "Where is the nearest naval ship?"

"That way," he said, pointing downstream.

Captain Hathaway moved quickly, running out into the street

behind them and shoving a fellow from his horse. He leaped on the back of it and rode furiously for help.

And most notably ahead of the ship, but for how long he could keep that lead . . .

For a time, there was nothing to be done but watch, as the boat caught the current and began to move.

Lady Muscoates smiled smugly at them, while Craddock seemed to take great joy in giving Roselie a rough shake from time to time.

Brody pulled out his pistol and was about to take aim, when there was a rustle of silk behind him.

"Whatever are you aiming at?"

Brody stilled at the question that rose up from behind them.

"I mean, you might hit Miss Taber," she added.

He spun around and couldn't believe the sight before him.

Bedraggled, hair all loose and looking as if she'd been tossed about, it was *her*. Roselie.

"Oh, how is this?" He hauled her into his arms and for a moment all he could do was look at her. Then of course, all he could do was kiss her, devour her. Reassure himself she was real.

And after a perfectly convincing kiss—yes, indeed this was Roselie—he held her out at arm's length and said those very words—in a rush to have them out and done.

"Oh, Rosebud, I love you, you impossible minx."

She grinned. "I love you, as well."

Then Brody got back to business. "Where the devil did you come from?"

"The warehouse," she told him and glanced over her shoulder. "Oh, yes there is Miss Taber! How wonderful, she gets to take a sea voyage after all."

Roselie stepped around him and waived quite gaily at Lady Muscoates, as if she was wishing the villainous woman a hearty *bon voyage*. "Do take care, my lady," she called out.

At the railing of the ship, Lady Muscoates gaped, as did her cutthroat partner.

Craddock spun around and yanked the hood off the figure beside him, only to discover a gagged Miss Taber, her face twisted with rage.

"I don't think Miss Taber wears that color as well as you do, Lady Rimswell," Miss Manx added, having come up alongside them.

"Mariah!" Chaunce cried out and looked ready to take her into his arms, but in the end stuck out his hand and she shook it. "Well done, I mean to say," he managed.

Roselie cast a sideways glance at Brody that was quite telling.

Yes, well, that was a story for another time.

Just then, there was the boom of a cannon.

"I think my brother located help," Chaunce said, grinning down the Thames, where several of the sailors onboard Lady Muscoates's ship were jumping over the rails rather than find themselves purloined into the Navy.

It wouldn't be long before everyone on board was going to find themselves either soaking wet or in irons.

And given the murderous look on Lady Muscoates's face, Brody guessed the woman couldn't swim. The cat with nine lives had finally found herself without a place to land.

He turned back to his wife. His wife. The one he loved with all his heart. So many things he wanted to say.

But first . . . he had one very important question.

"How ever did you manage to escape?" Brody asked, no, demanded. Good God, he was furious with her. He had quite the list of grievances, starting with the fact that she wasn't supposed to get caught in the first place.

"Well, I undid my bindings just as I was taught," Roselie said, smiling over at the Honorable. "You see it is all in the wrists, and how one holds one's hands."

"A handy trick, for certain," the Honorable acknowledged with a slight bow.

"Indeed, I thank you," she said. "And then a bit of a diversion," she said, winking at Captain Reddick. "Like switching cards when no one is looking."

"I never—" he began.

"She did," Mariah told him. "And yes, you have."

Reddick shrugged.

She smiled at Brody. "And then I held on to my courage and thought of you. Thought of how you took on those men in the street. Miss Taber was going to kill Mariah, and I couldn't—"

"No, I don't suppose you could," Brody said, pulling her close again. Oh, he was furious with her for taking such risks, but then again, he'd known this was going to be the way of things when he married her.

For as much as he'd thought he could forbid her, or stop her—there was no saying *no* to Roselie.

Not when she set her mind to something.

"Nor did I have any notion of dying," Mariah informed them.

Roselie laughed. "No, she didn't. She kicked up quite the fuss—and once Mariah began, Miss Taber was perfectly diverted. She never saw me coming. Then it was a matter of my mother's old trick of a new hat. But in this case it was a new gown." Roselie sniffed at the green silk she was wearing and then shrugged as if it couldn't be helped.

"You could have been—" Brody began.

"But I had to save Mariah—for Miss Taber intended to sell her to the nearest—" Roselie paused. "Well, I assume we all know what sort of place Miss Taber intended for Mariah."

Mariah shuddered and shook her head. "Certainly it would have been a horrible waste of my education at Miss Emery's."

Once Lady Muscoates, Craddock and Belle were in custody, Brody gathered Roselie into his carriage to take her home.

For good.

Chaunce and Captain Benedict had Mariah—both insisting on

getting the credit for returning her unharmed to Lady Essex. If only so the old girl would have no cause to make some dramatic report to their mother.

Now, finally alone, Brody turned to her. "What were you thinking—getting yourself captured—"

"It was all part of my plan," Roselie told him, lifting her nose in the air.

"Truly?"

He needn't sound so skeptical. She leaned over and put her head on his shoulder, twining her fingers with his. He was warm and strong and solid. Her Brody. Hers always. "Well, I did trust that eventually you would find me."

Brody leaned back in the seat, chest puffed out, his arms crossed. "I did, didn't I?"

"You did," she conceded, slanting a smile at him. "We make an excellent team. But in the future—"

At that, he scrambled upright. "Future? Oh, no you don't! Your days as that creature—"

Roselie laughed. "I have no intention of becoming her ever again."

"Never?" he asked, winking at her. "She might like to come out periodically. In private. Or just the mask. I do so like that mask."

She blushed at the implication, but also let the heat in his glance, the desire so plainly written on his face ignite her own passions. She might don one of Asteria's gowns and mask, but she'd wager she wouldn't be wearing either for long.

But to a more practical point, she continued, "I only meant to say that if we are to find the duke's heir, we'll need to work together."

"If you think I am going to let you gallivant off to who knows where to find—"

Her brows rose and she gave him her most imperious glance. "Let me?"

His lips pursed together.

She sat back, now it was her turn to cross her arms over her chest. "I daresay I can go alone."

"I would find you," he shot back.

Roselie smiled at him. "I'm counting on it."

Epilogue

Love is never impossible.

Roselie Garrick, Baroness Rimswell

Garrick Hall, Hampshire
1820

Lord Rimswell led his wife out onto the patio where their entire family and a good number of friends had gathered for a grand picnic out on the lawn beyond. He smiled at his guests, happy and content to have gained so much in his hasty marriage to Roselie.

His Rosebud.

He surveyed the scene before him again and grinned. Family by blood and family by ties that ran as deep—Louisa and Piers. Tuck and Lavinia. Mrs. Rowland. The Honorable. Lord Charleton and his wife, the former Lady Aveley. Blessings all of them. Even his mother, who—with the arrival of grandchildren—had come around and inexplicably softened, as if touched as well by all the love that filled their home.

He looked over his shoulder and saw another carriage coming up the drive. Lord and Lady Roxley. Brody cringed a bit, for whenever Harriet and Roselie put their heads together, all of England had best take notice. The house would now swell to overflowing with their addition, but oh, it was such a good thing to have so much joy.

So much love.

"Everyone is here," Roselie said happily, leaning her head against his shoulder, her hand clutched in his. Children darted all over the green. Tuck and Lavinia's trio of sons, Louisa and Piers's handful of rowdies—three girls who all looked like their mother, but had inherited that Stratton spirit, and the newest addition, a son, just a toddler, trying his best to chase after his exuberant siblings.

And his own brood. Michael stealing tarts from the table, young Hero playing cards with his godfather, the original Hero, while baby Leopold lay snug and happy in Bernie's arms. Nor would Leopold be alone for long, for from the way Roselie was eating, it seemed Leo would have a brother or sister by early next spring.

Adding to the happy, joyous chaos of their growing family.

Nine years of marriage. And always Roselie with her heart in the thick of things. Not even three children could stop her from keeping her promise to the Duke of Ranworth. By the time the war with France had ended—and Napoleon was safely dispatched a second time—she'd already managed a handful of leads as to the whereabouts of the Duke of Ranworth's heir.

A promise is a promise, she'd said when the peace accord was signed, and no matter that the duke had died the year previous, they packed their bags and for three years hunted all over India for Edmund Vaile, until one of the clues she'd collected took them all the way to Calcutta, and there they found the duke's nephew, making reports to the East India Company as to his most recent explorations—travels that had taken the man all the way to China and back.

Now he was back home, and would soon be declared the new Duke of Ranworth.

"It's ever so good to be home," Roselie said with a soft sigh.

"What, Lady Rimswell? No plans for our next great adventure?" he teased back as they stepped off the patio and onto the thick green grass.

"I rather like being here," she told him. "And you must admit, it does make me easier to find."

"I'll always find you, Rosebud."

"I'm ever so glad of that. I'd be lost without you. You are my love. My heart."

"As you are mine," he said, pressing a kiss to her forehead.

But that brow was furrowed and her gaze fixed at a point off in the garden.

"What is it?" Brody asked, looking up and trying to see what had her attention.

"Hero just stole Uncle Charleton's pocket watch."

"Isn't he getting rather old for those sort of tricks—"

"Not that Hero. *Our Hero*," she said, her lips pursing together.

Brody laughed. "I told you not to teach him how to do that—"

Instead of denying it, Roselie stormed off in order to make the lad give back his purloined treasure.

"You impossible child—" she called after the little scamp.

Some things, it seemed, never changed. And Brody hoped they never would.